translated from the Hebrew by
HILLEL HALKIN

The Jewish Publication Society of America
Philadelphia 5739-1978

Whose
little boy
are you?

Whose
little boy
are you?

Whose little boy are you?

a novel by

Hanoch Bartov

First English edition
Taken from the Hebrew edition of Shel Mi Ata Yeled,
published by Am Oved *Publishers, Ltd.*, *Tel Aviv, 1970*
ISBN 0-8276-0112-3
Library of Congress catalog number 78-56551
Manufactured in the United States of America

Designed by Adrianne Onderdonk Dudden

To my father and mother

Whose
little boy
are you?

1 | *Being burned*

The room fairly hummed with preparation, with hectic expectation of that unknown, mysterious something in honor of which his mother had risen in darkness and toiled noisily ever since, turning everything upside down, running frantically to the kitchen and then out to the yard and back again like the wind, flushed and irritable with the effort of getting ready for that something called family which was about to descend on them at any minute and fill the whole house with its uproar of people and talk, none of which Nachman would be able to understand, though his heart still throbbed with excitement.

She had awakened him unusually early too and dragged his bedding out to the yard with everything else. Even when she flung the shutters wide open, the room remained shrouded in darkness; yet she persisted in dressing him with firm hands and sending him outside. Nachman strove to outwit the confusion, to hide from it. His mother had draped their eiderdown quilt over the bench beneath the fig tree, and now he thrust his head into the feathery mountain. He liked best of all to lie in his parents' empty bed surrounded by the fragrant warmth that was pent up beneath the quilt. It had two linings, a white outer one full of lacy holes that his mother had just stripped off and a red one underneath. The red one was stiffer and more colorful to look at, and the sharp white points sticking through it tickled his fingertips. Feathers. Nachman picked one gingerly with his fingers the way his mother plucked the skin of a chicken, raised it to his nostrils, held his breath, and crossed his eyeballs downward to see if anything moved. His mother had scolded him more than once and said that this was only if someone had died and that besides, if he kept squinting like that, his eyes were sure to get stuck and stay crossed forever. You musn't, she had warned him. But the more she threatened, the more he felt the need to put everything—his breath, his eyes, the coins that jingled each time in a different corner of the quilt—to the test.

The coins. This was the strictest of his mother's prohibitions and the one he felt most driven to break. Each time he heard them ring from their hiding place in the feathery mountain he wanted to know all about them. They were for luck, his mother had told him. Before they left for Palestine, grandmother had given them the quilt with the silver coins hidden inside it. For luck. Nachman had wanted to know what kind of luck. Luck to bring money, his mother had smiled while her eyes filled with tears. Nachman had hurried away so as not to cry too. He already knew that whenever his mother spoke about money she started to cry. But if the quilt was full of coins that brought luck, why did she always complain that she didn't have a piaster to her name? What made them ring the way they did? Whenever they jingled, which always took him by surprise when he had already dug his way into the pillowy darkness, Nachman would start to hunt for them. If only he could get his hands on them once through the mountain of feathers, he would carefully steer them to one corner of the quilt, make a small hole there with a fork, and take one of them out, just for a second, to see what a lucky coin looked like. But each time, just as he managed to feel their padded hardness between his fingers, his mother would come into the room. It was the coins themselves that had luck.

This morning, however, his thoughts refused to stand still, and throwing off the quilt, he went off to see what his mother was up to so busily. She had put on a housedress over her embroidered nightgown and was running barefoot back and forth, spreading the linens on the fence, on the branches of the trees, on the railing of the porch. She stood the chairs upside down on the table, dragged out the beds on their squeaky legs, dashed to the kitchen where she made a clatter with the pots, peeled something with a knife, chopped something with a cleaver, cried over an onion, fiddled with the kerosene stove and the burner that she had borrowed from Madam Mendelevitch, sped back to the room again to wash the shutters with soapsuds, scrub the windows with old newspapers, furiously polish the oval mirror in the closet on whose smooth surface she had discovered a fly dropping, which she spat on, scratched with her fingertip, and rubbed with a dry cloth, before returning to her pots in the kitchen again, and once more to the yard to beat the pillows and the pillowcases, and on and on without end.

Everything was so hectic that it infected Nachman too. Why didn't whoever was expected come already? Who were they anyway? They were from Europe, his mother had told him. They were family, she had said. But who were they? Uncle Rifael was family too, yet he didn't come to them each time from Europe but from the place beyond the vineyards and the jackals and the sand. Only the devil knew where it was. Uncle Rifael came nearly every evening, sat drinking tea with his mother and father on the front stoop or under the fig tree, and left riding on his donkey. Mother said he was a *poyer*—a peasant. But she said the same about young Mendelevitch, who rode on a mare, wore high boots, and wasn't like Uncle Rifael at all. Who was this family from Europe that they were awaiting now, for which his mother was crossly turning the house upside down while declaring that she would die of shame? Nachman trailed after her from place to place, seeking to make himself part of her wondrous doings. No sooner did she shoo him away from her in one spot than he was again squirming under her legs in another.

The kitchen. The kerosene stove wheezed loud and then soft like the breathing of some strange beast. Elongated blue fingers flickered beneath the large pot and grasped it from below, turning into yellow tongues where they licked it further up. Suddenly the fire went out with a sibilant whistle. Imperturbably, his mother stuck a narrow needle down the nozzle of the burner and with the help of the air pump and other incantations brought it whispering thinly back to life. Then she lit a rolled-up piece of newspaper from the alcohol lamp, touched it to the nozzle of the stove, and a many-fingered blue ring of fire sprang forth once more. Its wheezing filled the kitchen again. Nachman couldn't take his eyes off the crackling flame, yet his mother was already lifting the lid from the giant pot, from which a cloud of imprisoned steam shot up. She stuck her head into it and blew, then lowered a large spoon into the depths of the pot, raised it carefully, touched it to her lips, blew again, and sipped from it with a whistling sound. Brrr, crept Nachman's flesh, yet he wanted to take part in it too. The pot cover wobbled on the tin tabletop, and Nachman reached out to touch it, to feel the hot vapors, but his mother beat him to it with nimble, impatient fingers, resealed the steam in the pot, and swept back to the other room. For a second Nachman couldn't decide between the stove and his mother, but in the end he chose the latter. He made his way to the open porch and from there back to the room. A strong smell of kerosene tickled his nostrils as he passed through the door. His mother moved back and forth above the bed, rubbing the metal bedstead and the spring with a rag dipped in kerosene, dripping oily drops on the worn floor tiles. Wherever they fell, spreading into dark, shiny circles, the tiles regained their old color. Nachman kneeled on all fours and twisted his neck to peer up at his mother from below, through the metal bedsprings that resembled the fence around Mister Blackman's garden, which he was strictly forbidden to enter. His mother's face, bent over the bed, looked as though it had been washed with beet juice. Through her open nightgown Nachman could see her breasts as he had never seen them before, two round, ivory balls that bounced up and down with each scrub that she gave to the bedstead and spring. Openmouthed, he put out his hand to touch the two white balls. Just then, however, his mother caught sight of him. Without his knowing why, she turned on him with a great cry, then straightened up, adjusted her dress, and ordered him outside at once. "All I need now," she shouted, "is for you to poison yourself with kerosene. You'll get the spanking of your life if you don't get out of here. The day is slipping right through my fingers, and I haven't done a thing yet. All I need is for the Sabbath to come and the whole family to arrive and find me like this. I'll die of pure shame."

Nachman crawled out from under the bed and escaped outdoors. His mother was perfectly capable of spanking him. Standing on the porch and looking toward Mister Blackman's house, where neither Mister Blackman nor Missus Blackman could be seen, and toward the barn at the far end of their yard, which was also deserted now because Abed had taken the cows out to pasture, he couldn't stop thinking about those unknown, mysterious creatures, the family, who were about to drop in any minute. He made up his mind to descend the front stairs and wait for them, the family, right there by the wide entranceway between the two cypresses, but before his foot had touched the first step he again heard the singsong wheezing of the stove. The smell of kerosene was still in his nose. Suddenly, right before him, ground into the dust of the yard, he noticed a pack of his father's cigarettes, the butterfly with the spread wings on the wrapper. Nachman remembered something that he had always wanted to do, climbed down the steps, picked up the pack, and opened it. There were no cigarettes inside, but his fingers detected at once the thin, transparent paper in which they were always wrapped. Sometimes his father would roll this paper up, stick it in Nachman's mouth, and say, "Here, have a puff!"

Nachman stole silently into the kitchen, rolled the waxy paper into a cigarette, and dragged the stool over to the table in front of the stove and the burners. Imitating the way his father lit a cigarette from the glass bowl of the kerosene lamp, he pinched one end of it between his lips while bringing the other to the blue flame, which just then stuck out a yellow tongue at him. Just like his father. He tried to inhale, breathing into his mouth, but there was still no smoke, and so he brought his head even nearer, plunging the cigarette directly into the flame and breathing as deeply as he could.

Years later, when Nachman's memory groped its way back to its starting point—to that palpable moment of which it could be said, Here, this *I* really remember, here *I* already was, on a Friday morning, in a high blue room with my father and mother—this same scene would come back to him. Many other moments flashed before him too, like bits of broken mirrors out of a total darkness in which there was neither an after or before, but each time Nachman returned in the end to this particular morning. In no time, with that same inhalation, his face was plunged into a raging, acrid fire that both choked and blinded him at the same time. He tried to chase it away, to drive it off like flies, but because he couldn't see, he felt that his whole body was on fire. He wanted to scream, but he hadn't any voice. He turned to run, but everything disappeared underneath him as though it had turned to smoke. He collapsed in smoke, striking the stone floor. His hands groped along it, his eyes on fire with tears, his face and mouth being burned.

With this fall the memory that carried Nachman back to the starting point cut to another scene. Now little Nachman was being seen by his older self, who stood to one side as though looking down from above on somebody else, as though his own private memory—which started with this moment, with his stubborn insistence on starting at the beginning—had become intertwined with another, family memory. This little Nachman was carried in his father's arms, a large towel covering his face. (Women were shouting through the towel, "The white of an egg, the white of an egg! Smear him with the white of an egg!" And Missus Blackman's voice rasped, "From the sun cover him up! His face don't touch!") His father ran down the street through the sand. Even through the towel the sun shot burning darts at Nachman's face, and he screamed into his father's shirt. Without stopping to catch his breath, which got shorter and shorter, his father kept whispering, "We're almost there, *ketzele*—my kitten—we're almost there, Nemmale, we're almost at the doctor's, *yingele*—my little boy."

Nemmale—his favorite nickname—was woven too into that race down the street in the burning sun and the sand. Beyond this was an empty blank once more, and then the pungent memory of many days of pleasure and indulgence. Whether the relatives for whom his mother was waiting so expectantly ever arrived and who they were anyway—none of this seemed to matter in Nachman's memory. What he did remember was that for days on end he lay in semidarkness, while around him people whispered, caressed him, told him stories. He remembered someone saying that the boy, God forbid, might lose his eyesight completely and that one had to pray that his face would not be scarred and that he would be all right in the end. And he remembered Mister and Missus Blackman, who refused to budge from his bedside and plied him with candies. Yes, the memory of his being burned had about it a certain prolonged, festive intensity, as though it were then that he had really been born.

And his mother. At no other time, neither before nor after, was she ever the same again. He remembered it well. His face was bandaged; he was swathed in bandages and darkness. Before leaving for work, his father would take him in his arms and carry him to his warm bed. Then the door closed behind him and his mother would come to his side. He would lie on his back, and she would put one arm under him and draw him to her body that gave off fragrance and warmth. Tell me a story, he would say, and she would answer that she couldn't think of one just then. Instead, she sang him a Polish song in a soft voice. It was a song, she said, that she used to sing with her friends when they went for walks in the forest. Nachman asked if a forest was like the eucalyptus trees that grew behind the Mendelevitches' barn, and his mother laughed.

"A forest isn't like that at all. In a forest, a Polish forest, you can walk deeper and deeper, for hours, for days, and never see anything but trees. And when the winter is over and the snow melts, you can't even see the ground. All you can see is grass and flowers and berries. And the smells—what smells! You can never forget those smells. Your grandfather was in charge of the whole forest."

"Which grandfather?"

"My father. You are named after him."

"A grandfather like Mister Blackman?"

This time he heard his mother's loud laugh with all his body, perhaps because there were bandages over his eyes. Nowhere in Nachman's memory was there another day when his mother had laughed the same way.

"My father wasn't like that at all. In the first place, he was very young, and as tall as a tree, and handsome and strong. He had a beard that was as black as tar, clipped short, and he always wore leather boots and a coat with a fur collar. Everyone looked up to him. He was in charge of the whole forest, and the Poles had more trust in Pani Herzlich than in one of their own. No one lifted a finger in that forest without asking Pani Herzlich first. He was a very well-educated man."

"And were there berries in the forest?"

"What a question! Poland is full of them. Berries. And mushrooms. Everything."

"And geese?"

"Geese too. But not in the forest. That was in the villages, by the water. Did you know that Poland was full of water?"

"How many geese does it take to make a quilt?"

His mother burst out laughing again and hugged him until he could actually feel the warmth being poured from her body into his.

"I never counted. A lot. But praise God, there's no shortage of geese there." And suddenly, in another voice, "I have to go now, Nemmale. I have work up to my neck."

"What kind of berries are there in the forest?"

"All kinds. *Yagdes*—blueberries. And *malinas*—raspberries. And others too."

"And what's *grivn?*"

"Fried goose fat. Nemmale, I have to go."

"Mama!"

"What?"

"When will you teach me Polish, mama?"

"I'll teach you."

"Why doesn't papa let you speak Polish?"

"Papa says that in the Land of Israel we should only speak Hebrew."

"Why?"

"Because it's our language."

"But you told him you don't always understand."

"You'll teach me Hebrew."

"Teach me Polish, mama! You promised."

"I'll teach you. But I have to go to the kitchen now."

"Mama!"

She had already risen from the bed, and Nachman wanted to stop her. His eyes were bandaged, but he could sense her by her warmth.

"What does a forest look like?"

"Like a forest."

"Tell me."

"What do you want from me? I have work. When will I ever get it done?"

"Tell me."

She returned to the bed, lay down by his side, and told him. He lay there with his bandaged head on her breast, listening to the magical names of the trees, the berry bushes, the flowers that pushed up through the snow, wanting it to go on forever and ever.

This was the earliest memory Nachman was able to salvage from the bottom rung of the ladder that stood in dense fog—a memory that was all his, not transmitted through the memory of his family or built up with the help of analogies and deductions. Of this he was certain: his memory began with being burned.

2 | *Whose little boy are you?*

And there was also perhaps, somewhere back at the starting point, a faraway evening of scattered pieces all mixed together, many pictures and words that in the end fitted into an unmistakable something that made Nachman shiver each time he remembered it, as though it were still an unsolved mystery.

"Whose little boy are you?"

Evening. Dusk flowed into the yard from every direction, carried by the warm wind, loosed from the throats of the distant jackals. The glow that had been reflected a moment ago in the windows of Mister Blackman's enclosed porch now vanished and was gone. The glass panes seemed to darken, and the colorful ribbons in the sky faded away above the eucalyptus trees behind the barn.

"Whose little boy are you?"

Evening. He was trapped between Mister Blackman's prickly knees. Mister Blackman's white pants against his legs, and the smell of his clothes, so like the old wicker trunk in which his mother kept all kinds of clothes, annoyed Nachman so much that he twisted his neck and drew his face back as far as he could. Yet his eyes kept coming back to the brightly colored round tin on the table. On it, promising and menacing at once, Mister Blackman's hand rested. The tin was full of English toffee.

"Well? Whose little boy are you?"

Nachman made no attempt to escape from between Mister Blackman's knees. He kept his eyes on the colorful tin and said nothing.

"Well, whose are you? Whose?"

"Leave the boy alone already. Give him his toffee and stop driving him crazy!"

The rasping, voiceless words came from behind him. They were spoken by Missus Blackman, who had lost her voice in Zud Afrika.

Darkness continued to fill the yard, rising as high as the tops of the eucalyptus trees. There was a different light now in the sky, a light of many stars. Pinned by the rough cloth of Mister Blackman's knees, Nachman kept silent. Though it was now completely dark and there was not a sound beneath the fig tree, he knew that people were sitting there, on the wooden bench that circled the tree's trunk. He knew they were sitting and quietly laughing.

"Did you ever see such a strange child before?" said Mister Blackman to the fig tree, behind Nachman's back. And turning back to Nachman, he declared, "You're not getting a thing until you tell me whose little boy you are. Well? Whose?"

Mister Blackman's head, which smelled like his mother's wicker trunk too, was so close to him that he could make it out clearly even in the dark. All around his square skullcap Mister Blackman's tousled white hair fell over his forehead and into the completely different hairs of his beard. These were clipped short and were nearly colorless like the bristles of the hard brush that his mother dipped in tea and cleaned his father's black suit with on Sabbath eves. They got into Mister Blackman's nostrils and covered his lips. He even had hair sticking out of the middle of his nose, as though he were stuffed with it under his skin, like Nachman's mattress, which was filled with dry grass everywhere and not just where he had punctured it with a fork. The beard made him strangely afraid, and he held his breath and lowered his eyes to keep from having to look.

"Well? Don't be stubborn! Well? Whose little boy are you?"

As though on their own, the words spurted from Nachman's lips. "I'm my father's and my mother's."

Behind him he heard Missus Blackman's rasping laugh, or perhaps it was Adon—Mister—Mendelevitch's mare whinnying in the dark. In the dark, too, under the fig tree, someone was laughing and clapping his hands.

"You are?" Mister Blackman pinched Nachman's ear with two cold fingers, pulling it toward him. "Your father's and your mother's?"

He paused for a moment, Nachman's ear between his fingers, before thrusting his face forward until Nachman could feel the rough stubble of his beard.

"That's what you think, *oremer kind*—poor child! That's what you think! The truth of it is that they bought you. Yes, bought you! See for yourself. Just look at your hair. It's like a Bedouin's! And your eyes! Does your father have eyes like yours? Eh? Does your mother? And your face! Just touch it with a finger and the black comes right off like chimney soot. I may be Blackman, but you're really black. They bought you from the Bedouin. Yes, they did."

A dry laugh grated out of the narrow slit in Mister Blackman's beard and turned into a cough that turned into a wheeze. Mister Blackman let go of Nachman's ear. He opened his legs and hugged himself tightly around the chest while jerking his body and making strange sounds. Nachman was frightened. Yet, though no longer trapped between Mister Blackman's sharp knees, he did not turn to run but simply retreated a step and stood there staring at him. Mister Blackman stared back. Wheezing and coughing up phlegm, he reached for the round tin of toffee and motioned to Nachman to come closer.

"Come here, *arabchik!* Come over here, you Bedouin! Oy, I'm choking. *Oy!* Come, have some English toffee. It's the real thing. *Oy!*"

Now Nachman was terrified of the old man, but he was irresistibly drawn to the tin of toffee, with its gold bands between the different colors glittering even in the darkness. Its contents held him spellbound. He stuck his fingers into the tin and pulled out a toffee in its waxy wrapper.

"Take another, *arabchik. Nu,* take another. Take two, blackie."

By the time Nachman had taken a third toffee, the old man had fully recovered from his coughing and, seizing Nachman's wrist with his cold hand, pulled him back between his rough pants.

"Shalom!" he called out at the darkness under the fig tree, where Nachman's father, his mother, Missus Blackman, and still some more people were sitting. "Shalom, let me buy this little Bedouin from you. How much did you pay for him, eh? Five pounds? I'll give you fifty! Well, what do you say? You can buy ten more Bedouin for the same amount."

"Please, Mister Blackman. I really wish you'd stop talking like that in front of the boy."

Only now, suddenly, did his father's presence become real to him. All at once he felt it all over. Holding the toffee in clenched fists, he listened to him coming forward in the darkness, a quiver of anger in his voice. A sudden fierce desire overcame him to break away from the pressure of Mister Blackman's fingers and run to his father. He tried to worm free, wriggling and striking with his fist at the old man's white sleeve, but the cold hands were too strong for him. The wicker-trunk smell twined itself around him, and Mister Blackman coughed wheezingly again through his scraggly beard.

"I love this little *arabchik,* and I want to buy him . . . kkchhhh, *oy!* I'll give you fifty!"

"Please, Mister Blackman, let the boy alone."

Two strong hands gripped Nachman by the elbows and swept him cleanly into the air, far from Mister Blackman's straw chair. For a second he sailed free, held by nothing at all, and then he landed straight in his father's lap. He lay there enveloped by the ticklish hands, the strong smell, the rough cheeks. The breath he held while flying through the air had exploded in a loud laugh as he sifted through his father's arms, but now, with his face hidden in his father's coarse shirt, the laughter turned without warning into an unfathomable fear, a high-pitched, continuous sob that ended in a torrent of tears. Into the blackness came his father's whisper, as the stubble on his father's cheeks scratched at his ear and throat. "That's enough, Nachman. That's enough. Look at me. I'm right here. Your mother's here too. Nemmale, our son, our only one."

His sobs continued by themselves in the blackness of the shirt, but through them he heard his father say sharply to Mister Blackman in another, harsher voice, "Those are no games to play, Mister Blackman. I'm asking you for the last time not to say such things to the boy. I'd lay down my life a hundred times over for the little finger on his hand. Look at papa, Nemmale."

His tears dried up and vanished as quickly as they had flowed in the first place, but his face remained hidden. The longer he kept it pressed into the hideaway of his father's shirt, the longer his father would keep whispering the words that he couldn't hear enough of, "*You're ours, ours.*" Just as he liked to do when he was alone with his mother under the feather quilt.

Now too he curled himself up like a porcupine against his father, whose firm voice continued to protect him. "The boy is shaking all over. Why must you put such ideas into his head, Mister Blackman?"

"You're worse than a woman, Shalom! What on earth did I say? *Arabchik?*"

It was this word that stuck in Nachman's memory. Nothing, he felt certain, went back further or came before. *What did I say? Arabchik?* Yet the more he tried to untangle the skeins of the knot, the less it came apart, so that no matter how often he tried to plumb the mystery to its depths, he was left in the end with the same summer evening in the yard and the question, "Whose little boy are you?"

"You're ours, you sillyhead. Of course you are," whispered his father's voice in his ear, but Nachman was thinking of Abed, their neighbor Adon Mendelevitch's herdsman, and of all his black children in the barnyard where the eucalyptus trees began. Perhaps he too was Abed's child? Perhaps his mother and father, too, like Mister and Missus Blackman, hadn't had children of their own, and Abed had sold them one of his, who was none other than himself, Nachman. Or perhaps he had been switched after being born, so that his father and mother were really bringing up a black Bedouin boy, while he, the real Nachman, was left to himself among the cow dung behind the barn, without a father or a mother, barefoot and dirty and covered with flies.

Try as he might, this question remained unanswered. Even when years later in his memory he again curled up like a porcupine in the darkness of his father's rough shirt, he could never descend below this rung on the fog-bound ladder.

"I'm yours, papa! Papa!" From the side he could see his short arms hugging his father's neck, though they couldn't reach all the way around it.

"Who else's could you be, you sillyhead? Whose?"

3 | Enter Uncle Rifael

Enter Uncle Rifael into Nachman's memory: from out of the gloom, which during the daylight was the cattle gate with its dust ground up by the hooves of the herd and its giant cypresses, Uncle Rifael suddenly appears riding his little donkey. The donkey's footsteps vanished into the dust and its gray hairs were swallowed by the darkness. Visible only were Uncle Rifael's white work clothes, his legs that dangled far apart and half touched the ground, his rolled-up shirt sleeves, and his cap encrusted with dried cement. He guided the donkey with a poke of his pointed stick beneath its tail while flicking its ears with the end of the rein. Nachman ran after him, careful to keep a safe distance, and watched him tie the animal to a fencepost in the yard. Then he escorted Uncle Rifael to his seat on the warm stoop by his father.

Uncle Rifael was his father's brother and his father was Uncle Rifael's brother. All the questions that he asked his father and mother about this only made them laugh, and Uncle Rifael laughed too when he was told about them; yet they were real questions all the same. Nachman's eyes would shift back and forth from his Uncle Rifael, who revealed a head of kinky hair when he took off his cap, to his father, who uncovered his head only in bed, at which times it proved to be mostly white forehead even where it should have had hair. The glass of tea Nachman's mother had brought him in one hand and a spoon in the other, Uncle Rifael would sit and slowly stir his drink, peering into the glass all the while as if to see what he had accomplished. The yellow light of the kerosene lamp that hung high on a nail in the porch wall fell on Uncle Rifael from above and behind, highlighting his hair, which had been pressed beneath his cap all day long, gummy with sweat and cement. The light fell too on his thick arms, which were covered with black grass, but failed to reach his face bent over the glass of tea. Nachman's father would talk, and Uncle Rifael would listen and not say a word. The lamp shone on his father's face, while Uncle Rifael's slipped deeper into the shadow as he silently sipped his tea. Sometimes his silence would make them all just as quiet, so that they could hear the water pumps ticking far off, and almost, too, the whisper of the Lux lamp in the Mendelevitches' open window. Suddenly Nachman was startled by a loud heehaw, which sawed up and down as though someone had rammed a large nail under the donkey's tail. Uncle Rifael stirred and even laughed a broken laugh, which had a funny, wheezing sound, "Hey there, you *shofar*-blower! The High Holy Days are still a long way off!"

The donkey's bray set Adon Mendelevitch's large donkey braying too, and they were joined one after the other by more distant companions. Uncle Rifael rose from the stoop, handed Nachman's mother his empty glass, and said, "The poor fellow's right—animals too have to sleep."

He quieted the donkey with a flick between his ears, untied it from the post, and pulled it after him into the darkness. Nachman and his parents walked with him past the gate. It was night already, but it had gotten lighter too. Stars were scattered all over the sky, and a red moon rose behind the mountains. Uncle Rifael hugged the donkey's neck, clambering on his belly up its back until he was in a sitting position, and took the prod from the saddlebag. He flicked at the donkey's left ear while jerking its head to the right with the rein and said, "You wouldn't be breaking any law if you visited us some day too."

"We will," said Nachman's father. "It's just hard to take the child so far at night."

"Take him for a walk on a Saturday morning. It won't do you any harm. There are worse sins than walking too far on the Sabbath."

Nachman's mother kept quiet, but his father called out after Uncle Rifael, "Tell Tsipoyrele that it wouldn't harm her either if she were to drop in on us some time when she's in town."

But the donkey had already slipped its moorings and lost itself soundlessly in the darkness, beneath all the stars, among the shadow cast by the moon as it rose over the dirt path.

This was how Uncle Rifael first entered Nachman's memory, on his almost nightly visits on his way back from the work lineup in town. But was it only these visits that Nachman remembered and not all those other times too when Uncle Rifael's name was simply in the air? There was hardly anything into which it wasn't dragged, and whenever it was, it was always with some hidden innuendo, which became inextricably mixed up in Nachman's memory with this small man himself riding on a donkey, his father's brother.

On one such night, Nachman remembered, after they had seen Uncle Rifael off, his father stopped to chat with Mister Blackman, who was lying in his beach chair in the dark. He said, Nachman didn't know why, "We were the two youngest, Rifael and I. Our older brothers used to say that even as a baby there was something wrong with him, that he used to take things from the house and give them away to strangers. My mother said that he was sure to be swindled some day out of everything he had. Someone would steal the shirt from his back and he wouldn't even notice."

"She saw what lay ahead," mused Nachman's mother in a whisper, as though to herself.

"Exactly what was it that she saw?" There was suppressed anger in his father's voice.

Instead of replying, his mother took him by the hand and led him inside. Yet later, as he lay in bed, his face pressed against the bars, he could hear her say, "But he's all dried out, he's shriveled like a raisin! He's afraid even to sit with us for half an hour!"

"It's her fear that he's afraid of. She spends the whole day out there by herself, surrounded by sand dunes, in the middle of nowhere."

"If she'd do some work herself, her time would pass more quickly and he wouldn't turn into such a wreck. How can anyone carry on as he does from dawn to dusk, and tend a farm too, and walk here and back every day—and all by himself! He even has to buy his own food. Did you hear him say 'the animals'? He meant himself and the donkey!"

At this point a different note crept in, which Nachman knew was not from the same evening but from another conversation. He could see—he was ready to swear to it—his father confide to his mother, his voice choked with anger, "But he's literally turning into an animal, like a blind horse turning around its tail or some dumb ox. He's lower than the lowest *goy*. Believe me, every Yanek Khlepko is more of a Jew than he. How on earth, I ask myself, and it tears me up inside just to think about it—how on earth did such a *zhlob* ever grow up in my father's house? No God, no Sabbath, no holidays, no family! I swear to you—here and now, by your life and mine and Nachman's—I'll throw him out of here like a dog if he ever dares show his face in my house again!"

This oath had a frightening effect on Nachman and apparently on his mother too. "Shalom, you should be ashamed of yourself. You musn't swear that way. He's your brother."

"I don't want to hear about him any more. I have no brother."

"How many brothers do you have here that you can afford to write him off so easily?"

"I left them all behind when I came here. All of them, all my brothers, the whole family. Let's get it into our heads that we're alone here. There's no one else and there never was."

How, how could his father have been so cruel?

Nachman's memory was full of riddles, blind exits and entrances that made no sense. As though he had literally vanished or never existed, Uncle Rifael ceased to appear with his donkey in the yard in the evening. But his name lingered on, and the day didn't pass when it wasn't brought up along with all his sins. Each detail that Nachman heard was linked to another, and his imagination filled in the gaps. In years to come, whenever he returned—which was over and over—to those first, distant days, to that dawn of his life, his memory refused to distinguish what he himself had experienced from what he had heard or managed to piece together. Just as he had done with the feel of the house and the yard, the rays of the sun, being burned on that Friday, Mister and Missus Blackman, so he took in whatever his father's and his mother's memories gave out, what each remembered separately and the family memory of both. His keen senses were ever alert—record, absorb, connect, put together, and constantly feed his own memory. There came days when it seemed to him that everything, from the hour of his birth and even before, everything was his own, something he himself remembered.

And yet it was not the same thing. There was still a difference. Only who was to say whether it mattered or not?

4 | The family memory

The family memory credited everything to Uncle Rifael, in good times the good, and in bad times the bad. His mother's memory, though, had nothing to say of him in good times at all, whereas in bad it would snap. If Rifael hadn't put all kinds of ideas into your head, there would be a different face on things today.

In the picture album his mother kept on the top shelf of the clothes closet there was a photograph of Uncle Rifael that Nachman, who had leafed through the album many times and tried to breathe life into each picture, knew so well that it seemed he himself had been there, in Kaplan's photography shop, when Uncle Rifael had posed for the camera. How different the man in the picture was from the Uncle Rifael who rode into their yard at night mounted on his little donkey: his face was soft and round, without its black stubble, and his large, luminous eyes bulged slightly outward instead of squinting beneath lashes encrusted with gray cement. He was wearing a long, Polish-looking coat that came down below his knees and had a starched collar around his neck and a broad tie that emerged beneath his chin and vanished somewhere underneath his coat. White dots were reflected in the picture from the shiny surface of his eyes and the tips of his shoes.

According to the family memory, this photograph had been enclosed by Uncle Rifael in his first letter home after he had suddenly gone off to Palestine. The letter itself, the family memory told, had been just like the picture: festive, full of enthusiasm, all milk and honey.

If it hadn't been for those letters, said his mother's memory, and Nachman knew what she was getting at, things today would have a different face.

That, his father's memory angrily interrupted, had nothing to do with it! I would never have gone to America in any case. Really, that's all we needed, to have to go through what happened to Elyakum in Chicago!

It's pointless to talk about it now that it makes no difference any more, said his mother's memory. But his father insisted on reconstructing it all from the moment their ship had dropped anchor in Haifa, so that Nachman felt certain that he had seen his parents standing there with his own eyes, lost and penniless on one of the city's streets, looking in vain for Uncle Rifael, who was supposed to have met them.

We should have known right then and there who we were dealing with, said his mother's memory. But we couldn't even afford to give him a piece of our mind, because on the train, in Romania, we were robbed of all our money, and we arrived in Palestine without a penny to our name. There we stood in the middle of the street, surrounded by the dirt and the noise and the Arabs, and on the hottest day that anyone could remember. It was all I could do to keep from jumping back into the ocean.

At this point his father's memory sought to correct his mother's by pointing out to Uncle Rifael's from the moment of their arrival in the Land of Israel. Yes, we were robbed, it would say, but it wasn't so terrible. We weren't given a Rothschild's fortune for a dowry in the first place, and we still had some money left in our pockets, so that we didn't have to go begging right off the boat.

All of a sudden, his mother's memory stubbornly went on, to fall straight from Poland, from my family, from my mother's house, into all that heat and dirt, with all those Arabs and flies, and not a single familiar face to welcome us or tell us what to do in that wilderness. It was pure luck, a miracle, that I had a few dollars sewn into the lining of my coat, so that we could at least take a room in a hotel and not have to die of hunger and shame in the first few days. *M'shtayns gezogt*—imagine—dollars. I think I must have been so upset over being robbed that I already took sick on the boat, because I came down with an upset stomach and was very weak, but when I came ashore and took a good look around me and saw that Rifael wasn't there, I felt that *ikh vell dos nisht oyshalten*—I simply wouldn't survive. And in the hotel I took sick for real, with a high fever, because of the heat and the bad water and all the excitement. How could he possibly have abandoned us like that? How could he have been so heartless?

It really didn't matter much, disagreed his father's memory when his mood was good. So we spent a day or two at loose ends in Haifa. Was that really so terrible? There are better places than a port for kissing and hugging anyway. Just as we made our own way from Warsaw to Haifa, we could make it from Haifa to town. That wasn't the worst part. It wasn't as if we didn't know that people grew callous in Palestine and became hard-boiled and dried out. The worst part happened later. That I can't understand, I can't forgive to this day.

If it didn't end in tragedy, his mother's memory continued, it was only because of old Widow Simkin. The minute she looked into my eyes she knew I was ill. She took me to our room (at least he did get us a room, said his father's memory, and his mother's memory replied, How awfully grand of him!) and undressed me and washed off all the filth that had accumulated on the way. Then she rubbed down my back and chest with alcohol and gave me a cup of special tea and a steam kettle. She wouldn't even let me get out of bed.

It was because of the widow, his father summed up with a trace of ceremoniousness, that we felt we were really in the Land of Israel. It's over with now, but all in all it's best not to think back on those first few days.

But those first few days fully occupied the family memory, from which they spilled over into Nachman's own recollections, until it seemed to him that he'd actually taken part in them, though he hadn't even been born then. Most of all they erupted when times were bad, which was often enough.

We had a room, all right, and even work, his mother's memory bitterly continued. Right away, on our second day here, Uncle Rifael came to inform me that in Palestine a person had to work. He was afraid, her memory added, that we might become his charity wards.

By then I couldn't have cared, said his father's memory. I didn't even ask him why he hadn't come to meet us. He tried to apologize and say that that's how it was, that in Palestine a day of work was too sacred to miss, that it had taken long enough to get the old colonists to agree that a Jewish worker could hold his own with an Arab, and that when you got a day of work you didn't pass it up. And to work you had to be healthy.

You should have seen his face when he saw that I was sick, his mother's memory said. You have to be healthy to work. As if I were pretending, as if I haven't worked enough since!

I heard him and kept quiet, said his father's memory. And I didn't say anything either when he told me that I was going out to the fields with him the next day. True, I wondered how I could possibly leave Leah all by herself, in her condition, with a fever, and in a strange country. But I didn't say anything. I was a Shpiegler too, and if my dear brother was doing all this to test me, he was welcome to try. We would see which one of us looked bad in the end. And the fact is that I started to work on our second day in Palestine, and I'm proud to say that I've been working ever since. And Leah too—two days later she was up keeping house on her shaky legs.

It was only because of the widow, his mother's memory said, it was only because of her that I got through those first few days. The state I was in! She was like a mother to me, even more than a mother. She not only took care of me, she taught me how to live in this country, how to cook filling meals that wouldn't cost too much money, where to buy, how to bargain with the Arab women who went from door to door selling vegetables and eggs, how to run a household in general. She was a very clever woman, and she had been living here in town right from the start, for over forty years. In the whole town there's no one like her anymore. Despite everything she had gone through, she still had a Jewish heart. It was because of her that I began to feel a little *nisht azoy elent*—not so lonely. There's no point in discussing it now, but if it hadn't been for her, who knows if ever I would have gotten through those first days.

That was how the family memory spoke when times were bad, when Uncle Rifael stayed away from their yard and visited them only in thought. But suddenly, one day, he reappeared on his donkey out of the gathering dusk, his legs dangling down on both sides and his cement-caked shoes half touching the powdery dust. Once again he sat on the front steps slowly stirring his hot tea while Nachman's father talked in the yellow glow of the kerosene lamp. On evenings like this the family memory would tell such completely different stories that it was practically impossible for Nachman to connect them with the bad ones he had heard. On one such evening, Nachman remembered, his father retold how Uncle Rifael had once had one drink too many and forgot to watch his tongue. Or could it be that his father had told the story to a third party, while Nachman himself had personally witnessed Uncle Rifael's rare outburst of talk? No, it could not be, for it was clear from the story itself that he, Nachman, was not even then a twinkle in his mother's eye.

We had just finished building our first house, his father's memory related. That is, it was the first that I myself helped build. The owner brought wine for all the workers, which was the custom. It was the end of August, right before the Jewish New Year. My hands and feet were calloused and full of cuts and all banged up from the hammer, but I was in seventh heaven. We drank a *le'hayyim,* and then we went with the rest of the wine to old Widow Simkin's yard. It was the kind of evening that I used to see in my imagination when I dreamed of the Land of Israel. I nursed my wine along, but Rifael drank glass after glass as though it were tea. At first he drank and kept quiet as usual. Then he began to sing with us, and suddenly he remembered that the Day of Atonement was near. He threw himself on my neck and began to beg for forgiveness: Forgive me, Shalom. It wasn't right of me, Leah. I don't know what the devil got into my head. It was I who persuaded you to come here and join me because until you came I didn't have a single living soul. I did nothing but work like a mule from dawn to dusk. I don't know what got into me ever since you came. Maybe it's that here you have to—I mean—there isn't any choice, you have to harden yourself like a stone. And really, I had an image of you as being made out of silk, a mama's little boy who talked a lot and had a handwriting like a scribe. Believe me, I swear to you, I don't have a soul here without you. It's so good to have you here, Shalom. How like a stone I have been, Leah.

His father's memory was fond of this evening, while Nachman himself, even when he had heard about it for the hundred-and-first time, never failed to sympathize with Uncle Rifael, both when the story was told to explain how his father and Rifael had suddenly made up, and when it came to introduce the period that followed, in which the two brothers quarreled again and went their separate ways.

It was a labyrinth that Nachman was never able to penetrate successfully. I was in the habit, his father's memory told, of praying with phylacteries every morning, and Rifael used to grumble about this and tell me that because of it we were always late for work. And so to teach him a lesson I changed my routine and started taking the phylacteries with me to the field in my lunch basket. When it was time for the morning break, I'd go off by myself and pray. This infuriated him, but there was nothing he could do about it. Instead, he began to arrange things so that on Friday afternoons we would finish work as late as possible, which meant I had to pass through the town in my work clothes after the Sabbath whistle had already sounded. One Sabbath eve we began to argue so furiously that we nearly struck each other with our hoes. I couldn't understand it—I never will—there were times when he was just like Cain!

In any case, his father's memory concluded the episode, that same day I swore that from then on I'd look out for myself and not work with Rifael any more, even if Leah and I had to go hungry. And that wasn't just a figure of speech. When the Arab workers left the town during the riots, all the farmers took an oath in the synagogue to employ only Jews, but time went by and the oaths were forgotten and the groves and farmyards were full of Arabs again. Whoever lost his job in those days joined hundreds of others who literally had nothing to eat. I didn't have any skills, what little money we got for our wedding had been stolen in Romania, and except for the Herzlichs, who came after us and settled in Tel Aviv, we had no family here at all. But still, I said to myself, the less I have to do with Rifael, the better. We'll get along the way all the other pioneers do.

Here his father's memory waxed expansive and related in detail and with considerable pleasure, which Nachman shared because he knew whom it involved, how they had come to move into the Mendelevitches' yard. In the end, his father's memory went on, I didn't go to pieces, thank God. I began looking for odd jobs and I found them, sometimes as a yardhand, sometimes in the orange groves, sometimes in the building trade. And I was able to make ends meet without ever having to work on the Sabbath. Little by little I made friends, and people in the town came to know me. They learned that here was one pioneer who was not ashamed to do any kind of work and to do it as best he could, yet who was also not ashamed to be seen in the synagogue.

It was actually there, his memory continued, that I met old Adon Mendelevitch, who was really quite a personality. One Sabbath he did something that was totally unheard of between us and the old colonists: after the service, he came over and invited us, Leah and myself, to have tea with them later that afternoon. We went, and right over there—here his father's memory always pointed to the corner of the yard with a backward jerk of his thumb—I saw Abed working by the barn. It made me terribly angry, but I didn't say anything. He wanted to talk books with me, which was the reason he was attracted to me in the first place, because even though he'd been a farmer for forty years and had a reputation for great physical strength—I wouldn't want to be on the receiving end of it even now that he's old—he had an intellectual side too, and was the only one of the old colonists to have any real culture. He had a memory like a steel trap, and even later, when I came to know him better, he sometimes astonished me by reciting some piece from world literature by heart, or by telling me about some philosophical conversation he had with Bialik or Rabbi Kook, or with the Baron de Rothschild in Paris, or with everyone who was anyone, and in such detail, as though every word had been engraved in his brain. That was one side of him, but on the other, he was a tough, flint-fisted farmer whose fields and groves and yard were full of Arab labor. Anyway, that Saturday I steered the conversation to the fact that I was looking for work, any work. The old man, who didn't much care for the new brand of pioneers with their high-flown talk, pointed to Abed and asked sarcastically, "You want to work like him, Shpiegler?"

"I want to work in his place, Adon Mendelevitch."

"Don't be a fool, Shpiegler. Leave that kind of nonsense to your brother and his friends."

"And what am I to do in the meantime? Do you want me to go back to Poland, or should I maybe try Australia?"

"Go find a job in Tel Aviv, or enroll in the Teachers Seminary in Jerusalem. When you graduate, you can come back here and teach. Your hands are too delicate and your eyes are too bright for anything else."

"Right now, as of tomorrow morning, I need a day's work in town."

"Do you really think I'm crazy enough to put you up on a pile of horse manure together with that Arab peon?"

"Not at all. Invite Abed for tea and I'll do the work by myself."

Each time his memory reached this cutting reply, his father looked up at his audience to observe the impression it made. Each time Nachman was filled with admiration all over again. It was little wonder that old Adon Mendelevitch had been so taken with his father that he found work for him in his orange groves. When their lease was up they left old Widow Simkin's—that is, the neighborhood in which Uncle Rifael still lived before he crossed the sea of dunes—and moved into the Mendelevitches' yard.

This story had a permanent place in Nachman's memory for yet another reason. It was connected with a crucial event in his life: his birth. Times were very hard then, his mother's memory related, and so I hid my pregnancy from Shalom for as long as I could, though there were days when I practically panicked because I didn't know where our next meal was coming from. Once we moved to the Mendelevitches', though, and Shalom whitewashed the room himself, and we bought two beds and a used cabinet with a large mirror, and he had more or less steady work, I couldn't keep it a secret any longer. And I knew too how hurt Shalom felt by his quarrel with Rifael. When he wrote letters home, he was ashamed to mention that he hadn't seen his brother for months. I was sure he'd run to tell Rifael right away and then they'd make up. And so I told him.

I was so happy, said his father's memory, that I ran right out into the street, because I was sure that at that hour of the evening he would be standing around with all the other unmarried workers who were alone like him and never knew what to do with themselves at night. I embraced him right there without a word, kissed him on both cheeks, and told him the news. Deep down he too was a Shpiegler, soft and sentimental. He kissed me and wiped the tears from his eyes, and the two of us went to see Leah in our new house. We talked and celebrated and were together again.

What happened after that, Nachman didn't know. In his memory he clearly recalled those summer evenings when Uncle Rifael would appear on his little donkey out of the gathering dusk. He would drink a glass of tea with them and disappear on his donkey back into the darkness beneath a mass of stars. When had he stopped coming again, and why? Although the gaps in Nachman's memory were now growing less frequent and confusing, or perhaps because of this, Uncle Rifael's new disappearance made no impression on him. Their new house with its kitchen and porch, the yard, the stable, young Madam Mendelevitch's parlor, Mister and Missus Blackman—these now filled Nachman's world, though they too no longer formed its horizons. He could also remember excursions to the various acquaintances, to the town square on summer evenings, where they stood in a crowd and listened to the firemen's band play on a high platform from which the polished brass trumpets glittered extra brightly under the electric lights, or to a large yard on Saturday nights, which was paved with big pebbles and had a giant swing in the middle, where they ate cold yogurt, and the air was filled with music from the gramophone, and the pebbles grated under their chairs, and they all said together, "Oh, that Josef Schmidt." And far, far away at the end of the village—Nachman was certain that this was his own memory and not his family's—beyond the square and the band, beyond the big building with the large, brightly lit windows from which came a din of voices that belonged to the workers who had no homes of their own to eat in, there was his first trip to a movie. They stood in an unfamiliar yard, among high eucalyptuses, in front of the open door of a corrugated tin hut in which people were sitting in darkness, except for the shaft of white light that streamed above their heads as though it had burst from a fireman's hose, though it was made of glowing dust in which all kinds of night bugs were dancing. Nachman stood outside with his father—or was it his mother?—who picked him up and sat him on his shoulders, while at the far end of the strange hut he saw giant figures come and go, approach and recede. A machine whirred near his ear, and Nachman saw that the dusty light was flowing from it through the door of the hut and over the heads of the people to illuminate the giant figures who came and went and kept changing their number and size. Nachman couldn't remember what else there had been, but the movie stuck in his mind. That, and still more. There was an exciting trip in an autobus to Tel Aviv through sand dunes and orange groves and hedges of prickly pear and black Bedouin tents to visit his mother's relatives who had come from abroad. That same summer, almost entirely on his own, he had begun to read whatever was written in letters and words. Each day was crammed full of things that were indisputably his and that his memory took for its own, while Uncle Rifael and Tsipoyrele no longer appeared except in the scary stories that he told himself at night while lying in his barred bed, his face to the wall, pretending to sleep as he listened to the family memory, which had neither beginning nor end, which was something apart from Nachman and yet never ceased to be absorbed by him and to become part of himself.

And then, all of a sudden, Uncle Rifael appeared once more to stand at the center of a complete, unforgettable scene that perhaps marked the end of the period of fog.

5 | *Dreams don't lie*

Early that evening Nachman's father took a pinch of ashes from inside the heavy steam iron on whose prow a black rooster raised a stiff comb, rolled a hard-boiled egg in them, and told Nachman that the ashes were to remember the Temple that had been burned to ashes on this day and the egg was to remember the Exile, which went round and round like an egg. They hurried through an early supper, so as to be through before the sun set behind the eucalyptus trees, and set out for the synagogue. As they cut through the empty lot across the street, a moon as white as the hood of a Lux lamp shone high above in the sky. It was hot, without a breath of wind, and the trees stood silent as stones. A smell of smoke hung in the air, as though someone had been burning brambles. In the street by the Mendelevitches' house they saw three horses pawing the fine sand. Young Adon Mendelevitch was mounted on one of them, but Nachman's father didn't wave hello to him because on the fast day of Tisha B'Av it was forbidden to greet anyone while mourning for the Temple that was destroyed. Father didn't greet old Adon Mendelevitch either, who was standing by the wide gate among the cypress trees, but he did pause to whisper something in his ear. Nachman held on to his father's hand, and they stood there for a moment looking at the horsemen. All three had broad-brimmed hats on their heads, and the butts of their rifles stuck up from their saddles. Suddenly young Adon Mendelevitch's horse bolted from its place and started at a gallop down the sandy path toward the vineyards with the other two horses after it.

"Abed hasn't come back yet," said his father, and Nachman didn't know whether it was a question or a statement of fact.

"No, he hasn't," said old Adon Mendelevitch, already turning away from them as he walked slowly back to the yard. Now Nachman recalled that earlier that day Mister Blackman had asked Adon Mendelevitch where Abed and his family had gone. On Friday, his mother had whispered to Mister Blackman, all the Arabs had vanished from town. They had disappeared together, every last one of them, and God only knew what trouble was brewing. If even Abed, who spoke Yiddish and was friendly with the Zionist Workers Club—if even he had disappeared, then someone was up to no good.

Nachman felt his father's firm, dry fingers sharply against the palm of his hand. It was an effort to keep up with his father's legs on the narrow path among the thistles. The thorns scratched his bare arm whenever his father swerved slightly, but he didn't let go of his hand. The moon cast a milky light on the flat mountains, which seemed unusually close and clear. There, in the mountains, was where the Arabs lived. That was where they had gone on Friday, and it was from there they would come. Nachman had heard the story that old Adon Mendelevitch told long ago to his father, how they had come by the thousands with their donkeys and their sacks and their oil cans to burn the town down, how young and old Adon Mendelevitch and a few other men had driven them off on horseback, and how one of the watchmen had been found dead in the orange groves with his belly split open and his shoes stuck into his belly. "But don't think," old Adon Mendelevitch had said to his father, "that we didn't even the score. We evened it all right, and in a way they'll never forget." All this rushed through Nachman's mind while his legs ran after his father's. The synagogue was already in front of them, lamplight falling through its open windows into the bluish glow of the moon outside. They crossed a thorny field and followed the path to the courtyard with its large trees. Nachman's father reached out to catch a branch of a chinaberry tree and plucked a handful of hard, green balls. *Bombalach.* He put them in his pocket and said to Nachman that he could have them in the synagogue to throw. At people? On Tisha B'Av, his father explained, it was allowed. Under the windows, in a patch of bluish light and milky shadow, the children ran about shouting and throwing *bombalach* at each other. Nachman was drawn to them, to the tumultuous center of things, but his father pulled him up the steps and into the synagogue. He had been here before, but a strange, puzzling picture now met his eyes. The benches and chairs had all been laid on their sides, and on them sat the worshipers, almost on the ground, their feet unshod. His father too had left his shoes among all the other pairs on the open veranda and now walked about in his socks. There was barely room for them to squeeze onto the end of a bench. Nachman's father took a prayer book and began to leaf through it. The synagogue was filled with an odd murmur, as though everybody on the benches was praying for his life or mourning for something stolen, which made Nachman forget the three horsemen and the crowd of children throwing *bombalach* outside. Only at that exact moment, almost, so Nachman remembered, a great cry was heard from the high veranda of the synagogue. "Fire! Fire!"

The service stopped. Everyone rushed outside in his stockinged feet, crowding on to the veranda, fighting to get to a place from where he could see. Now Nachman was outdoors too, astride his father's shoulders, his eyes, like everyone's, turned to the distant mountains. The milky air was red right up to the sky, as though the moon had lost its light. Below, where the mountains began, a large fire could be seen.

"It's beginning," someone said.

"On Tisha B'Av of all days," said someone else.

Then they were back in the synagogue again, on the upended benches, chanting lamentations. His father took the *bombalach* from his pocket and urged Nachman to throw them at the worshipers, but Nachman was no longer in the mood. The old man sitting in front of them kept mumbling into his prayer book in a singsong wail while tossing his head back toward Nachman's father and saying in time to the prayer, as though this too were printed in his book, "Oy, on Tisha B'Av! Always on Tisha B'Av!"

That night, so the family memory was to relate in years to come, his father's father died. That night too, his father's memory would relate with an odd sort of pride, he had a dream. In it he saw Nachman's grandfather, his own father, stretched out on the floor in their home in Europe with two black candles by his head. They had gone out and were smoking. He tried over and over to light them with matches, but it wasn't any use. The flame wouldn't catch, and only the smoke kept rising like thin bits of string. When Rifael came to the house and handed me the letter, whispered his father's memory, my head started to spin and I fainted because I knew right away what was in it.

All this was told by the family memory, which Nachman did not really need, because he remembered it clearly on his own. They were sitting and eating on the porch, a horde of mosquitoes and night bugs fluttering about the kerosene lamp that hung on the wall, circling around it, colliding with the wall, biting them on the ears, the neck, the feet—when suddenly Uncle Rifael emerged on his donkey right in front of their eyes. Before he could dismount, Nachman's father jumped to his feet, and his mother, after an uncertain moment, rose from the table too. They stood there motionless, waiting. As always, as in the days when he had been a steady visitor, Uncle Rifael carefully hitched the donkey to a fence post before approaching the house.

Nachman's father could contain himself no longer. "Something has happened, Rifael!"

Uncle Rifael's cheeks were blacker than usual, as though the darkness from which he had just materialized had rubbed off on them, and his grimy cap came down over his ears, covering most of his forehead. Still he said nothing, shifting from foot to foot, parting his lips as though gasping for air. Suddenly he fell on Nachman's father, resting his hands on his shoulders and burying his face in his shirt, shaking all over, emitting strange noises.

His father fought free of Rifael's embrace.

"What happened, Rifael! Tell me the truth, what have you heard?"

"Shalom," he whispered, "*der tateh*—Father . . . "

"*Der tateh,*" echoed his father, as though he had been expecting it. "Yes, I saw him."

Nachman's eyes raced back and forth from his father to Uncle Rifael, both frightened and entertained at once. It was an unexpected sight, coming as it did after the long time that Uncle Rifael hadn't been to see them, and after all that had been said about him and Tsipoyrele. He looked so funny with his black face, and his clothes that were gritty with cement, and the comical way that he cried. From time to time he wiped his stubby fingers before bursting into tears again. In between he fumbled through his pockets, pulled out a creased envelope that he handed to Nachman's father, took a stool, turned it on its side as though it were Tisha B'Av, sat down, unlaced his shoes, which were as gray and heavy as blocks, removed them, and remained sitting there in his gray socks, with his heels and his toes sticking out through the large holes. Nachman's father was very quiet. Standing by the lamp, he took the letter out of the wrinkled envelope and read it slowly, soundlessly, to himself. When he was through, he folded it again, put it back, and said, "Dreams don't lie. They certainly don't."

Only then, as though he had been stricken by a sudden pain, did his face contort and the sobs spurt from his stiffened lips like water from a broken main. They spurted and stopped. He went back to the table, picked up the bread knife, stretched his shirt taut at the collar, and slashed it with the knife until it tore along a long line.

"Papa!" Nachman ran to him, frightened by the sight of him cutting himself with the knife.

His father muttered some incomprehensible words, just like in the synagogue. He put the knife back on the table and seized Nachman, hugging him tightly to him.

"Your grandfather," he began, and already he was bitterly weeping again, even as he spoke. "You don't have a grandfather, Nemmale, you don't have one anymore."

"Don't frighten the child," whispered his mother, who had tears in her eyes too. But he was already accustomed to them.

"It's something he has to know. If he never had the chance to see his grandfather, let him at least remember when he died. Let him know that there was a man, Reb Aryeh-Leib Shpiegler."

Now all three of them were crying, and Nachman too would have liked to join in, except that he hadn't any tears. Just then the yard was rocked by the bray of the donkey, which sounded right in his ears. Uncle Rifael leaped up in his socks to quiet it, and Nachman could scarcely keep from laughing. Now Adon Mendelevitch's big donkey was braying too, and soon the whole lot would be one great chorus. Suddenly he spied Mister Blackman, who had been roused from his beach chair by the noise and the tears, shuffling toward them in his slippers. Only as he approached the circle of light did it occur to Nachman that Mister Blackman too could die, just like his grandfather. His mother's father, after whom he was named Nachman, had died too. Nachman stared at Mister Blackman and wondered how he would die, already overcome with the sadness of it. If Mister Blackman dies, he thought, I'll cry like papa and mama and Uncle Rifael. And if papa and mama die, I'll cry too. As he continued to picture the death of the people he knew, a lump formed in his throat. He ran to Mister Blackman and began to weep savagely, clinging to Mister Blackman's white pants. "Don't die, Mister Blackman, please don't. . . ."

6 | *Bluma's garden*

"A child like you is a disaster around the house. If I should ever collapse one day and not get up again, I want you to know that it's only because of what I have to go through on account of you. I don't have an Arab woman to wash and clean for me like Madam Mendelevitch, and your grandfather didn't leave your father any grand estate. Just to save a few pennies I have to get up every morning at four o'clock and run to the marketplace while it's still dark out, in God knows what kind of weather, to drag back two big baskets of supplies that cut my hands raw. All day long I'm on my feet, running home from the store and back again, waiting on customers, cooking, washing, putting things in order, standing in the store until ten in the evening, and then slaving on until midnight to make sure that your jacket is starched and pressed and that you aren't dressed any worse than that little Lord Balfour. And now you jump right into the mud in your white pants and your shiny new shoes. . . . Put down those raisins, Nachman! I'm going to give you a licking one day that will make your teeth pop out and then you'll really have something to pick up with your hands! I'm going to explode, I'm eating my heart out, and he—he doesn't even listen, he just stands there eating raisins! Just whose son do you think you are, Nachman? The Baron de Rothschild's? Do you think I'm up wearing my eyes out until all hours of the night, stitching and ironing and going through every piece of clothing for the tenth time to make sure it looks clean and neat, just so you can go and roll in dirt with your little Arab friends? Get your fingers out of that halvah, or I'll slice them off for you, Nachman! How long are you going to go on being a baby? You're already three years old, thank God, going on four. I just don't have the strength to carry it all on my back anymore—the store, the house, your father, and you. Everyone thinks he's a prima donna here, everyone has to be pampered. But who's ever going to pamper me for once in my life, I ask you? Maybe if I collapsed one day and didn't get up anymore, if this life of mine just finally came to an end, *maybe* you'd realize then that I was just a human being too, nothing but a weak woman. Maybe there in the grave I'll finally get to rest a little. . . . What's the matter, Nachman? What is it? What are you crying for all of a sudden? Either he's wallowing in filth like a pig or he's bawling like an infant! Stop it this minute, Nachman! If you don't, I'll crack you so hard across the face that you'll really have something to cry about. . . . I said that's enough. Enough already! Here, Nachman, have a piece of this chocolate halvah. He stands and cries as though it were my funeral. . . . There, Nemmale, come, *ketzele*, come to your mama. What did I ever say to make you cry like that? You have a soul of silk like your father. One has to cater to their every whim, but just try telling them something and you've wounded them to the quick. . . . There, that's enough. Come here, *yingele*, tell mama what you're crying about. My poor little thing, my little orphan. . . . "

They now owned a grocery store at the far end of Mister Blackman's property (ever since when? ever since when?). It was a colorful, exotic world, full of things that he coveted with his eyes but wasn't allowed to touch. His mother's flood of words generally swirled past him and left him untouched, but now they were more real than the riches around him. One day mama would collapse and never get up again. Never. She would be dead like grandfather. She would lie on the ground like the dog that young Mendelevitch had shot with his rifle. Nachman knew that his father had taken to vanishing from the house for days on end and reappearing without warning. Those nights when the two of them were home, he would hear them arguing angrily with each other, and when they were not arguing and the dark room was quiet, his mother would lie on her bed and silently weep. He would listen to her cry, his face to the wall, pretending to be asleep. All the long evenings when she stood by herself in the store or labored at home her eyes had tears in them too. They were like the kitchen faucet, which always had a drop at one end. One day she would lie down and not get up anymore, and there would be no more tears in her swollen red eyes. Nachman involuntarily burst out crying, stricken with invisible fears. He clung to his mother's dress and pleaded in a choked voice, "Don't die, mama!"

"So help me, I swear! Is that why you're crying?"

"Don't die, mama."

To Nachman's amazement, his mother burst into one of her rare, unexpected laughs. "Where do you see me dying, you silly? Do you think it's so easy to die? You have to go through hell first and get sick and grow old before they let you die. . . . Oy, you're such a silly thing, Nemmale, such a silly thing. . . . Already he has me in the grave! I was just carrying on because I was tired and upset—and he takes me at my word! Here, suck on this candy rooster. There, that's how I like to see you. . . . Sit here on this sugar bin and be a good boy. Give mama a kiss and don't worry. I'm not dying yet."

Now the two of them sat in the store, from which the daylight had already retreated as far as the doorway, where it lingered sunless and pale. With the fading of the light, the smells in the store had grown sharper. There was the cool smell of the bin of white sugar, the thick smell of the yellow barrel of oil, the ticklish smell of the dill that his mother had put in the large pickle jar, the muffled smell of the large raisins and the clear smell of the small pitless ones, the gross smell of the herring barrel, and the dusty smell of the sacks of dried beans, the sea smell of the salt bin, and the warm smell of the basket of bread. All this was now mixed with the smell of his mother herself, who was leaning over him and urging him to blow his nose into the creased handkerchief she kept in her apron pocket. Taking out the round comb that was always tucked into the back of her bobbed hair, she ran it over his head. The long teeth with points sharp as nails scratched his scalp, but Nachman didn't even say ouch because he had just spied Missus Blackman, who was standing in the open doorway.

At long last his mother released him to concentrate on his candy rooster. He licked and sucked the rough sweetness until his tongue had polished its solid red face to a fine, windowlike transparency. If he held it up to his eye now, everything he looked at turned a lovely red. In the meantime, however, the rooster had attracted a large fly, which now circled above it looking for a place to land and join in the fun. Nachman stuffed the rooster far into his mouth and tried to drive the fly away. It finally drifted off among the topmost shelves, somewhere up near the ceiling, where Nachman's eyes came to rest on the spiral strip of paper that hung festooned with dead flies. He was curious to know what this fly's fate would be. Would it continue to circle endlessly in the air of the store, or would it suddenly tire and alight on the flypaper, to stick there helplessly with the first touch of its legs, buzzing and buzzing until it died? The light taxed his eyes but sharpened his ear, which now tuned in on what his mother was saying to Missus Blackman. "Like father, like son—one minute the sun is shining and the next it's raining cats and dogs. You should have seen the size of the tears on his cheeks—like grapes! But what can I tell you? When he cried, I felt better. At least I know now that he'll cry by my grave."

In the dim light Missus Blackman's rasping voice sounded as though it were coming from the grave itself, but he struggled to catch every word. "A young girl like you, healthy as a horse, and talking such nonsense! How can you even think of dying when you have such a gem of a child? It's worth living just to be able to look at him, luv!"

"Of course it is, but where am I to get the strength to run after him and wait on him all day long? Now he sits there like an angel, playing the perfect innocent, but take your eyes off him for a second and there'll be the devil to pay."

"Be more careful of what you say, luv. I know what it's like to live in a house without children."

"I dressed him all in white. I put new shoes on his feet. I just don't have the strength for it. I'm going to send him to Bluma's kindergarten."

"He's too small for it, Leah."

"I'm only human myself. This way at least I'll have a few hours of rest to myself."

"He's too small. The big children will murder him there."

"If he keeps on staying home, he'll murder me. Nothing will happen to him there. Bluma will make a man out of him."

Nachman had pretended not to hear, but he couldn't control himself any longer. Fear made him spring to his feet and run to his mother. "I don't want to go to Bluma. I don't want to."

"You'll go to kindergarten, Nachman, as soon as the school year begins. And Bluma will make a man out of you."

"I don't want to. I don't want to."

"All the children go to kindergarten, luv." Missus Blackman's rasping voice unexpectedly seconded his mother's dark designs. Her dry fingers passed through his hair like his mother's comb. Hadn't she just said herself that the big children would murder him there? He felt a wave of anger in his eyes. He clenched his two fists and lashed out at Missus Blackman's body.

"Nachman!" His mother raised both her voice and her arm at him, then turned back to Missus Blackman and said, "Well, there you see my gem of a child. If he goes on sucking my blood like this, I really will die young. No, the best thing for both of us is to send him to Bluma's kindergarten."

And so one morning (where was his father? who was minding the store?) she scrubbed his face carefully with a wet towel, inspected his fingernails and ears, put on his blue velvet pants and his starched sailor's middy, which had portentously sat out in his room overnight, pulled a pair of white socks and his black patent leather shoes over his feet, squarely placed his sailor's hat—whose two silk tassels dangled down in back to the broad collar of his jersey—on his combed head, fastened a white handkerchief to his breast pocket with a large safety pin, gripped his wrist in her steel-fingered hand, and set out straight ahead—through the door, across the yard, down the street, to the center of town. She didn't look back even once to see whether Nachman was still paddling after her or whether it was only his wrist that she continued to grip in her hand.

"I don't want to go to Bluma," he screamed, holding on to the table, the chair, the doorknob, the railing of the porch, the bars of the fence. "I don't want to, I don't want to," he had howled, digging his feet into the fine dust that formed every year as the dry summer drew to a close, being hoisted up and pulled along by his mother's strong grip until he found a toehold again, only to be yanked forward once more and dragged behind her long legs all the way down the street.

"I don't want to go to Bluma, I don't want to."

"What don't you want? What?" She spoke through her teeth without looking back. "You don't even know what it is you don't want."

"I don't want to go to Bluma. I don't want to go to kindergarten."

"You don't even know what a kindergarten is," she said through her teeth without pausing for a second.

What kind of a garden it was he didn't know, but he knew why he was being banished from the store. His mother had told him time and again: because he would be the death of her yet. And he also knew what awaited him there: Madam Mendelevitch's son Balfour. Missus Blackman had said that the big children would murder him, and he knew that Balfour could do it. When Balfour was around the yard, Nachman didn't dare leave the store by himself. Now his mother was going to leave him with Balfour and the other big children, and there would be nowhere for him to escape. He had already stopped crying and trying to brace with his feet. His eyes were studying the new street where they were walking, which was packed hard with a kind of red dirt that looked like the rust scraped from old iron. They kept to one side of the street on a wooden walk, then on the footbridge, whose planks groaned as they passed over them. Now they were among tall eucalyptus trees, amid fragrant morning shade, but before Nachman's eyes could climb to the topmost branches, his mother stopped short—and he with her. In front of them stood an iron gate with a wire screen stretched over it. Through it he saw a huge house, which was terribly tall and long, bigger even than the Great Synagogue. The sound of children singing reached him through a row of high, open windows, beneath which ran a cracked, peeling wall studded with nails and colored with charcoal to give it the appearance of a dusty melon rind. Beyond it sang the children. This was Bluma's garden?

"Just see how we're late because of your monkeyshines. What will Bluma say? And on the very first day!"

His mother rattled the gate with her powerful fingers, throwing the full weight of her body against it. Perhaps she wouldn't manage. Nachman hoped against hope while beyond he heard the children singing and saw a huge, paved courtyard in which there grew not a thorn, not a single blade of grass. Yet suddenly the gate was wide open, and his mother lurched through it dragging him after. They climbed a broad flight of stairs and came to a closed door, which she gingerly touched, half knocking with her finger. He could feel his heart pound, yet it was already too late to do or say anything. The door swung wide open and a fat lady now stood in its place. Nachman's mother whispered something in her ear while she bent down over him with her puffy cheeks and multiple chins. When she drew very close to him, though, he saw only her eyes, which gleamed like the afternoon light that streamed through their slatted shutters at home. A smile danced among the folds of her eyes, and Nachman smiled back. But now he also began to make out the shrieks of the children who were tumbling all over the fat woman's body. The smile disappeared from his face.

"Good morning, Nachman. My name is Bluma."

"Say good morning to Bluma," his mother prodded him. But Nachman, who was conscious only of the screaming children, gritted his teeth and backed away with his head down.

"Aren't you a big boy now, and don't you want to learn with the other big children? Don't you, Nachman? You have the name of a very great rabbi, Nachman, Rabbi Nachman of Bratslav. Your mother told me that you know how to read already, and if you study hard, some day we'll have another Rabbi Nachman, an awfully sweet and jolly one."

"It's enough for me that he should become a man."

"He's already a little man. I like his eyes. Especially when they smile, the way they did a minute ago and will in another. Come, Nachman, all the children are waiting for you. They want to get to know you, Nachman."

Nachman's hand sought to clutch at the hem of his

mother's dress, but she was already on her way down the stairs and he was still pressed tight against Bluma's big body while her eyes went on dancing. Without knowing how it had happened, the door was now shut tight behind him, and he found himself in a room full of children who sat or stood on low chairs. A dead quiet prevailed among them. Gone were the noisy shouts and the singing, which had made his head spin a moment ago and pulled him this way and that between the gate and the school building. Now he was imprisoned in a closed room, stared at by a lot of strange children. Balfour was here too. They would murder him.

"This is the new boy, children. The smart, sweet boy whom I told you about. Say hello to Nachman."

"Hello, Nachman," the children called out.

But suddenly one voice chimed on its own, "Nachman–Achmed, Achmed–Nachman!"

Nachman wasn't sure why this made all the children laugh. Only now another child took it up, "Nachman–Achmed, Achmed–Nachman!"

Together all the children burst into laughter, their raucous peals repeating in chorus, "Nachman–Achmed, Achmed–Nachman, Achmed–Achmed!"

All at once Nachman realized what seemed so funny and why they were laughing so hard. He was Achmed. He was a little Arab. Beyond the children's shrieks he now heard Missus Blackman rasp how they would murder him. And beyond even that, long, long ago, he heard Mister Blackman laugh too. They bought you. Your father and mother bought you. They bought you from the Bedouin.

"Mama!" screamed Nachman, turning to face the closed door.

The chorus of children, which Bluma was trying to hush, flicked at his back like a whip. "Nachman–Achmed. Achmed–Nachman." He pushed against the doorknob but nothing gave.

"Mama, mama, come back!"

From behind and above him came Bluma's heavy voice. Her warm hands covered his face, seeking to turn it back into the room. "The children are only joking, Nachman. They're saying you're welcome here. Look at them, Nachman. There are other new boys and girls here besides you. Look, Nachman."

"Mama! I want to go home. Mama!"

"Your mama has gone home, Nachman. Now I'm everyone's mama. Isn't that so, children?"

"I want my own mama! I want my own mama!"

He pushed against the doorknob. He pounded on the door with his fists and kicked it with his new shoes, but it was as solid as a wall.

Bluma tried to calm him, her warm hand caressing his neck and cheek, but he buried his face in his hands and pressed it hard against the door so as not to hear. Suddenly both her voice and hand were gone. Behind him the room resounded with the notes of a piano, which forced their way through his hands and into his stopped ears, from where they rippled through his body and filled it with that same whatever-it-was he felt when he sat in young Madam Mendelevitch's darkened parlor and watched her fingers embroider their wonderful textures of sound on the keyboard. The children had stopped shouting and were singing along with the piano, and the music tempted him strongly to turn around and join in. He kicked at the door once again so as not to give in and called out, "Mama! Mama, come back!"

The music stopped. He heard the turn of a key in the lock, and then the door opened little by little so as not to leave him unsupported all at once. He saw both Bluma and the open door out of the opposite corners of his eyes, and in his confusion he stood there without moving, scanning her face. She stood to one side, her arms folded over her breasts. Her twinkling eyes informed him with a smile that he was free to go. Nachman no longer knew what he wanted, but he descended the stairs on the run and headed for the gate. His fingers grasped the wire and shook it hard as his mother had done, but the gate remained shut and only its metal chain rattled. He let go of it—and the chain fell silent; he shook it again—and it jangled once more. The door of the kindergarten was closed now too, but the voices of grownups and children carried down to him from the high windows in the wall. The gate couldn't be forced. He leaned his head against the wire, padding its hardness with his sailor cap, and looked down at the blotchy sand by his feet. A ladybug was crawling through it, leaving thin lines in its wake. Nachman got down on his knees to watch the little black-and-red spotted globe. He was sure that its legs were even thinner than the needle of the kerosene stove. He picked up a dried eucalyptus leaf and blocked the ladybug's path with it, forcing it to climb on the leaf. How did a ladybug look from underneath? Did it have titties, like Mendelevitch's cows? He turned it over on its round back, enjoying the little creature's helplessness as it thrashed its legs in the air. He sat down in the sand and put down the leaf and the upside-down beetle to see if it could turn right side up. It couldn't. He breathed on it cautiously, to annoy it—but just then a great bell pealed sharply, louder and harsher than that of the kerosene man. Frightened, Nachman leaped to his feet and looked about.

The large courtyard, so trodden that not a single thorn or blade of grass could grow on it, was rapidly filling with droves of big and small girls. They shouted at the tops of their voices, chased one another, skipped rope, danced in circles, played hopscotch, and spread out all over the yard. Nachman ran toward them until he reached the other fence which divided the kindergarten yard from the school yard. He clung to the wire grill, his eyes running with the girls as they ran, skipping as they skipped, laughing as they laughed, dizzily revolving as they whirled round and round.

A noise sounded right in his ear. He jumped back and spun about, his back to the fence. Only now did he notice that the kindergarten children too had poured into the yard and were forming around him in a tightening circle. More and more children were joining it. They jostled and called to each other, voice over voice. One boy plucked at the handkerchief which his mother had fastened to the pocket of his middy, another sprayed sand with his foot over his shiny leather shoes. Nachman pressed back against the fence as though to squeeze through the large squares of the screen, yet the circle kept tightening, cutting him off and filling him with fear. He wanted his mother, the store, anything safe and familiar. So great was the need to escape that all at once he sprang from his place and charged, head down, right into the children, his fists flailing out, his teeth bared in a picture of fury.

How long did the great battle last? A minute at most. Already the dense circle was behind him and before him were the empty yard and the gate at its far end. Blinded with tears, Nachman made straight for the latter, head down and fists balled tight—only to run smack into Bluma's soft body. Her warm laugh penetrated the darkness around him. Strong arms swept him off the ground and held him dangling in midair, resting on her ample breasts.

"Now all the boys and girls have seen once and for all that you're not afraid of anyone. Not so big perhaps, but the bravest and the strongest of them all."

That much he already knew himself. He wanted to open his eyes and look straight into hers, but instead he wrestled with her, squirmed from her grasp, and landed once more on the ground, where he stood regarding his shoes.

"Now all the children have seen that they mustn't pick on you because you'll make them wish they hadn't. It would be such a shame if you went home now and didn't stay here with us to sing all the songs that we'll learn and to hear all the new stories that we'll tell. And you'll miss out on all our games too! We'd very much like you to stay, wouldn't we, children?"

"Yes," chorused the children, and Nachman's ears automatically perked up. He was already seeing himself sitting all day by himself in the store and missing the kindergarten. He was already feeling sorry for himself.

"See, the recess is over. Now we'll go back to the room. We'll play a little, learn a little, sing a little, and before you know it, your mother will be here to take you home. You'll see."

Bluma headed up the broad staircase with Nachman in one hand. The other children formed a line and followed double file. He and Bluma led the way by themselves.

"Does anyone here know how the dry sand dunes and the terrible swamps turned into oranges?" Bluma asked the children after they had taken their seats. And turning to Nachman, she asked, "Did you ever hear the story, Nachman?"

"My Uncle Rifael lives in the sand," Nachman said proudly.

"And has it already turned into oranges?"

Nachman wasn't sure about that, but he did know something else. "My papa worked in the orange groves and brought home sacks full of oranges."

"Yes, your papa worked in Adon Mendelevitch's groves among the dunes. But who knows how the dunes turned into such lovely, juicy oranges in the first place? That's the story I'm going to tell you right now. It's a very wonderful story, and when you tell it to your papa, he'll give anything to know where you heard it. Here, here's a chair for you. Sit down and pay close attention."

7 | *"You have to think twice when there's a child involved!"*

Something bad had come between his father and mother, something that tasted as bitter as the lemon salts his mother sold in the store. Nachman tried to guess what this something was, but it was too much for him to fathom. Of one thing he was sure: part had to do with the store that they had suddenly acquired. But Nachman knew too that Mister Blackman had only built it for them after something else had gone wrong, so it wasn't this alone that stood between them. Early one summer morning, before there had been any store, before there had been any kindergarten, his mother had aroused him from bed. Red-eyed and tight-mouthed, she dressed him with hard, unyielding fingers in his best clothes, picked up the suitcase, which was already standing shut and tied on the porch, and set out for town with it in one hand and Nachman in the other. When Nachman asked why his father wasn't coming too, she silenced him gruffly. "We're going to my family, to Tel Aviv. You'll like it there. You're always telling me how Balfour goes to the seashore. Now you'll go to the seashore too."

She said no more, neither when they boarded the bus nor all the long way to Tel Aviv. Nachman asked no more questions either, for from here on he was totally absorbed in the journey itself, which was the first one he was to remember well. A constant stream of novelties flowed by the window, and when there was nothing new outside, there was sure to be some interesting commotion in the bus itself. From time to time they would all be catapulted from their places by a great bump, which sent heads crashing into the rooftop and bodies sprawling into each other's laps. Bundles and boxes were tossed back and forth, while the passengers shouted, groaned, and talked at the top of their voices to make themselves heard above the noise of the vehicle. Nachman didn't take his eyes off any of this, yet he didn't miss what was going by outside either—orange groves hedged with prickly pears, black Bedouin tents and black Bedouin children screaming and running bare-bottomed in the sand, a camel dining on thorns, a hill cut in two (a quarry, his mother explained), small houses like those in town, and then all at once, nothing but sand dunes as far as the eye could see. (Like Uncle Rifael's? Nachman wanted to know. Not at all, his mother explained. These were already the sand dunes of Tel Aviv.)

The bus stopped bouncing from pothole to pothole with its careening passengers. Suddenly the noise died away, like a kerosene stove when turned off. The bundles, boxes, and suitcases were taken down, and the passengers descended through the rear door. Nachman and his mother set out among houses and huts, but it was not at all like in town. There was a different smell to Tel Aviv. You can feel the sea, said his mother, but to Nachman it seemed that he was smelling peepee. They came to a long, narrow strip of sand between houses, in which sticklike branches had been planted and surrounded with another circle of sticks to protect them. Nachman wanted to ask what kind of trees could grow in so much sand, but he could see that his mother was in no mood to be questioned. The sun overhead beat down on them and on the thin sand that burned its way through the soles of Nachman's shoes. His mother was red with perspiration; not even the broad straw hat on her head could ward off the heat. She walked without stopping, pausing only to transfer the suitcase from hand to hand, at which times Nachman would circle to her other side. Where was Uncle Herzlich's house? he wanted to know, but she didn't answer. Almost all of Tel Aviv already lay behind them. Beyond the last rows of houses stretched open fields where the great citrus groves began. His mothr now turned into one of these houses, and Nachman followed after.

The house looked just like all the others they had passed. It didn't have a yard or trees or anything. Straight from the sand they climbed two steps to a dimly lit passageway. Inside were more steps, which they also ascended. His mother set the suitcase down on the landing. She took a large handkerchief from her purse and cleaned Nachman's face and her own with vigorous strokes, then inspected herself in a small mirror. It was pleasant to stand and rest for a moment in the sunless hallway, except that the odor of peepee was here too. Nachman's feet were burning up and he bent to sit on the top step, but one look from his mother was enough to change his mind. Just then he heard a long, questioning cough like Mister Blackman's from behind a door.

His mother said something in Yiddish. The door swung open at once, and through the gloom Nachman made out two sparkling lenses in a thin gold frame, a red beard parted in the middle of the chin, a large skullcap on a bald head, and a shiny bathrobe, which a pair of elderly hands was trying to tie.

"*Oy vayz mir*—woe is me!" The old man held out his arms to his mother. "Leah!"

"*Fetter*—uncle!" said his mother tonelessly. "Everything is just fine."

"So why are you all of a sudden in Tailoviv, Leah?"

His mother was still standing in the doorway, but in her

labored breathing Nachman could already detect the tears to come. Though she and the old man spoke Yiddish, which Nachman didn't understand, he knew everything they were saying.

"You'll have to excuse me, *fetter*, for coming like this unannounced. But there's no one. I don't have a single soul besides you to whom I can even come to pour out my heart." The large handkerchief, which only a moment ago had wiped the sweat from both their faces, was now over her eyes. "I'm so alone, *fetter*."

"*Reboyne-shel-oylem*—Oh, my God!" the old man cried. Small and frail as he was, smaller and frailer than Nachman's mother, he snatched up the heavy suitcase and directed them both to come in at once. Nachman's mother tried to retrieve the valise from his hands, but he was already inside while she followed clutching in vain at the suitcase with Nachman trailing behind. The old man kept talking, half to her and half to himself. "*Reboyne-shel-oylem*, what's there to cry about? You have a *fetter* and a *mimeh*—an uncle and an aunt—in Tailoviv, thank God, so why apologize that you've come to them? Sit down, the first thing is to sit down. First of all, maybe you want a glass of water from the icebox? Maybe some cold seltzer?"

They were in a large room. The blinds were down on the windows, and there was the same smell of old people that he knew from Mister and Missus Blackman's. But Nachman was already wishing that now that they were in Tel Aviv and close to the sea, *fetter* Herzlich might comfort his mother in a hurry so that she would stop crying and take him to the beach that same afternoon. The old man sat them down at a large table in the middle of the room and continued to ask his mother questions, while shuffling from the parlor to the kitchen in his peculiar house slippers. Even though Nachman's mother swore to him that they weren't hungry or thirsty and would gladly wait until *mimeh* Herzlich returned from visiting her daughter Toybe, he insisted on serving them with a large siphon of seltzer and a bottle of lemon syrup with two glasses. His mother was against letting Nachman drink seltzer until his body had cooled off a bit, but this only increased his thirst for the cold soda water, which he did not see everyday in so huge a container. *Fetter* Herzlich stood at his side, where he first poured a little lemon syrup into a glass and then squirted it full of foamy, bubbling liquid. His mother, who had been sitting with her head in her hands, frantically reached out to push *fetter* Herzlich's hand away from the spigot.

"He's a delicate child. All I need for him now is to catch cold in his stomach."

Nachman's eyes were already accustomed to the dimly lit room with its dark furniture and to the person of *fetter* Herzlich himself. Not only was the parted beard all red, but his high forehead underneath his skullcap was covered with freckles that looked like smudges of dirt on his white skin. His neck was freckled also, as was the skin beneath his ears and on his hands, which were speckled with rusty blotches from his nails to the cuffs of his shiny robe. (Nachman now noticed that this was not black but green, like the smooth rind of a watermelon.) The rusty fingers pinched Nachman's chin and raised his face to meet *fetter* Herzlich's, whose eyes were red too.

"You understand Yiddish, young fellow?" Nachman pretended not to hear. Instead he lowered his lips to the half-full glass of seltzer and hurried to drink it while it was still cold and sparkling with little bubbles, which pricked at his tongue and fizzed in his nose. He heard *fetter* Herzlich say to his mother, "Now then, Leah, I want to hear everything, the whole truth. What has that *zaddik*, that saint of yours, done now? What new *meshugas* has he got into his head?"

"Later, *fetter*. The boy is listening to every word. As it is, he's seen and heard more than is good for him."

"Just one thing: is he still working in Mendelevitch's orange groves?"

"What is there to do in the groves in the summertime? They try to be nice and give him a few days pruning, a few days irrigating. That isn't my greatest worry. It's that I myself am turning into an old rag there, in Mendelevitch's yard. I've decided to go back, *fetter*."

"To Poland? Have you gone out of your mind? A divorce you want to get, with a child around your neck? Leah, I don't want to hear another word about it."

"Not now, *fetter*. Later."

And indeed, this was the last Nachman heard or remembered of it. Meanwhile, they continued to live—for a long time, it seemed to him—with the Herzlichs, whose apartment was roomy and large. The old couple slept in the bedroom, and he and his mother on the big couch in the parlor. Every morning *fetter* Herzlich went out in a suit and a round straw hat which he called a "panama," both of which looked as though they had once been white before they rusted, and the rolled-up umbrella that served him as a cane and without which he never went anywhere. Nachman was none too sure what *fetter* Herzlich's business was, for he went to work late and returned home before lunchtime and never wore work clothes at all. His father and mother used to say that he had managed to bring some money with him from Poland, and now—his father would add with contempt—he bought and sold land in Tel Aviv. Nachman didn't understand how *fetter* Herzlich could buy and sell land in Tel Aviv every morning, but he enjoyed living in their house, especially on account of *mimeh* Herzlich, whose kitchen and large glass cupboard in the parlor were always well stocked with good things, not to mention the large corn on the cobs fished from a steaming bucket and the cold ice creams that he licked and nibbled down to the last of their soggy cones each time he went with her to the beach. There were really two aunts: one for leaving the house, who was tall and had a dark dress that came practically down to her ankles and a head of hair piled high, with sparkling jewels in it and a single pearl that gleamed at the end of a long pin; and another for staying at home, who was short and wore an old frock, while her head, which was wrapped in a kerchief from eyelid to earlobe, seemed only half its other size. Nachman knew her secret—one morning he had slipped into the old couple's bedroom and had seen her whole head of hair on a chair by their unmade bed. How, he wanted to know, could she possibly remove all her hair and put it back on again, and what did her hairless head look like without the kerchief? At night he would lie on the couch with his eyes shut, trying to stay awake, in the hope that a bareheaded *mimeh* Herzlich might suddenly emerge from the bedroom on her way to the kitchen. But he waited in vain.

There were all kinds of other new things at the Herzlich's too. On Sabbaths *mimeh* Herzlich covered the table with a white cloth and set it with tableware that was hidden away in the closet the rest of the week—fancy dishes, glass goblets over whose sparkling surface the candlelight played, heavy polished forks and spoons. All day Friday his mother and *mimeh* Herzlich stood cooking in the kitchen, and toward evening *fetter* Herzlich put on a black shiny coat, which hung down to his shoes, and clapped on his head a hairy hat, which was not, however, like *mimeh* Herzlich's head of hair, but like the fur on the fox wrap that his mother kept in mothballs in the large wicker trunk. When they sat down to eat, they were joined by their daughter Toybe and her husband, who lived nearby. They remained for a long time at the table, eating and singing Sabbath hymns at the top of their lungs, and when they had finally said the grace after meals, they moved to the balcony, which overlooked the street facing the orange groves. More guests would arrive, and they would all speak Yiddish and drink tea and crack pumpkin and sunflower seeds until it was time to go to bed. The Sabbath day passed the same way. *Fetter* Herzlich went to synagogue and always returned with a crowd of men, who drank wine and munched on *mimeh* Herzlich's black honey cake. When they had gone, the family sat down to eat, after which they shut all the blinds the carnival gaiety made him oblivious to everything else. He forgot why they had come to Tel Aviv in the first place, forgot his mother's tears, forgot the whispered exchanges between her and the Herzlichs about going back to Poland, forgot his own father who had stayed behind at home.

In front of the door they carefully wiped the sand off their feet before entering. *Fetter* and *mimeh* Herzlich were sitting at the table with his father. Tel Aviv and the sea had made Nachman forget him; now he made Nachman forget all that. His father ran toward him, but his mother grabbed him by the hand and pulled him back. His father hoisted him high and showered his face with kisses. His mother crossed to the other end of the room and stood by the window.

"I came to take you home," his father said to him.

"This time you are mistaken," said his mother. "I'm through with all that."

Fetter Herzlich stood up and shuffled across the floor in his house slippers to Nachman's mother. "Leah, first of all, listen. Shalom hasn't come just like that. Everything has been arranged for the best."

"No. The best for me and for him is that we put an end to this situation. The sooner the better."

"*Fetter* will help you a little too, to get on your feet," said *mimeh* Herzlich. "You have to think twice when there's a child involved."

"I've talked it all over with Shalom, and I tell you—after all, I'm your *fetter*—that it's all been arranged for the best. I'm going to let you have fifty pounds to stock a store and to see you through for a while, and when you earn it back, you'll return it to me, God willing, with the interest."

"He's told me twenty times already that it's all been arranged for the best. When a person hates his own life, when he can't stand another person's face anymore, how can it be for the best? The summer was the last straw for me. I don't want him to agree now to any store for which I'll have to end up paying for the rest of my life."

8 | Kaddish *for Mister Blackman*

Now too, when he was already in kindergarten, he still liked the store best of all, more even than playing with Balfour in the Mendelevitches' big house, more than the expeditions to the middle of the eucalyptus woods, more than his visits with Mister and Missus Blackman. Especially in the wet winter. So as not to have to run back and forth in the wind and the rain, his mother had brought the kerosene stove to the store, where she would cook a hot meal for them when business was slow. The burners gave off warmth and drove away the patches of moisture that appeared on the whitewashed wall. Even when she dressed warmly and wrapped herself in her red wool shawl, his mother was always cold. All winter long her nose was running and her hands were like ice. Nachman was never cold, for his mind was on other things, such as the customers who came in and out, or the women who gossiped about each other, or the stories his mother told—when she was feeling good—about winters in Poland. But even when the store was empty and her mood was bad, so that it was dangerous even to talk to her, there was enough to keep Nachman busy and take his mind off the cold.

His father had taught him to read long ago, and just as he loved to smell all the boxes and bags in the store, so he longed to decipher what was written on them. The problem was that most of this writing was not in the letters he had learned, but in others, which were like Polish. The lump sugar came from Egypt, the loose sugar from Poland, the white flour from Canada, the butter from Latvia, the sardines from Portugal. Everything was from another part of the world, and when Nachman looked at them, he saw not only the products themselves but all the places from which they had come by ship, wagon, and train. He fingered the bins, sacks, and barrels as though they were a gateway to their countries of origin, but for all that, he had despaired of getting his mother to teach him to read Polish. If his father were in the store, he would teach it to him just as he had Hebrew, but Nachman could sense that something bad had come between the two of them again, though he didn't know what it was. It was like a dog waiting to bite you in the dark: even if you couldn't see its face or hear its voice, you knew that it was lying there, black against black.

Nachman liked to sit in the store, but his mother's silence could be eerie. Days now passed in which he didn't see his father at all, but even when he was at home or in the store, whatever it was that was wrong would only get worse, and Nachman would slip outside. If the weather was nice he would hang about the yard or in the big empty lot with the other children, while if it rained or got dark out, he would be glad to be invited by Balfour to play in his house. They would light the large Lux lamp with its pleasant hiss and play lotto and drink cocoa. Sometimes young Madam Mendelevitch would join them too, and play for them on the piano or put a record on the phonograph.

Sometimes too he would tiptoe out of the store and treat himself to a visit with Mister and Missus Blackman.

An intricate, intangible knot now bound him to Mister Blackman, whose claim that he had been bought from a Bedouin he had never forgotten. Nachman knew that it was Mister Blackman who had built the store for them and that it was only because of him that they had a well-stocked grocery and that his mother had not taken him to Poland. Whenever Mister or Missus Blackman stopped by the store to ask him to visit them for a while, his mother would prod him to accept, and Nachman knew that it was his duty to do so. Yet it was not just because of that that he went. He had learned a new secret: Mister Blackman did not even have to offer his father fifty pounds to buy him. On the contrary, by the law he actually belonged to Mister Blackman, from whom his father had ransomed him with a large gold watch that he had been given for his wedding.

"Yes, indeed," Mister Blackman would insist. "According to Jewish law the eldest son belongs to the *kohen*—the priest. You are an eldest son, and I am a *kohen*. Yes, indeed."

"That's not exactly the whole truth," smiled his father, but all his explanations took away nothing from Mister Blackman's revelation. Once, father explained, before the Torah was given on Mount Sinai, people used to sacrifice their eldest sons. Yes, sacrifice them—burn them on the altar. But this was in the distant past, long, long ago. Now it was just a custom, a kind of performance, really. When a boy was born, you invited a *kohen* who held the child in his arms, and the newborn's father pretended to ransom him.

"With a gold watch?"

"It can be done with a watch or with money. It's just make-believe. He didn't even keep the watch. I gave it to him, and he returned it. See, it's here among the sheets in the closet."

"But he's really a *kohen*?"

"A *kohen!* What does it mean to be a *kohen* these days? Absolutely nothing!"

His father had an answer for every question, but none

of it disproved what Mister Blackman had told him. A *kohen* was not absolutely nothing. In the synagogue it was the *kohanim* who blessed everyone from underneath their prayer shawls. Only the *kohanim* knew how to spread the fingers of their hands two-by-two in the priestly blessing. In the Temple only the *kohanim* could enter the holy of Holies and see God. Anyone else dropped dead on the spot. Mister Blackman was a *kohen*, and this wasn't absolutely nothing.

Nachman felt that somehow it was all connected—the something bad that had come between his father and mother, the store, Mister Blackman, the young and old Mendelevitches. Whenever his parents sat wordlessly together, whenever he couldn't bear his mother's tears any longer, he would open the door to the Blackmans' house and step inside.

He was always made to feel welcome. They would hurry to open the toffee tin for him, stuff him with chocolate, ply him with slices of bread spread with citron jam, and, as the feature attraction, tell him frightening stories. Mister Blackman had a large album full of pictures from Zud Afrika, and since he knew that Nachman loved stories better than anything else, he would tell him the story of every picture. In the end he always came to the same photographs of children, who were sometimes smaller than Nachman and sometimes bigger, about as old as eighth graders. There, Mister Blackman related, were his own boys, and had they remained alive to this day, they would be older than Nachman's own parents. "But both of them, may their souls rest in peace, were taken from us, first one and then the other, and now they live in heaven with all the little angels. For many years we sat and cried over them, and in the end we decided to come to Palestine. But now we don't cry anymore because soon we'll see them again."

Of all the frightening stories, the scariest was this one about the children in the pictures who had died and were now little angels in heaven whom Mister and Missus Blackman would soon see again. Whenever Mister Blackman leafed through the heavy, dog-eared pages in the album, Nachman would wait with baited breath for the snapshots of the children and their stories. Mister Blackman would carefully repeat everything he had told him the last time and introduce some new detail that was the creepiest and most hair-raising yet. One day, when they had been sitting and looking at the little children and Mister Blackman had suddenly glanced up and begun to say something to Nachman, he was seized by a spasm of coughing that choked off his speech and brought tears to his eyes until they rolled down his scraggly beard. The coughing scared Nachman more than any of the stories, but just because it did he couldn't take his eyes off Mister Blackman's ashen, purpling face. When Mister Blackman was himself again, he wiped his lips and beard of the phlegm that had collected there and said, "Oy, another minute and I would have been with my angels. The one thing still keeping me here is the fear that I'll be buried without a *kaddish* said after me."

All of a sudden Mister Blackman opened his robe, unbuttoned the shirt underneath it, and pulled out a kind of yellow hair shirt to whose corners were tied fringed knots like those on his father's big prayer shawl. He put the knots to Nachman's mouth and said, "I have a deep secret to tell you, Nachman, but first kiss the *tsitsis*."

A bad smell, the smell of the wicker trunk, registered in Nachman's nostrils, but his desire to hear the secret was even stronger than the smell, and he kissed the fringed knots.

"Now repeat after me, word by word: 'I swear by the holy Torah.' "

Nachman repeated it, word by word, his knees shaking with fear. Mister Blackman scratched Nachman's cheeks with his scraggly beard, kissed him on the forehead, and whispered in one ear, "When I've lived to be one hundred and twenty years old, Nachman, everything—this whole house, the yard, and the store, too—will be yours. And you'll be our *kaddish*."

Mister Blackman's precautions, the words of the oath, the kissing of the fringed knots, the house that would some day be his—all this made his imagination run riot, like a stone cast into a dovecote. But what did it have to do with the *kaddish*? Was Mister Blackman going back on his agreement with Nachman's father when he traded him for the gold watch? What did it mean, being Mister Blackman's *kaddish*?

Mister Blackman picked up the prayer book that was lying by the rocking chair, and with it his eyeglass case. Putting on his glasses, he leafed through the stained, well-thumbed pages of the book, beckoned Nachman to his side, and pointed out to him a passage printed in fat letters, which he proceeded to read out loud, signaling to Nachman to follow, "*Yitgadal. Veyitkadash. Shmey. Rabba. Bechayeichon. Uvyomeichon. . . .*"

This was the secret that he had sworn by the knotted fringes not to reveal to his father or mother or anyone in the world. Nachman would repeat the words after Mister Blackman, half reading them from the book. They went over the *kaddish* often, and his rendition of it grew more and more perfect. By the middle of that winter, when black rainclouds drove away the daylight and evening came early in a spatter of raindrops on the lowered blinds, Nachman was swallowing chocolates the likes of which he had never seen in the store and declaiming the *kaddish* from start to finish without even pausing once. Missus Blackman had joined their pact now too. The two of them would sit and stare at him until forced to turn away to brush the tears from their eyes. The fact that his reading of the *kaddish* could make them so moist eyed was a source of intense satisfaction to Nachman, who never needed to be asked twice to say the prayer all over again from beginning to end. But no sooner had he proclaimed the last "Amen" than Mister Blackman would bend over to kiss him on the forehead, and Missus Blackman would press another toffee on him. And then—it never failed to happen—Mister Blackman would touch the tip of Nachman's nose with his finger, whose skin was as leathery and gray as the pages of the prayer book, and demand, "Your oath! Do you still remember your oath?"

"Leave the boy alone," Missus Blackman would rasp. The rain beat on the shutters as though it had fists, and a wail that sounded like a jackal hiding beneath the window cut through the air. Missus Blackman took the ends of the blanket that she had draped about her shoulders and wrapped herself up in it. If it weren't for the rain, he would run back to his mother in the store. But he didn't budge except to move his head from right to left.

"Put your hand on the *siddur*," said Mister Blackman.

"That's enough," Missus Blackman said. She added a few words in the language of Zud Afrika, which sounded like Yiddish but wasn't.

"On this holy prayer book . . ." Mister Blackman began.

"On this holy prayer book . . ." Nachman repeated after him, swearing to himself that he would never again cross the threshold of their house.

His fear was real enough, but the secret pact between him and the old couple, the incomprehensible words of the *kaddish*, which brought tears to their eyes, the repeated oaths, the promise that everything, the house and the garden with its fruit trees, would one day be his—all these were even stronger than his fear. And yet at the same time, he felt a conflicting desire: something inside him told him that if only he could reveal the secret that Mister Blackman had whispered in his ear to his father and his mother—in the strictest confidence, of course—whatever it was that had gone wrong between them would vanish, just as the dog who lay in wait in the dark was not even the shadow of a memory the next morning. What was an oath? And yet if he should tell his parents what Mister Blackman had made him swear not to, who knew what might happen to him? But it wasn't easy to keep silent, either. His mother questioned him about what the Blackmans had said to him after each visit, and his father tried to keep him away from their house. If only he could tell! But he was sworn to darkest secrecy. He felt torn between the desire to tell and his vow to say nothing. What if he did? What if he didn't? Suppose Mister Blackman should die, and he should stand by his grave and say the *kaddish*? Suppose the whole garden should be his, all the trees, the pineapples, the guavas? Suppose his father should overhear him saying the *kaddish* for Mister Blackman the way he himself had said it when grandfather had died?

What a fix Nachman felt he was in!

9 | Hanukkah candles

Nachman's memory could retrieve only moments from his kindergarten days. (Years later, a young man, a diamond polisher, crawled on the floor, gathering up the dust with a soft brush and sifting it carefully through a flour sieve. Suddenly the tiny gem that had jumped the wheel reappeared with its hard glitter from out of the dust, its one-sixtieth of a carat gleaming like sunshine.) Moments hard as diamonds, polished seventeen ways, the sun glancing off their facets as though it were only yesterday—no, tomorrow, when the stormy night would be over and the sky wouldn't have even a single thunder scratch to show for it: yes, tomorrow was the day of the fabulous Hanukkah party.

The very road seemed joyful, as though it had dressed itself up for the occasion. The cypresses were greener, the roof tiles were redder. The muddy path sparkled in the sun. Large drops fell from the treetops onto their heads. The thin grass had turned green in the early winter rain, which had beaten down the last shriveled thorn stalks of the summer before. Everything, the path, Nachman himself, was bursting with anticipation for what lay waiting in the kindergarten, where the children were already noisily donning their costumes for the play amid songs and chords on the piano. Everything, the whole world, was getting ready for the party, even the blue mountains, whose freshly sponged slopes seemed this morning to come right down to the edge of town.

Yes, everything—a needle flipped over in Nachman's memory—was already full of the pain of that morning's end, when his tongue had stuck fast to his mouth before the menorah, with the pain of the days that preceded it.

The preparations for the holiday (when had it been? during his first year in kindergarten? or was it already his second?) had taken many days. The classroom was full of shiny reds, blues, and greens, the softness of crepe paper contrasting with the metallic glitter of the gold and silver tinsel. And the scissors. And the pots of glue. And Bluma and the children snipping and coloring and pasting armor and helmets for the wicked Greeks and swords for the brave Maccabees. With silver and gold they carefully covered the menorahs they had made from strips of wood and soda caps and the giant tops that would hang from the ceiling. The fat pianist taught them Hanukkah songs, her big bottom rippling over the round piano stool while Bluma prepared the show and rehearsed everyone's lines. The part of Mattathias the High Priest went to Balfour, who was the tallest and the plumpest in the kindergarten. Nachman now sat in the Mendelevitches' parlor and watched Madam Mendelevitch sew Balfour's long silk gown and try on the beard she had made for him from the leftover flax in which the citron had been wrapped for the holiday of Sukkot. Nachman would have liked to have been one of the Maccabees himself, perhaps even Judah Maccabee, or Eleazar, who had single-handedly killed the elephant, but he had to wait quietly for Bluma to cast him. She had already given a part to everyone else. If only, he thought with a twinge, his father were a *poyer* like young Adon Mendelevitch, who was the head of the local defense force, he would certainly have been chosen for Judah. He suffered in silence until Bluma turned to him at last, fixed the beret on his head, and announced, "And Nachman, boys and girls, will do what the rabbi does. He'll light the Hanukkah candles and say all the blessings."

"I don't want to," he answered at once, without stopping to think. And by then he really didn't. Anything but that.

"But why not? You'll sing the blessings beautifully. Nachman's father knows all the prayers and the blessings just like a cantor in a synagogue and he'll teach him to say them perfectly."

It was music to his ears to hear his father's praises sung, yet at the same time it frightened and infuriated him. He wanted to be a Maccabee, not a cantor. And besides, what if he wouldn't remember all the blessings? Though on the other hand, if he had learned to say the *kaddish,* why shouldn't he learn to say the blessings just as well? He declined again, but Bluma refused to change her mind. Instead she spoke to Nachman's father, who sat him down on Sabbaths and each night before going to bed and coached him on everything that had to be said when lighting the Hanukkah candles (which meant, Nachman's memory affirmed, that his father was home at the time). "Both your Hebrew and your voice are better than a lot of cantors'," his father told him, "and besides, I'll be standing right by you in case you should need me."

All this was the prelude to that rain-washed morning of the Hanukkah party. His mother slipped a sweater over his good clothes and insisted, despite his protests, that he wear his rubber galoshes and not his best shoes, which he could put on inside the kindergarten. She herself was wearing her Sabbath dress, over which she put on the coat with the fur collar that she brought from Poland and kept carefully stored in the wardrobe with her fur wrap. It was only when they were already out of the yard and Nachman noticed that the store was locked that he realized his father was not coming too.

"Your papa had to go to the marketplace. He'll join us straight from there," his mother said. But Nachman knew that she wasn't telling the truth. In her voice he could detect those bitter outbreaks between her and his father whose sudden occurrence was never predictable. His mother was lying now, and his father had lied all along. He'd said he would come and he hadn't.

"I'll be there with you, Nemmale. You'll light the candles and say the blessings and it will be just lovely." She bent down over him, her cold lips brushing his forehead between the eyes. Her fur collar tickled him and made him draw back.

"He promised. He promised he'd come."

Without warning his mother exploded. "Why must you always torture me like this? I'm right here, I'm not going anywhere. Right here, six feet underground, where my days aren't days and my nights aren't nights." And then just as suddenly—Nachman felt it keenly—she swallowed her anger and whispered submissively, "Come, Nemmale. I'll be right by you."

He wasn't a baby anymore. Far from it. He understood perfectly well that his mother had no business leaving the store untended, especially at this hour of the morning, when men on their way to work were in the habit of stopping by for fresh bread, some halvah, a slice of smoked fish, a few olives, a bottle of buttermilk. A customer had only to find the store shut down once to switch to the new grocery that had opened down the street. They should thank their lucky stars, his mother said, that they had the store at all. It was all that kept hunger from the door.

Nachman stood his ground and said nothing. He knew that he had to go to kindergarten, but how could he stand in front of the menorah without his father? What good would it do to have his mother there—though on the other hand, how could he go through with it all by himself? Just then Balfour and his mother appeared among the cypresses. The special silk gown that Balfour's mother had sewn for him was tucked away under his coat to keep it from getting muddy, but you could tell from his white beard and Arab headdress that he was Mattathias. Something unknown to Nachman had also come between his mother and Madam Mendelevitch, who no longer shopped in their store but went to the new one down the street. Now, though, she greeted them warmly, to which Nachman's mother replied with a faint hello. "Will you come on!" she said with incomprehensible anger, clutching his arm. But just as Balfour and Madam Mendelevitch were about to pass them and Balfour had stuck his beard into Nachman's face, wagging it this way and that while extending a hand, Nachman decided, "I'll go to kindergarten by myself. With Balfour."

At once he broke away from his mother and the three of them hurried on, stepping on the wooden sidewalk wherever there was one and on the hard, reddish sand where there wasn't, hopping among the puddles and carefully skirting the high, waterlogged grass. Laughter and Hanukkah songs accompanied each skip and jump. Madam Mendelevitch was quick on her feet, and every summer she and young Adon Mendelevitch rode in the great annual horse race along with the Bedouin. Her gay grace made Nachman forget all about his father and mother and the lighting of the Hanukkah candles. Now they were already crossing the footbridge under which flowed a black, foamy bilge that ate away at the red soil of the creek. Now they were in the classroom.

Swords in hand and helmets or Hanukkah crowns on their heads, the armor-bearing children milled about with their mothers in the decorated room. The fat pianist was already sitting on her round stool. Any minute now Bluma would clash her cymbals. The children sat down while the mothers lined the walls and joined the children and the piano in loud song.

Only when Nachman's eyes came to rest on the giant, silver-and-gold-plated menorah did he remember that in another minute Bluma would call on him to light the candles. His fear came back all at once. Father hadn't come, and he didn't remember the blessings, didn't remember a thing. The children sang on. Now Bluma clashed the cymbals and walked through the crowded room looking for something. She was looking for him. Unconsciously, Nachman reached out for Madam Mendelevitch's warm hand. She drew his head to her body, and he breathed her pleasant fragrance, like the blossoms of some unfamiliar tree. His fear had no voice, yet he could hear it above the singing of the children, above the piano itself. His father had lied. He had promised to come, and he hadn't. He would hold on to Madam Mendelevitch and stay right where he was.

Bluma raised the cymbals high overhead. She put her finger to her lips and sang in a whisper:

Hush, hush, watch the fire
Whispering and getting higher.

They were all whispering together now, even the piano. Nachman shut his eyes tight. He wasn't there at all any longer, he had vanished into the darkness. Yet his fear was still there, like a jackal primed to howl outside their window. Through the darkness came Bluma's voice. "And now we're going to light the Hanukkah candles. They'll be lit and blessed by Nachman."

If he opened his eyes now to be caught in Bluma's twinkle, there would be no way out anymore. She would light the first candle and put it in his hand. He would have to say the blessings, and he wouldn't remember a thing. He could already hear the silent darkness being broken by the children's loud guffaw. "Nachman–Achmed!" they would sing in a chorus, to the accompaniment of the piano. "Achmed–Nachman!"

He would just stay hidden in the darkness and never come out.

"Go ahead, Nachman," whispered Madam Mendelevitch in his ear. A fragrant warmth caressed his cheek, the blossom-smell of that tree he didn't know.

"Come, Nachman," he heard Bluma say. Her hand lifted his chin. "Come, Nachman, let's bless the candles. You know the blessings so well. Come, we'll bless them together, Nachman."

Voices murmured in the dark, rose to a crescendo. Many voices calling out, "Whose boy is this? Where's his mother? How can they let such a little boy bless the candles?"

Madame Mendelevitch's soft voice caressed his ear. "You'll sing the blessings beautifully. Bluma and I will sing with you. You're so brave, Nachman."

He felt sorry for himself that he hadn't stayed in the store, sorry that he had shut his eyes and let himself be cornered by so many voices and stares. But to get up and light the candles was simply too much for him.

And then, straight into the darkness, came his mother's furious voice. Her hard fingers dug into his arm, and her choked voice slashed at his face, "Why must you always do this to me, Nachman? Do you want me to die of shame?"

His ears tingled with pain. His mother's whisper stung like a burn. He opened his eyes to see hers looking into them from very close. Only they weren't eyes at all but two red, tear-washed wounds.

"Go light the candles this minute!"

"He's a big boy," said Bluma. "He'll go."

"We'll sing along with you," Madam Mendelevitch caressed him.

"Papa promised me. He promised."

"Your father is in Jerusalem. He isn't here."

"But he promised."

Why must they crowd him so? What did they want from him? They had tricked him. They had lied to him. He wanted to run away from them all, from the kindergarten, from his father, from his mother, from the store, to some place where he would be by himself, like in the darkness, but without any voices, without anything at all.

Had he really gotten up then and run, as his memory related, slipping through the arms of the three women surrounding him, passing through the open door and out the gate, over the path lined with tall grass and pitted with puddles of water, running with the Hanukkah crown on his head, sweaterless, bootless, as far as his home and farther yet, on and on toward the sands where Uncle Rifael lived, toward the mountains, toward the end of the world?

The family memory told a different story, which was different itself whenever it was repeated. One point alone was stubbornly clung to: how appealing Nachman had been when he had stood and sung all the blessings, how perfectly he had said them, how well he had stayed on tune! And—the family memory added, though Nachman had his silent doubts about it—his father had been there, too, just beside him. He hadn't forgotten at all. He had had some important business to attend to, after which he had run to the kindergarten as fast as he could, arriving in the nick of time. These were the plain facts.

But if it really were so, Nachman often wondered, why wasn't it in *his* memory too? Why was it that he clearly remembered his mother shouting after him, "Stop, Nachman, stop, I'll die of shame!" while he kept running toward the dunes, toward the mountains, toward the end of the world, running so that no one would see how small and frightened he was, though as he ran on by himself, away from Bluma, away from Madam Mendelevitch, away from his mother, he could feel his limbs being charged with a new energy that was entirely his own, his alone, while a voice beat time in his heart: this is what *I* want, this is *me*, me, me?

Why would he remember what hadn't happened and forget what had?

10 | Cold eyes

Mister Blackman was no longer the same person as before. He now spent the whole day indoors, lying in bed or sitting in the rocking chair in his flannel pajamas and heavy robe, a blanket over his feet and a round woolen cap, gray, like the one the mailman wears, on his head, passing the time on the enclosed terrace, his eyes fixed on the tall windows, though they no longer seemed to see a thing. Only when Nachman entered did they flicker slightly, like Sabbath candles that had burned down to the last drop of wax and were about to go out. His beard had grown sparser and scragglier, like a brush that had lost its bristles, and his wrinkled face looked like a crumpled candy wrapper that someone had tried to smooth out. All day long he didn't set foot outside the house. Gone were the days when he could be seen, cane in hand, on his way from the marketplace, striding ahead of Missus Blackman, who carried the full shopping baskets behind him. No more did he argue under the mulberry tree with old Adon Mendelevitch or visit the store he had built for Nachman's parents to lecture them on how to run a business. By day his lifeless eyes stared at the window, while by night his coughing filled the yard, slicing through the walls and jabbing its way like a needle through the blanket that Nachman pulled over his head. With every cough it seemed that right then and there he was about to stop breathing forever.

In the store and the yard it was talked about quite openly. His lungs, it was said, were already no good in Zud Afrika, though no one seemed to know why or what he had done there to harm them. It was common knowledge, in fact, that the air there was excellent, though on the other hand, the country was full of gold mines, so that perhaps he had gone off prospecting somewhere and had breathed in too much dust. Yes, everybody knew what gold dust did to the lungs, to say nothing of diamond dust, which was even worse.

"All I can say is that it's a mystery to me," said Nachman's mother, who had taken to defending Mister Blackman ever since they had gotten the store and would let no one criticize him. "My father died of the exact same thing, and he was young and strong as an ox. Every cough tears another bit of blood from his lungs. My heart goes out to him."

"It's her my heart goes out to," said old Madam Mendelevitch. "She never had an easy time with him, but I don't envy her once he's gone."

Missus Blackman too, said Nachman's mother, and everybody agreed, had been looking poorly as of late. A strange expression had settled over her eyes, as though she were already in the other world.

"It's the fear of what will be once he's passed on that keeps haunting her," said old Madam Mendelevitch. "When I see Rabbi Kutter troubling himself to sit with Mister Blackman every day, I can see why she's so frightened. God only knows what she should ask Him for, to keep him alive a while longer, or to hurry and take her first."

When Nachman looked in Missus Blackman's eyes, they seemed no different from before, yet it was true that her rasp had deteriorated into a thin whisper, as though the head she laboriously carried on her bowed neck were pressing against her throat and cutting off the air. He didn't dare refuse now either when she came to the store or knocked on their front door to beg him to drop in on Mister Blackman—who, she said, missed him terribly—but he tried to evade her when he could. An impalpable fear now overcame him whenever he stayed at their home. Above all, he was afraid that Rabbi Kutter would walk in while he was there.

Nachman couldn't remember when Rabbi Kutter had first begun to appear, but he knew that it had been before his father's trip to Jerusalem. Rabbi Kutter would sit in the back yard with old Adon Mendelevitch, peeling an orange or sipping his glass of tea, and sometimes Nachman's father would join them too, if he happened to be off from work. His mother loathed Rabbi Kutter from the moment she laid eyes on him. "In the first place," she would say, "why does everyone call him a rabbi when he's not one at all but simply one of those bearded Jersualem Jews who pretend to be? He's just a Talmud Torah teacher and I don't like his looks, though don't ask me why. It's nothing I can put my finger on, but I'd watch out for him like the devil, even if you do call him rabbi. I admit that he wears a long coat and a long beard and long sideburns wrapped around his ears and a skullcap that sticks out beneath his black hat just like any pious Jew, but he has cold eyes."

"You!" Nachman's father would answer angrily. "You find reason to suspect everything and everybody. You see everything in the worst possible light. I've never checked to see if he's actually an ordained rabbi, but that he's a learned Jew I can see for myself. What's so strange about the fact that a scholar like him, the head of a Talmud Torah, should want to bring a ray of light into the last dying days of a childless man? For forty years Mister Blackman knocked about Zud Afrika doing God knows what, and now the fear of Judgment Day has suddenly gotten into him. He wanted to have something to show for himself when the time came, and so he began to spend his days in the synagogue and even to give money to charities and the Talmud Torah. And now that he's housebound all the time, what crime is it if Rabbi Kutter comes to sit with him a bit and tell him some story to keep up his spirits? On the contrary, it only proves that he's a truly religious man."

"We'll see in the end," replied Nachman's mother. "I'm a simple soul just like Mister Blackman, but this much even I can understand: it's not to tell Mister Blackman stories that Adon Kutter visits him all the time. His eyes are as cold as ice."

One day Nachman overheard Missus Blackman whisper something to his mother that put the fear of those cold eyes in him too. "He wasn't always like this," she whispered, "going from one synagogue to another like a saint, holding a prayer book in his hands all day long, giving money to the Talmud Torah. All of a sudden he's concerned for the little children, but when his own children were alive he hardly ever saw them. When did he ever have time to be at home? I know what Rabbi Kutter smells in our house. But the old fool just sits there and stares at Rabbi Kutter's beard. To think that there hardly used to be a Jewish custom in our house! I had to remind him when it was Yom Kippur so that he shouldn't go off on the road. I've tried to reason with him, to tell him that the man is after only one thing, but he just sits there as though in a trance and stares glassy-eyed at Rabbi Kutter's beard. I can already see myself being put out in the street."

"No one's putting you out in the street," said Nachman's mother, "but I don't like the looks of him. He has cold eyes."

As though he were her last hope, Missus Blackman would suddenly pounce on Nachman and beg him to come home with her to make the old man happy. "He does miss you so, luv," she would say, and Nachman couldn't refuse.

They sat in the enclosed terrace, but Mister Blackman no longer leafed through the old album or told stories about Zud Afrika and his two little angels in heaven. He didn't even ask to hear the *kaddish*. Nachman was already tired of the candies that Missus Blackman kept forcing on him and was waiting for the first excuse to slip away when Rabbi Kutter stepped into the house. He filled the terrace with his tall frame, over which a gray coat descended from his broad shoulders to beneath his knees. A round black hat (a Jerusalemite hat, his mother said) was sliding down his forehead as though to hide the cold stare of his eyes. Mister Blackman came instantly to life and sat up in his chair, his eyes alert once again. Rabbi Kutter unbuttoned his long coat, exposing the fringed knots that protruded from underneath his gray vest. At once he began to talk in a low, deep voice, which enchanted even Nachman. Mister Blackman was suddenly seized by another coughing fit, but he managed to hold it in, spitting his phlegm into a pot and motioning to Missus Blackman to bring some tea and citron jam. Wiping his whiskers and scraggly beard with a handkerchief, he leaned over toward Rabbi Kutter. Nachman tried to peek into Rabbi Kutter's eyes to see if they were really ice cold, but when he found them beneath the hat brim, they were closed. As he talked, the upper half of Rabbi Kutter's body swayed back and forth. Nachman tried to follow what he was saying but all he could make out were words: We read in the weekly portion. Our Mother Rachel. Rejoice O barren one. Let me have sons. God's commandments. Angels. The study of Torah outweighs all. Heaven. Hell.

Dusk drifted over the terrace, and Rabbi Kutter's incomprehensible phrases filled Nachman with boredom. No one was paying any attention to him, and no one would notice if he got up to go. Yet no sooner had he touched the doorknob than Mister Blackman's voice brought him up short. "Reb Nachman! Where are you off to, Reb Nachman? Come over here."

Nachman went over. Rabbi Kutter removed his black hat and tilted the black skullcap beneath it down over his forehead. His eyes were open now, and Nachman could look right into them. They were as bright and smiling as Bluma's, and Nachman smiled back. Who said they were cold?

"Reb Nachman," said Mister Blackman, "is something of a scholar himself. He could already be going to Talmud Torah."

"You don't say!" The eyes stared at him. "Then tell me, Reb Nachman, what's the proper blessing to say over toffee?"

The eyes bore right into him, and Nachman now began to understand what his mother had meant. What was the blessing for toffee?

"And do you know the *shema* by heart, young man?"

"Of course he does," Mister Blackman defended him. "He already reads books."

"Jewish books?" asked Rabbi Kutter, and now Nachman was sure what his mother had meant. (Cold, cold!) He didn't know the *shema* but he did know something else.

"I know the *kaddish*." And without further ado he stood and declaimed in a clear, fluent voice, "*Yitgadal veyitkadash shmey rabba*."

It wasn't until the words were already out of his mouth that he saw the black cloud descend on Rabbi Kutter, who recoiled in his chair while clapping one hand to his head to keep his skullcap in place.

"*Kaddish?* The mourner's *kaddish?*"

Mister Blackman pressed his hands to his chest in a vain attempt to stifle a cough. Nachman knew that he had done something wrong, that he had gone back on all his oaths.

"The boy still has his parents, may they live to be one hundred and twenty. Who taught him to say the *kaddish?* It's strictly against the Jewish law."

Mister Blackman wanted to speak, but his cough filled his chest and covered his lips with froth until he began to turn purple. Having just put down a cup of tea and some citron jam before Rabbi Kutter, Missus Blackman hurried to Mister Blackman's aid as he bent above the spittoon. Nachman glanced back and forth from Mister Blackman, who looked as though he were about to breathe his last each time he cleared his lungs, to Rabbi Kutter, who refused to let the subject drop and kept returning to it time and again. "How can you say the mourner's *kaddish* when your father and mother, may they live, are still alive? It's strictly forbidden. Only if, God forbid and preserve us, something should happen—it's only then that you say the *kaddish.* The mourner's *kaddish,* Reb Nachman, is not a children's game."

Rabbi Kutter's words seemed seven times scarier against the background of Mister Blackman's unstoppable cough. Threads of saliva hung in his scraggly beard, and the veins swelled beneath his wrinkled skin. Afraid to witness what seemed about to happen any second, Nachman ran to the door and escaped outside. There he felt better, though a dog was barking in the darkness. As fast as his legs could carry him he ran to the store, which was hardly twenty steps away. He has cold eyes, his mother would say. It was forbidden to say the *kaddish.* And did he think it was permitted to make Mister Blackman cough like that?

He had intended to tell his mother everything that had happened, but now that he was already in the store's circle of light he changed his mind. No, he wouldn't say a thing. Not to anyone. He would keep quiet. And when Mister Blackman died, he'd say the *kaddish* to himself. Quietly. So that no one else could hear or say a thing. Just like that.

11 | At young Madam Mendelevitch's

Nachman's father went more often now to Jerusalem and came back less often, leaving his mother chained to the store. By the time he rose in the morning to go to kindergarten, she had already been to the market and back, while the store would still be open when he went to bed at night. If he didn't fall asleep before she came home, he would see her bent over the black ledger entering her customers' debts or laboring at the endless job of keeping house. She was always busy and tired and never had time for him anymore. Yet Nachman too needed her less now. He dressed himself in the morning and undressed himself at night, and the hours in between never seemed long enough for all the thousand and one discoveries that lured him outside everyday, farther and farther into the ever expanding world.

Balfour was now Nachman's best friend, and the two were inseparable. Balfour was so big and strong that even the regular schoolchildren didn't dare start up with him, and Nachman knew no fear when he was with him. Together they went to kindergarten, together they came home, together they played in the afternoons and evenings. Every day Balfour chose a new way back from the kindergarten. In wintertime they would stand on the wooden footbridge and watch the water stream by in the creek below, foaming like a saucepan of chicory mixed with milk. They would try sailing paper boats and search for some interesting object that the water had washed up. As it came down from the mountains, Balfour explained, the current was so strong that it could sweep along a horse with its rider, or a herd of sheep, or even tear up whole trees by their roots. In summer they climbed down into the dry waterbed and dug in the ground, hoping to find some buried treasure that the winter rains had carried from afar. Once they found a few rusty bullets, which Balfour said were from an English rifle, because the Turks and the English had fought here once. Balfour knew about such things because his father, young Adon Mendelevitch, and his grandfather, old Adon Mendelevitch, had rifles and Mauser revolvers and were great heroes. To this day Arab sheikhs came to consult them in their yard, and whatever old Adon Mendelevitch told them was law in their eyes.

From the bridge Nachman and Balfour sometimes proceeded along Mohilever Street to look at the pictures in the window of Sirkin's photography store, or else they headed in the opposite direction toward the new road that was being paved on Lovers of Zion Street, where they watched the workers smashing huge rocks with their hammers and the steamroller belching smoke from its chimney while its giant drums crushed the big stones together with gravel scattered from rubber baskets and boiling tar poured by the bucketful over everything. Or if they didn't get that far, halfway home they would come to the animal market, where Arab women squatted in the dust, noisily selling eggs packed in baskets layered with straw, chickens with their legs and wings tied together, figs, melons, huge, overripe yellow grapes, plums, and watermelons, olives ready for pickling—all depending on the time of year. Here one could have a grand time, and Balfour was always full of ideas: one minute he was ramming a long stick under a donkey's tail to make it angrily kick up its hind legs, the next he was sneaking up to an old woman on the ground and pinching something from one of her baskets. What it was didn't matter. There was never a dull day with Balfour.

Eventually they remembered that they had to go home for lunch. This was the one thing that Nachman's mother was strict about: he could run around outside or spend the time with Balfour as he pleased, but to eat in anyone else's house—in other words, at young Madam Mendelevitch's—was firmly forbidden. "We have food of our own," she would say. In the rainy season, when she tried to avoid running back and forth from the house to the store so as not to catch cold, she cooked in a corner of the store and served lunch on a clean kitchen towel spread over a crate. There was always a bowl of hot potato, buckwheat, lentil, or bean soup, followed by a meat patty, or stuffed cabbage, or eggplant that was either sliced and fried or grilled whole on the fire and chopped fine with a cleaver together with an onion and a hard-boiled egg. On other days there might be spinach cake, which was full of iron and grew muscles on little children. In summertime Nachman's mother fed him great amounts of yogurt and homemade cheese, borscht, grated carrot, heaping salads, and whatever fruits were in season. And whatever she served, he was expected to eat—either because it was good for him, or because it was the best she could do with what little money they had, or because one simply didn't let food go to waste. "Back in Poland," she would say, "we used to eat meat every day, and food in general was terribly cheap, yet we still never threw anything out." The greatest sin of all was to throw away bread, even if it was hard as stone, for stale bread was even better than fresh bread. There were several reasons for this. In the first place, the fresh bread was sold to customers, while they themselves could make do with the half- and quarter-loaves left over from the day before. But it wasn't just a question of money. Not only was stale bread more economical, it was actually healthier and less harmful to the digestion than the fresh bread that Nachman craved. Even in summer, wrapped in a towel and kept in a closed place, it would still be good after three or four days. Yet even if it were all dried out and hard as a board, it still could be used: white bread by being shredded on a scraper and added to a meatloaf, hallah to gefilte fish, and black bread by being soaked in water and fed to the chickens. Nachman ate whatever his mother put before him, above all because the minute his plate was clean, he was free to run back into the yard.

"The yard" was everything. It was the sandy hill thick with eucalyptus trees right behind the barn as well as the vast empty lot which stretched in front of the house, down to the Hasidic synagogue and even farther—all the way to Guberman's dairy and the wooden cottages that were like black patches against the open skies. In summer they played in the yard until dark, while in winter there were games in Balfour's parlor. Nachman's eyes never tired of this room and its contents. Its walls were plastered with broad stripes of a silver-spangled green alternating with narrower stripes of an indeterminate shade that seemed brown or red to Nachman in the daytime and the glossy color of stewed plums by the light of the Lux lamp at night. Along one wall was the black piano whose keys Nachman wasn't allowed to touch. But just as fascinating was a magnificent cabinet, whose decorations were wondrous to behold. The lower half consisted of legs and columns with patterns of leaves and clustered grapes, which were repeated on the doors. Above them rose two towers on thin, carved supports with panels of polished glass, against which the rays of the setting sun broke into all the colors of the rainbow as they passed through the blinds. Between the two towers was a mirror in which the whole room was brilliantly reflected, so that it seemed that not one Lux lamp was spreading its white light but two. And in the mirror too could be seen a marvel of a clock, on whose cylindrical gold base rested a transparent glass cap, through which one could see all the cogs and wheels that made the hands go round. Nachman loved the parlor and everything in it and the hours when Madam Mendelevitch joined them and filled the air with that special fragrance of an unfamiliar blossom that came with her. He could never get enough of it all, yet the time would always come when he suddenly fell into a mood, as if it were somehow wrong to be constantly away from the store, as if by staying in Madam Mendelevitch's parlor he was making things still harder for his mother because that bad something still existed between her and his father, just as it did (only, what?) between her and young Madam Mendelevitch herself. It wasn't just that Madam Mendelevitch had stopped buying from them, either, and now patronized the new store down the street, but rather something (but what?) more serious. He would have gladly stayed on at the Mendelevitches', but in the end he got up to leave, even though it meant missing the piano or the gramophone with the music coming through its horned speaker.

"No, thank you," he would say, "my mama already made me cocoa and salad and a hot *pita*—round Arab bread. I'd better eat at home."

In summertime the hours flew by almost unnoticed, but in winter it grew dark early, and his mother continued to sit in the cold store, which was lit by a kerosene lamp, huddling by the burner on which a teakettle emitted a thin jet of steam, waiting for the last of the workers to return on his way back from the nightly lineup in town. Those who would go to work next morning might drop by and make a purchase, and she could not afford to close as long as that other store down the street remained open. Nachman didn't mind this, however. On the contrary, he liked to sit on the cushion that his mother made up for him between the sacks in the corner, near the small stove, where he drank cocoa and ate a piece of the warmed-up *pita* (this to lure him from Madam Mendelevitch's) and sucked on a sugar cube while listening to customers' stories. Sometimes not a single patron would enter the store for hours, but then he had his mother's unending movements to observe: she would scrape the dried mud from the floor with a stiff brush, sweep it, and swab it with a wet sack that made her hands turn red from the cold, polish the copper scales with that acidy fluid until the yellowish light of the lamp would gleam back from the burnished plates, set a trap for the mice, tidy up the shelves, write down tomorrow's orders with a thick-stubbed pencil, and total the day's sales in her black ledger (whispering in Polish the figures she was adding up: *yeden, dva, tchi,* or *shti,* or *shtchi,* and the funniest number of all—*shcheeri*). Only then would she sit down to rest for a minute, going over to the kettle to warm her hands by the thin line of vapor rising from its spout or against the towel that she put on it to dry. This, Nachman knew, was the hour of magic, the time when she would have liked someone to tell her how tired she was and to beg her to rest for a while.

"Mama, sit down," Nachman would say. "Rest for a while."

A hint of a smile passed over her weary face. She took off her apron, spread it on the soap crate, and sat down. It would be a good evening. If it had been preceded by one of those looked-forward-to days, when a letter arrived from Poland, now would be the time to ask her what was in it. She was sure to have read it several times already, and she would read it as many times again before the next letter came. Now, though, she read out loud what grandmother had written in Yiddish and what Nachman's uncles had written in Polish, translating into Hebrew as she went along. Every sentence was a pretext for Nachman to ask a question and for his mother to reply with a story. Each day he came home from kindergarten he was careful to ask if a letter had arrived, because if it had, it was certain to be a good evening.

But even when there weren't any letters, which was most

long winter nights, he liked to stay in the store as long as he could. He liked to be with his mother when the sky was suddenly split by lightning as far as the distant mountains while a thunderclap burst above the roof. On clear nights, too, he tried to stay in the store and not go to bed by himself. Even when his eyes began to close, he would lean his head against the rice sack and doze off. It was better yet to lie half awake in his mother's arms and even better than that to awake by surprise in the morning under the eiderdown quilt with his mother's warm body beside him.

Best of all were Saturday mornings. Then Nachman and his mother (there were Sabbaths now, and sometimes two in a row, when his father would be away in Jerusalem) would lie in bed until late. His mother would get up in her nightgown to bring him some cocoa and a piece of cake, and then get back into bed to sleep or read the thick Yiddish paper—*Der Amerikaner*—that she regularly borrowed from Missus Blackman. In the afternoons they would go out for a walk or drop in at somebody's house, where they would have tea and talk Yiddish and Polish until it grew dark outside and it was time to go home. Then Nachman's mother would change from her Sabbath to her weekday dress and open the store.

One letter was different from all the rest. One Sabbath was different from all the others too.

12 | *Beyond the sea of sand*

That whole evening was sad. His mother lit the candles and spread a white cloth over the table, but they ate in haste, without blessing the wine, without Sabbath hymns, without gefilte fish, without the grace after meals, without Nachman's father. When they finished eating, his mother told him to go to sleep early because in the morning they were going to visit Uncle Rifael.

Nachman's parents were always talking about the wooden shack that Uncle Rifael had built beyond the sea of sand and about the hell he went through at the hands of Tsipoyrele, on whose account he no longer came by their house at night astride his little donkey. Nachman had heard so many times about that shack beyond the dunes that he had not only pictured all its horrors in his imagination but had actually come to feel that he had lived in it, among the bare walls through whose cracks the wind wailed, surrounded by the orange grove that Uncle Rifael had planted at night while Tsipoyrele lay in bed like a countess and didn't even dip her little finger in cold water because all she did was suck Uncle Rifael's blood and burn down his life like a candle.

And yet the truth of the matter was that he had never even been there. At night it was impossible to go, at one time because there had been some trouble with the Arabs and two Jews had been killed when walking through the groves on their way back from work, and now because of the store. While on Sabbaths it was forbidden to walk beyond those wires which mark the town limits, not to mention all the other reasons, such as that they would never pay a visit to Tsipoyrele until Tsipoyrele visited them first.

All of a sudden none of these reasons counted any more, and now that his father was away, they were even free to walk as far as they liked on the Sabbath. Nachman rose first that morning and kept urging his mother to hurry, not quite believing they really were going until they set out among the cypress trees in the same direction that Uncle Rifael and his little donkey used to disappear in at night. The night's rain had packed the sandy trail hard, and their feet skimmed over the ground. The sun shone down from a cloudless sky on the freshly washed world with its fields of high grass that were dotted with red, white, and yellow flowers. His mother, who never stopped worrying about the weather, had insisted that it was still winter and that Nachman wear his heavy sweater, while she herself had put on her Polish coat with the fox collar over her Sabbath dress. Tall and elegant, she walked with measured steps over the packed sand, patiently enduring the battery of questions with which Nachman assailed her.

Though he had learned to wander from the yard with Balfour, Nachman had never been so far on foot before. Everything he saw seemed newly created, like the broad field they now passed amid whose tall grasses stood twisted, burned-looking stumps. This, said his mother, had once been old Adon Mendelevitch's vineyard. Now it no longer paid to grow grapes, and the vineyard was slowly being turned into building lots. They sold off a lot at a time and that was how they lived.

Farther on a bit, the packed sand path climbed a flat-crested hill, whose red earth had been furrowed by the rain, and began to meander beneath a shady canopy of acacia hedges that bordered the orange groves on either side. Here the sand was deeper and softer, and the latticework of branches overhead resembled the roof of a very long *sukkah*. The air had a brisk aroma, and the silence around them was so complete that they could hear the sand squeak under their feet. Thin lines of light threw an embroidered pattern on the carpet of shade. The smells among the green, green trees kept changing with every step: there was the wet smell of the shade and the dry smell of the light, the smell of the orange groves through the acacia branches, the smell of fallen oranges rotting in the irrigation holes and of the fruit that was still on the trees, and the smell of the first new blossoms of the awakening year. And all the flowers growing under the trees in the wet grass, the yellow ones with petals like tiny suns and even tinier blue ones that could hardly be seen at all. The sharp trill of a bird pierced the perfect silence, and then another and another. Bluma had told them about the birds that flew away to the Land of Israel every winter from their homes because it was terribly cold there and the ground was covered with ice and snow, and the sun hardly shone, so that it was night all the time and so terribly dark and sad. Bluma had told them too about a man called Hayyim Nachman Bialik, who stood by his window in that faraway land and saw a bird coming back from the Land of Israel and envied it so much. "Hail to thee, O pretty bird, O traveler from the south," sang Hayyim Nachman Bialik. Then why did his mother always say how beautiful it was there, and why did she read every letter from grandmother over and over and tell him about the wagons that traveled on snow without wheels and about the warm house in which they sat with windows closed, embroidering pillowcases and singing and playing cards? Nachman bent down to pick a blue flower, only to be angrily snapped at by his mother that it was forbidden on the Sabbath.

This made Nachman angry too, and he almost blurted

squint and looked as through his mosquito net at the dark green and red earth and at the Bedouin tents dotted upon it like a herd of black cows. From here up to the mountains, and on the mountains, and everywhere, there was nothing but Arabs. And Bedouin. A sea of earth and of Arabs. But where was that sea of sand beyond which lived Uncle Rifael?

Once again they were on a sandy path that girdled a hill of reddish sand. "Those," said his mother, pointing at some slender saplings that stuck out in rows from the sand, "are the orange groves." Uncle Rifael's? Nachman wanted to know. Some of it, said his mother, a few dunams of land. Not the groves. The groves belonged to everybody.

The path now led them between two rows of black shacks. Nachman blinked in amazement at the unaccustomed sight that met his eyes. The men and women standing in front of the shacks, his mother explained, lived in those buildings. But they didn't look at all the way people should on a Sabbath morning. One of them, a man in short pants with a summery tan on his shirtless back, was working away with a hoe that he held in one hand. On the Sabbath! In front of another hut two men were pouring cement into a wooden mold. They were adding a porch to their hut, Nachman's mother explained, without mentioning the day. Directly before them a two-wheeled wagon pulled by a donkey was bearing a load of fresh hay. By its side, the reins in his hand, strode a man in time with the donkey, his muddied pants tucked into his rubber boots, a patched shirt sticking out of his belt, a cap like Uncle Rifael's dangling brim backwards from his head as though it hung from a nail. Nachman glanced at his mother's face, but she walked on impassively with long steps, merely transferring her heavy coat, which had come off with Nachman's sweater long ago, from one arm to the other. It was so warm, so lovely a morning, and there wasn't a sea of dunes in sight.

His mother walked swiftly and surely as though she had been here often before. Turning off the path with Nachman after her, she headed down a narrow lane that had been cleared through the tall grass until she came to a shack so small that it seemed more like a shipping crate than a house. The walls were covered with black tarpaper and capped with a slanting roof of gray tiles. On one side was a door, and above it an awning of tin. With the joy of recognition Nachman spied Uncle Rifael's little donkey. Black and red chickens scattered in their path, fleeing to the safety of the laundry that hung on a long line between two high poles. From behind it came the sound of someone hammering. Though she was already in front of the door with one hand poised to knock, Nachman's mother now changed her mind and headed in the direction of the sound.

"Oy *vay*, he'll feel a little uncomfortable," she murmured as though to herself, but she was already passing between the clothes that hung on the line.

He stood there barefooted, in a tattered undershirt and heavy work pants that were caked with dried cement, banging away at a great, glistening sheet of tin, which he was joining to some kind of enclosure in the yard that was too big to be an outhouse and too small to be a room. Suddenly he glanced back over his shoulder, as though he had heard Nachman's mother between hammer strokes. When he saw her, he literally leaped from his place, and lines of gladness furrowed his sunburned face.

"I swear to God! Leah! I knew you'd come."

"Exactly what did you know?" Nachman could hear the suspicion in her voice.

"What? I didn't know anything. But my heart, something told me. Just this morning. I don't know why. Hello there, Nachman. Ah, it's good to see you, Leah. I had a feeling!"

"So it goes. One person has a feeling—and another takes the trouble to come."

"There goes the needle already! Rest a little first. Have a glass of tea." Uncle Rifael talked quickly and a lot, unlike the way Nachman remembered him, and the twinkle that danced in his narrow eyes seemed suddenly like his father's. "I swear to you that I knew. Ask Tsipoyrele if I didn't say to her this morning . . ."

"There's no need to swear, Rifael. Whether you were waiting for me or not—here I am."

"You're right to be angry. But what can I do? I work day and night. I'm supposed to be getting two cows, and I haven't anywhere to put them, so I'm building this thing here. Where am I supposed to find the time?"

"And that's all you ever think of, day and night, seven days a week."

"This isn't work. This is Sabbath relaxation." Uncle Rifael's belly shook again with a staccato laugh, and the wrinkles in his black face engulfed his eyes completely. His whole body—his chest, his neck, his shoulders, the big holes in his gray undershirt—was covered with black wool. He ran barefoot to the hut and shouted, "Tsipoyrele! We have visitors, Tsipoyrele!"

Turning back to Nachman's mother, he confided, "She didn't get a wink of sleep all night. The child wouldn't stop crying. Nothing we tried helped quiet him."

"Is he teething?"

"He has too many teeth already. We don't know what it is. Maybe a stomachache. Tsipoyrele's afraid that he might have caught cold in his ears. The way she is, you know, the child's already on its death bed."

"That's no way to talk, Rifael, not even as a joke."

But this only made Rifael laugh harder. He was already on his way in when a small, thin woman in shorts appeared in the doorway, her long, long hair falling over her shoulders and back. Nachman squinted at her in the sunlight. Could this be her?

"*Shabbat shalom,* Leah! Don't look at me. I look like a witch and the room is a mess. Don't ask what kind of a night we had."

"You can tell her about Amos's diseases later. First invite them inside."

"Come in, come on in. So this is Nachman!" Only now could he make her out clearly. Her shrill voice pierced his ears, and for some reason he looked down at the floor and stepped back.

"Let me see your eyes, Nachman. Why, they're just like Shalom's! Shalom didn't come with you? What's the matter, he won't walk on a Saturday?"

"Tsipoyrele!" said Uncle Rifael harshly. Nachman pricked up his ears. "You must want something to drink."

"I'll give them something to drink in a minute. First let me comb my hair and tidy up the room. Show them your estate first, Rifael. I'm embarrassed to let you come in, Leah."

She disappeared through the doorway. Uncle Rifael stood silently glowering for a moment, then turned on his heels and said, "Really, it's one of those mornings—it's nicer to sit in the sun." He relieved Nachman's mother of the coat and sweater, went in, returned with a stool in his hand, and only after she sat down he too sat down on the doorstep. He looked at Nachman's mother and Nachman looked at him. Now they would talk about yesterday's letter.

"Go play in the yard a little, Nachman," said his mother. And Uncle Rifael added, "Why don't you say hello to the donkey. Look behind the shed, maybe one of the hens has laid an egg."

Nachman wanted to listen to what they would say, but he also wanted to have a good look at everything. All the way to Uncle Rifael's he had kept imagining that black shack beyond the sea of sand, in which he was buried alive, working day and night for Tsipoyrele, who was both a countess and a witch. Her hair came down to the middle of her back and she was walking barefoot in the winter. Could this be her? And where was Uncle Rifael buried? Here, among the chickens and the donkey, among the vistas that stretched as far as the distant black tents, as far as the mountains and the sky? Nachman went looking for the donkey.

Balfour had taught him to watch out for a donkey's hooves, so he took care not to approach from the back but crept up to it from the side, patting it first above the stomach, up to the mass of yellow-gray hairs that was the donkey's neck before carefully approaching the tail, which kept angrily waving at the bothersome flies and whisking this way and that. He debated with himself whether to try Balfour's trick of poking a long stick up under its tail, or whether not to, both because he might suddenly get kicked from behind and because Uncle Rifael might get mad.

Uncle Rifael was talking about his father now, and Nachman cocked his head and struggled to make out what he and his mother were saying. He pretended to be busy with the donkey, to be looking for lost eggs, to be ferreting out the yard's secrets, but all the time he kept within earshot, narrowing the distance the more quietly they talked. Because they spoke in Yiddish, it was doubly hard to find some word he understood among all the meaningless syllables, such as the name of a person or place, or a Hebrew phrase that might suddenly crop up and enable him to fathom what came before and after. His ears strained to hear, while his brain broke down and put together, imagined and guessed. They were talking about his father. About Jerusalem. About Rabbi Kutter. The letter from Chicago had not been mentioned, though Nachman was sure that it was somehow connected with their having come to see Uncle Rifael.

Nachman listened.

"I realized a long time ago that the situation was hopeless. I took the boy and went to the Herzlichs with the idea of going back to my mother."

"You're talking like a little girl. To your mother! Is that any solution—to your mother?"

"And to go on like this is a solution? How long does he think I can take it? Every other day he starts his life all over again."

"Don't be angry with me, Leah, but the store was a great mistake."

"I knew you'd throw this at me! As though I enjoy standing on my feet sixteen hours a day!"

"That isn't the point. In the first place, Shalom never was a businessman and never was meant to be, even if he wanted . . ."

"So what was he meant to be, I ask you? A store he doesn't want. To work in the orange groves—you yourself saw what kind of a field hand he made."

"It isn't easy for someone like him. But you knew all that when you married him."

"What did I know? I didn't know a thing. Did I know what Palestine was? He said there was only one condition—that we go to Palestine. Fine, I said, if that's what you want, we'll go to Palestine. But a body has to eat here too. I myself, all right, I followed him of my own free will, but why is the child to blame?"

"Shalom cares about the child too, believe me. He's searching for something. He's in Jerusalem because he hopes to become a teacher."

"A teacher? A drudge in Rabbi Kutter's Talmud Torah! Is that what he came here for? I ask you, Rifael, what does he want? We had a stroke of luck with Mister Blackman that was positively unbelievable. He built us a store, Uncle Herzlich put up the money to stock it, and now—we'll never be rich, but at least we have something. So what is he searching for now? Why does he have to ruin everything all over again? To be a *melamed*—just a teacher—for Rabbi Kutter?"

"It's a terrible thing, Leah. He doesn't understand you, and you don't understand him."

"I understand him very well: he's ashamed to be a grocer. What's there to be ashamed about? In my own family everyone was in business, and believe me, they were good, respectable people. I could wish that Shalom were respected here the way my family was there. That's just what I can't understand—here everything is twisted, upside down."

"That's it, that's just the thing you have to understand.

To turn the world upside down is exactly what we want to do here."

"I don't want to have to insult you, Rifael!"

"I can imagine how."

"Anyway, here too you have the same world, and the same people. In this country too there are men who live with their families like human beings, and there are others who themselves live upside down and force this kind of life on their families. Only here they want to put into your head that this is really best for you, to stand on your head!"

"If you were trying to insult me, Leah, I'm not insulted. Let's say that I'm an upside-down man and so is Shalom. But let me tell you, Leah, and mark my words—here the world really does revolve around people who are turning our lives upside down."

"You don't even know what you're talking about, Rifael. How upside down can you get? Here, see for yourself."

Nachman held his breath and stole a glance at the letter from Chicago which his mother now took out of her purse. He mustn't miss a word now.

"Read it. Read it for yourself and tell me if the man hasn't gone completely out of his senses."

Uncle Rifael held the torn envelope between his pudgy fingers, the nails black with dry dirt and hammering, and without removing the letter said, "What has my crazy brother written to Chicago?"

"Don't ask me. Read for yourself."

Uncle Rifael held the thin blue sheet of paper, the kind that came only from Chicago, between his thick fingers, while his lips moved slowly and soundlessly. Nachman's mother sat on the stool, wiping her eyes with a handkerchief that she had taken from her purse. Even when he was through reading and had refolded the letter and replaced it in the torn envelope, Uncle Rifael remained silent. Only his sunburned face seemed to grow even darker. Suddenly he bent over, his hand skimming the ground as though looking for something.

His fingers found a piece of cinder block, which he grabbed and angrily hurled at the donkey grazing beneath the clean laundry.

"*Nevayleh*—unclean beast!" he exclaimed in a mixture of Arabic and Yiddish. "*Padleh! Yallah!*—Beat it!"

The donkey sauntered imperturbably away into the high grass at the other end of the yard, in perfect submission.

"This is already too much for me to understand," said Uncle Rifael. "To go to America? What does he want with America? Now? And with conditions there the way they are? Elyakum himself writes that no one's licking honey there these days."

"It's I who ask you! And you're telling me that the world is upside down. This man is upside down! He's absolutely determined to ruin our lives. I ask you: a store never, but America yes? You call that normal?"

Suddenly, without warning, Uncle Rifael did the unexpected: he tore the envelope and the letter inside it into tiny shreds and sent them sailing over the grass.

"First of all, then: Elyakum just never answered his letter. That's first of all."

"Tearing it up doesn't solve anything. When Shalom sees that he hasn't gotten an answer, he'll sit down and write again."

"You don't know him, Leah. The same day he wrote to Elyakum, he regretted it. I'll bet he's already sent him a second letter going back on everything he said in the first. It will say that he never wanted to go to America to begin with, that it was just a moment of weakness, and so on. That's the whole problem—the man is forever starting out and never getting anywhere."

"But how can anyone live like that? What am I supposed to do? I don't even have anyone to talk to. I can always go to the *fetter* in Tel Aviv, but believe me, I'm ashamed. I'm so alone, and everything falls on me: the store, the house, Nachman. . . ."

The handkerchief covered her eyes. She blew her nose. But her tears got the better of her. Nachman's glance shifted back and forth from her to Uncle Rifael, all his senses working furiously, digesting, selecting, hypothesizing, putting together. He knew that this Saturday morning's visit to Uncle Rifael was very important, and this became even clearer when Uncle Rifael said, "I'll have a talk with him, Leah. After all, I have the right to make him listen to me. I'll go see him. Tomorrow. Tomorrow I'll go to Jerusalem."

Afterwards they must have gotten up and gone home.

That is, he couldn't be sure. Nachman was always to remember this Saturday visit well, though it was only with time that he was able to filter out and place many things retained but not understood. There was a picture there of Tsipoyrele too, coming out into the yard in an inky blue pinafore that widened about her previously uncovered thighs and legs, her messy hair plaited into a thick braid, a small child in her arms. Nachman's mother started back toward the path, carrying her heavy coat and his sweater over her arm. Tsipoyrele begged them to stay for lunch. His mother stubbornly refused, though Nachman would have liked to stay longer in Uncle Rifael's yard.

"I've left the food on the stove," his mother said, "and I'm afraid it will burn."

"You're hurting my feelings," said Tsipoyrele. "At least have a glass of tea. The boy walked all this way and needs something for the way back. At least let me give him a glass of juice."

Yes, this he remembered, and the inside of the hut with its plank walls that were plastered a greenish color and its broad couch in one corner with a white crib next to it. In another corner some clothes hung behind a drawn curtain. They sat on the couch, his mother noisily sipping her tea and preserving a veiled silence between sips, while he drank his fresh, unstrained juice as slowly as he could so as to stay a while longer in Uncle Rifael's yard.

Then there was the long way back. His mother walked quickly, transferring her coat from arm to arm, while Nachman ran after her through the squeaky sand, through the damp grass now dried by the sun, through the shade of the acacia trees now heavy and hot. What happened to the food that his mother had left on the stove he didn't remember.

He was never to forget this day, which was woven into his memory. In the family memory, on the other hand, it was never alluded to. And yet, when his mother sometimes exclaimed in one of her moods, "And even when we swallowed our pride and went to visit them, when we walked all the way through the orange groves past that sea of dunes, that witch Tsipoyrele wouldn't even let us through the door or offer us a glass of tea"—whenever she talked that way, Nachman thought back to that brisk Sabbath morning, thought back to Uncle Rifael in his bare feet and tattered undershirt, to the glistening sheets of tin that he was using to build a shed for his cows, to the vistas that stretched onward to the clear mountains, to Uncle Elyakum's letter, which Uncle Rifael ripped up and scattered in the grass. Had his father really wanted to move to Chicago? And what would have happened if they did? And what had he done when Uncle Elyakum's answer never came?

13 | *The Talmud Torah*

His father's face was now disguised by a black beard that was trimmed back to its bristles along the cheeks but that sprouted to a hairy hemisphere around the chin. Each Friday afternoon, as soon as he returned from the Talmud Torah, he took off the jacket of his black suit, extricated himself from the bow tie that was bound around his neck with a strip of elastic, removed the stiff collar from his shirt, took out the long scissors from the table drawer, sharpened them with a special flat stone, tested the blades on the nail of his left pinky, which was longer than those of his other fingers, and struck a stance before the oval mirror on the wardrobe door. It was fun to watch him intently cutting back his rough cheeks, carefully gliding the scissors over his beard, curling his upper lip, pruning and plucking the hairs that had grown on his throat, on his Adam's apple, and in the opening of his shirt, clearing a space for the air to enter freely into his nostrils. Nachman would look at him and wonder about that other, beardless father of his, the one who was now hidden behind the new face that was awfully like grandfather's in the portrait on the wall, except that it was a little darker below the chiseled nose and a little brighter above. The scissors never missed or cut too much, and his father never regained his old face.

How long had it been since he last had it? Every morning now he put on his black suit, encased his neck in a stiff collar and bow tie, brushed his shoes with a strip of velvet from a pair of Nachman's old pants, put on his hat, and seized his briefcase in one hand and Nachman's hand in the other to drop him off at the kindergarten on his way to the Talmud Torah. Their promenade together filled Nachman with great pride, as if his father's being a teacher in the Talmud Torah had made him more important and grown up. He would have liked very much not to have to say good-bye at the gate of the kindergarten but to continue to the place that was the subject of so much discussion between his parents and Uncle Rifael and Rabbi Kutter, who was now father's friend: the Talmud Torah. He'd rather go to Talmud Torah, Nachman kept telling himself. Its mysteries were all he could think of. He'd rather that than anything at all.

And yet how had it actually happened that he was suddenly no longer in kindergarten and was sitting squeezed among new children at a high table, on whose nail-scratched, knife-carved, penciled-in surface rested a great pile of open and shut, bound and bindingless books? How had he so quickly become a Talmud Torah student?

Nachman was certain that he could remember the change from kindergarten to Talmud Torah, but in fact his memories of it were very much like his family's. All of a sudden, recalled his mother, he had begun to complain stubbornly that he was bored in the kindergarten, that there was nothing for him to do there, that he could already read and write and would rather go to the Talmud Torah. "More than once," his father proudly recollected, "I found him in the courtyard listening under the window. We kept insisting that he go to kindergarten, and he kept running away to the Talmud Torah. We saw that it was hopeless and that it really was a shame for him to waste a whole year singing and playing games when he already knew more than plenty of second-graders, and so in the end we gave in. At least in the Talmud Torah I could keep an eye on the little rascal."

He himself remembered only the long room with its high table and its masses of books, which smelled like the books that his father brought from Poland and were kept in a case in a corner of the room and taken out only once a year before Passover to be aired. That, and the raised platform of the teacher with the Holy Ark behind it, which was covered with a red drape embroidered in gold letters, and the calendar that hung crookedly from a nail in the wall, with its big print and small print and the smallest print of all, and the tiny specks that had been left by the flies on the faded paper, which looked as if it had been torn right out of the naked, crackled wall.

Most of all he remembered sitting on a hard bench in front of a table among children who were not like those at the kindergarten at all. Secretly missing the kindergarten was indeed his earliest memory of the Talmud Torah. Here you couldn't sing or play or look up into Bluma's twinkling eyes. Here you took your seat every morning along one of the table's long sides while the teacher—who never actually sat down on his raised platform—paraded around the table twirling a ruler in his hand, jabbing it into this boy's back or whacking it over that boy's neck or fingers or ear, stalking back and forth and reciting out loud, slightly ahead of the children staring at their prayer books but in the same singsong rhythm, "Happy are they who dwell in Thy House, for they shall praise Thee forever, Selah."

The teacher kept time to his drone by banging his ruler on the plank table, while the children chanted prayer after prayer, page after page, morning after morning, with barely a chance to catch their breath in between. There were all kinds of boys in the class, some small like Nachman and others big and strange. The latter opened their large mouths wide and bellowed at the top of their lungs, but all the while their hands were busy elsewhere: working a forked lemon twig into a slingshot by peeling it with a penknife, grooving the bark, and tying a thick rubber band to the prongs with strong wire; swapping marbles—peewees, shiners, jewels—or stamps or empty boxes of Lateef, Matossian, Simon Arzt, or still cheaper brands of cigarettes; carving initials and drawings into the table; hunting and spearing flies on safety pins; or, for lack of anything better to do, pinching and poking the smaller boys, who had no choice but to go on shouting in the same rhythm as before, ". . . for Thou hast not made us like the nations of the world or set us among the families of the ea–a–a–r–rth. . . ."

Nachman tried to be like everyone else, to keep up with the prayers and master the verses in the weekly Torah portion so as not to lag behind the bigger boys in the Talmud Torah, where his father (alas, he now knew!) was one of the teachers. He tried not to think bad thoughts, but deep down he already knew what a terrible mistake he had made. Deep down too he was angry with his father for not having prevented it.

He spent the days squeezed in between Peterzail and Kashani. Peterzail had white hair and white eyebrows and white eyelashes, but his skin and eyes, whose corners were filled with yellow pus, were pink and his nose was always dripping snot, which he either snorted noisily back up or wiped with the back of his hand. When he wasn't harnessing flies to paper chariots, he was hunting them down amid the sores on his elbows and knees for the sole pleasure of tearing off their wings and leaving their crushed bodies on Nachman's book. All the boys knew that Peterzail's father was crazy and that one day he had gotten angry—just like that—and broken a bottle over Peterzail's mother's head. It hadn't killed her but she had been cuckoo ever since. Peterzail lived in one of the new cottages beyond the dry creek. His mother sat around the house and did nothing all day except beat Peterzail's little brothers and himself.

Kashani was the biggest and strongest boy in the class, and even the teacher, Adon Pollak, was afraid to lay hands on him. He never paid attention or talked to anyone, but just sat there with his hands beneath the table, drilling holes in apricot pits to turn them into whistles or making flutes from straws or reeds. When he grew tired of this, he simply laid his head down on the tabletop. Adon Pollak never raised his ruler at him, and once, when Kashani's red tea box with all his marbles and apricot pits fell on the floor, Adon Pollak kept quiet and let him crawl under the table to pick everything up. All the boys laughed to themselves but were careful to hide it from Adon Pollak, whose ruler was a menace at such times to everyone but Kashani. All the boys knew that Rabbi Kutter had once hit Kashani and sent him home from school. That same day he had a visit from his father, who worked as a porter and liked to lie between one job and the next under the eucalyptus trees near the Great Synagogue across from Roitman's liquor store, either guzzling from a bottle and crooning out loud, or else going to sleep with his porter's headrest as a pillow and his discarded slippers resting by his bare feet. He came to the Talmud Torah, his thick porter's rope wound around his hips above his baggy Arab pants, and shouted, "Where's Adon Kutter? Where's Adon Kutter? I've come here to kill him!" Since then no one dared touch Kashani. The more he drove Adon Pollak crazy, the more the other boys knew to watch out.

Nachman sat between Peterzail and Kashani, hemmed in by the flies of the one and the industrious elbow of the other, looking from his book to Adon Pollak pacing around the table while imagining himself back in the kindergarten with Bluma, singing along with all the children to the piano, putting on shows, listening to stories. The book before him grew luminously bright and its cramped letters seemed to shrink and vanish into the page. The Talmud Torah and its noises seemed far away now, like the distant sounds of a Sabbath morning, when one heard them (did he really?) filtering through the slats in the lowered shutters, up which those noises climbed on a slender ladder of light.

Nachman's ear was on fire.

He jumped from his dream, in which he had just been reliving the moment the paper cigarette had burned his face, only to find himself suddenly toppling over without support and landing on his backside on the floor. He opened his eyes—and there was the class, standing on the benches, roaring with laughter. Without lifting his head he could see Adon Pollak above him, ruler in hand. Nachman's ear burned fiercely and his backside hurt too. He silently cursed the whole rotten class and that ape, that bespectacled frog, Adon Pollak.

"On your feet, Shpiegler." Adon Pollak's ruler pressed against his neck. "On your feet, make it snappy."

Nachman stood up and lifted a leg to return to his place on the bench.

"Come here."

He was too frightened of what Adon Pollak was planning to do to him to budge. And in front of all the boys. Let them burn, let them all burn in hell.

Adon Pollak gripped the collar of Nachman's sweater with one hand and his chin with the other. Adon Pollak's beard was as yellow as the thread with which water pipes were lined, the color of flax and rust. His red nose was peeling as usual, and there was blood on his chapped lower lip. He stuck his face into Nachman's as he talked and slivers of spit like spiderwebs formed between his lips each time he opened his mouth. "What did we learn in *Pirkei Avot,* Shpiegler?"

Nachman twisted his head to one side to dodge the spray of spit.

"Look me in the eyes, Shpiegler! Too much sleep, Shpiegler, too much sleep, we learned, drives a man from the world. That's what we learned. Sleep drives a man from the world, but how can the world drive a man from his sleep, eh? Or better yet, how can we drive sleep from a man, eh? Why, the same way the Lord took us out of the Land of Egypt: with a strong hand! With a strong hand, Shpiegler, and with much fear. And don't think you can go running to your father. On the contrary, just because you're not one of these wild beasts, just *because* you're Adon Shpiegler's only son and he said to me himself, the boy is in your hands now, just *because* of that I'll drive the sleep from your head. There'll be no mercy, Shpiegler, there'll be no favorites here. Get it into your head: your father told me in so many words to show you no mercy."

Nachman knew that the red monkey was lying, yet at the same time he couldn't be sure. Just as all the while he was in kindergarten he couldn't wait to go to his father's Talmud Torah, so now his father's stature seemed to shrink from day to day. Previously he had seen only how honored he was by everyone. Not just by Mister Blackman, either, but even by old Adon Mendelevitch, who deliberately sought him out, though Nachman had heard his father emphatically tell Uncle Rifael that he wanted nothing to do with the Mendelevitches—neither with the old man, who was one of the founders of the town, said to have been a great hero in the old days when it was a tiny settlement in the malaria-stricken marshes, nor with young Mendelevitch, who was now head of the local defense force—because they had shamelessly gone and taken back Abed and his entire family into their backyard after all the Arabs had done during the recent riots. Now that Nachman went to the Talmud Torah and Balfour to regular school, they too no longer saw each other. All day long he was in the classroom while at night he would sit with his mother in the store or else read in bed. There were things in books that weren't anywhere else.

But his days were spent in the Talmud Torah, where he

was forced to hear things he didn't want to, such as the terrible stories that were told by the boys, the worst of which concerned the teachers. All the boys knew, for example, that at night Adon Pollak snuck off to Crazy Sima's mud cabin and did things to her there which Nachman wasn't sure of, though he knew it was shameful even to talk about them. He realized now too that it was not only his mother who thought that Adon Kutter had cold eyes. All the boys knew that he had only to look a hen in the eyes while holding a lighted candle to paralyze her completely, like a stone, and even after she recovered she would never lay eggs again. He had such power in his eyes, the boys said, that if he just looked at a pregnant woman her child would be born dead. That was how powerful Adon Kutter's eyes were.

Worse yet, Nachman now began to hear his own father made fun of. The things that were said about him were so awful that he began to keep away from the other boys so as not to have to hear them. During recess he would retreat into some corner, while after school he would try to run home as fast as he could, or to find a route that the other boys didn't take—but in vain. The older boys would find him in the end and do what they could to torment him.

"Just look at this little boy. He's Shpiegleh's son, this little boy."

"Shpiegleh! Come over here, Shpiegleh!"

Nachman walked faster. He was already past the wooden bridge, past the eucalyptus trees. He was almost on his own street, almost home safe, but now someone grabbed him by his knapsack and yanked him back. He tried to wriggle out of the straps and run, but it was too late.

"What's the matter, Shpiegleh, you deaf?"

"He didn't know we was calling him. He thought we was calling Adon Shpiegleh. This is Shpipeleh!"

The name made the boys laugh, and they tried to outdo each other in inventing even better ones.

"Not Shpipeleh—Pipeleh!"

"It's the other way around—Shpipeleh is Shpiegleh's pipeleh!"

The big boys surrounded him, pulled at his knapsack, laughingly passed him from one to another. They told terrible stories about his father, mimicked the way he talked, made fun of his announcing that he had never struck a student and never would.

"Just let him try," said the biggest of the bullies.

"Show us how high he comes on you," said an admirer.

"I'll show you how high," said the bully. His father's humiliation was Nachman's too, and he made up his mind to escape. He would leave them the knapsack and run. Anything so as not to hear his father disgraced anymore, so as not to see their dirty gestures. Nachman made a move, but the bully's voice lassoed him by the neck.

"Pipeleh! What's the big hurry? Stay where you are!"

He stood where he was and helplessly listened to them say that his father was like a woman, that he was a shrimp, that he wore shiny shoes, that he used the nail on his pinky to make marks in his notebook and to prick the boys' hands, that he was a pain with his funny Hebrew and his outings to orange groves and exhibitions and his big words, "I never, I never struck a student and never will."

"Let him try!"

"Shpiegleh!"

"Shpipeleh!"

Nachman would stand there until one of the teachers or some other adult saw what was happening and rescued him. Then he would take to his heels and run home.

He tried as best he could to avoid being caught on his way back from school, though despite all his fear he took pains not to be seen in his father's company and so not be teased even more. During recess, however, there was nowhere to hide. Like a pariah he would cower in a corner, the last to leave the classroom and the first to return. A sudden movement by one of the older boys was enough to make him tremble. Worse yet, against his will he was beginning to think of his father the way the boys did and to call him Shpiegleh in his mind. He measured his father with critical eyes: Rabbi Kutter was a good two heads taller and even Kashani looked as though he could finish him off with one blow. His thoughts buzzed in his ears like mosquitoes, and the more he chased them away the more they came back. An abyss had opened between him and the other boys. A wall had gone up between him and his father.

14 | *Bava Metzia*

He was no longer a beginning student and was now studying the book of the Talmud called *Bava Metzia*. (Could that mean that he was already in third grade?) In the trunk where his father kept his religious books there was an entire set of the Talmud, between whose yellowed, tallow- and wine-stained pages—when they were taken out to be aired before Passover—they had found long, rust-colored hairs. "These must have been my grandfather's," said Nachman's mother. "My father inherited the set from him, and since he passed away there's been no one to make use of it. Now it will be for you." Those were her words. Yet when Nachman began to study *Bava Metzia* his father took him to the same stationery-and-book store where he had bought him his first reader, his first pencil case, and his first knapsack, and purchased a brand-new copy for him, a thin, redolent volume whose cardboard cover had a ringed design like a tree trunk. Its pages were gray and not like other books. Instead of running all the way down and across, the lines formed a square of large letters in the middle of the page, around which were narrow columns in a peculiar writing that looked like an army of ants. Nachman tried to read some of it, but he couldn't decipher the strange Talmudic language or the tiny letters on the side of the page that looked like Rashi script. And yet it was his nature to get all excited over every change in his life. A change meant something new, and anything new could only be for the better. Now he would be learning what the big boys learned, and this would make him big too.

The Talmud didn't fit into his knapsack, and so he held it under his arm on his way to school, displaying it for all to see. Like all the novelties in his life that Nachman always looked forward to, however, this one too proved a disappointment and already in the very first lesson. Rabbi Kutter's husky voice buzzed like an angry hornet through the high-ceilinged classroom, one minute dropping to a whisper and the next gathering strength and rising to a crescendo that broke against the windowpanes in a flood of meaningless words and incomprehensible arguments whose starting point Nachman had lost track of long ago and whose end was never in sight. He was mindful of one thing only: to keep his head in his Talmud and watch out for the buzzing hornet.

". . . bzzzz . . . thiszzzzz one says I found it and it's mine . . . thiszzzzz one says I found it and it's mine . . . divide it! Thiszzzzz one says half of it is mine . . . thiszzzzz one says . . . divide it! Thiszzzzz one says . . ."

The flies refused to learn from their predecessors' fate and continued to flock to Peterzail's sores, drawn by the pus that oozed through the cracks in the hard scabs, while Peterzail himself indefatigably continued to trap them. They were no longer studying in the same room or around the same table, but the difference between one year and the next, between one class and the next, had grown blurred. It was all like one long day, in which there were no songs, no stories, no walls that were decorated for each holiday and season of the year, no Bluma with her twinkling eyes. Nachman had no friends anymore, either. There were only the bigger boys who picked on him because he was his father's son and viciously trampled on the father in his heart. Nachman would have liked to go to school with Balfour, but he had learned to keep his desires to himself, to preserve a watchful silence and stay abreast of what was going on around him. Now he kept his eyes on Rabbi Kutter as he paced up and down the room, an open Talmud in his hands, buzzing like a hornet while his cold eyes lay in wait for the students. Nachman watched him close in on Kashani, whose head was in the Talmud but whose eyes were intent on his latest homemade throwing top.

The top season was now at its height and there was no end to the different models: the most common was pear- or onion-shaped, or somewhere in between, and varied in size from as big as Nachman's fist to only half as large. The choice of a screw or nail to go into its sharp, spinning end was a science in itself. Some preferred a round, slightly flattened screw, while others insisted that the pointier the better, though of course it made all the difference whether the top was released on a surface of concrete, packed hard dirt, or wet or sandy ground. There was also an element of pure luck, for even a perfectly balanced top carefully wrapped around with exactly the right amount of "spaghetti"—the same thin builders' twine that was attached to plumb lines to see if walls were built straight—sometimes staggered and collapsed like a drunk after the first few turns. But Kashani's top had a new shape entirely. It looked like a heavy carrot, and the twine—"spaghetti special"—was wrapped in such a way that the top was thrown not with the usual circular windup and release but with a quick forward thrust and an equally sudden backspin just before it hit the ground. The major innovation, however, was something else: rather than simply watching the spinning top go round, its owner now stood above it and nimbly whipped it on with the special twine, making it go even faster.

One couldn't help sneak a glance at Kashani's top,

though Nachman was careful to keep one eye on Rabbi Kutter, who had already singled out his prey and was now creeping softly up on Kashani from behind without stopping his hornetlike buzz. Even had Nachman wanted to warn him, he wouldn't have dared. What would happen to Kashani and his top now? The answer was nothing. At literally the last moment, as though he had eyes in the back of his head, Kashani glanced up, noticed Rabbi Kutter, and slipped the top into his sweater sleeve. He now made believe he was following in his Talmud, but Peterzail giggled uncontrollably. Rabbi Kutter looked at him coldly, but his ruler remained by his side. Perhaps, the kind thought passed through Nachman's head, he was showing mercy.

The Talmud lesson seemed endless, but it too finally came to a close. With the first chime of the bell the rest of the Talmud Torah jumped to its feet. Their own class, which was taught by the principal, however, remained seated, patiently listening to the galloping footsteps on the long terrace outside. Soon, they knew, Rabbi Kutter would shut his Talmud too, tilt his square skullcap down over his eyes, and depart from the room. As soon as he did, the boys all rushed noisily out the door to the terrace or the busy yard. Nachman took his time and left last. Carrying his lunchbag, he looked for an inconspicuous corner, far from bullying eyes. At the far end of the yard a large, two-story building was going up, one of the new houses on reinforced concrete stilts that had lately begun to rise in town. He found a shaded corner at the back of it, sat down on a pile of building sand, and took out the lunch his mother had prepared for him—bread and butter, some slices of radish, a skinned, halved cucumber, and two tangerines that practically peeled themselves. He ate in silence while his imagination traveled to far places and met and talked at great length with all kinds of strange people. His father had bought him a new book for Hanukkah, *King Solomon's Mines,* which had a yellow cloth binding and a paper jacket to protect it, and Nachman was entirely absorbed in the adventures of the treasure hunters and of Gogol the Witch, in the dangers they faced and the gold, which he himself would have had no trouble knowing what to spend on. The Talmud Torah seemed so distant that it had simply ceased to exist.

"Who's that hiding in the corner? Can it be Pipeleh?"

Ozer Lichtig and several of his galley slaves suddenly appeared from behind the building. Nachman jumped up to escape, but they were already in front of him, blocking his way. He looked behind him. The building stood on its reinforced columns, a black void beneath the concrete first floor. He took two steps back. Perhaps he could hide somewhere under it.

"Don't try to run, Pipeleh. If you do, we'll run after you. And down there in the dark you'll be even sorrier."

Ozer Lichtig was in the seventh grade, though according to his age he should have graduated from the Talmud Torah long ago. He had already been thrown out of every other school, here in town, in Tel Aviv, everywhere else. His father, the boys said, owned orange groves and land, and would have sent him to school in Beirut, or even in Germany or England, except that no place would take a holy terror like him. So only the Talmud Torah was left. His cheeks and forehead were strangely puffy, as though they'd been bitten by bees, and were punctuated by bloody pimples and blackheads and the first beginnings of a beard. Going over to Nachman, who stood pressed against the concrete wall, Ozer removed the beret from his head, dusted it off against his pants, and replaced it carefully on Nachman's head like a loving mother.

"What a lovely child!" said Ozer to his slaves, who were now crowding in on Nachman too. He ran his fingers over Nachman's cheeks. "What smooth skin. What a delicate face. He's not like a boy at all."

"Maybe he isn't a boy!" said one of the slaves on cue. Nachman stood petrified. "He has a face like a girl!"

"He goes to the Talmud Torah, he's dressed like a boy, and he even has a boy's name. Pipeleh!"

"But he has the face of a girl," insisted the slave.

"Why don't we ask Pipeleh himself," said Ozer. "Tell us, Nachman, are you a boy or a girl?"

Nachman kept silent.

"Pipeleh isn't talking," said Ozer. "Maybe he isn't talking because he's ashamed to tell us, and maybe he isn't talking because he doesn't know the difference. Didn't Adon Shpiegleh ever tell you if you were a boy or a girl, Nachman?"

"Adon Shpiegleh doesn't know the difference himself," said one of Ozer's slaves. "He has a beard, but he's just like a woman."

"Have you been circumcised, Pipeleh?" asked another slave. Nachman stood riveted to his place in fear, looking frantically out of the corners of his eyes. Perhaps someone would come along and save him. He wanted to yell papa but he was ashamed to open his mouth.

"Why don't we examine him ourselves," said Ozer, "and then we can tell him what he is." The idea was received enthusiastically, and the whole gang tackled him at once. Ozer grabbed his elbows while another boy reached for his pants. Just as on that first day in kindergarten, Nachman was seized by a blind impulse to break through the circle of humiliation, to run from it all so as not to hear his father mocked any longer or suffer disgrace for his sake. As on that day in kindergarten, he sprang forward with his head hunched between his shoulders and his fists leading the way, biting and scratching and butting at the solid wall around him. But the wall wouldn't give. Hands grabbed his wrists and ankles and heavy bodies sat on him. He was flat on the ground, powerful fingers pressing on his throat, threatening to choke him. Nachman twisted his head and his chin met an unidentified hand. He lifted his neck and sunk his teeth into it. There was a shout of pain from Ozer Lichtig. His throat was free now, but his hands and feet were still pinned by the bullies. Ozer got hold of his head and forced it to one side, grinding it into the dirt. Now they were all sitting on him and he had ceased to exist, except that he could still hear them talking.

"He hits with his hands open, like a girl. Ha, ha, ha."

"He bites, he scratches, he's just like a girl."

"He's got to be a girl. Look at his nails, just like Adon Shpiegleh's."

"Come on, let's have a look!"

In vain Nachman squirmed and writhed like a worm, his mouth, nose, and eyes in the dirt. Hands unbuttoned his pants and pulled them down over his knees. Nachman said a prayer with the last of his strength, but he still couldn't move. Now, when it was already too late, he shouted papa, papa, into the dirt, but the sound was stillborn. His shame was complete. He was beyond human help.

Suddenly the heavy weight of the bullies' bodies was off him, and they were gone. He lay alone on his back in the building sand as though of his own free will. He looked around, got to his knees, hiked up his pants, which kept falling as he rose, and stood on his feet. The first thing he saw when he opened his sand-encrusted eyes was the yellow beard of his old first-grade teacher, Adon Pollak, whose own eyes seemed to float behind the thick lenses of his glasses. Adon Pollak bent over him and offered him a hand, grumbling something about Ozer Lichtig and his gang of thugs, but to Nachman, who was still not standing quite erect, one hand clutching his pants to keep them up, it seemed that behind Adon Pollak stood the whole Talmud Torah, grinning as one man with mocking, malicious glee. As though he were simply continuing what had been interrupted before, he began to run mindlessly without caring where he was going.

He was already in the street, past the grain store and the smithy, his fly buttoned up and the sand shaken out of his face and hair (his cap was lost for good), slowing down to a walk so as not to stand out as he passed the animal market, the synagogue, the big sandlot, Guberman's dairy, then running again, out of breath, once more in tears, away from the shame of it, away from it all. He crossed the wooden footbridge over the creek. A flow of dirty water still snaked down the gulley below. (Yes, it had happened in winter, right about Purim time.) Long ago, when he had gone with his mother to visit Uncle Rifael, they had crossed this same bridge. And there had been one Saturday when he and his father and mother had crossed it again on their way to visit Arele Holzberg's parents, who lived in the new cottages beyond the creek. Where should he go now? He would go to the orange groves, to the dunes, all the way to his Uncle Rifael.

He paused at the level top of a hill. There was nobody else in sight. Back where he had come from the whole town was now spread out—its houses hidden among the tall eucalyptuses, cypresses, and other trees, the Great Synagogue with its glittering dome, and the white water tower denoting the very center. Nachman could even make out that grove of eucalyptuses on the low sandy hill beyond the Mendelevitches' yard. In the opposite direction, just in front of him, lay an open valley, old and new orange groves, grassy fields one sees only after the rains, the black Bedouin tents. The mountains, however, looked ominous. Shadows were drifting over them, now darkening them terribly, now lighting them up with a bluish glow. Nachman glanced up at the sky. Beyond the town, where the sun sets, and rains come from, the horizon was already turning black with clouds, and they were making straight for the open foothills, where he was standing. A cool breeze blew, and Nachman wiped the sweat and the itchy sand grains from his face and his neck, listening to the wild pounding of his heart. He rested a while, letting the wind caress him and watching the play of light and shadow on the mountains and among the Bedouin tents. He made up his mind to go on to the nearest orange grove. Perhaps he'd find some fallen fruit there to quench his thirst.

A wagon full of damaged oranges emerged from one of the acacia hedges, climbing the hill. The wagoner walked by the draft animals, urging them on with shouts and lashes of his whip. Nachman managed to hide in the nick of time, slipping off into a side path that skirted the grove along the cypresses and acacias. It was perfectly quiet here in the cool shade, and the wet earth and the tall grass and trees gave off a reassuring smell. His mother always said that he mustn't sit on wet ground because he might catch cold in a nerve or a bone and develop rheumatism. Nachman found a log that was black from decay and sat down on it. From far away, through the quiet, came the sounds of the packinghouse. Each noise carried so distinctly through the clear winter air that Nachman felt as if at any moment he would be overtaken by the voices he had fled from. Shpiegleh. Shpipeleh. Pipeleh. From even farther off, but achingly clearly, he heard the children's voices from Bluma's kindergarten. "Nachman–Achmed. Achmed–Nachman." Suddenly he was convulsed by a paroxysm of tears that burst from his nose, eyes, and throat as though from a broken water main. Only now, away from all eyes and ears, could he really cry freely, for his own helplessness, for his father, for he no longer even knew what. I'll never go back to the Talmud Torah again, he whispered to calm himself through his tears. Never. Not to my papa, either, or to my mama. I'll never go home again, ever. I can stay right here, in the orange groves. No, I'll run away to the Bedouin. I'll go to them, and they'll see right away that I have eyes like them, and they'll take me and teach me to ride and to shoot. I'll wander all over with them, far, far into the desert, and no one will ever see me again. Except that one day there'll be a great horse race in the village, and the Bedouin riders will be invited too. And I'll come on my noble stallion, with a *kaffiyeh* over my face, and I'll finish ahead of them all. Balfour will be in the race too, like young Adon Mendelevitch and old Adon Mendelevitch used to be, and I'll beat him too. Everyone will want to know who is the but rather as though whole mountains of sheet metal were exploding in turn, as though the sky had collapsed and all the waters in heaven were pouring through. The single drops were now a solid wall of rain, a flood. There was no longer any sky or clouds or avenue of trees to stand under—the whole world had become one impenetrable ocean of rain and he was at the bottom of it. This was the rain that swept away horses with their riders, that drowned whole herds of sheep, that had already covered up whatever he had imagined and resolved a moment ago. There was only one place to hide from such terror: home. He was already on his way there as fast as he could run, which was faster even than his flight from the Talmud Torah. Lightning flashed through the rain, and after each bolt came the thunder. Nachman ran along the bottom of this sea, his head and face in water, his clothes soaked with water, his shoes shipping water. The sandy path, which had smelled so good and been so easy to walk on, was now a series of streams and pools. He had no idea whether he was running on or alongside it. He had no idea if he would manage to find the bridge or plunge straight into the creek.

The slimy flow that had snaked beneath the bridge before was now a soapy, foaming, black torrent. Luckily, the bridge could be crossed—in mortal fear, in sopping wet shoes, in a stream of water that cascaded down his head to rejoin the rain. The cottages passed dimly and quickly before his eyes. Perhaps he should knock on one of the doors and ask for shelter, like the people in stories who were lost in snowstorms, like the picture of Eliza skipping over the broken ice in *Uncle Tom's Cabin*. He stopped for a minute in the rain under a mulberry tree, but suddenly he remembered that here, in one of these houses, lived Peterzail's mother, who had been crazy ever since Peterzail's father had broken a bottle over her head, and he began to run once again. It wasn't worth stopping, he told himself. Soon he would be home, though it seemed to him that he would never get there and that the flood would never stop. Not until he saw the store distinctly before him did he notice that the rain had let up and that the drops were falling more lightly and widely apart. Right in front of him, in the middle of the street, stood his father, a sack on his head doing double duty as both raincoat and hood, looking like one of the penniless Bedouin who hung out in the square. His father ran toward him, his face and suit drenched with rain. Without a word of rebuke, without even a question, he scooped Nachman up in his arms and called to his mother. (Here he was, thank God! The main thing was that they had found him!) Together they hurried him inside, where they stripped off his waterlogged clothes, rubbed him down with towels, massaged his hands and feet to make the blood warm up and flow, covered him with the big quilt, and stuck a hot-water bottle under his feet and two big pillows beneath his head. Then his mother came and lay down next to him, just as she used to do long, long ago, when he was still a baby, and the warmth of her body was siphoned into his own.

And then what had happened?

There had been a medicinal smell in the house, a smell of the Sloan's Liniment which they rubbed into his chest and back, of hot olive oil and of a wick dipped in alcohol to heat the cupping glass. They soaked bandages in warm olive oil and alcohol, wrapped them in oilcloth, and put them around his neck, covering the entire compress with a large towel. The big kerosene burner was lit all the time and on it sat the kettle sending up puffs of white steam. They poured boiling water over dried, crushed, yellow-green chamomile blossoms and forced his head into the bitter-smelling vapors beneath a canopy of towels to keep in the fumes and the heat. "Breathe in," his mother would command him, "breathe in as hard as you can."

That much Nachman remembered: the smells in the closed room. And afterwards it was already the day before Passover. His window stayed open all that day and from the yard outside came the scent of citrus blossoms and jasmine, of the eucalyptus trees and the barn. The air was full of smoke smells too, as it always was before Passover. The neighbors were all doing a grand wash, borrowing each other's blackened boilers, and deep tin basins in which the laundry was left to soak in hot, soapy water, and flat basins for rinsing and bleaching the linens. The whole town smelled of thin smoke and boiling soap-water, and echoed with the pre-Passover cries of the Arab tinkers calling out in Yiddish as they were passing through the streets, "*Vaysen kesalach, vaysen balyes*—kettles repaired, washtubs repaired," and of the Arab women hawking eggs, which would be eaten in great numbers during the seven days of the holiday. The noisy, sun-drenched hubbub outside excited Nachman. He was no longer confined to his bed but could walk about the house by himself, and when the sun was warm enough—but not too hot—and there was no wind blowing or any other danger to his regained health, his mother allowed him to sit in front of the store. Just so long as he didn't wander about. Or perspire. Or drink cold water. Pneumonia is no laughing matter, everyone told Nachman. It's a sheer miracle you pulled through.

Two more miracles happened before that Passover, which made Nachman try to get well as fast as he could.

His father had bought a dunam of land, which would be their own property, where the new black wooden cottages were being built on this side of the creek. They would also build on it a huge one-room cottage of their own, which would belong to them too. Uncle Rifael came and went often these days, and all day long there was talk of the dunam and the cottage and the "prosperity" that everyone was enjoying these days. There had never before been so much building going on in Palestine, they were saying to one another, and construction workers were making a fortune. In Tel Aviv skilled labor was being snatched off the street, and if you contracted for one big job you could manage to get on your feet in the course of a single summer. His father and Uncle Rifael—Nachman heard the news with a burst of joy—would form a plastering team.

This was the second miraculous development. Also, it meant this would be his father's last year as a teacher. He had come to Palestine to be a worker, he said, not a drudge for those enemies of Zion, those parasitical religious fanatics in the Talmud Torah. He would be a plasterer, and they would live on their own land, with a whole quarter of an acre, a whole dunam, on which to raise vegetables, or build a small chicken coop, or perhaps start a nursery for sweet lemon or bitter orange grafts. They would live like human beings for a change.

And Nachman?

He too would not go back to the Talmud Torah. They were registering him in the Yavneh School for Boys. If the doctor permitted, he would begin there right after Passover, but it was more likely that he would have to stay home until the end of the school year.

Yes, the new year would usher in great changes—no more grocery store to come between his parents, no more Talmud Torah. His father would be a plasterer, and they would move to their new cottage, while he would never again have to face the retributions of Adon Kutter and Ozer Lichtig. Sun and high hopes and tantalizing smells announced this Passover eve, this gateway to the prosperity ahead.

His mother watched over him with eagle eyes, but Nachman didn't mind her prohibition against running around with the other children. Everyone pampered him and gave him whatever he wanted, and nothing could be better than the books that he could now read voraciously. The whole summer still lay ahead of him, but he was already preparing for the coming year. His father brought back his knapsack with all that was in it from the Talmud Torah, but his *Bava Metzia* had been left behind on the table among the great pile of books. Every day Nachman reminded his father to bring it, and every day his father forgot. "Why do you keep pestering me?" he asked. "If you want to study the Talmud, we have a complete set right here in the trunk, thank God." Nachman didn't answer. In his own mind he was working out a plan.

One day—the Passover vacation was over—he stole out of the house and made his way to the Talmud Torah by various shortcuts and detours, following fences, sneaking through back yards, cutting across empty lots, and circling behind the large building that was still under construction. He had calculated in advance that at this hour even the eighth graders would have been dismissed, leaving only the janitor behind. Indeed, there wasn't a soul in the yard, nor a sound in the Talmud Torah itself except for the squeak of the benches and tables that the janitor was moving about.

The squeak of the benches and tables and the thump of his own nervous heart. He silently slipped into the building, climbing first onto the terrace, which smelled of dry dust, and from there into the classroom, after making sure that the janitor was off somewhere else. The sun burned fiercely through the open windows, its rays baking the empty room. The walls were more faded than he had remembered. The drape over the Holy Ark looked like an old curtain and the gold letters embroidered on it were worn from use. The sunbeams glanced directly off the calendar, which was still hanging crookedly from its rusty nail. Nachman hurried to the long table and began going through the dilapidated books there, the Bibles, the prayer books, the volumes of the *Shulhan Arukh* and of *Bava Metzia*. He searched all the benches and the lectern up front and wouldn't give up even when he heard the janitor's broom on the terrace outside. Here it was—the new *Bava Metzia* his father had bought him. One corner of it was broken, the ringed cover with its tree-trunk design was spotted with fingerprints, pencil marks, and stains, and the binding itself was warped by the heat of the sun. But this was it. It even had his name on it—Nachman Shpiegler. He grabbed it and made for the door, peeking outside. The janitor was still sweeping the terrace, sending up clouds of

15 | *The fortune that flew like a bird*

That summer, that summer they would move from the Mendelevitches' yard to their own cottage, this side of the dry creek, beyond the big empty lot and Guberman's dairy. From now on Nachman's life would become less opaque and its inner logic more consistent. The family circle would continue to surround, nourish, and protect him, but he was beginning to feel how a kind of shell was growing and hardening around his unformed self, out of which he might occasionally still sally but to which he always returned. The circle of the family still impinged upon him, but this hard shell would soon divide circle from circle, one set of memories from the other.

In the summer they would move from the Mendelevitches' yard, and Mister and Missus Blackman, who had been wasting away before their eyes, would cease to exist. Even if Nachman later felt an urge to revisit them—as indeed, from time to time, he did—he would no longer be able to because they'd be gone. Yet the family memory would still sometimes pierce his hardening shell like a searchlight shooting a sudden beam into a darkened corner, illuminating obscure dreams, opening underground passages from the present to the past, which remained suspended in his memory like a thick fog, full of endings without beginnings, landings without takeoffs, entire scenes that maybe happened this way and maybe that. Into this oblivion the family memory would dig, like the lapping of waves against the sand on the seashore. The watery mixture would drip upon his own memory, forming a slender sand castle, the legend of Mister and Missus Blackman's stolen wealth, which was also the legend of the fortune that had rested like a bird in Nachman's palm and then flown off never to be seen again.

Any small matter, such as the appearance of the bill collector from the water department in the town hall with a threat to shut off the water or the arrival of a slip of paper from the bank with the words "Final Warning" printed on it in red letters, would be enough to pit the memory of Nachman's father against that of his mother in a duel over the fortune that might have been, the poverty they might have been saved from.

It would take even less than that. Nachman, for example, might have gone out to play with the other kids. How could anyone run through the sandy street with sandals on his feet? It could happen to anyone—it happened to Nachman—that he came home one evening barefoot, and in his hand a single sandal.

"Everyone took off their sandals, everyone! I looked for it in the sand, everyone helped me, but we couldn't find it. It was somewhere in the sand, but we couldn't find it, and then it began to get dark. What could I do?" Nachman angrily asked when his mother refused to stop badgering him over what he would wear on his feet tomorrow, "What?"

"You can cut a few strips of skin out of me and make yourself new ones," said his mother, "that's what. I just bought you a new pair for Passover! Where am I supposed to get the money from now for another, tell me that, will you?"

Nachman had looked in the sand until dark. Tomorrow

he would look again, but how was he to blame if his sandal was lost? What could he do?

"What do you mean, what can you do? Just who do you think we are that you can go around burying a new pair of sandals in the sand? What am I supposed to do now? A pair of sandals costs seventeen and a half piasters. Do you know how long a person has to work to make seventeen and a half piasters? A whole day pruning or picking, and you don't make that much even then. Who do you think we are that you can throw sandals away like that? If we were rich I'd be happy to buy you a new pair every month. But we're not rich, and we're never going to be. We had our chance, we could have gone on to something better, but we let it slip through our fingers like a bird. Some people were just born to be poor. You can serve them money on a silver platter, and they'll push it away with both hands."

His father was sitting to one side, figuring out accounts by the lamplight. A long while passed in which he seemed not to hear Nachman's mother at all, so absorbed was he in calculating the wages that were due to his plastering team, but suddenly—without looking up from his black ledger—he remarked as though to himself, "Well, what do you know! We're back to Mister Blackman's fortune again."

"Do you mean to say it isn't true? He didn't want to leave all his money to Nachman?"

"Do you mean to say that he did? The rabbis knew what they were talking about when they said that an ignoramus can't do right and an uneducated man can have no sense of sin. I hope that wherever he is now he'll forgive me, but what kind of man is it that can be so cruel to his own wife, who slaved for him all her life as though she were some African kaffir, and not even leave her a plugged penny in the end? And not only that, but to go and appoint that scoundrel Rabbi Kutter as his executor! What reason have I to believe for a second that he seriously intended to leave anything to Nachman if he was capable of behaving that way to his own wife? Even in novels you won't find anything as pitiful as what happened to that poor old woman in the end!"

"It's very interesting how everyone remembers what's convenient for him," answered his mother. The sandal and Nachman were forgotten now, and his parents' memories fought between them, pursuing once again the various versions of the legend of the lost fortune. "One can be a scholarly Jew like Rabbi Kutter and a scoundrel, and one can also be an ignorant but a decent man. They loved Nachman like their own. I can remember perfectly well the birthday parties they used to make for him year after year and the presents they gave him. How many times did he tell you and me how Nachman was a ray of light in the darkness of his old age? He wanted to leave Nachman everything, and he would have too, but we, just like that . . ."

"We what?"

"You know very well what I mean."

"Ah, so that's it! But then why do you say *we* if it's all because of me? It was me who wouldn't let that old idiot make a laughingstock out of us! It was me who didn't permit him to twist and deform the boy's tender soul! It was me who refused to bow and scrape in front of him!"

"How can you be so ungrateful, Shalom! When we lived in this house without work and were being eaten alive by our own frustration and poverty, who was it that helped us in the end? Adon Mendelevitch? Madam Mendelevitch? Who took us and put us back on our feet if not him? Your own father wouldn't have done any more for you. How can you forget such a thing?"

"Fine, I remember. It wasn't by chance that he put the idea of a store into your head. He wanted so badly to turn me into a shopkeeper that he took his own money and built us that box."

"It wasn't a box. It was a nice, big store."

"I can see how you miss it."

"Why ever should I? So that I can stand eighteen hours a day on my feet again?"

"Then what are you carrying on like this for? What's so terrible now? On our last plastering job I cleared seventy or eighty piasters in a single day, maybe more. You call that bad?"

"I don't mind suffering, and I've done my share of it without complaining. But where in the Good Book does it say that you have to work like a mule all your life? It's too late now, but when I think that you had a fortune right there in your hands, that Nachman's future would have been all taken care of. . . ."

At this point his father would lose his temper and jump to his feet, nearly knocking over the inkwell as he pounded his fist on the table. "Good God, there's just no talking to you! She gets an idea into her head and no matter how many times you prove to her what a cock-and-bull story it is, she just won't give it up! We lost a fortune!"

"How can you say I got it into my head? He said so himself in so many words, and not just once."

His father's clenched fists waved in the air, as though they were about to rain down on his mother's head, or upon his own, but instead he headed for the door, opened it in a burst of fury, and shouted in a choked voice from the threshold before slamming it: "A man can go out of his mind! Not only didn't he have the slightest intention of leaving us his house, but even if he had put it down in black and white in a will—do you hear me, Leah, if he had put it in a will—I would have torn it to shreds. I didn't come to this country to live off the inheritance of some old man from Zud Afrika who made his money in God knows what shady ways. I came here because it was high time that we Jews stopped making our living from buying and selling, because I wanted to live from an honest day's work with my hands. And I will too, whether you like it or not. I tell you, I will!"

Now the two of them were alone in the perfectly silent house, his mother with her soundless tears, Nachman with the legend of their lost wealth. Nachman nursed a preference for his mother's version of the story, which stoked his imagination and made him dream of all the things he could have bought, the journeys he could have taken, the lives he could have lived, if only the fortune hadn't slipped through their fingers like a bird. He liked to think of himself as a prince who had been banished from his father's palace and handed over to the swineherds, or as a wastrel like in *Yossele*, or *Oliver Twist*, or *Hershele*, or *David Copperfield*, or *The Seven Good Years*, or the story about the three wishes, or about the fisherman who found a pearl in the belly of a fish. It all revolved around the legend of Mister Blackman, which his mother's memory kept alive in Nachman's own.

Sometimes, though, his father's version would convince him and—temporarily—erase all doubt from his mind. On those hot summer evenings under the stars, or those wintry Sabbath afternoons, in the twilight that was no longer day yet in which it was still too early for a lamp to be lit, when his parents sat with their friends around the table, drank tea and cracked seeds, and talked about all kinds of things—they might suddenly remember the Blackmans and their melancholy end. At such times his mother's memory fell silent while his father's worked fast and furiously, spitting out words like a galloping steed, unshakable in the force of its opinions. With colorful pathos he retold the story of how Rabbi Kutter wormed his way into Mister Blackman's ignorant soul like a termite that can eat through the hardest wood, how he had played on the old man's most sensitive heartstrings, how he had exploited—and with the most utter cynicism!—his fear of being punished in hell, how he had bewitched him with his cold eyes—actually bewitched him, there was no doubt about it!—and robbed him of everything.

"Why, we saw with our own eyes what he did to Missus Blackman," Nachman's father would say, his burning glance catching the eyes of his audience. "He left her without a penny to her name, she literally had nothing to eat. For her own good, so he said, he drove her out of her own house and put her in some old-age home, even though Mister Blackman had explicitly said that the house was not to be sold as long as she lived. They sold it, knocked it down, and built a new one in its place, while Missus Blackman, who had meanwhile run away from the home and come back here, had to take a room with some old woman in that tumbledown clay hut behind the Great Synagogue and to support herself from the rotten fruits and vegetables that merciful people gave her in the marketplace. Leah used to go there sometimes to look after her and bring her a hot meal, but she was a broken woman, crushed physically and spiritually. They couldn't bear her being around for everyone to see, so they stuck her in some institution in Jerusalem, and that was the last we heard of her.

"And to this day," Nachman's father would thunder, "we haven't been able to trace her. I don't know whether she really went crazy or whether the same gang that threw her out of her house and robbed her of everything didn't also put her away somewhere so that she couldn't prove in court that they had taken advantage of Mister Blackman's innocence and ignorance to make him sign papers he never even read. Not only that, they made off with what wasn't even his to give—what belonged by right to Missus Blackman. And these are supposed to represent Jewish religion, to act only for the glory of God, mind you! Oh, how I have hated the mealy-mouthed hypocrites ever since I was a boy! Even then I vowed that I'd live differently. Either I'd go to Palestine and live by the true faith, that of the prophets Amos and Isaiah, or else I'd throw it all over. To perpetuate this kind of Jew that Exile had bred—never more. Not me. And so I came here—to find them here too. I went to Rabbi Kutter, I threatened all kinds of scandals, I even went to Jerusalem to look for her, but I was never able to find her. I've even heard it said that she took her own life in her misery and that these bandits—for they are extremely strict in observing the Law—buried her near the cemetery wall as the Law says suicides should be buried. That's what became of her. And then people wonder why the present young generation rebels against religion and breaks away from our sacred tradition to become Bolsheviks or our own homemade Left-Zionists with all their foreign doctrines. When I see men like Rabbi Kutter, I begin to understand what the prophet meant when he said, 'They kiss the cow and slaughter the man. . . .'"

His father sat at the head of the table surrounded by his friends, who nodded in total assent. Nachman too was won over by his father's memory. He remembered the Talmud Torah and Adon Pollack and Ozer Lichtig and his slaves and that faraway winter day when he caught pneumonia, and he agreed with everything his father said.

And yet, on the other hand . . .

On Sabbaths his father wore a white shirt, and when he spread out his palms on the table, Nachman could see the plaster peering out between the cracks on his fingers and from underneath his broken nails. With his sunburned face, the wrinkles that fanned out from the corners of his eyes, and the contrast between his deeply freckled forehead and the receding bald spot that was hidden under his helmet while at work, he now looked like Uncle Rifael. But in his memory Nachman still recalled the unmistakable look of a different father: in a black suit and bow tie, with a round beard on his face, which he had trimmed before the mirror every Friday afternoon. Had he really once had such a father, or was it only a dream?

Whatever his parents' memories retold trickled into Nachman's own, but the violent transitions confused him to the point that not only were different images of his father forced to compete with each other in his mind, but he himself seemed sometimes to be one Nachman and sometimes another.

That summer they would move to their new cottage, and everything that had come before, from his earliest memories to the legend of the lost fortune, would come to rest in the depths like a sunken cargo of gold. He himself would be up in the sunlight, but the family memory—his own memory too, all he had dreamed and imagined—would partly continue to lodge in the dark, watery depths, amid the silence of shipwrecked, gold-laden galleons.

That summer they would move to their new cottage, and everything would begin all over. When you took a bitter orange sapling for transplanting in some grove, you drove the spade into the ground far from the root and pulled out the plant as though there were a flowerpot around it, so the soil continued to cling to the thousands of fine roots and enabled them to grow once again when put in fresh earth. To the amputated roots it must have felt as though they were still nursing from a reality that no longer existed, for the growing sapling made them attach themselves to different soil. There a new, fruit-bearing branch would one day be grafted on. Everything seemed to go on as before, but what would be was not what had been, was not what had been at all.

16 | *Roof tiles*

His father's shoes gripped the top rung of the ladder, which was coated like them with cement, with a firm, intrepid tread as though they and it were one solid mass. His two outstretched arms lifted a tile to Uncle Rifael, who bent down from his place on the roof. Nachman's father handed him the tile, and Uncle Rifael set it on the white rafter so that its lip would fit the hollow of the next tile in line, while its wavy ridge matched that of the tile on its left. Another patch of gray roof bit into what remained of the skeleton of white beams, which now seemed even smaller than the hole that old Adon Mendelevitch punched every year in the roof of his porch and covered with branches in order to make a tabernacle for the holiday of Sukkot.

Uncle Rifael set the tile in place and his father's legs, which had seemed molded to the topmost rung of the ladder, moved nimbly to the bottom, where he leaned over toward Nachman's mother to take another tile from her hands. Until his caked shoes came all the way down, his mother continued to lean against the ladder with all her weight, holding on to it with both hands as though for dear life. She handed up a bottom-row tile, exposing one more full strip of the clean sand left from the fill that had been laid on the floor of the cottage before it was tiled over so handsomely. A single column of roof tiles was now all that remained. "If all goes well," his father had told his mother earlier in the day, "we'll finish the roof today, and then the cottage will be nearly done." Now, as he climbed nimbly back up the ladder from rung to rung, he winked at Nachman, whose own eyes narrowed in a kind of wink too as they followed his father's shoes up and down.

In a way he was glad that the cottage was almost done because he was impatient to live in it, but at the same time he wished that the tiling of the roof weren't ending so quickly. In a little while, when Uncle Rifael set the last tile in place, it would no longer be possible to see the sky from the inside. Nachman wondered how much of it was still visible. Since his neck was stiff from looking at the ladder, he decided to have a look inside. There was no need to open a door because neither the doors nor the windows had been brought yet by the carpenter, and there were only the white, wooden jambs with their shiny steel hinges screwed into them. Once windows and doors hung on them, the cottage would be a real house. Smells tickled his nostrils even before he reached the front step: the smell of rafters, of sawdust, and of the unplaned planks that were nailed to the house beams from floor to ceiling to make the walls. The flat heads of the nails were smooth and cold and smelled the opposite of the drops of sap in the knots of the wood. Nachman ran his fingers over the planed surface of the jambs and over the rough wall planks and the nails. The entire cottage, even the horizontal and transverse joists, was held together by nails. The floor tiles touched the bottom joist and the roof rested on the top one. Between them ran the rough planks, three meters high in the corners of the room and four at the peak of the roof, which was the real height of the cottage. "It's nothing but boards and nails," his mother had said, "and if someone gives a good push the whole thing will slide right off the cinder blocks." Nachman leaned against a wall and pushed as hard as he could, but the cottage was very strong and didn't even creak. Overhead he could hear the clink of the tiles as Uncle Rifael set them in place. The square patch of sky was very small now, and anyway, it was quickly getting dark. He'd better go outside again to see how many tiles were left.

Yet he liked it in the big room that was full of smells. Light no longer came through the frames of the doors and windows, but rather darkness, streaming through the open spaces from everywhere on their dunam of land. By the time the doors, windows, and shutters were installed, their old lease would be up. They could wait until the end of summer to tarpaper the walls against the rain. It would be lovely to hear the rain outside while they sat in their dry new house. Now, though, there were still chinks between the planks, one of which had a knothole. Nachman peered through it and spied his mother's strong legs as they braced to support the ladder. Now that the roof was all tiled and it was almost nighttime, he might as well go outside.

He was out under the ladder now, and his father was scolding him from above. "Get out from under the ladder, Nachman! A tile can fall, and then you'll be sorry."

He felt an irresistible urge at the sight of his father's bare arms. Bending over the dwindling pile of tiles, he took one beneath his fingers and held it up high. It wasn't heavy at all.

"Papa, here's a tile!"

Both his parents turned on him at once, one voice rising above the other. "Put down that tile immediately, you rascal! That's all we need—all winter long he lay sick in bed, and now he wants to go rupture himself or crack open his head. Go for a walk in the yard, Nachman, we're almost done."

His mother snatched the tile from his hands and pushed him aside. Did they think he was still a baby? If they left the ladder behind, and there would be no one to see or stop him, he would climb it all by himself, right to the very top. He wasn't afraid. Take the time he had run away from the Talmud Torah because he couldn't stand it anymore, all the way to the orange groves, or the way he now sat by himself on the hill under Mendelevitch's eucalyptus trees. They didn't scare him, but he was sick of their shouting. Perhaps he'd really better go and survey their new dunam.

He wandered about while the light lingered in the sky. Where in wintertime there had been white and yellow flowers and green flowerbuds, there was now nothing but scorched, scratchy thorn stalks. Only by the puddle that had collected about the leaky faucet was green grass still sprouting. A castor-oil plant was growing in the grass. It was still small, but his father had said that it could spring up overnight. That was what had happened to Jonah, over whom a beanstalk had grown to shade him from the sun. Perhaps it wouldn't happen overnight, thought Nachman, but by the time they moved and settled in they would already have a tree—not one like the Mendelevitches' mulberry or fig, or like a carob, which didn't even bear fruit until it was seventy years old, but a tree nonetheless. He couldn't wait to see their dunam surrounded by trees and planted with rows of vegetables and a nursery for the bitter orange and sweet lemon his parents planned. Nachman had intended to reach the far end of the dunam and then circle back, but darkness was already everywhere, and snakes and scorpions might be hiding in the thorns. They liked to come out when it was night, his mother had told him. Even in the dark, though, he knew exactly what was on their property. One way past the empty lot was where Kashani the drunk lived, while the other way, past the creek, was the cottage where Peterzail lived. There Arele Holzberg lived too. His father and Nachman's came from the same little town in Poland, and Arele would be in the same class with him when summer was over. In Yavneh School.

Overcoming his fears, he carefully advanced through the thorns, treading them down one by one and crushing them under his sandals. Once they moved, said his father, he would take a hoe, weed all the thorns, and burn them. Then he would turn the earth under ("That's no work for you," Nachman's mother had said. "You should hire some Yemenite to do it," but his father refused to hear of it), root out the finger grass, and plant all kinds of things. What couldn't be done with a dunam? "First we'll plant cypresses and palms, and when they grow we'll have a green wall all around. In front we'll plant fruit trees, all different kinds—figs and pomegranates and oranges and grapefruits and tangerines and guavas. In the back we'll grow vegetables, and we'll have a large nursery for sweet lemon and bitter orange. We'll build a chicken coop too, so that we'll always have fresh eggs. Just wait and see," his father challenged Uncle Rifael, "if we don't have a whole farm here one day. And when we finish paying off our debts, we'll cast concrete walls and add a second room as well as a toilet and a septic hole for the sewage, so that it will be a real house. When a man owns his own land, there's no end to what he can do with it. The main thing is that every penny he puts in it is left with him. Everything in good time."

The high trees in the center of town were now a solid wall of darkness, but the sky was still like thin gauze and the air had an acrid, smoky smell. Nachman strained his eyes, but all he could see in the sky were two or three glittering pinpoints. A sudden breeze brought yet another smell, which along with the smoke-bitter air and his thoughts about their new house left Nachman with an intoxicated feeling. Something cold and clear was rising beyond the low mountains, lighting the edge of the sky, driving the darkness back toward the wall of trees in the center of town, where the burning sun had set before. Now, all at once, the moon would shoot up. At first it would be huge and red like a blood orange, but as it pried itself loose from the mountains it would grow smaller and paler until it hung halfway between them and the Arab villages, shining through a mesh of still air. His father would look at it and say, "It's going to be hot tomorrow."

But just then, as though right by his side, somewhere among the thorns on their dunam, a fierce, angry bark cut loose and drew quickly nearer. Nachman turned and began to run—no, to walk, but fast—to the ladder. Trying to pretend that nothing had happened, he got there just in time. The dog was still barking, but his father had already descended the ladder, and Uncle Rifael too was groping his way down, his legs dangling before him, from rung to rung.

"We're finished," his father called up to Uncle Rifael's legs.

"That does it!" answered Uncle Rifael from the ladder, his staccato laugh tumbling down the rungs.

"May we live to see good times in it," murmured Nachman's mother from the side.

"They're already good," his father exulted.

The two brothers stood side by side, the veiled moonlight shining on their perspiring faces, on their hairy arms, and on their undershirts that were gray and full of holes by daylight. The two of them lowered the ladder, seized it at both ends, and laid it on its side, resting it against the house. Nachman's mother handed them their shirts and they dressed in silence. Uncle Rifael fumbled for something in his pocket, but Nachman's father drew his own cigarettes first.

"Here," he said, "have one of mine."

Each rounded and squeezed a cigarette, licking it at one end. His father lit a match, and only now could one see how dark it really had gotten. They inhaled smoke and the ends of their cigarettes glowed. His father stared up at the roof. "You've been a great help."

"After all the quarrels between us, one roof isn't terribly much."

"I just hope other people come to live here too," said his mother. Didn't other people live here already? Nachman wondered. But the darkness now covered all up.

"Nowadays they're building everywhere," said Uncle Rifael. "And it's not like when we first came with nothing but a few rags. These German Jews bring huge packing crates with them, and they're used to living well. Germany isn't Poland." He puffed on his cigarette and blew smoke at the rising moon. They now stood back from the cottage, looking half at the moon and half at the finished roof.

"I don't like the looks of that ring around the moon," said Uncle Rifael.

His father nodded. "It's going to be hot tomorrow."

His mother hugged her arms to her chest and shivered. "I can feel the dew already. The dampness is bad for the child."

"We're going," said his father, but he didn't budge. He and Uncle Rifael continued to puff away. Dogs were barking again now, but in the distance, the wailing, drawn-out howl of Arab mongrels. The ticking of a pump could be heard too. As though mimicking it, Uncle Rifael unexpectedly burst into one of his broken laughs.

"You'll never guess who I just thought of. Elyakum!" He laughed again.

"Elyakum?" asked his father. Nachman pricked up his ears.

"The reception that *fetter* Eizik gave him in Chicago."

"Why now of all things?"

Nachman wanted to ask the same question. The mention of his Uncle Elyakum brought back that Saturday morning when he had gone with his mother to visit Uncle Rifael, who took Uncle Elyakum's letter and tore it into bits, which he scattered all over the grass. On the Sabbath.

Don't ask me why, but I suddenly saw the whole scene in my head: how Elyakum came to Chicago and went to the address that *fetter* Eizik sent him, and when he asked for Mister Eizik Shpiegler, he was shown into a room full of *unterveltniks*—gangsters—playing poker around a table . . . a pretty picture."

"A fine uncle we had there in Chicago."

"But just think of Elyakum, the minute he stepped into that . . . into that place and suddenly discovered what Reb Aryeh-Leib Shpiegler's brother was up to in Chicago."

Nachman's father laughed now too. "The land of opportunity. *Oy vay.*"

"This dew is bad for the child," said his mother, changing the subject. "He's still susceptible, and he shouldn't be out after dark."

"We're going," said his father.

They turned away from their cottage and began to walk, Uncle Rifael and his father leading the way and Nachman and his mother in the rear. The yellow light of the kerosene lamps could be seen through the windows of the houses across the empty lot. The white light of the Lux lamp lit up the open windows of the Hasidic synagogue, while far away, in the center of town, another single light flickered like a giant star. Uncle Rifael and his father talked in loud voices that drifted through the dark over the empty field, reminding each other of the details of a story that each already knew.

Nachman had often heard about Uncle Elyakum, and he had even perhaps heard the story that was now being told, but he stuck fast to the two men so as not to miss a word. *Fetter* Eizik had sent Uncle Elyakum an affidavit to come to Chicago, and he went straight to the address that was sent him, where he found all the *unterveltniks* sitting and playing cards. *Fetter* Eizik didn't even lay down his hand when Uncle Elyakum entered the room, but just nodded hello and signaled to him to take a chair and join in the game. Then he motioned to a waiter to bring Elyakum something to eat and went back to his cards and the mountain of dollar bills that lay stacked on the table before him. Uncle Elyakum ate in silence and *fetter* Eizik played cards, as though they had last seen each other just the other day and not years before when *fetter* Eizik left for America and Elyakum was still a small child. In the end they threw down their cards and *fetter* Eizik stuffed the dollar bills into his pocket and got up to go with all the *unterveltniks* after him. They piled into a taxi, Uncle Elyakum too, and rode through the streets of Chicago until they came to the shore of some lake. There *fetter* Eizik stuck a revolver into Uncle Elyakum's hand and told him to stay in the taxi and keep an eye out. Those were the first words he spoke to him. Here in America, he added by way of explanation, everyone is expected to pay his own way, and you may as well get used to it right now.

His father mimicked *fetter* Eizik while Uncle Rifael's laughter broke beneath the magical light of the moon. "God willing, everything will go smoothly. But if you see any cops, give the trigger a squeeze. Don't be shy, don't be shy, give a good squeeze."

"And everything went smoothly," said Uncle Rifael.

"With God's help," said his father.

Now the two of them laughed as one man. This was the laughter that they saved for their stories about the family, for that part which existed only in their tales. Nachman wanted to know how they knew what had happened in Chicago, and why, if it had really happened as they said, his father had wanted to join Elyakum, but he didn't ask.

"He managed to survive that evening with *fetter* Eizik," said his father. "But you can't say that he had much luck on the whole."

"America. Everything is built on a bluff there."

"And he wanted us to come too. That's all we needed. America!"

Uncle Rifael didn't answer. The evening sky, the full moon with the wide ring around it, the infinity of stars—all seemed to deepen with the silence. The thorns on both sides of the trodden path were very bright now, as though the silvery moonbeams had been caught in them. Perhaps, Nachman thought, this would be the last time that they would return through the dark to the Mendelevitches' yard. Now that the roof tiles were laid, all that remained to be installed were the shutters, the windows, and the doors. He turned to look back, but their new home was lost in the distance, and even the moon couldn't help. When they lived in it and the light of their bright Lux lamp—or maybe even electricity—passed through its open windows, it would be easily seen, even from much farther.

17 | In praise of a dunam

Thus far he had been merely a tiny ant, imprisoned in a world of antennae and smells, but henceforth this world and its domains—the cottage, the dunam, the neighborhood, the spreading town—were to widen and expand. Nachman now saw, investigated, considered, remembered. Whatever had come before their new house rested in the depths like a sunken ship, while a new life of openness began from here on, and his memory branched off from his family's for good. Years later, when he sought to return to that time and place, scenes from the little market would swarm before his eyes like a series of old sun-prints.

"The little market"—those who knew it didn't need it explained to them, while those who didn't could hardly be expected to distinguish between its two dozen cottages and the other small yellowish houses and black wooden cottages all around it. A new little market had suddenly sprung up here by the side of the cattle exchange, and this is what the new neighborhood this side of the creek came to be called by everyone. Everyone, that is, except people like old Adon Mendelevitch, who insisted on calling it "the new threshing grounds." In the early days, he used to tell Nachman's father, before the great craze for citrus took over, even before the days of vineyards and almond trees, the local farmers had grown sorghum and barley and wheat and used to bring them at harvest time to the old threshing grounds, which have since been turned into the soccer grounds, just behind the Yavneh School. Nowadays, of course, no one needed a threshing floor at all, but then even one had not sufficed, and so a new one had been established right here, exactly where the cattle exchange stood at present.

But that was later. Now Nachman was overjoyed with his new home and everything that came with it. They moved on a fiery hot day, the day that their lease was up, with a wagon drawn by a team of mules on which were their belongings—the disassembled beds, the mattresses, the wardrobe, and the large washbasin with all their pots and pans inside it. His parents walked beside the wagon, between the thorny wild grass and the grooves cut by the wheels in burning sand, carrying two lamps, a basket full of plates and glasses, and their alarm clock. Nachman carried their old broomstick, which his mother couldn't bear to leave behind, on one shoulder, though she had already bought a new one and soaked a sugar sack in water to be used as a mop. They marched on and on through the hot sand as though to some faraway land. Yet before he knew it, everything was unloaded and inside the cottage, and they were arranging their furniture in the cavernous space, trying out each wall to see what it was best for.

"At least we'll have plenty of air," said his mother, who was already worrying about the rains though it was still the middle of summer.

They put the huge double bed by the window facing the back, while his crib was placed by the adjacent wall, away from the rainy west and the window, so that he shouldn't be in the drafts. The wardrobe went against the same wall but to the window's right, where according to Nachman's mother it would be protected from the sun, which was bad for its polished finish. Now the table was set in place with its four chairs around it. And still the room seemed very empty. His father counted the floor tiles and did sums in his head. The room was six meters by five and awfully high, and the porch and kitchen together were the same length. The kitchen was walled all around, not so the porch, which had just two—the outer walls of the room and the kitchen. The eaves of the roof extended over it, supported by rafters, and it had a cement floor, whose dimensions were four meters by two (they were actually a little less, said Nachman's father, after he had measured them once and then again with the folding wooden ruler he never went anywhere without).

Nachman's mother, who couldn't get the winter off her mind, insisted that having sunk so much money into the cottage already they should have done things right and also closed off the porch, which faced the rain side. This would do double duty, she argued, because in the summer the porch would be flooded with sunlight all afternoon, but in wintertime it would fill up with water, which would make it impossible to use and would seep into the kitchen and main room. His father acknowledged that they might have to suffer through one hard winter until their debts eased up a bit, but a winter in Palestine, after all, was not a winter in Poland. Snow there wouldn't be. "We'll see," said his mother, "we'll see. If we had invested a few more piasters, we could have had another little room. On an enclosed porch it's possible to eat, to store things, even to put up a bed for guests. And to judge by the letters we've been getting, there's going to be no lack of guests. But the main thing is the rain."

In the meantime, however, it was the middle of summer, and the cottage was a constant pleasure. The rough wooden planks of the walls were faint green on the inside, and the floor was a veritable work of art. Each tile by itself was simply a differently colored pattern of stripes or curves—some a bituminous red, some green like banana leaves, others orange like the inside of a pumpkin—but together they formed a luxuriant carpet of wonderful cubes, leaves, buds, and flowers. In summer his mother sponged the floor every day and waited until the sun sank behind the eucalyptus trees before she opened the shutters. It was delicious to sit in the darkened room—and when she wasn't looking, to stretch out on the floor—and to read, daydream, or just look around. Here Nachman's imagination could run free.

The biggest advantage of the plank walls of the cottage was that if you wanted to hang a picture, you simple drove in a nail and put it right up. When someone brought Nachman's mother a piece of embroidery sent by his grandmother in Poland, they took the long strip of linen, which resembled a thin towel, stretched it against the wall and stuck four tacks into its corners, thereby brightening a whole corner of the room. The house was now filling up as though on its own, so that its walls were no longer empty and bare, and the strange, sharp smell of quicklime no longer dominated as before. Nachman's father brought home two boards of planed white pine and sawed them to make a bookcase, which he attached to the beams of the remaining free wall from the door to the corner. In it he put the books he had inherited from Nachman's mother's father, Reb Nachman Herzlich, and next to them the new books that he bought or borrowed wherever he could. Over his parents' bed, on his father's side, hung a photograph of his own father, Reb Aryeh-Leib Shpiegler, and next to it, on his mother's side, a photograph of her father. Nachman remembered him from her stories, but there were no boots or fur coat to be seen in this picture of him. It had been brought by Volush, mother's relative, who had come with the Polish team to the Maccabiah athletic games, though he himself neither ran nor jumped nor excelled in any sport. Neither Nachman nor his mother had ever known that such a photograph existed, and now she sat looking at it as though she too were seeing Nachman's grandfather for the first time. His father had taken the picture to be enlarged and framed, and now the two grandfathers hung together on the wall. One of them was very old, and nearly all his face, from the eyes and nose down, was hidden by a spreading beard that blended indistinguishably with the yellow background of the picture. This was Grandfather Aryeh-Leib, his flesh a faded color and an expression of great weariness in his dimming eyes, whom Nachman's father had seen dead in a dream. Grandfather Nachman, on the other hand, had round, slightly protruding eyes, and a short beard the exact color of which—black according to his mother, but lighter and even younger-looking than his own father's as imagined by Nachman himself—could not be determined because of the peculiar tone of the print. Nachman liked to look at this picture both because of his mother's stories and because it resembled the many photographs that adorned the reading room in the public library. With a tarboosh on his head, Grandfather Nachman would have looked exactly like one of the town's heroic founders. It was funny to think that he was his mother's father and that he had died while she was still a little girl. In another country.

The cottage was an inexhaustible pleasure, and Nachman liked best to lie in his bed, which was already too short for his growing body, with eyes and ears open, especially on summer evenings, when silence filled the world and streamed through the open windows. At such times the cottage had a life of its own. A wall groaned as though its stomach ached. Something cracked in the stillness. Nachman knew that this was the nature of the wood, which "worked" all the time, alternately drying and splitting from the sun or swelling and warping from the rain, yet at night all the walls stirred together, and not just the wood. The quicklime was working too. His father had mixed a bright green into the whitewash, and working with a very large brush he had covered the walls from the inside. He had been praised by all for the masterful job he had done. A few weeks passed, however, and the dry lime began to peel off and fall—on the floor, on the plush bedspreads, over the books. No less than the walls, it too had

misunderstand her, God forbid! She wasn't complaining. Not at all. She had enough to do around the house as it was, making pickles in large jars and curing olives in a tin can; buying up several rotels of ripe Arab grapes, stuffing them into an apothecary jar, sprinkling them with a few cups of sugar, covering the mouth of the jar with a piece of torn sheet, and putting it on the kitchen windowsill to turn into wine; hoeing the weeds that grew around the house; baking hallahs for the Sabbath and sweet cakes for tea; and doing all kinds of other things too. No, she wasn't complaining.

At night, when Nachman's father and Uncle Rifael sat figuring their day's wages and his mother served them cookies and tea, Nachman felt that the something bad that had passed between his parents was now gone. His mother might threaten to catch pneumonia, but she never failed to add, "Never mind, soon things will be better." His father was now earning sixty, eighty, even ninety piasters a day, and his mother told Uncle Rifael that she was scrimping on every bit of it, because each piaster of debt they paid off brought them closer to the day when they would no longer owe anyone anything. If only times didn't get worse.

One day Nachman's father didn't go to work. He went to the marketplace instead and came back with two huge Syrian egg crates that were as high as the porch. He whipped his wooden ruler out of his pants pocket, measured something, jotted something down, made a mark with his pencil, broke up the crates into their wooden slats, sawed them still further, took a builder's hammer, filled his mouth with nails, and began to join the slats to the beams of the porch. In a single day he closed in the whole short end of the porch and the bottom half of the long end and even made a kind of temporary door. In the top half of the long wall there would eventually be windows, but for the time being he enclosed it with strips of wood and old sacks. There was no way of knowing what would happen when it rained again or a strong wind blew up, but in the meanwhile they had added another room to their house. Come what may, Nachman's mother lauded his father's work in front of all their guests.

There was so much to be done. Where would they ever find time for it all? And as if getting the house in order were not enough, their yard too was taking on a different look and being transformed strip by strip from a fallow patch of weeds into a proper vegetable garden. They turned under all the topsoil, pulled up the white root-nests of finger grass, built elevated furrows, and planted carrots, red radishes, cucumbers, and scallions. Winter came and went, and the following summer the rows were covered with carrots, radishes, and parsley. The scallions were the first to push their spearlike heads above the ground. The creeping cucumber plants stretched out their hairy leaves. The tomatoes, which had been droopy and faint when planted, rooted, gathered strength, and climbed rapidly upward. Nachman loved those summer evenings when there was time enough to do everything: to water, to hoe, to thin out the rows, and best of all—to eat. There was no greater pleasure than sinking one's teeth into a tender carrot freshly plucked from a row, washed beneath the outdoor faucet, and devoured on the spot. Nothing tasted better than the cucumbers stealthily ferreted out by his fingers and eaten peel and all, to say nothing of the salads that his mother prepared on the porch, into which went whatever had just been picked, plus sour pickles, a spot of oil, a pinch of salt, and green olives from the can. And every bit of it was homegrown! How had they managed to do it all, and when would they ever find the time to do all the things that they were still planning on those summer evenings in the yard, Nachman's mother in the easy chair, his father on the box, and he himself on the warm stoop, cracking dry watermelon seeds, squashing mosquitoes, listening to the tick-tock of the water pumps, and looking up at the infinite stars that lit up the sky? Prosperity was abroad in the land, and not only did every new house that went up need to be plastered, but every new orange grove that was planted, whether Jewish or Arab, required fresh saplings for stock. They could sow sweet lemon and bitter orange seeds on their dunam, let them sprout under glass, plant the saplings, and sell them to the orange growers when they reached the right size.

It wouldn't mean much work, Nachman's parents agreed, but where were they to find the time?

There was a busy, confident air to their home and yard, as if the same fortune that had been put in the palm of their hands by Mister Blackman only to fly away forever would now be restored through his father's prowess on the scaffolds of the new buildings rising in Tel Aviv and from the treasures buried in the soil of their dunam.

In school they had read a story about a man who had bequeathed a buried treasure to his son, who dug and dug for it without finding a thing until he finally came to understand that his father was alluding to the earth itself and to the wealth of those who worked it. It was the same with their dunam.

Despite his father's entreaties, his mother would no longer hear of preparing the sandwiches for his lunch the evening before, for the bread lost its taste when forced to sit sliced and spread overnight. Instead she got up before him and put water to boil on the stove, made coffee with chicory and milk in a small saucepan, buttered some sandwiches (Nachman's father worked hard, his mother explained, and had to eat well), hard-boiled some eggs, peeled a cucumber, took out a radish, some scallions and two tomatoes, and packed everything in a closed jar along with a pinch of salt, carefully wrapped it all in newspaper, and added a bottle of tea, some oranges when in season, or bunches of grapes in the summertime. Once up she did not go back to bed again. The vegetables in the yard were best watered early in the morning or at sunset, and if she was not busy in the garden, or running to the market, or doing the big wash, or cleaning the house, or cooking for the Sabbath, she would go off to the Holzbergs to sew. Arele Holzberg's father was a plumber who made money hand over fist. The Holzbergs lived in a cottage that was tarpapered on the outside and paneled on the inside with painted plywood so that it really seemed like a house. A large icebox stood on their porch, which was enclosed with big windows. Arele's mother never had to take her cakes and hallahs to be done in the bakery because she had a *wundertopf* oven of her own that sat on top of the stove, while in the main room stood a Singer sewing machine, which was so modern, Nachman's mother said, that even young Madam Mendelevitch had nothing like it. When it wasn't in use, it resembled a chest, an elegant piece of walnut furniture whose shiny finish Arele's mother kept covered with an embroidered cloth so it wouldn't fade or be scratched. In order to sew, she removed the cloth and lifted half of the chest's top to reveal the machine, which lay on its side. Taking it by the neck, she twisted it upward by its bearings, replaced the top lid, and set the machine upon it. All that remained to do now was to sit before it with one foot on the filigreed metal pedal and to sew. Nachman's mother's greatest dream was some day to own a Singer too. Then she would be able to sew all their clothes by herself.

She wasn't just dreaming, either, but was confidently calculating what would come next, once they had paid off some of the money that they owed on the cottage and the lot. A sewing machine. Tarpaper on the outside and concrete walls within. At the very least, plywood paneling. And also she wanted Nachman to learn to play the violin. Among the new arrivals from Germany, she told his father, there was a teacher who had many pupils, including Balfour. Nachman's father liked the idea but decided that they would have to wait one more year. If things got no worse, they would be able to afford both the sewing machine and the violin lessons.

His mother had another dream too, which she no longer mentioned with tears in her eyes but rather with every expectation of imminent fulfillment: she would wish at least once, just for a short trip during the summer, to visit her mother. The idea no longer astonished anyone, not even Nachman's father. One constantly heard nowadays of people visiting back and forth. Volush had come with the Maccabiah team and stayed, but there were others who came and went back. And there were young men too, even among the sons of the citrus growers as well as enterprising Yemenites, who went to Poland for their summer vacation. The citrus packers, for instance, who made enough money during the winter season to last them the rest of the year, in summertime could do—especially if they were bachelors—whatever they pleased. One of them, who was an acquaintance of Nachman's parents, traveled every summer to Paris. To paint, they said. Not walls, pictures. Just like that. Nachman knew that Paris was where the Baron de Rothschild lived, and though he didn't know why you had to go all the way there to paint pictures, the idea stirred his imagination. Last summer, however, this same packer had gone to Poland instead and married a young girl there. That is, the girl had wanted to come to Palestine and hadn't had a certificate, and he married her so that she could come as his wife. Whenever Nachman's parents talked about the young men who went to Poland to get married, they called the weddings a *fiktsia*—a fiction. Some of the young men who were married in a *fiktsia* had their travel expenses paid by the parents of the bride and got a free trip for themselves. Only it sometimes happened, his mother related, that after the *fiktsia* the young man fell in love with the girl and refused to divorce her, and then there was nothing that could be done, because a *fiktsia* was just like a real marriage. What was the difference? Nachman wanted to know. "There's a difference, that's all," said his parents with the kind of smile that Nachman knew it was pointless to challenge.

"It's really not such a big thing anymore," said his mother. "They have special excursions for tourists now that cost only thirteen pounds. You go from Haifa to Constanza by ship, and from there by train nearly all the rest of the way, and it only takes about five days."

"It's really not that expensive," agreed his father. "If this year should be no worse than the last, maybe you can go next summer with Nachman."

"That's what I'd like best of all," said his mother, "that the family see Nachman and that he get to know them. We have a son, and no one has ever seen him. And apart from the travel expenses, it won't cost us a single groschen. Everyone will go out of their way to be good to us. We've got a big house there," she said to Nachman, "not far from a brook. And right near there lives my closest friend, Maryla, and they have a huge garden of fruit trees and a sawmill across the brook. Yes, you can walk to the forest from our house. You can't imagine how green it is in the summer. And all the cows. And the fields. And so much water. How many dunams do we have there? In Poland there aren't any dunams. There are morgs and hectares. Kilometer after kilometer of fields. I'd like to visit there just once, just one more time."

The idea of such a trip was no longer too much for Nachman to fathom. Circle was giving way to circle, and his field of vision was rapidly expanding to take in all kinds of people and their obscure ties with his parents. Volush was followed by another relative, Ruzha, who spent the whole summer with them, sleeping on a folding bed on the porch. Besides Toybe, the old Herzlichs had other children who had stayed behind in Poland and were now beginning to arrive too. His father and Uncle Rifael too had endless stories about their enormous family, with its ten brothers, its innumerable uncles, its brothers-in-law and sisters-in-law. The sons of the oldest brothers were as old as Nachman's father himself, or only a few years younger. Now they too were coming, first one, then another, dressed in the heavy, peculiarly cut clothing of all newcomers. One got a job with a printer in Tel Aviv, another at the Haifa port, yet another took a room with a couple of other young pioneers not very far from their cottage. New faces were seen everywhere now, and they too were expanding Nachman's circle.

His father no longer prayed at the synagogue they had at the Talmud Torah, nor at the Hasidic synagogue just across from the empty lot. That kind of synagogue, he now said, was simply a place where the hypocrites went to kowtow to one another, some getting to sit in the most sought-after seats up front, others to recite the *maftir* after the reading of the Torah or to be honored with the *musaf* service. "According to the original, pristine tenets of our faith there's no need to say one's prayer in any specially dedicated house. Any ten Jews can make up a *minyan*—a prayer quorum—as long as they have a room with a Torah scroll in it. If we are given one day of rest a week, which should be given over to holiness and one's better self, why should I have to spend it in the company of those peasants or boorish traders who pray at the Great Synagogue, or those Hasidic bigots? For the new Hebrew living in Palestine and earning his bread by the sweat of his brow, the Sabbath too should have something special, something original about it."

And in fact, when his father put on his Sabbath clothes and his mother spread the green silk tablecloth that Ruzha had brought them, one felt at once that this day was different from all others. On Saturday morning they went to the Yavneh School where Nachman now studied, one classroom of which had a simple wooden ark with a Torah inside. There they were joined by Holzberg with his son Arele; Kravitz, his father's and Uncle Rifael's plastering partner; Sharoni the teacher, who lived next to Guberman's dairy; another teacher from the girls' school; Adon Karniel, who was an official in the Anglo-Palestine Bank and wrote for the newspapers; and a few other men from the little market. The prayer began late and ended early, and every Sabbath a different member of the congregation served as the cantor, though all agreed that Nachman's father was everyone's favorite. When Nachman grew tired of listening to the service, he wandered off through the empty school building and found some book to read, or went out to play in the yard with Arele and the other children. Nachman liked going to pray every Sabbath, but they didn't always go. Sometimes his father's sleepiness got the best of him, and by the time he was able to drag himself out of bed, it was already too late. Then the three of them rose together, poured boiling water from the kettle that had stood on the burner all night over a teaspoon of coffee, ate a piece of the honey cake that Nachman's mother had baked, and went off to visit Uncle Rifael. There was no longer any talk of walking too far on the Sabbath when they crossed under the wire cable strung between two poles to show the limit past which a pious Jew was not supposed to go. Even if they found Uncle Rifael in his work clothes, his bare feet covered with mud, weeding or watering or feeding the chickens in his yard, nobody said a word. They all went inside, and Tsipoyrele served them tea and sugar cookies, oranges in winter and grapes in summer, and pumpkin seeds all year round, and they sat and joked and told stories and wondered what it would be like in the good times that lay—that had to lie—ahead.

Nachman's world kept widening, and soon it would split off entirely from that of his parents. He was already roaming far beyond their cottage and their dunam, but he was still firmly connected to them, almost as if by an umbilical cord, and it was this total dependence that he now strove to break. On Saturdays in winter, following an afternoon nap under their quilts, they again put on their good clothes and went for a walk along the main streets. The whole town was out promenading and cracking nuts and seeds, everyone greeting and looking at and chattering with everyone else. They walked past the Great Synagogue, past the old well and the water tower, past the fenced soccer field where a noisy, good-natured crowd had gathered even though it was forbidden to play ball on the Sabbath, and past the kibbutz on top of the hill until they came to the Beckers, who lived in a single room at the back of their store.

There was hardly a Sabbath on which they didn't stop in to see the old couple, or on which the Beckers—who prayed in the Hasidic synagogue—didn't drop in on them. Nachman's father said that even though they weren't family he felt as though they were, and that it was a duty and a good deed to visit them, as they didn't have a living soul in the country. Old man Becker was funny. He went about all year in his leather boots, whose tops were like huge wooden screws, and gray-bearded though he was, he walked with a vigorous step and held his body perfectly erect. Whenever they came, he placed a small bottle on the table whose contents looked like water, but which Nachman's father said was firewater. His father would cover his empty glass with the palm of his hand while the old man would refill his own, toss it down his throat with a single gulp, and wipe his beard and whiskers with the back of his hand. A miraculous change then came over him, and he began to tell long stories in Yiddish. To Nachman it seemed that he told the same story each time, working in the same Russian phrases in a loud voice while pacing back and forth between the furniture that ran around the room like a fence. Sooner or later he always stamped his boots and broke into a wordless song that kept insistently repeating the same syllabic refrain, "Tum-ta-rarum, tum-ta-rarum, ta-ra-ra-ra, tum-ta-rarum." Nachman didn't understand all the Yiddish that was spoken between the Beckers and his parents, but what little he did he was sure he had heard before. He was tired of always sitting around the same table until dark, tired of the tea, of the crumbly cakes, of the Yiddish, even of old lady Becker herself, who had won his heart in the beginning with her songs that she sang in a trembling voice and her stories that she read from a Yiddish book called *Sholem Aleichem*. Both she and her husband were funny. Nachman's parents told him that when she was still a young girl she had run away from home and gone off to Breslau to be *eine Schauspielerin*—an actress. When the spirit moved her, she would take out her picture album

18 | "Yes!—Yes!—Yes!"

At the far end of their property, past the vegetable rows and the hothouse where they had planted bitter orange and sweet lemon seeds, past the soil that the Yemenite hired hand had turned over, weeded, and prepared for transplanting, stood the outhouse—a little wooden hutch that was so narrow that even Nachman could touch both walls at once when he stretched out his arms. It stood over a simple pit they had dug at the end of their dunam, and its seat was a square crate with a round opening cut into the top. When you squatted on it with your pants rolled down, you had to be careful not to get splinters in your behind. In effect, the outhouse was the boundary of their dunam, though to be more exact the actual border lay two steps beyond it, where a metal rod set in concrete formed one corner of the fence that ran between deaf Baylin's yard and Tuvim's bakery.

This too, however, was only an approximation. Not until later, when Nachman's father decided to fence in their own yard so that grazing animals couldn't eat all their vegetables and saplings, and the great feud broke out between them and the Chupchiks, did they discover the iron marker that had been driven into the ground by the official surveyor appointed by the town council and the British authorities, which showed the precise spot where their dunam came to an end.

But this came later. As of now, their dunam was whatever had been hoed as far as the outhouses. There wasn't any fence, and if you kept going straight, you ended up in the little market, among all the yards and the children and the sandy lanes. It was simple, really. On his way home from the Yavneh School, Nachman always walked with the children who lived in the little market and beyond the dry creek, accompanied by Arele Holzberg. He threw his knapsack down on the porch, ate lunch standing up (now that his father was a hard-working plasterer who had to eat well, the big meal was in the evening when he returned from work), and ran to the little market or to Arele's house to do homework, coming back later by himself.

It was simplicity itself: suddenly he was a grown boy like the others, footloose and fancy free. Before supper his mother would send him to Tuvim's bakery to buy fresh bread for his father's lunch the next day, and Nachman would ask—and sometimes be allowed—to buy a *pita* like all the other children. Without having to be told, his feet knew the way over the packed dirt path that led to the bakery through Chupchik's yard and back again, through the yard once more and along the sandy path that crossed the footbridge over the creek to Arele Holzberg's house. Nachman knew that Peterzail lived in one of the nearby cottages, and once he had even seen his idiot mother sitting on her front stoop in a dirty smock, her pasty-white arms and legs covered with sores like her son's. Nachman told himself that he was no longer afraid of the boys from the Talmud Torah, but nevertheless he tried to avoid being seen by Peterzail, or Ozer Lichtig, or Kashani, whose father's drunken yodeling and petrifying screams he sometimes heard from their yard in the twilight stillness. He wanted to forget, as if he had never studied in the Talmud Torah in the first place. Arele Holzberg was a fine friend and he liked to spend his time in the Holzbergs' cottage with its bright green plywood walls. Arele had two older sisters and their yard was always full of boys and girls. He could go there whenever he pleased too, because Arele's parents and his own parents were friends. In the summer they flew *kifkes*, paper kites made out of old notebook pages folded diagonally with great precision, over once, and then a second and a third time. The margins left by the first fold were snipped and shaped into a long, thin tail, without which the *kifke* spun around like a top instead of gliding smoothly through the air. Or else they played hide-and-seek, or five stones, or games where someone was "it." Suddenly a yoyo craze might develop, or the girls would play jump rope while the boys fought with sticks, or the girls would bounce a ball under their legs and sing *van, too, tree a-leary* while the boys stole into back yards to pick mulberries. There was no limit to their games, which changed with the season, and ranged all up and down the neighborhood. Together the children roamed from yard to yard and street to street, separating and regrouping, inventing something new every day.

Above all, he was no longer shut up like a baby inside the house. One day he and Arele quarreled and stopped talking to each other. After school Arele walked home by himself and Nachman by himself. He was already feeling sad that he had no one to share his adventures with. All the rest of the day he moped around the house. He finished the book he had borrowed from the library. He took the hose and watered the vegetables. But all the while he couldn't stop wondering what the other children were doing now and what he might be missing. Without having even to ask, his mother told him to go to the bakery and buy himself a *pita*. He wandered away from the dry creek, the warm bread in his hand. Todros Chupchik was sitting in front of his house on a broken cinder block and looking at him. In the distance the smoke of a bonfire could be seen rising from the open field this side of the creek. Nachman couldn't decide between the bonfire and Todros, and just stood there for a second.

If Arele were with him, they would go to the bonfire, where all the big boys from the little market would be roasting potatoes and telling scary stories about movies they had seen, or about the Great War between the Turks and the English that had been fought right here by the creek, or about the old days when the town was the only Jewish settlement between the mountains and the sea and thousands of Arabs had come down on the new town, just after Passover, and old Adon Mendelevitch and his sons and that other hero who had lived here for a while—a desert Jew who had a huge Arab sword and spoke only Arabic—had cut them to shreds and driven them off like dogs. Nachman wanted to join the big boys, but he didn't dare go by himself.

Neither did Todros, who wore thick glasses and couldn't see a foot in front of his nose when somebody grabbed them. That was why Todros preferred to stay home and sit by himself on a cinder block when the whole neighborhood was gathered around a bonfire. Nachman felt sorry for him, and this made him feel sorrier yet for himself, but beyond that he felt an urge to have another look at the large painting that hung in the Chupchiks' house in a frame (so Todros swore) of real gold. Todros's house was different from all the others. It too had once been just a tarpapered cottage, but now its walls were poured concrete and were not plastered the usual bright green but were a swirl of bright, colorful patterns such as only a master plasterer like Chupchik knew how to make. Taking up nearly half the wall of this unusual room was the picture, which Nachman had seen many times and longed to see again. He turned away from the bonfire and headed for Todros.

They sat in the room, Nachman staring fixedly at the picture and Todros talking about it. Todros said that his own father had painted it, and Nachman didn't even care though he knew that Todros was a liar and was making it all up. In the picture, Todros explained, his father had painted what it would be like at the end of time, after the Messiah came. Trees as blue as indigo climbed above others whose leaves were as broad as banana fronds and wound around each other like strange snakes. Bushes sharp as javelins grew out of the ground. At the top, in one corner, hung a red sun that looked like half a watermelon. A monkeylike man, covered with hair, fondled a bare-fanged wolf with one hand while his other rested on the mane of a lion. By his side stood a woman, completely naked except for a shaggy braid of hair that fell between her breasts all the way to the tiger that crouched at her feet. Nachman's eyes kept returning to this woman, who was unlike anyone he had ever seen. Sometimes while lying in bed at night he would pretend to be asleep and wait for his mother to undress, but even when she was sure that he was sleeping and had turned down the lamp, she would face the other way. He had once seen Ruzha naked without meaning to when he had gone to return the watering hose to the hut they used as both a shower and a storeroom, but he had been so shocked that he couldn't be certain of what he'd really seen. Now, though, it occurred to him that the woman in the picture looked very much like Ruzha, and this frightened him so that he looked away to keep from betraying himself. Just then the roar of many children came pouring through the open windows, and Nachman, who knew from the sound what was happening outside, jumped to his feet and ran to the door. He stopped for a moment with his hand on the doorknob to look back at Todros, who continued to sit on the sofa.

"Todros, it's Yes!"

Todros didn't budge. Nachman now noticed how dark the room had gotten, so that Todros's eyeglasses shone with a strange glitter. The rhythmic chant of the children reached them from the street again: "Y–e–s! Y–e–s! Y–e–s!"

Nachman couldn't contain himself any longer. This

time, between Todros and the commotion caused by the lamplighter in the street, he chose the street.

Electricity had already come to the town center, both outdoors and in many of the houses, but not to the little market, though Nachman's father had said that they would soon be erecting power poles here too, and that electric wires would then run straight to their cottage. Along the two streets of the little market there were at present different, shorter poles, with lanterns in square glass boxes at the top. Every day, at that same fleeting twilight hour between darkness and dusk, the lamplighter passed through the neighborhood, a long ladder over his left shoulder and a large can with a long spout on his right. The first child to set eyes on him dropped whatever he was doing and announced with a loud cry, "Y–e–s!" At once the word spread from child to child and in no time at all would be running together toward the lamplighter with a single rhythmic chant on their lips, "Y–e–s! Y–e–s! Y–e–s!"

The lamplighter was a curious fellow. He carried a tall ladder and climbed to the top of the lampposts, but he himself was small and shrunken beneath the gray smock that hung on his thin frame as though on a scarecrow. "Yes!" never appeared in the neighborhood except at this time of day of neither day nor night, and his whole appearance was as nondescript as the hour. His face was gray, and there were deep indentations beneath his cheekbones and in the skin of his neck that was ridged like a turtle's. But his sunken cheeks and the fireless pits of his eyes were a total blur underneath the broken visor of his cap, leaving his thick nose alone to jut out over his toothless mouth like a long spinning top. He took his time, oblivious to the swarm of children running before and behind him, jumping up and down in the sand and shouting "Y–e–s!" in a single voice. Halting in front of the first lamppost, he leaned his ladder against it and prepared to climb, taking no notice of what was happening around him. The children did not doubt for a moment that he would live up to expectations as he always had in the past, yet they knew too that it was their task to egg him on until he did. And so they shouted even louder, redoubling their cry that was half challenge, half plea, "Y–e–s! Y–e–s! Y–e–s!"

His one leg was already on the first rung of the ladder, the oil can in his right hand, and his left hand reaching for the rung above his head. Now he began to rise, his other leg leaving the ground too, and dangling for a second in midair. All of a sudden, as though on command, his audience grew deadly silent. At that exact moment a single blast of air rang out in a high, trumpeting tone to be greeted by thunderous cheers. The lamplighter had done it again, proving once more that he had yet to lose his command over his nether organ. His admirers swarmed about the ladder, cheering and calling for more. Yet his face remained as shaded as the time of day. Oblivious of everything, he ascended the ladder, opened the glass box, took out the lamp, filled it with oil, trimmed the wick, lit it with a match, replaced the lamp in its box, and descended. The applause, the loud flattery, the catcalls, the pleas, all broke against his dusky, shrunken face. He re-shouldered the ladder without a word, picked up the oil can, and walked to the next lamppost, still deaf and blind to the crowd of children, big and small, running after him through the sand in sandals and bare feet, cheering in frantic cadence. Though they already knew that in a minute he would lean his ladder against another lamppost and repeat his entire act, they went on shouting hoarsely like the acolytes of some pagan god, "Y–e–s! Y–e–s! Y–e–s!"

The lamplighter planted one foot on the bottom rung while the other paused in midair. Once again, as though on command, the voices died down all at once. All ears strained to hear in the perfect silence.

"Y–e–s!" came the admiring shout once again. He never let them down, the lamplighter.

"Yes" was the open street, and the street was the world that renewed itself day by day in ever-expanding circles. "Yes"

19 | *A book a day*

A rhyme kept running through Nachman's head. It was a birthday rhyme:

Down a cloudy path
One cloudy afternoon
Rode a cloudy man
Fiddling a cloudy tune.

Why a birthday? Why these words which kept rhyming over and over in his head?

As though out of the family memory, a distant scene passed before him. A warm evening, before the autumn holidays. The stores in town were still open, but they already had their lights on. Women were carrying full baskets and dragging about chickens with their legs tied and their wings interlocked. The sandals on his feet were badly worn and last winter's shoes had grown too small for him, yet they had passed by the shoe store without going in because his father hadn't taken him for shoes. They had passed the hat shop too. Nachman's beret had faded completely over the summer, and a good look at it showed just how rumpled and full of holes it really was, but they had not come to buy a new beret either. They had come to buy a book for his birthday.

Was this the first book his father had bought him in Halevi's bookstore, a large, beautifully illustrated volume called *Cloudy Pants,* or *Cloudy Boots,* or was it maybe *Cloudy Shoes?*

Down a cloudy path
One cloudy afternoon
Rode a cloudy man
Fiddling a cloudy tune.

Along the street they were on, Lovers of Zion Street, stood the town's oldest houses, built of baked clay and thatch. They too had been plastered on the outside and even nicely whitewashed, but one could tell them right off by their low roofs, their narrow entrances, and their sagging, cracking, hunchbacked walls. Now that the street had been paved with asphalt and the wooden sidewalk on its shopping side replaced by large flagstones, the clay houses seemed to have sunk into the ground, so that you had to descend two steps to get to Halevi's bookstore. The outside of the store was unimpressive, and its narrow show window, when the shutters were up, had nothing but a few notebooks, a High Holy Day prayer book, a Hebrew calendar, a half-faded roll of crepe paper, a single pencil case, and a lone knapsack. But inside it was another story. The smell of books already engulfed you on the first step down. Adon Halevi would emerge from a corner into the circle of yellowish light made by a bulb hanging from the ceiling on an overhead wire to greet Nachman's father with a faint smile underneath his gray mustache, his quiet glance would brush Nachman's face, and he would say, "So, it's little Nachman's birthday again."

Even he knew that every year his father bought him a

new book for his birthday in Adon Halevi's store. That was to say, his memory was not of the first time it had happened, nor of that book that was called—he was almost sure of it now—*Stars in a Bucket.* His father had already taken him to Adon Halevi's bookstore many times before, always at the same warm hour of the evening, at the summer's end, shortly before the New Year. His father would intend to buy a book for Nachman, but no sooner did he spy the overflowing shelves than he forgot why he had come and began to take down volume after volume, feeling and examining and rapidly leafing through each one as though trying to swallow it all. "There isn't one of them I wouldn't like," he would say to Adon Halevi, "and if I had the money I'd buy them all."

Adon Halevi would smile back fondly and urge him to pick a book. "Take something," he would say. "You can have it for nothing. Pay me when you can afford it."

"No," his father would say, "I never take anything for nothing, not even a book."

"Take something anyhow," Adon Halevi would say. "You can pay me in weekly installments."

"No," recollected his father, "today I've come for a special reason. For Nachman's birthday."

"In that case," said Adon Halevi, "I have a book for him that he can't possibly have read yet because it just came out. A very nice book."

But no, he was confusing two different times. This conversation had come later. When his father had bought him his first book, he had said something else.

"A child's first book," his father had said, "should both look nice and have something in it to stimulate the imagination. Something to make him want to read more."

"He'll read." Adon Halevi raised Nachman's chin and looked him in the face in the peculiar evening light. "I can tell by the gleam in his eyes, by the way they run down the page. He'll read all right."

"I hope so," said his father.

Nachman saw himself then, holding a book, *King Bob,* whose illustrated jacket looked like one of the pictures on its brightly lettered pages: thin branches of strange trees snaking down the margins of the page, baby monkeys hanging by their wriggly tails, big and little elephants, and all kinds of birds. Yes, he wanted this book badly. With it he could gallop off to faraway lands on an elephant's back, leaping like the monkeys from tree to tree, from world to world. The cottage, the dunam, the little market—these had been the first big breakthrough. Books were the second, and they were to last him longer and take him further.

How it had happened, what came before what, he no longer remembered. The bookcase that his father had built out of boards and braced against the wall had always been within reach, and there was always something there for him to find. *Ben Hur*—a book without a binding, missing the beginning and the end, yet how many times had he read it! *The Complete Legends of Israel. The Diaries of Doctor Theodor Herzl.* A thin volume of strange tales, one especially, "The Story of Little Rabbi Gaddiel," which Nachman reread whenever the books were taken out to air or he was searching through the bookcase for something new. The first two sentences were engraved forever in his mind: "Little Rabbi Gaddiel was born because of the Torah, which his father taught to Jewish boys. And when Rabbi Gaddiel first saw the light of day, he was so tiny that it was difficult to tell whether he was a real human being or not."

There was another thin volume, too, in a paper binding that was graying and stained from use, with red letters on the cover that said *Echoes.* In it was a story that Nachman felt certain was about their own town, especially the following lines, which he sometimes wasn't sure he really had read or possibly had heard from his father on one of those summer evenings when they all sat outside and were bitten hand and foot by the mosquitoes: "Squat before us rise the Mountains of Ephraim, the very same that were unfaithful to the zealous and vindictive God of Israel, that lay with their alien Cuthites like some foreign presence, like the flesh of some wild beast in the living body of the nation."

There were the first, interconnected breakthroughs to come to him through the fog. Through the fog rose another day too with a wonderful tang. Once more it was the end of the summer vacation. Nachman had gone with his mother to visit their relative who was working in the port in Haifa.

"It's a perfect disgrace," she had announced, "that we have family here whom we haven't visited even once."

She hated to travel, unless it was to go see her *fetter* in Tel Aviv, and the relative in Haifa was on Nachman's father's side. But this time she prepared herself thoroughly, baking a cake and filling some jars, before taking Nachman and setting out. The journey, which took the better part of a day, cut over the mountains on a road that was one long succession of potholes and rocks through the frightening Arab towns of Tulkarm and Jenin, and from there to Afula across the vast valley that was as fiery as the inside of Tuvim's bakery, past settlements where his mother said there were pioneers and malaria, and finally to Haifa, high above the sea. Nachman remembered only three things from their entire visit: the huge boulders that he saw being cast into the sea to add landfill to the city; a boy standing in a window across from the apartment where they were staying and playing a violin ("We'll get you one too," his mother had promised as always); and the mailman who knocked on the door one morning to bring him a rolled paper cylinder, on which it said Nachman Shpiegler.

Perhaps it was because this was the first bit of mail he had ever received in his life, perhaps too because inside the wrapper was a copy of *Young News*, the children's newspaper that his father had subscribed to as a surprise birthday present for him. Every Friday from then on the mailman arrived with the same stamped, postmarked roll of paper on which it said Nachman Shpiegler. Could it be this was even the same birthday that for some inexplicable reason kept running through his head together with the rhyme, *Down a cloudy path, one cloudy afternoon, rode a cloudy man, fiddling a cloudy tune?*

One way or another, driven by his passion for books, Nachman now blazed a new trail for himself—to the public library. During the long weeks after his illness and the months between schools that followed, his father had brought him books all the time, but now that he was a pupil in the Yavneh School he wanted to get them on his own. Adon Zusskind, the principal, encouraged him too.

One evening they had gone to his house. He was sitting at the head of a table on which a flowery oilcloth was spread, before him a glass of tea, a sugar bowl, a plate full of assorted biscuits, an eyeglass case, and a newspaper, which he folded and laid aside when they entered. Despite the great heat he was wearing a vest, which barely buttoned over his stomach. On his bald head, which was round like his paunch, a circular skullcap was perched. His glasses too were circles within circles, and his tiny eyes, which were round as well, peered from the innermost of these circles. Only the beard on the tip of his chin was pointed. He quickly flicked back his glasses and stared at Nachman to form an impression, while conversing at the same time with his father in a low voice about what was in the newpapers, about the new immigrants from Germany who wanted to send their children to the Yavneh School, and about Hitler, might he roast in hell, whose hysterical shouts had been heard the night before over the radio in Rosenwald's kiosk. Suddenly he turned to Nachman and asked, "So, young man, you'd like to attend our school?" Nachman nodded and hung his head. "And how do you get along with the twenty-two letters of our Hebrew alphabet?"

"He reads more than he should," his father was quick to boast.

The principal leaned back without rising from his chair, took down a red book with a much-handled cover, opened it, thumbed through it, and placed it before Nachman.

"We're waiting on your words, young man."

He had already read this book, *And It Came to Pass,* once before, the story of the demon Asmodai and King Solomon. Now, however, he read hastily, eager to show off, frightened of failure, rushing from word to word and line to line.

"That's enough," said the principal in a gentle tone of voice. Nachman stopped in the middle of a sentence without looking up.

"If I do say so myself," his father praised him again, "he reads very nicely."

But the principal didn't react. "Don't hide your face from me, Nachman," he said.

Nachman stirred and looked straight in the principal's eyes, which seemed to recede behind their thick lenses, lens within lens.

"And how are you at kicking around the old football?"

Nachman said nothing, not knowing what the right answer was.

"If anything, he's been overdoing that too ever since we moved to our cottage. He's out running around until dark every day."

"Good. Studies aren't everything. We want to raise a generation here that will be like the disciples of Rabbi Akiva, healthy in both body and mind. Try to be one of the biggest and strongest boys in your class, so that no one can push you around. You'll go into third grade." The principal noticed the look on Nachman's face. He wanted him to stay back a grade. "I can see you read well enough to go straight into fourth grade. But you're too young. You'll keep on being the smallest in your class all the way through eighth grade, and that won't be good at all. What would you like to be when you grow up?"

Nachman didn't answer. He felt hurt that the principal was changing the subject.

"The principal asked you a question."

"A worker," he said.

The principal laughed gently, and Nachman's father joined him. "Let him be what he likes as long as it's not a teacher," said the principal. He rose from his place, and Nachman and his father rose too. Only now did he realize how short the principal was and how his stomach and buttoned vest were at war. He put a hand on Nachman's shoulder. "The most important thing of all is to be a man, healthy in body and mind. You should be a good Jew and a loyal son of Zion." And when they were already in the doorway, he asked, "Where did he learn to read so well? Does he take books from the public library?"

"I bring him books from wherever I can."

"That's not good enough. A boy in third grade should be able to look after himself. Bring any big book from your father to leave as a deposit, Nachman, and take out a library card. We have an excellent public library here that doesn't have an equal in the entire country, not even in Tel Aviv."

The attractions of the library revealed themselves to him slowly over a period of months and years. First there was the walk there with Arele and the other children, with all its incidental pleasures: the glass showcase with scenes from the new film at the theater, the bus from Tel Aviv that stopped to let off all its passengers, a fight between two wagon drivers at the station, the new store exclusively for young people recently opened by some German Jews who had settled in town, and finally the large, two-story town hall with its broad staircase that led to the huge balcony on the second floor. The greatest fun of all was to stand on the balcony itself, in front of the barred railing, where the mayor stood to address the meetings that gathered in the yard below, and where once the British high commissioner had stood in a white suit and a cork hat and spoken—with a mouth that sounded full of stones—to all the schoolchildren, "Rau-rau-rau! Doo-voo-doo, hau-hau!" A mulberry tree grew below in the town hall's fenced garden—a fence whose gate was never shut, though even if it were, the berried branches hung out into the street within easy reach.

Yet all this was nothing compared to the library itself, on the ground floor of the town hall. The underside of the balcony, which was supported by four metal columns, created a roofed-over space where the children gathered whenever the line inside was too long or during a winter cloudburst. Here too was the entrance to the library, that is, to the narrow corridor past which the children were not allowed and which was separated by a gray wooden partition from the reading room, where the books stood row after row. The children were permitted as far as the partition, along which ran a shelf piled with catalogs where all the books were alphabetically listed in black ink in a large, clear hand. At one end of the partition was a slanting table, like a cantor's podium in a synagogue. Behind it stood the old librarian Adon Ivri. For Adon Ivri to see him, Nachman had to climb on the bench that had been put there especially for this. The first time he saw Adon Ivri face to face, it was all he could do to keep from jumping back down. One couldn't really tell whether his bare head was shaven or bald, but between it and the collar of his shirt there wasn't a hair except for his bristling eyebrows and the tufts that stuck out from his nostrils and ears. Adon Ivri's bare scalp looked like a piece of transparent leather pulled tight over his skull, beneath which the twitching veins threatened to burst any minute. Add to all this the sight of his ceaselessly working bottom jaw and his lips that kept sucking and making strange slurping noises and you had—Gogol the Witch, straight from *King Solomon's Mines!*

The boys and girls jostled in line and jockeyed for position, but exemplary order reigned in Adon Ivri's library, and the children were summoned before him in strict accordance with the sequence of their returned books, which were piled with the first on top and the last on bottom. Glancing at the next book and card, Adon Ivri chewed on his lip and remarked, "You just took out a new book yesterday, Adon Shpiegler. Before supper. You couldn't have read it."

Nachman said nothing. It was annoying to have to stand like this on the bench with all the children crowding behind him.

"Go home, read it, and come back tomorrow."

"I've read it," Nachman said without moving.

"I see that we're not only liars but insolent too, Adon Shpiegler." He pushed his thin, silver-framed glasses down from his forehead over his eyes as though to get a better view of the insolent liar. The veins swelled beneath his skin and his scalp reddened. Saliva flew from his lips and he shouted, "In that case, my distinguished friend, tell me what you read! And be quick!"

Fine. He would tell him. From start to finish. It was a thin book, for babies, which he had read in its entirety on his way home. There was once a boy, in England, named Robinson Crusoe, who wouldn't listen to his father and his mother but ran away from home and went to sea in a boat that was shipwrecked. Robinson was saved by a miracle, yet still he didn't go home but continued to set sail until one day he was stranded on a desert island. He lived there for many years all by himself, and to keep track of the time he cut a notch in a piece of wood every day. Not until the twenty-fourth year did he find his savage servant, Friday, who was given that name because . . .

"That will do, Adon Shpiegler, that will do. So." The librarian lifted his glasses and went back to sucking and chewing on his lips as though they were a marrowbone, delaying his verdict. "In other words, you don't just want to take something out, tear and compare. Yes, that's very, very interesting. Let's see how long you keep it up. Let's wait and see."

This was his ticket of entry into the immeasurable world of the public library. What didn't he read? *Legends of the Balkans. Son of the Navajos. To the Mountains of the Moon. Pinocchio. In the Evening* by Feierberg ("A pack of wolves was racing through the forest and heading straight for him. . . . Their eyes glowed like fire and their mouths and sharp fangs were a terrifying sight. . . . Yet they couldn't cross the circle. . . . And now came a marvelous melody, wafted on the wings of the unsullied wind. . . ."). *Captain Hatteras,* all parts. *Treasure Island. Hershele, A Sad Story. Hershele of Ostropolye. Memoirs of the House of David,* all parts. My *Journey to Tibet. Overland to India. Michael Strogoff. The House of Aguilar. Baron Munchhausen. The Animal Book* by Mendele Mocher Seforim. *Pharaoh's Daughter. Varda. A Thousand and One Nights. The Myths of Greece.* Mapu's *The Love of Zion. David Copperfield. Oliver Twist. A Tale of Two Cities. Tom Sawyer. Uncle Tom's Cabin. Leatherstocking Tales. The Life of Solomon Maimon. The Black Tulip. The Early Explorers. The Later Explorers. Tales of the Brothers Grimm. Salvation* by Sholem Asch. *Kidnapped. Herod and Mariamne. Taras Bulba. Captain Grant's Children,* all parts. *With Fire and Sword,* all parts. *The Deluge,* all parts. The Ahiasaf Library, The Tushiah Library, The Stiebel Library, The Little Library . . .

Nachman didn't read all these and many other books in a day or even a year. Before long, however, in a year or two, he had joined the select few who were allowed to ask for a book from the catalog even though it was meant for an older age group, or to pass beyond the wooden partition without asking permission to help Adon Ivri arrange the returned books in his inner sanctum and look for those that had been requested by the children on paper slips. There could be no greater honor or enjoyment. What didn't Nachman find among the stacks of books? Old volumes that had grown gray and spotted with the years, that had crumbled from use and been rebound after having their margins snipped off and their pages refastened with strips of white paper, strange old journals, *Ha-Maggid, Ha-Zeman, Ha-Shiloah, Bustenai, Do'ar Ha-Yom, Ha-Or, Ha-Me'orer, Ittonenu Li-Ketanim, Ittonenu Le-Gedolim* . . .

There were books and there were titles. Every book was

first and foremost a puzzle of words, a new mystery which Nachman couldn't wait to unravel. The words rubbed off on him even when he never got beyond the title page. But when a book intrigued him, it was impossible for to wait until he got home. He kept his eyes glued to it, his knapsack on his shoulder, his feet guiding themselves along the familiar path from the library home. In those early days when Adon Ivri still insisted on limiting him to thin children's books, he would have reached the last page by the time his feet touched the front stoop. His mother would scold him for being late again from school, for reading too much, and worst of all, for reading while he walked. "You'll ruin your vision, and then you'll be sorry for the rest of your life."

Nevertheless, having acquired the taste for books, there was no satisfying him. He even read through the handful of books in the house. The two bound volumes of *Ha-Tekufah* and *Ha-Shiloah.* H. G. Wells's *The Science of Life*. Together with Holzberg his father now subscribed to the daily paper *Davar,* and with the weekly Sabbath supplement came a children's section too. What wonderful stories were there! And in *Ittonenu Le-Gedolim* they were serializing *The Theft of the Gulf Stream.* And there were jokes. And riddles. To say nothing of Uncle Rifael's home, where much to his surprise, Nachman discovered books he had never even heard of. Without noticing the transition, he was now racing through volumes meant only for adults. The title of one small, greenish volume tempted him in particular: *In the Name of Rabbi Jesus of Nazareth.* What nightmarish stories! The Gentiles tortured the Jews, just as they always did in stories, but such blood-curdling descriptions as these his imagination had met nowhere else. They poured tar over the Jews' hands and lit them like Hanukkah candles or forced them to sit on sharp stakes. No, he hated these stories and did not even want to think of them, though he could never again forget them either.

His reading bug, as his mother called it, had other motivations too. The simple pleasures of the little market no longer delighted him, and Nachman increasingly found himself steering clear of the riotous gang of boys who tumbled in the sand of the neighborhood's two streets and in the empty lots along the dry creek. He no longer ran with the boys behind the lamplighter to shout "Y–e–s! Y–e–s! Y–e–s!" or eagerly volunteered his services to sit in the house of some woman in childbirth and pray for the angels to protect her in exchange of a handful of peppery chickpeas and two sucking candies with fillings. He even took a roundabout route now to Arele Holzberg's, though by no means because on his way there one evening he had run into some toughs in the company of Ozer Lichtig, who was now—despite the reputed riches of his parents—working as an apprentice in the bus company's garage. As soon as he saw him Ozer reached out with both arms to grab Nachman, who barely managed to slip away while Ozer's voice followed after him. "What are you running for, Pipeleh? No one's going to touch you. Pipeleh, send my love to Shpiegleh!"

No, it had nothing to do with Ozer Lichtig. He had simply grown up, quickly. There would still be several more such unpleasant incidents, but his passion for books came first.

There was a good feeling in the cottage nowadays, and he liked to sit in it, especially when it rained. How delicious it was to read at such times, when the room was like Noah's Ark in the midst of the flood! How many times had he run despite the rain, through the rain, to the library not to be left without a book! How many times too had he come home soaked to the bones to be met by his mother, who rushed from her post by the porch window (yes, the porch was now enclosed by a real door and real windows), wringing her hands and shouting at the top of her voice, "One case of pneumonia wasn't enough for you! Take off those boots at once. Master of the Universe, you must have walked right through all the puddles. And just look at your new knickers! They feel as though they've been soaked in a tub. They're English wool and now they'll shrink completely. I'll get a heart attack from this child yet! In rain like this you have to run to the library? Your father doesn't spend enough money on books as it is? It's just too much for me. You're wet through to your underwear, and the color on your flannel shirt has all run. Take off those clothes immediately, and get into your pajamas and into bed."

What a magnificent punishment! By the time his mother had put the kerosene stove on the stool in the middle of the room and the kettle had begun to steam, by the time she had brought a plate of cabbage stuffed with raisins and chopped meat and rice along with a bowl of buckwheat soup and a glass of tea to his bed, he was already at the far end of the world, in Patagonia, at the Cape of Good Hope, beyond the Arctic Circle, in Tierra del Fuego, reading to the accompaniment of the hail that drummed on the roof. Let it rain, let it pour! He didn't even care if he finished the book before the day was done because his father had borrowed a new book from Adon Sharoni, and though he had expressly forbidden him to read it, Nachman knew that the temptation would prove too much. What an irresistible title too: *The Great Madness* by Avigdor Ha-Meiri!

20 | *The whole cloth*

Like one of Ruzha's embroidered cloths, so streets, houses, and people now joined to form a single vivid pattern in Nachman's mind: the town. On winter evenings they sat around the table, a kettle steaming in the middle of the kerosene stove. The large, green-tinted lamp cast a soft light on Ruzha's fingers, drawing silk and woolen threads through tiny holes in the stiff linen, green threads and yellow threads, blue threads and silver threads and gold threads. Ruzha was as beautiful as the pictures in books. She not only did marvelous embroidery but could also sew dresses, measure a meter of fabric, draw a charcoal pattern on brown paper, cut the fabric spread out beneath it on the table, and pin it and baste it with a needle. It was a pity that she hadn't a sewing machine, but even Nachman's mother had yet to get the Singer that his father had promised her. Sometimes Ruzha went to Arele Holzberg's mother to sew, but if she had a machine of her own she could easily have made a living at it. As it was, she worked in the orange groves, wrapping fruit in the winter and pruning the trees in the summer. The skirts and dresses that she sewed were only for Nachman's mother and herself. Nachman couldn't take his eyes off her when she dressed up with a beret on her head, hiding one ear while disclosing the short, bobbed haircut over the other. He wasn't the only one. Volush, the other member of their family who was sharing a rented room with some friends, now came often to visit them too, and Nachman knew without even having to eavesdrop on his parents' whisper that he was in love with Ruzha, though he agreed with their opinion that she deserved someone better than this young man who liked to sit up to all hours of the night jabbering in Polish. Ruzha wanted to learn Hebrew, and Nachman would have been happy to teach her, but the opportunities were few. During the day she worked, and at night, if she wasn't sewing or embroidering, she was off somewhere with Volush, at the Workers Club or the movies. Soon she would move to a room of her own, or perhaps even to Tel Aviv, and at the thought of it Nachman felt an unfamiliar emotion that he had previously known only from books. It was a pity that he was so young and Ruzha was already eighteen. If only, just suppose, he were four years older, and Ruzha, just suppose, were four years younger.

At night Nachman sat and watched Ruzha's nimble fingers amid the jumble of colorful threads. Suddenly she stood up and pinned a piece of embroidery to the wall of the cottage so that everyone could see it from a distance. It was a handsome picture. Blue smoke curled up from the black chimney of a red-roofed house. Near it stood a green tree with branches full of white storks, whose feet and bills were embroidered red. A golden-braided girl carried a bouquet of flowers. While Nachman stared at the scene, the whole town formed in his mind into a picture too, so that he knew with perfect clarity where every house and street belonged, where the settlement had first started between the Great Synagogue and the council and library, where the colonists had built their large houses that were now hidden behind tall cypresses and palms, and where on the outskirts stood the wooden one-room cottages of the Bukharans, the Yemenites, the young pioneers. A whole cloth.

Whole—yet constantly changing.

It was not only in their own cottage that new relatives were coming and going all the time. The entire town was filled with new faces. Like Rosenwald, who converted his packing crate into a candy-and-newspaper stand and hooked it up (a first for the little market) to the electricity system, so that music from his radio attracted the entire neighborhood at night. Or like their next-door neighbors, the Saubers. There were six of them, five men and a woman. The men were all tall and broad, starting with the youngest, who was a grown man himself, and ending with the oldest, who walked around with a bulging paunch and a curved pipe in his mouth and was the father of the family. No one knew what they did for a living. To Nachman's father they said that they had been farmers in Germany and wished to be the same here, but in the meantime they did nothing at all except go twice a day, all five of them, to the back of Rosenwald's kiosk, where two folding tables had been set up under a large, colorful awning. Nachman's mother couldn't get over it. They didn't work, they were always complaining about Palestine, and yet they were too lazy to boil their own coffee and had to go to the kiosk whenever they wanted a cup! It had nothing to do with laziness, Nachman's father explained to her. It was simply the way Germans were: they liked to sit for hours in cafés, eating *kaffeekuchen* and drinking *bier* and talking. That was their idea of a good time.

There were other newcomers too. There were the Berkovitzes from Romania who lived in an old packinghouse in one of the orange groves and whose son Pesach was in Nachman's class. They had an egg stall in the market, and it was from there that his father had brought the big crates to enclose the porch. The stall was tended by Pesach's mother and one or two of his older brothers. Pesach's mother was a bulky woman who bore her weary body around all day long on a pair of puffy legs and always wore men's work shoes that were laced with short pieces of string. The stall was run entirely by her and her eldest sons because Pesach's father was a mule driver, though he had originally been brought from Romania (so Nachman's father claimed) along with other Jews like him to work from dawn to dusk in the orange groves for coolie wages, and the family still made its home in an abandoned packinghouse. That was his father's version of the story; his mother had another. "He's already feeling so sorry for these Bessarabians that any day now he's going to go out begging for them in the streets. But I tell you that less than a year after coming to this country they're better off than we who have been buried here in this town for ten years and more!" They were strange creatures, she maintained, who lived in a packinghouse and put all their children to work in the egg stall, wrapping oranges, or in the foundry, while they walked around in rags and never even bought a single book. What wonder was it if after a year they had a business of their own and a wagon that made good money too? But Nachman's father disagreed. They were simple folk, he said, the kind of earthy Jews that the country needed. They worked hard and didn't complain. What difference did it make if they were Bessarabians?

It was a rich and colorful cloth, and Nachman found something new in it every day. The five tall Germans who lived next door to them and went twice a day to Rosenwald's kiosk, for example, were tenants of the mother of Mute Baylin, who wasn't really mute at all, as everyone well knew, but simply had a thing about not talking.

Nachman's mother told his father that she had heard from Baylin's mother that as a young man he had charmed all the girls not only with his good looks but with his clever repartee. He had read a lot too, both in Russian and in Hebrew, and was an unmatched conversationalist. But books had proved his undoing, Mute Baylin's mother claimed, and Nachman's mother stressed this point as though with some motive in mind. It was from books that he got all his crazy ideas. One day he simply shut his mouth for good, and since then you couldn't pry a peep out of it with tongs. Yet there wasn't a greater expert on citrus grafts in all of Palestine, and the orange growers literally fought over him despite his persistent silence, the khaki shorts he wore summer and winter, and various other peculiarities, such as his insistence on taking cold showers even in the middle of February. Mute Baylin tickled Nachman's fancy, and he liked to lie in wait by the cottage window in order to catch a glimpse of his sunburned face and his long legs that were covered with black fuzz. Perhaps he might even be able to discover what had made Mute Baylin stop talking. Nachman longed to hear some of the things that he had read in his books and said to the girls, but Mute Baylin never spoke. On principle. Not to anyone.

His counterpart in the neighborhood was Blind Koppel, who never stopped talking for a minute, not even when he was laboring along by himself in the heat of day with a basket full of rotten fruit and vegetable peels in one hand and his lemonwood cane in the other. Mute Baylin wasn't really mute, and Blind Koppel wasn't really blind except in one eye. Strangely enough, though, the eye that was blind, which was covered by a bluish cataract, was more open and visible than the eye that could see. Koppel talked about one thing only, the Messiah. The Messiah, he said, a glint in his blind eye, should already have come. There was no doubting it, and even a blind man (Nachman's father quoted these words mockingly when he repeated them to his friends) could tell that this was the meaning of the great wars of the Russians against the Japanese, the English and French against the Germans, the Japanese against the Chinese, and now of Hitler, might he rot, against the Jews. Nachman's father mocked Koppel, but he couldn't resist debating with him anyway. Why should the Messiah have waited to come until now, he teased, instead of after the expulsion of the Jews from Spain? Why not after Chmielnicki's massacres in Poland? Why not after the pogroms in Russia? Koppel had an answer to every question, and Nachman's father challenged every answer. Koppel said that the impious Zionists were holding the Messiah up, to which Nachman's father replied that every Jew was his own Messiah. This made Koppel lose his temper, so that he spit into the yard, brandished his lemonwood stick, and departed. In the evenings his father would sit with Uncle Rifael and their partner Kravitz and mimic Koppel's speech and even the look in his blind eye. Perhaps Koppel was the prophet Elijah, the Messiah's herald, he would say, and the three of them would burst into laughter that made Nachman uneasy. A *meshugener*, said Uncle Rifael, a crazy one, and Nachman's mother remarked, "He may be blind and he may be crazy, but if he really expects the Messiah any day, what does he need all that money for? He has a house. He owns land. Everyone knows that he owns houses in Tel Aviv too, and that he's such a tightwad that he walks all the way there on foot when he has to go once a month to collect the rent. And he hangs around the market all day long looking for rotten fruits and vegetables. Who can believe that a person like that expects the Messiah to come at any moment?"

Nachman wasn't so sure. Every day when they recited the morning service in the Yavneh School they came to a part that said, "And even if he lingers I will surely wait for him to come every day," and in the *Yigdal* prayer too they sang, "May He send His Messiah at the end of days." So who was to say? Nachman knew that his father rarely bothered to go to synagogue on the Sabbath anymore. He hardly ever prayed with phylacteries in the morning, he shaved his cheeks clean with an ordinary razor, and he went about bareheaded after changing clothes when he came home from work. No, Nachman wasn't so smug about Koppel's white eye or the lemonwood cane in his hand. Just as he wasn't really so blind, who could be sure that he wasn't really so mad?

This was the cloth. The center was still the little market,

but its colorful threads reached as far at one end as the house of old man Becker, who stamped his boots and guzzled fire-water and sang, "Tum-ta-rarum," and at the other end to where the Berkovitzes from Romania lived in the abandoned packinghouse beyond the dry creek where the orange groves began. Until recently the creek had marked the end of the world, like the legendary river Sambatyon. There the English had fought against the Turks, and who knew how many corpses were buried in the sandy red loam along its banks. After every heavy rain that coursed down its bed, the children went out to hunt for war trophies. Nachman himself once found a rusty helmet and salvaged it at great peril from the slippery mud. The grown-ups who inspected it noted the bullet mark and pronounced that its bearer, an English soldier, must have spilled out his brains at this spot. They also found bits of shrapnel, military buttons, and other indisputable evidence that here, at the end of the world, on this river Sambatyon, the great battle between the English and the Turks had indeed taken place. Here the children of the little market went to war too, some firing cannons, others riding horseback or advancing with drawn sword. When they weren't fighting, they would descend to the creek bed to search through the refuse there, under the piles of rubbish, the old rags, the rusted scrap iron, and the fresh mud.

Two eerie experiences, though, frightened Nachman. In the display window of the movie house he had seen pictures from the film that Ruzha and Volush had gone to see. Children were not allowed in, but from these scenes and Ruzha's descriptions Nachman was able to imagine the vast cemetery under whose rows of crosses lay the innumerable soldiers, thousands upon thousands of them. Suddenly the graves opened and the soldiers emerged—the dead, the lame, the amputees, the blind—and began to advance in the darkness toward the audience. Ruzha had also told him about the speeches against war that she had heard at the Workers Club, and she had even recited several lines that stuck in Nachman's memory: "O *the boots, boots, boots! They rise and fall and rise,* O *the boots. . . .*"

The dry creek. The movie. *The Great Madness*. (Yes, he had read it, his father's strict ban notwithstanding.) And Feyvl Tuvim, who was swept with his horse and bread wagon into the creek. Nachman knew Tuvim's bakery well because he went there practically every day, cutting through Todros Chupchik's yard, to buy fresh bread for his father's lunch and a hot *pita* for himself. Sometimes he went just to sit in the bakery and see how the bread was made, how two bags of flour were first emptied into a deep trough on which water was poured from a bucket, how the great lumps of dough were kneaded like cement with wooden implements and bare hands, how the long breads were next laid in rows on shelves sprinkled with flour, and how each was slashed with a sharp knife in three places and dashed with cumin or poppyseed. There were round loaves too, and flat *pitas*, and rolls. Best of all were the braided Sabbath hallahs, which were woven with marvelous dexterity, braid after braid, and smeared with a feather brush that had been dipped in a deep bowl of egg yolks. Even better were the High Holy Day hallahs, which were not braided at all but kneaded into a floury sausage and then rolled thinner and thinner and then coiled into a round tower. Nachman liked to watch the bread being made and even more, being baked. The mouth of the oven was narrow and long. At one time it had been heated with coal and wood, but now a pipe brought oil from a can out in the yard and spit a long, sibilant tongue of fire deep into the oven. Only when the oven was hot enough did Tuvim arrange the loaves on a long baker's shovel and slide them inside. As soft and white as paste when they went in, they emerged a golden brown, neither burned nor doughy but perfectly done.

All this was the job of big Tuvim, whom everyone called Shmiel. His entire world was the bakery, where he spent all hours of the day and night, so that Nachman's mother dismissed him with the remark that he was a workhorse who was good for nothing but baking bread. The business end was run by his younger brother Feyvl, whose one leg was shorter than the other, which made him rock back and forth when he walked. Feyvl distributed the bread in his covered wagon, purchased the flour, and kept all the accounts. If Shmiel was asked anything that did not bear directly on the nature of his bread, he referred the questioner to his younger brother. As far as Nachman was concerned, Shmiel was a good-natured fellow who let him sit in the bakery and watch whatever he wished, while Feyvl was a meany whose appearance on the premises made him slip immediately away. Though he had begged him many a time, Feyvl refused to let him ride with him in his wagon, and Nachman cursed him roundly for this and imagined how it would be if his horse were to limp and rock back and forth on short legs like Feyvl himself.

The accident happened that winter. It had rained without letup for an entire week, and the creek was a foaming river. Feyvl had actually been warned, so the story was still being told years after the calamity, not to drive his wagon across the wet wooden footbridge, but he was a stubborn soul. Nachman imagined him sitting in the driver's seat, a sack over his head to protect him from the furious rain, while his horse struggled slowly along the water-soaked, muddy path, dragging the wagon full of hot bread. The horse saw the water pouring down the creek and dug its heels into the mud, but Feyvl whipped it on and forced it up onto the bridge. Suddenly one hoof slid on the slippery boards. The horse keeled over on one side and struggled to right itself, but its feet lost their grip and sent it crashing into the bridge's shaky railing, which broke under the weight, so that it plunged over the side and pulled the wagon full of hot bread after it into the raging torrent. Perhaps Feyvl tried to leap from the wagon, but his short foot made him lose his balance and he caught himself in the reins and toppled into the water.

Feyvl was never seen again, and there was no repressing

thereafter the sensational news that he and his horse had died in the creek, in that stormy Sambatyon at the end of the world where the Turks and the British had fought. From then on Nachman had kept away from the bakery and from Tuvim's yard, as though the whole incident could thereby be forgotten or never have taken place. The little market was never the same again.

Nachman now clearly saw the embroidered pattern and yet it kept changing all the time. New electric poles were going up. Roads were being paved with asphalt. And with the roads, everyone suddenly started to talk about the boundary of his dunam. Who gave anyone permission, people wanted to know, to take from their dunam to make a road for all the world to use? To put an end to such a state of affairs everyone now hurried to fence in his property. And not just with a few eucalyptus stakes from which two or three lines of barbed wire were strung, but with real fences that had concrete foundations and metal posts and wires stretched between them and iron gates through which you went in and out.

Ruzha finished the pattern she'd been working on and took a new piece of cloth as stiff as cardboard on which a new picture was outlined, but before she had made up her mind what color threads to use, along came Volush and invited her to go with him to the Orient Fair in Tel Aviv. Even though she had already promised Nachman that she would take him one day, she accepted Volush's offer. Nachman stalked out, and she let him go without a word of apology, as though she had never promised in the first place. He walked to the back of the yard with tears in his eyes and sat down behind the shower on half a cinder block, biting his lips with chagrin. He didn't even answer when he heard her clear voice call his name in her funny accent, in which every "*ch*" resembled an "*h*." *Now* she remembered! Now she would suggest that he tag along after them, while they yacked away in Polish all evening long, *pabchshch* and *vatshchy kecham*. He wanted no part of Ruzha and her embroidery and her dresses with their pleats and lace and fancy bows. She had lived in their house long enough. Why didn't she marry Volush already and move to Tel Aviv? He would have gone to the bakery now, but it was off limits. He would have gone to Arele Holzberg's, but he didn't want to cut through Chupchik's yard. He would have taken a book and read, but he didn't feel like returning to the cottage. Ruzha was nearing the shower and would discover him in another minute. He ran along the row of bitter orange plants to the end of their dunam, slipped between the fence's two black wires, and sped down the path between the bakery and Chupchik's house to the street leading to the creek.

It may have been the last time he took that route, for the battle of the fences was already in the air, though Nachman had no way of knowing.

21 | The great fence feud

Chupchik's property bordered Tuvim's bakery on one side and the Saubers' land on the other, while its far end came up against the end of the Shpieglers' dunam. To keep off the stray cattle that grazed in the empty lots, Nachman's father had stretched three lines of barbed wire between eucalyptus stakes, though this hadn't prevented the neighbors from cutting freely back and forth across their yard. Not the Saubers, though, who like typical German Jews had gone and put up a high fence of wire netting which they attached to metal posts set in cement. When their fence was finished, a strange thing was revealed: the Saubers' corner post did not stand flush with the fence between the Chupchiks and the Shpieglers. The Saubers' dunam, it turned out, was two meters longer than the Chupchiks'.

"I saw right away that there'd be trouble," said Nachman's father looking back. "I was sure that Chupchik would think that I'd stolen the two meters from him. I even thought of going to show him the deed so as to erase all doubt from his mind, but since he kept quiet about it, and their dunam was covered with thorns anyway, I told myself that perhaps

I was suspecting him unfairly. On the other hand," he continued, "it was hard to believe that he would simply accept the fact that his dunam was shorter than Sauber's. I knew there'd be trouble."

And in fact, no sooner had Nachman quarreled with Todros than the fence feud began.

Todros was an albino. His pinkish skin was allergic to the sun and his eyesight was poor. Todros kept away from the other children in the neighborhood because he was afraid they might grab his glasses, without which he was as blind as a mole, or poke fun at his white hair and pink skin. Nachman had visited Todros's house a number of times, mainly to look at the picture that hung on the wall, but also to listen to Todros's stories, which were all big fibs. But it was hard to be friends with Todros. Try borrowing a book from him, and he would remind you that yesterday you hadn't waited for him and had gone off with Arele Holzberg instead. Try looking at the picture, and he would make you promise first that you would stay with him all afternoon and not run down to the creek. And as if that wasn't enough, Nachman was constantly being bothered by Todros's mother, who had white hair like him and whose pink skin was covered with red blotches as though it were rusting away. Whenever she saw him going to the bakery or cutting through their yard on his way to the creek, she would pester him to play with Todros, and if she didn't see him for several days she would come looking for him in the yard. She was a great nuisance, and Nachman tried to keep away from her and Todros together. He was sick of them both.

Nachman avoided Todros's yard, but when he wanted to go to Arele's, or to play with the children down by the creek, he would wriggle through the barbed wire and walk down the dirt path through the Chupchiks' rather than go the long way around, just as the Chupchiks did with them. One day he ran into Todros blocking his way.

"This is our property."

"Don't be an idiot. I'm just using the path."

"The path is on the property, and the property belongs to us. I'm not going to let you through."

"The path belongs to everyone. You cut through our property too. Get out of my way."

"We do not cut through. Soon my papa's going to put up a fence like Sauber's, and then no one will cut through. Not to the bakery or anywhere else."

"Fine, but now get out of my way."

"I will not."

"Don't be a dope," said Nachman. But Todros, who was generally a great coward, spread his arms and stood his ground.

"It's our property."

"If you don't get out of my way, I'll break your head."

"I'll break your ass."

"At least I don't wear glasses on mine."

"So I'll tell you what your mother has in hers!"

At this point Nachman lost his temper. He charged at Todros, who was standing there with his arms out, grabbed his glasses in one full swoop, and began to run back home.

"Let's see what you are going to do now, you monkey!"

Todros didn't even try chasing him. Instead he headed for home, screaming at the top of his lungs, "Mama, mama, they stole my glasses! Mama!"

Nachman panicked and ran back after Todros to return them, but Todros either didn't hear him or pretended not to and kept running and wailing for his mother. "Mama, they stole my glasses!"

What was Nachman to do now? He didn't dare go to Todros's mother and give her the eyeglasses back. But he couldn't just leave them in the yard either. He was afraid to go tell his mother what had happened, but he couldn't think of anything else. He went and related, not with the utmost precision, how one thing led to another.

"I wanted to give them back. But he ran away. He went to snitch to his mother."

"What do you mean, you wanted to give them back? What were they doing in your hands in the first place?"

Nachman didn't want to repeat the dirty words and mumbled something vague that incensed his mother even more.

"Go return them immediately before we have a scandal on our hands! Wait a minute, I'll go with you. All I need now is for that pink witch to start up with me."

She hurried outside with the glasses in one hand and Nachman in the other, but Todros's mother was already coming toward them across their land, wobbling on her thin bowlegs, her face the color of raw meat.

"There's the little bastard!" she shouted from afar. "Just you come here and say to me what you said to Todros. So we can all drop dead, can we? You *pisher!* We'll see you all dead first. They must think they're somebody special, these people!"

Nachman's mother, whose fingers had been gripping his wrist like metal tweezers, now gave him a push back toward the cottage.

"Go inside at once, Nachman! Make it snappy. I don't want to see you here now."

From here on Nachman listened to the screams of the two women through open windows, just like the rest of the neighborhood. The eyeglasses were all but forgotten.

"I'll break both his arms if he comes near Todros again!"

"What child would want to come near him? I had to drag him to you each time, against his will and mine."

"Don't you worry! He'll never set foot on our land again, and neither will you. This is the last time he'll steal from us ever!"

"Watch what you say about my son, you witch!"

"Of course he stole! And it doesn't surprise me that he

goes wandering about other people's yards as though they were his own. You set him a good example."

"Take your glasses and get off our property."

"Your property. Tonight you'll move the fence a few meters more and call that yours too. Some people have no shame. And they go around with their heads in the air yet, as though they were somebody special."

"Get off our property before I sweep you off with a broom, you filthy bitch!"

"Even Lysol can't clean out your mouth!"

"Get off our land!"

"I'm standing on the land you stole from us!"

They stood there shouting insults until the neighbors came out of their houses and persuaded Nachman's mother to go back to her cottage. When his father came home and heard what had happened, he scolded her for her lack of self-control and lectured Nachman for not realizing that Todros was just a pathetic case who quarreled with him because he missed having him come to visit. He refused to listen even when Nachman's mother told him what Todros's mother had said about the land, that they had stolen from the Chupchiks' dunam. "Chupchik is a decent fellow," he said, "and I'll go over there now and make peace. We're neighbors, after all, and not Polish peasants who kill one another for a penny."

Nachman never found out what Todros's father and his own father said to each other, but his father was shaking with anger when he returned, and it was clear that things had passed the point of reconciliation. He went over to Nachman's bed and said in a choked voice, "Don't ever let me catch you stepping on those yellow scorpions' land again. Did you ever hear of such a thing, Leah? I deliberately moved the marker to steal two meters from them!"

"Now do you finally see?" said his mother. "Mark my words, our troubles are just beginning!"

And indeed, before many days had gone by, Chupchik, who already had one corner of a fence made to order—the corner belonging to the Saubers—unloaded a wagon of fence posts and wire netting at the end of his land. Nachman's mother told his father about it that evening, and added that the troubles were beginning even sooner than she had expected. "I'm willing to bet," she said, "that he'll start putting up a fence as soon as you leave for work tomorrow."

"There's nothing to worry about," answered his father. "We're in the land registry, and I'll call the police if he dares dig a single hole."

"I don't want any police," said his mother. "I just want to make sure they keep off our land."

"Then what do you want to do?" asked his father.

"I want you to stay home tomorrow," said his mother.

"And suppose he doesn't try tomorrow, but the day or week after, what then? Do you expect me to stay home all the time guarding our dunam? The one way to teach them a lesson is to call the police."

"What kind of nonsense are you talking? You know perfectly well that in the end you won't permit some English or Arab judge to decide between you. That's just what the roughneck is counting on."

His mother's hunch proved correct. His father rose early the next morning as usual, and she with him. He put on his work clothes while she packed his lunch basket, but he didn't leave for work. It was already past seven-thirty, and the two of them kept prodding Nachman to start out for school, for he too had delayed his departure so as not to miss the battle that was about to break out. He was already on the front step and had turned back for one last look when he spied Chupchik standing in their yard with a Yemenite worker, who had a hoe slung over his shoulder. "Here they are!" he cried out. His father and mother rushed outside, and the great fence feud was underway.

"I'm asking you for the last time, before I call the police, to get off our land." His father's voice shook and his face turned ash gray.

"I'm standing on my own land, and I'm running the fence straight from Sauber's corner. Start digging," said Chupchik to the Yemenite, pointing at a small cleared path among the thorns.

Nachman's father took a step forward and planted his foot on the path.

"I'm warning you, get off our dunam."

"How can you be such a blockhead?" Chupchik suddenly bellowed. "How can you expect anyone to believe that my dunam is shorter than Sauber's? It's me who'll call the police if you don't let us work!"

"I don't give a damn about Sauber. This is my dunam, and you're going to get off it right now!"

"Does your dunam have some kind of special color that you're so sure where it ends?"

"There's a marker in the corner of the lot that was put there by the government surveyor."

"Markers can be moved."

"Chupchik! Are you trying to tell me that I moved the marker? Deliberately?"

"I don't know anything about markers. Sauber has a dunam and so do I. My property ends exactly where his does. And I want a fence there. I've hired a worker, I'm paying him for the day, and I want him to begin."

All this while the Yemenite had stood leaning to one side against a stake of the old fence, twirling an earlock, sniffing tobacco, and taking care not to get involved. Now Chupchik ordered him to start digging the post holes, but each time he lifted his hoe Nachman's father got in the way. All of a sudden Chupchik grabbed the hoe from his hands and drove it once into the dry, sandy earth.

"I'm warning you, Chupchik! Force will get you nowhere. Let's ask the surveyor's office to come. They'll tell us who's trying to take what from whom."

"I've hired a man and he's going to begin working. As far as I'm concerned, the boundary is Sauber's corner post."

Meanwhile the noise of the argument had brought Nachman's mother and Chupchik's wife running too. A few neighbors came out into their yards and onto the path to listen. A great cry went up as Chupchik lifted the hoe again and Nachman's father, as gray as dust, planted himself in his way.

"Shalom, you're dealing with a murderer!" yelled Nachman's mother. She held on to him with both hands and began pulling him back to their yard.

"Thieves!" screamed Chupchik's pink wife from behind her husband's back. "They steal our land and then they cry murder. Tell the Yemenite to start digging."

"Just try!" said Nachman's father.

"I will!" said Chupchik. He took two steps forward, lifted the hoe, which glittered brightly in the morning sunshine, and was about to bring it down when Nachman's father sprang directly under the blade. The two women screamed at each other as though they were pulling hair. The neighbors came pouring into the two yards, the five tall Saubers, Mute Baylin and his mother, Sharoni the teacher's wife, even Shmiel Tuvim, who emerged from the bakery in his white baker's pants and an undershirt, his fingers sticky with dough. They physically had to force the two men back and apart. Then they tried to persuade them to arrive at some compromise—to go to the rabbi, or to pick an arbitrator acceptable to both sides, or to let the local engineer decide.

Nachman never found out what Chupchik had to say about this, but he heard his father's reaction more than once, for he repeated it each time in a trembling voice to whoever wanted to hear, the veins in his sunburned forehead swelling to form a grid over his spreading bald spot, the glasses of tea rattling in their saucers as he banged his fist on the little porch table and shouted:

"It's not a question of a meter of land! If that yellow scorpion can vilify me like that in public, if he can accuse me—the blackguard!—of moving the marker onto his property, then there's no room left for compromise or conciliation.

Let them look up the records, I say. There are deeds, there are subdivisions, let an Arab judge decide. If he rules that I moved the marker not two meters, but one millimeter, I promise to give five pounds over and above the court costs to the Jewish National Fund. It's too late for arbitration. If the land is mine, I want all of it, down to the last clod of dirt. The idiot. That pink witch drips poison in his ear, and he dances like a trained bear!"

But oaths and vows were one thing and the end of the affair another. Through the good offices of the neighbors it was agreed that Chupchik should build his fence in the middle, halfway between the metal marker and Sauber's fence post. Just so he could go on feuding, however, he insisted on paying for it by himself.

Thus the battle of the fences was settled, but for Nachman it had far-reaching results. The litle market was no longer a single open space and had now become a series of fenced-off yards, each with a gate of its own. All the empty fields were being parceled into lots, with houses on each. Some lots had been bought many years ago by people who had left no heirs, gone off to Australia or America, or had never come to Palestine in the first place. Whoever had built even a shack on such property and held it for ten years could now become its legal owner. Some of these properties were contested by a number of a settlers, and every contest raised one more fence. Not only did Nachman's legs rarely take him to the little market any more—his heart too now felt a stranger there.

22 | The cork helmet

Nachman was now a big boy, about to enter the fifth grade. Books were his closest friends, in addition, of course, to Arele Holzberg, whose cottage was always full of wonderful boys and girls playing interesting games. And there was Ehud Karniel too, whose father was an official in the Anglo-Palestine Bank and who wrote for the newspapers and attended the same Sabbath prayer group as Nachman's father. Nachman felt akin to Ehud, who was a voracious reader like himself and had an untold treasure hidden away in his room, an assortment of those forbidden penny novels: the adventures of the Tel Aviv detective David Tidhar, the Twentieth Century Series on Inspector Almog, as well as the loves and sufferings of *Sabina, Regina,* and *The Shanghaied Beauty of Tel Aviv.* All this drew Nachman to Ehud's house, but most attractive of all was the house itself, which was right next to the Yavneh School. To him it looked like an old mansion full of rooms (three or even four in all) and the kind of furniture they had at Balfour's home, except that there also was a huge bookcase, and Ehud and his older brother, who was already in high school, had a room of their own. Nachman liked to visit Ehud, but he was even fonder of Arele's cottage across the creek, with its off-green plywood walls, its whispering Lux lamp that cast a sharp, white light, its air of crowded warmth, the presence of Arele's sisters, the oldest of whom was already in her last year of school.

Nachman was now discovering a world of hidden things, forbidden words, concealed parts of the body, secrets that were best left to silence and the dark. Yavneh was an all-boys' school. Across the street from it, in the same building as Bluma's kindergarten—which still shone out from the darkness of his pre-Talmud Torah days—was the girls' school. The boys and girls went to school and came home in separate groups, studied separately, played in separate yards. Girls were silly geese, and it was best to keep away from them and make sure you weren't like them because the worst that could happen to one was the insult, "You run like a girl, you throw like a girl, you jump like a girl." Girls were for pushing, for bombarding with acorns, for pulling braids. Nachman was constantly reminded of all this because his parents' friends seemed to think that they were obliged to pet him constantly and tell him what a nice child he was, what smooth skin he had, what lovely eyes and long lashes and fine eyebrows and a delicate nose. They could all go to hell with such compliments. In fact he wished he had a face covered with acne, like Ozer Lichtig.

Yet he still felt drawn to Arele's home, even to Arele's sisters and their girlfriends. There was that special air to the games they played, to the songs they sang together and the tablecloths they embroidered, even if they weren't as pretty as Ruzha's. Arele's cottage was swarming with children and his mother's belly was swollen again, which meant they would soon be four. Nachman felt terribly lonely all by himself at home. Why didn't his mother have more children, he kept wondering. Everyone had brothers and sisters. He alone was an only child, which was almost as bad as being a girl. In the past he had annoyed his mother with questions about it, but now he was ashamed to, because at home no one talked or asked about such things, and if he did, he would get no answer.

It was different at Arele Holzberg's, whose mother was about to give birth to another child and whose home was full of grown girls who whispered to each other about everything. There was nothing that couldn't be said or done there. Nachman, for example, was afraid of dogs, just like his father, but Arele had a huge dog for which the children had built a kennel out of a soap crate, and they played and raced with it and even stuck their fingers into its mouth without fear of its sharp fangs. That wasn't the only thing, either.

Even though he was a member of Nachman's father's prayer group, Arele's father did things for which in the time of the Temple and the Sanhedrin you could have been punished by the four capital deaths—stoning, burning, choking, and hanging—and for which God now punished you by taking years off your life. When a neighbor's water pipe had sprung a leak one Sabbath, he himself had seen how Arele's father had taken a wrench and some flaxen thread and fixed it. He couldn't have let the water flow all day and cause a flood, he explained, but neither could he have turned off the central stopcock and deprived the whole neighborhood of water until Sunday. Lightning wouldn't strike him dead because of it.

Nachman was full of vague stirrings and muffled desires and felt the need to put himself to new tests all the time. None of the thrills of the little market gave him pleasure any more, unless perhaps it was sneaking through the fences across Chupchik's and Mute Baylin's yards and cutting across Tuvim's property above the dry creek to get to Arele Holzberg's. The creek, which had once been the end of the world, the fearful Sambatyon where the British and Turks had fought and in whose raging waters Feyvl Tuvim had drowned with his horse, was now nothing more than a narrow gulley that was rapidly filling up with refuse dumped by the garbage cart.

What was so special about it? Only the walk at night to Arele's and back was still an adventure that made Nachman's heart beat faster and put his courage to the test.

He hadn't forgiven Ruzha for breaking her promise to take him to the fair and going with Volush instead. From that day on, Nachman snubbed her and all her attempts to make up. Until then her presence had given the cottage a kind of permanently festive air: her beauty, her taste in nice clothes, the special knack she had for making you feel good, the way she had decorated the enclosed porch with a chest made of two orange crates covered with an embroidered cloth, colorful flowerpots, and a funny picture that hung on the wall, the magic in her fingertips (which were now, like her arms and legs, all cut up from pruning in the orange groves) whose every stitch coaxed something new and wondrous to behold out of invisibility, the fine fragrance that she sprayed on her neck when she emerged from the shower at night. Everything about her had been dear to Nachman. She alone had formed a living link between the world of books and the world of people he knew. Never to have had a brother or a sister, and suddenly—a sister like this! His head had been full of forbidden imaginings, and then this girl had appeared, whose every smile and touch had transformed him into a different person. Only now that she had taken up with that boastful babbler Volush, their relative from Poland, whom she had gone to the fair with and was going to marry, he wanted nothing more to do with her.

Then one day Ruzha moved out, and with her went her clothes, her hats, her embroidery, the fine smell of her perfume, and her nightly ritual of putting on fresh clothes upon emerging from the shower when Nachman, hidden in a corner, would throw stolen glances at the soft light around her forbidden body. Ruzha now lived in Tel Aviv, and all this was a thing of the past. She knew that Nachman had never forgiven her, that she was no longer the same for him, and she tried to win him back, but he rebuffed all her smiles, refused to let her hug him or sing him funny Polish songs, and wouldn't talk to her at all. Whenever she came to visit, he disappeared from the house.

Until one day she brought him a helmet for a present and bygones were suddenly bygones.

Nachman had always longed for a cork hat, the kind worn by that race of beautiful, heroic, legendary people. The whole world was crazy about such hats, which were called jungle helmets, or tropical helmets, or simply helmets for short. Some were very thin and had brims that widened at the back and slanted down over the eyes like those worn by the British policemen, while others were thicker with shorter brims that were rounded equally in front and in back. There were white helmets and gray ones and khaki ones. What they all shared in common was the thin leather band that was generally attached to the inside of the brim and could be pulled down over the chin to keep the helmet firmly in place, the flattened button on the top, and the cloth surface that could be refurbished with the kind of chalkstone that was used to whiten sneakers. It was a thing of beauty, a helmet, and it could change one completely, whether it was khaki like a soldier's, blue like a policeman's, or glittering white like old Adon Mendelevitch's, who wore it all summer long with his white suit and white shoes. And then there was the helmet Shirley Temple wore in the movies in India. With a helmet like that you could cross Africa like Stanley and Livingstone or Tarzan's father, or journey to Tibet like Sven Hedin. Helmets were the rage that summer, but each time Nachman passed the hat store with a longing gaze, one look from his mother was enough to keep him from raising the subject.

And then one day Ruzha arrived with a large paper bag bearing a picture of a hat. She gave it to Nachman and kissed him on the lips. A helmet. Of heavy cork. Khaki. Nachman ran to put it on in front of the mirror. How fabulous it looked! What a new face it gave him, what a look of daring in his narrowed eyes and firm lips! His parents scolded Ruzha for her extravagance instead of thanking her for the present. Nachman removed the hat and placed it on the table, where he kept it under his eyes. He waited patiently for the argument to end because he knew perfectly well that Ruzha was not going to take the helmet back to Tel Aviv. How pretty she seemed to him then in her white hat with its broad, blue-and-red striped silk ribbon, her short hair that fell barely over her ears, her silk kerchief that was tied under the collar of her white dress and hung limply over her breast. Her delicate fragrance bore into his nostrils, and he was ready to forgive her all.

The helmet was his, and he wanted to put it on and run straight to Arele Holzberg's, who didn't have anything like it. Even in Ehud Karniel's house it would be nothing to be ashamed of. If only his mother let him wear it to school, he would be a king there. But she didn't. Such a hat, she insisted, belonged in a paper bag in the wardrobe. It wasn't for wearing to school or playing with in the streets. It picked up dirt, the cork would break, and the cloth cover would tear at once if he so much as caught it on wire or thorn. Only when he stepped out with his parents in his Sabbath best was he to be allowed to wear it.

But that was only at first. Little by little Nachman convinced his mother that the hat could be worn on weekdays too, even if he were just going to Guberman's dairy, or to Tuvim's bakery, or out to play in the yard. He felt twice as tall when wearing it and a thousand times braver. He hated so to take it off even when it grew dark that his mother had to ask him whether he was by any chance afraid of moonstroke.

And so one day, with his new hat on his head, he set out for Arele Holzberg's. He was the king there. Everyone asked to try on the helmet, but he refused to let anyone dirty its fresh-smelling khaki with his fingers or leave grease stains from his sweaty hair on the broad band of leather inside. Only Arele and his sisters were allowed to wear it. Before he knew it, it was evening. This wasn't the first time he had had to come home after dark, though he generally tried to avoid it. Yet now, not only did he feel extra brave but also his concern for the hat increased his anxiety so much that he walked as fast as he could, hurrying across the open fields on either side of the creek to reach Tuvim the baker's yard. One might even say that he ran—and fast. The electricity was on in Tuvim's house, staining the darkness around it with light. He would be out of danger once he was there.

Just then, however, a dog howled so loudly that it seemed to Nachman the night itself was barking at him. His hair stood on end and he froze in his tracks, uncertain where the sound had come from. If he stood perfectly still, without moving, perhaps he too would vanish in the dark as though he were invisible. But the bark broke again, stronger and more persistent, as though the throat of the night had split open. Nachman ran toward the safety of the light, just like in the story he'd read about the boy who made a circle with his stick so the pack of evil wolves racing straight at him through the forest wouldn't be able to cross it. If only he too had a stick, or a stone, or even a clod of earth! Yet there was nothing at his feet but the summery sand and the dark. He ran on, bumped into something hard, and fell, his helmet rolling off his head. He groped for it, found it, picked himself up and ran farther. He was sure now that the dog was after him. It was somewhere right in front of him, yowling terribly. He had to drive it off before it sank its teeth into him and infected him with rabies, like that Russian in *The Story of San Michele* who went mad from wolf bites. Without thinking, as hard as he could, Nachman hurled his helmet straight at the dog. There was silence, as though the animal was gone. He thought of his new helmet and hurried to look for it, groping among the late summer weeds and withered thorns by the side of the path. Thistles pricked at his skin but he continued the search until he found it. Meanwhile, the dog began to bark once more, filling the night with the fearful sound, and he threw the hat at it again, advancing as he did. Another ten steps. And another. The darkness was no longer so thick. He could now make out a patch of light from the bakery. He made another dash. And another. And another. Now he was at the bakery's lighted front, and the dog was no longer barking, having vanished back into the night as though it had never been there.

He held his helmet, his elegant hero's hat that Ruzha had given him, in one hand. The cork was broken and its cover completely crushed. Done for. He no longer had a helmet and never would. He was furious at himself, at his fear, at the whole little market. He felt a lump like a large pit in his throat. He wished he had never gotten the helmet in the first place—the helmet that was supposed to make him brave but turned him into a coward instead. He didn't want to think about Arele, who would laugh at him tomorrow, or about anyone. He slipped through a gap in the barbed wire fence between Tuvim's and Baylin's properties and from there entered his own yard. If only he could steal straight to bed and pull the cover over his head so that no one would see him. Approaching the cottage, though, he heard his father's voice along with Uncle Rifael's staccato laugh and their partner Kravitz's loud boom. How would he ever face them? How would he go on living without his helmet?

23 | The fortress of yea and nay

Nachman mourned for his ruined helmet. Yet though the elegant cork hat was lost forever, his mourning was short-lived. That year, his third in the Yavneh School, was a marvelous one at home, and he was to recall it later as one long, endless holiday. Their cottage now had black tarpaper on the outside and concrete walls within, and the far end of their yard was no longer on the route of that stenchy wagon—with the large barrel that made everyone hold his nose when it passed; there was no need to empty the pit behind their toilet anymore because they now had a septic pit, which collected soapy water from the kitchen and the shower, and which was connected by a thick clay pipe to the shining toilet seat whose waters were flushed by a tug on the Niagara chain. All these years his parents had worn their good clothes from Poland on Sabbaths and holidays, turning and trimming and mending them again and again, but now Ruzha—who had come especially for several days from Tel Aviv—sewed his mother a new Sabbath dress and a brown winter coat, while his father, who never really wore a suit except on winter Saturdays, was planning to buy a new one if only the times got no worse.

Even now no one ever said that the times were good. If only they got no worse, they said. There was no shortage of work, praise God, and if the plastering team of his father, Uncle Rifael, and Kravitz had ten hands apiece they still could not have kept up with everyone's demand that they and they alone should do the walls. "Uncle Rifael sometimes scolds me because I'm too exacting on the job," said Nachman's father good-naturedly, "but I'm willing to make a few piasters less a day in order to keep our good name. You wouldn't find a single bump in any of our walls if you checked them with a level, or a single mark of putty, or a corner that isn't rounded right. That's why we're in such demand, so that in the Histadrut they think that we must be working for cutthroat wages. I can't remember when we last had to go looking for work. If only nothing bad comes from that war in Ethiopia, and the Arabs don't go on the rampage again because of all the Jews who are coming here now. Otherwise, praise God, I can't complain."

Regarding the Arabs, his father was doubly concerned. Their bitter orange and sweet lemon nursery was now a handsome source of income too. They had dug a few large rows, which they banked with boards and covered with large panes of glass. These they weeded carefully and spread with a special fertilizer. When the citrus season came around, they bought fruit by the sackful, squeezed it well, collected the seeds, washed them, laid them out on wet strips of cloth to soak up water, and set them out in rows the next day. It was demanding work because the young sprouts were sensitive to pests and cold. On frosty nights they covered the glass roofs with sacks. The sprouts were carefully thinned, and when those remaining were big and strong enough, they were cautiously dug up so as not to harm their thin roots, wrapped in wet sacks to prevent them from drying out, and planted in the raised rows at the end of the yard by sticking a kind of thick, hollow pencil of iron into the ground and pointing the roots through the round hole, making sure they were straight.

Only then would the saplings reach the right height for the orange growers to buy them. This past year they had sold twenty-eight pounds' worth to Arab customers alone. Praise God.

Everyday seemed like a holiday, though his father worked so hard that his skin was black from the sun and his hands had calluses that were as hard as shoe leather and were inflamed by the plaster and full of pus. A holiday, though besides doing all the housework his mother was busy with the nursery and the vegetables and the flowers they had planted beneath the cottage windows. They were managing to meet all their payments on the property and house, and next year, if only the times got no worse, his mother would finally get to see her old dream of visiting his grandmother in Poland come true. The mention of it no longer brought tears to her eyes but was the occasion of a detailed plan that she had carefully worked out: how they would travel, whom they would visit, and how much time they would spend with each. And most important of all, at what time of year they would go. If only it were possible, she would like to go for Passover and stay through the summer. Passover always came out in *Kwieczien,* the month of flowers. No words could describe how beautiful Poland was in this month and in the month of May. Yes, it was like when the oranges bloomed here, but there everything flowered at once—the buds that had been under snow all winter long, the apple, plum, and peach orchards, everything. In Palestine there was no spring at all. And the summer! To have one Polish summer away from the Palestinian heat! To stay in the woods, or to go to the mountains or the sea, to Danzig. The family would be so happy to see them it wouldn't know what to do for them first. "I'll go next summer. If only the times get no worse."

Nachman was in fifth grade now, and his father had a dream too, not for the coming summer but for the school year that followed. He'd changed so drastically ever since he'd become a plasterer that he no longer seemed the same person concealed in the fastness of Nachman's memory. He worked hard and was always so tired that he slept till all hours on Saturday mornings, but he was continually in good spirits and talked and joked a great deal. When friends or family didn't come to visit their cottage, they went out to visit friends. Not just the Beckers or Uncle Rifael. Sharoni the teacher, who lived near the dairy, was now his father's best friend, and they liked to argue with each other about books, about Hitler, about the Arabs, about the Russians. "I," said his father, "had a chance to see those Bolsheviks, those heirs of the Cossacks, over there. It's not to them or to our Jewish Bolsheviks here that I'll go to learn about socialism. Amos and Isaiah are enough for me. It's they who should be on the banner of the Hebrew workingman. But on the other hand, when I see those Orthodox hypocrites with their dodges and their simony, when I think of what Rabbi Kutter did to Mister and Missus Blackman, the whole thing makes me so nauseous that I don't wany any part of it either. I'll go my own private way, I'll earn my living by the sweat of my brow and bring up my son to be a proud, loyal Jew.

"To tell you the truth, it's harder for someone like me than it is for my brother Rifael. He's simply gone and changed one rabbi for another, so that now he believes whatever's written in the party newspaper just like my oldest brother Yitzhak-Hirsh believes in the Rabbi of Czestochowa. I myself don't have a rabbi at all, and the God I believe in doesn't need middlemen, because He reveals himself to each of us in a different light. Of course, it has its bad side, but it has its good side too. For the first time in my life I'm my own boss. I may work hard, but I'm earning good money and I can hold my head high. And that's how I want to raise my son too. He's a delicate boy who was badly hurt in the Talmud Torah—God only knows what its effects will be, and whether he won't throw out, in the end, the baby with the bathwater, like Rifael. But the Yavneh School isn't the right place for him either. It all depends on where you plant a child, in what soil, how well you weed around him to give his roots air, if you don't give him too little water, or, for that matter, too much, if you fertilize him just right. After all, it is during childhood that one's nature is formed. No, I've made up my mind: if only we can afford it, if the times get no worse, we'll send Nachman to the new private high school that's just opened here. The most important thing is for him to get a good education and not become a *chnyok*—a philistine—so that when he grows up he can decide for himself. I hope that he'll be more or less of a good Jew in the end, but the main thing is, he should learn to become a human being."

This news reached Nachman's ears unexpectedly one day while he was lying on the couch by the open window and listening to his father and Adon Sharoni talking in the yard. He had no complaints against the Yavneh School, but he wasn't particularly happy there either. He was in the same class as Todros, but it wasn't because of that, or even because of the many other children from the little market, which he rarely frequented anymore, who were in his class too. Something had changed at home, though Nachman wasn't sure when or how. All their new relatives who had come and kept coming, and who were so different from anyone he had ever known before, had enthralled him completely. They were like Uncle Rifael and Tsipoyrele, but younger and gayer. They wore short pants and rode bicycles and were called *halutzim*—pioneers. They laughed in loud voices and sang new songs from the radio and the movies.

Ever since he could remember, Nachman's life had moved among taken-for-granteds. Just as day was day and night was night, so meat meals were meat meals and milk meals were milk meals. Just as you didn't go out without your pants on, so you didn't go out without a hat on. Just as no one denied that the air existed because it couldn't be seen, so God existed too. Milk plates weren't just kept apart from meat plates but actually looked and tasted different. It was impossible to conceive of pouring a meat soup into the heavy, chipped bowl from which Nachman ate his semolina, his Quaker Oats, and his milk-and-noodle soup. Once a meat knife had mistakenly found its way to the dinner table and—God in heaven only knew how!—some milk had spilled on it. Nachman's mother was visibly shaken and didn't calm down until his father had taken the knife and thrust it up to its hilt into the moist ground by the water faucet in the backyard. Only after it had spent the night there would it be kosher again and fit for meat dishes.

So it was too with the complete set of dishes, bowls, pots, knives, forks, and spoons, which was packed away all year long in the large wicker trunk, wrapped in last year's newspapers, where it wasn't to be touched from one Passover to the next, for if the least bit of leavened food should fall on it, it couldn't be used anymore. One crumb of bread could ruin the entire Passover. Eating bareheaded was another sinful thing. Only a *goy* would think of gobbling down a slice of bread without first covering his head, washing his hands, and saying a blessing, or without reciting the grace after meals when he was done. Wearing a fringed undershawl was another thing. Or praying. Or not walking too far on the Sabbath. Or not picking berries from the mulberry tree on the Sabbath, or not drawing, even if it was just with a stick in the sand. Not on the Sabbath.

These were the taken-for-granteds, the things you would no sooner do than stick your hand in a fire. But there were more complicated things too. It was a sin to ride your bicycle on the Sabbath, but that didn't mean it was good just not to ride it. It just wasn't counted against you. To be counted for you, it wasn't enough not to sin. You had to do all kinds of other things too. You had to try especially hard like the great saints who not only did good deeds but also were as humble in spirit as though they did bad ones. And you couldn't cheat or get away with anything either, because God's notebook was always open and everything was written down there. Not just what you did but what you thought too. In school they were studying Jewish law, and their teacher had told them about a book called the *Shulhan Arukh.* The boys in class knew (there was nothing they didn't know) that all kinds of things you weren't supposed to talk about were written in the *Shulhan Arukh*. Just like you weren't supposed to talk about Rahab the *zonah*—the harlot—in the Book of Joshua. Their teacher had explained that Rahab sold food because the word *zonah* came from *zun*, to feed, but the children all giggled because they knew it meant something else, though Nachman didn't really understand why the two spies had spent the night with her in Jericho. You weren't supposed to think about it. And you weren't supposed to think about what he and Arele Holzberg had read in the *Shulhan Arukh* on the subject of men and women in bed with each other, either. It was a sin.

The sins and good deeds kept adding up, and when somebody died, his sins were put in one scale and his good deeds in another. If the sins were heavier he went to hell, and if the good deeds were heavier, he went to heaven, and if each weighed the same, his soul was sentenced to wander forever between them, like in the Hanukkah play they had seen. There were some particularly bad sins too, which in the days of the Temple had been punished by burning, stoning, hanging, and choking. Like the man in the Bible who gathered wood on the Sabbath. Or like Achan, who stole from the forbidden loot of war. And there was punishment by an early death too, which came straight from God. Everything came from God. A man couldn't lift his finger on earth unless it was first decided in heaven. When Feyvl Tuvim drowned in the creek, there must have been a reason for it, but Nachman was scared to think about it because God could read all thoughts. It was like eating in the dark with your head uncovered. Nachman was sure that God could see even better in the dark than in the light.

And yet cracks were beginning to show in this taken-for-granted world. Little questions had started crawling over its stony surface and eating into it like the ruby-jawed worms in the legend who split the rocks from which the Temple was built. What happened with the boys in the Talmud Torah had been such a worm. Another had been his father's accusations against Rabbi Kutter and the fawning hypocrites like him who trampled on every sacred Jewish ideal.

"Look at what they did to Missus Blackman," said his father with genuine emotion time and again to his friends. "First they robbed her of her last cent, and then they put her in the madhouse. No, that's not what I call Judaism. If I thought for even a single moment that these bearded charlatans were the true representatives of Moses and the prophets, I'd throw it all over in no time. Sometimes I understand now how one can lose all faith."

One could lose all faith. The ruby-jawed worms crawled on over the fortress of yea and nay, of good deeds and sins. A Jew was allowed to shave his beard. He might sometimes skip his morning prayers. He even didn't have to go to the synagogue on the Sabbath because it was just as good to pray at home. To light a fire on the Sabbath was of course a terrible sin, but to ask an Arab to do it for you or to turn on an electric light was just as bad. On the other hand, though, electricity (finally they were to have it installed in their cottage!) was a case apart, for how could the mere flicking of a switch be placed in the category of forbidden work? Nachman had long ago ceased to wear his fringed undershawl beneath his shirt. It wasn't right, his mother had ruled, to make a small boy wear a woolen undershirt in the hot summer, perspire, and develop a rash. His father was still careful to put on a hat when he sat down to eat or looked at a Hebrew book or went outside, but he didn't seem to care at all that Uncle Rifael and Volush and Kravitz ate bareheaded. There was nothing in the Bible itself, he said, about having to wear a hat. True, it was a very long tradition among Jews to wear one, and he for one wasn't going to break it, but it wasn't a horrible sin either if you didn't.

The ruby-jawed worm bit into the hard stone, chipping away at the world of taken-for-granteds. On Saturdays Nachman would stroll out of the orange groves with Arele Holzberg, as far as the new wooden cubes the pickers had recently built, or else go to the Maccabee Sports Club to watch a soccer game. On their way they passed young people watering their small vegetable gardens, riding bicycles, and kicking footballs, to say nothing of actually walking the streets with lighted cigarettes between their lips, profaning the Sabbath in broad daylight. Each of these sinners would have been stoned in the days of the Temple and was sure now to meet an early death. Yet Nachman couldn't bring himself to believe that all of these young, handsome pioneers, these muscular, sunburned workers, these marvelous football players were condemned men and would die young. It didn't make any sense. Was it possible then that not everything that was said to be forbidden was really forbidden?

There were even more serious offenses, which Nachman was forced to witness almost against his will. There was Mute Baylin, for example, who didn't go to synagogue even on the Day of Atonement, when the entire town lay under such a curtain of silence that the prayers of the congregation reached all the way to their cottage. He didn't even go to Kol Nidre. But then again, he was known to be eccentric and slightly mad, though the mystery of his muteness continued to make Nachman wonder. According to his mother it was because of the books he had read. What could he have read in them?

And then there were the Saubers, the four big sons, their father with his protruding paunch and his pipe that never left his mouth, and their mother who was tall too but very thin and whose clear gaze made Nachman think of what his mother used to say of Rabbi Kutter: cold eyes. The whole family, it was said in the little market, was barely Jewish at all. In their appearance, their giant height, their broad shoulders, their burly necks, and the queer German they spoke that was nothing at all like Yiddish—in all of this, said Nachman's mother, there was something definitely *goyish*. You couldn't find a drop of Jewishness in any of them. Nachman's father added that there had been many Germans in his part of Poland who looked exactly the same—they were all as healthy as horses, stuffed themselves with sausage and potatoes, and drank beer as though from a bottomless barrel. Nachman had never seen a *goy* and wasn't sure how one looked. Arabs weren't *goyim*, they were Arabs. Like Abed, who used to live with his children in the Mendelevitches' yard, or the peasants who came with their vegetables and fruits and chickens and eggs to the marketplace on Thursdays, or the rich *effendis* in their white *kaffiyehs* with a black silk cord, their dark, double-breasted jackets worn over long, striped robes and their broad girdles in whose folds they hid the purses from which they paid Nachman's father for the bitter orange saplings. The English too were not like the *goyim* he had read about in books. They were tall, slim policemen with trim mustaches and eyes hidden beneath the brims of their cork hats. A black billy club stuck out from the back pocket of their funny, knee-length pants, their shoes were shiny even through the dust, and they always walked in step. Nachman himself would have liked to be as tall and handsome as a British policeman, with a helmet of cork on his head. They were nothing like the Cossacks in the story *Salvation*, who took little Jewish children far from their homes to force them to be soldiers for the czar and tortured Jews in pogroms, which made Theodor Herzl dream of a Jewish state and his parents leave everything behind in Poland so that the *goyim* wouldn't spit in their faces and call them *zhyd* any more. His mother said that the Saubers were *goyim* too, and even though Nachman knew that this wasn't so, because they had come to live in town as a result of Hitler's persecutions, he still eyed them carefully, as though in hope of discovering what a *goy* really looked like.

That there was at least something *goyish* in them was evident from the fact they ate nonkosher meat. Todros, who lived next to the Saubers, beyond the new fence, swore that he had seen the old woman take a chicken out to their yard, lay it on a wooden log, and chop its head off with one stroke of her cleaver. Todros was a big liar who liked to make things up, yet the story haunted Nachman nevertheless. Nothing was impossible. Once he had heard about a butchershop where camel meat was sold and in books he had read how there were people who liked to eat horsemeat. Ehud's father had stayed in France years ago, before the War, and he too said there were special butcher shops there that sold horse. What manner of people the French must be! Or, pig. In books people always ate pork, and when Nachman mentioned this to Todros, Todros swore by the holy Torah that he himself had seen a baby pig hanging in the Sauber's kitchen. Nachman didn't believe this one bit, because no one who was even a little Jewish could possible eat pig. In *Memoirs of the House of David* he had read how even Jews who converted refused to touch pig. And how had the Greeks desecrated the Temple and caused the Maccabean revolt? By bringing a pig into the Holy of Holies. And when the Romans besieged Jerusalem, hunger was so terrible that mothers ate their own offspring, but when a pig was raised on the city walls, there was an earthquake that shook the whole country for five hundred miles around. He was sure Todros had made up the story about the pig, but the one about chopping off the chicken's head seemed likely enough.

Indeed, Nachman had never seen any of the Saubers at the old slaughterer's, or on their way there. His own mother always bought a plump chicken for the holidays, or else several smaller ones which she fattened on sorghum or old bread. On Thursdays, or a day before the holidays, the whole neighborhood would crowd at the door of the tiny shack, which served as the slaughterhouse. Apart, though, stood the eve of the Day of Atonement, after *kapparot.* When his father had finished swinging a rooster for the third time around Nachman's head and saying the last verse, "Let this one be in place of me, let this one be instead of me, let this one atone for me," Nachman joined his mother on her way to the slaughterer's. Most families would have a chicken for every member, roosters for the men and hens for the women. They themselves had only two because his father said that personally he objected to the custom, which he considered to be a pagan rite. One could just as well give money to charity, he claimed, which he did every Yom Kippur eve in the synagogue.

"On the other hand," he explained jokingly to Uncle Rifael, "that's strictly concerning myself. As for Nachman, I want him mostly to have an idea of what Jewish tradition is, and not to live as if he's sprung out of nowhere. And besides, our own father, may he rest in peace, used to do the same with us, and no one can deny that thanks to *kapparot* we are both still alive and in good health, praise God."

Nachman's mother disapproved of his father's levity, and Nachman felt that she took the atonement ceremony most seriously, not just for his sake, but for her own too when swinging the speckled Arab hen around her head and reciting, "Let this one be in place of me, let this one be instead of me, let this one atone for me."

Be that as it may, the whole neighborhood would be jostling in line at the old slaughterer's, holding out their birds as he stood in front of his shack in his long, stained smock, his glittering knife between his teeth. He turned up the chicken's throat, plucked its thick plumage which clung to his sticky fingers, mumbled a blessing through lips that were hidden in the thicket of his whiskers and beard, held the knife in his hand, and slaughtered the bird, taking care to bleed it into a tub full of sand. Then he hung it by its tied legs on a nail until it stopped writhing or tossed it through an open window into the yard where the feather pluckers sat. If Nachman and his mother were late in arriving, they would see all this by the bluish light of an alcohol lamp, which cast an eerie glow over the shack. On this evening too, the five tall Saubers and Frau Sauber were not to be seen. They didn't atone for their sins. They didn't go to the slaughterer. God only knew what they ate even on Yom Kippur. Perhaps Todros hadn't lied after all. Perhaps they were total *goyim.*

24 | One bad deed leads to another

It did no good for Volush and Ruzha to protest that it would mean too much work for Nachman's mother. His father refused to listen and said that it was his celebration no less than theirs, a joint affair. They were his cousins, neither had parents in the country—where else but in his house could they possibly get married? They might as well know, he concluded, that if they insisted on insulting him and holding the wedding in Tel Aviv, they would never see him again.

And so several days before the wedding, their cottage and the shower in the yard began to fill up with giant watermelons, honeydews, bottles of soda and siphons of seltzer. Nachman's mother soaked chickpeas in a large bowl and boiled up two big pots of them, which she salted and peppered, kneaded enough dough for four large batches of sugar cookies, which she had done at Tuvim's bakery, and baked a torte for the bride and groom in her *Wundertopf* oven, which she covered with chocolate frosting. His father went to the market and brought back pumpkin and sunflower seeds, sour sucking candies, and two bottles of red wine.

At first his mother had planned to cook dinner with all

the trimmings, gefilte fish, jellied calf's foot, chicken soup with noodles, meatballs, stuffed cabbage, and sweet carrots—except that to invite all the guests to eat was out of the question, and Nachman's father staunchly refused to ask only the immediate family and hurt everybody else's feelings. "Besides which," he explained, "it's pointless in any case. People don't get home from work until late, and if everyone waits to eat until after the ceremony, they'll all be dying of hunger. Let them eat first at home and then come here to make merry."

Ruzha, who had grown very thin and tan, wore a wide, pleated black skirt and a white peasant blouse which she herself had sewn and embroidered. Volush too came dressed up to the rabbi's house in a white shirt and his woolen suit pants from Poland. He was already under the wedding canopy before Nachman's father managed to clap a skullcap on his head, while the other young guests donned their work caps or hats improvised out of newspapers. The easygoing rabbi did not seem to mind that everyone joked and talked out loud all through the ceremony, and left it to Nachman's father, whose eyes sparkled with excitement, to call repeatedly for silence and keep after Volush until he had stamped on the drinking glass wrapped in old papers. Then they all set out for the cottage together, singing so loudly as they crossed through town that it sounded like a May Day parade.

The watermelons and honeydews had sat all day long in a tub of cold water, while the soda and seltzer lay chilled in a smaller tub, in the middle of which was half a block of ice wrapped in a sack. In no time everyone had fallen on the refreshments, salty and sweet, and eaten everything in sight. They finished off the fruit and drank straight from the bottles and siphons and broke into more songs: Sabbath hymns, "Titina" from the Charlie Chaplin movie, ballads in Russian and Yiddish, and "Camel, O Camel." Nachman's father surprised both his mother and the guests by producing a huge glass jug of wine from some secret hideaway. Uncle Rifael lifted it high and poured a jet of it straight down his throat the way one drank water from a clay pitcher. In a twinkle the jug was empty and the house was filled with the voices of the guests, which resounded to the starry sky and to the far mountains shrouded in darkness beyond the little market and the creek. Having done the unexpected once, Uncle Rifael shocked no one a second time—except Tsipoyrele, who clung to his shirttails in an effort to make him sit down again on the plank bench—when he got to his feet and announced that he was going to sing a song he had learned many, many years ago on his first night in the settlement:

O little blue flower
It grew in a row
And in my poor heart
Are sorrow and woe.

What makes my blood stir so?
One day I spied a fair young man
I plucked my flower and I ran
To put it in his eager hand.

No sooner had I turned away
My flower he threw down
It lay there by the dusty road
My fair young man was gone.

There stood Uncle Rifael—surrounded by Volush's and Ruzha's friends, by the Holzbergs, by *fetter* and *mimeh* Herzlich, by old Becker and his wife, who had run away to Breslau to be an actress, by Kravitz, by many other young men and women whom Nachman didn't know—singing! His face and stubby arms, coal black even in broad daylight, were invisible, and all that showed were his white shirt and the broadcloth pants that Tsipoyrele had brought for him from home. That, and his eyes, which were aglow with the wine and the stars. Who had ever heard Uncle Rifael sing before, and in such a loud, sentimental voice? It was the first time not only for Nachman but for everybody else. At the end of each stanza they all sang the refrain in merry disharmony:

O little blue flower
It grew in a row
And in my poor heart
Are sorrow and woe.

Nachman never forgot this summer night, though in the years to come he found it hard to say exactly what about it had impressed him so much, whether it was the wedding ceremony itself, or the tubs full of melons and bottles, or Uncle Rifael's singing, or the giant jug of wine that his father passed among the guests and even tippled from himself, or old lady Becker who suddenly rose to declaim a long speech in Yiddish while his father shouted at her, half in jest and half in earnest, "You're a Hebrew woman, speak Hebrew!" Or perhaps it was the snatches of conversation between Volush's and Ruzha's friends that he overheard in the course of the evening. How bright and gay and smart they seemed! Once again the ruby-jawed worm of doubt was abroad on Nachman's stone walls. Maybe it wasn't a question of forbidden or not after all, but of another division entirely. Maybe there were people who never smiled for whom everything was forbidden, and people who always laughed for whom everything was permitted.

His father and mother laughed a lot these days too. It hadn't been a bad year again, and if only next year proved no worse, they could finally begin to live like human beings. His father wrote long letters to Uncle Elyakum in Chicago and read them aloud to Nachman's mother and Uncle Rifael before mailing them. What a fine hand he had! There wasn't a halting stroke among the boldfaced letters: The promised land. Each man under his fig tree and his vine. We are growing citrus. The vegetables we eat are from our own garden. Nachman's mother nodded her head as he read and Uncle Rifael's eyes receded further and further into the deep furrows that the sun had cut in his face.

"If only the whole family were here now," his mother would say. "Then nothing would be missing."

"They'll come," his father would answer. "They'll all come. Those who don't want to will be made to by the anti-Semites." But his mother kept a dubious silence.

"We should at least bring mama here now," said Uncle Rifael. "We could really bring her now."

"We'll write to her," said Nachman's father. "We'll add another room, and she can live here with us. When Leah goes to Poland next summer, she'll tell them everything. They can live very nicely here."

"If only the times don't get worse," said his mother to squelch the evil eye.

Nachman knew, though, that she too believed in her coming trip, for which she was already making preparations. He had suddenly discovered that the *fetter* and the *mimeh* had not only a daughter, Toybe, but two sons who had just sold their businesses in Poland and come to Tel Aviv. One Saturday during the Hanukkah vacation he went with his mother to visit them, and to see Ruzha too.

The new Herzlichs all had reddish skin covered with rusty blotches and spoke only Polish and Yiddish. One had a son named Milik, who was exactly Nachman's age, while the other had several children, one of whom, a pretty girl named Lola, was almost as old. Like the typical newcomers that they were, though, all Lola and Milik wanted to do was play in the storage shed of the new house that was being built at the other end of the street for the whole family. Nachman missed Ruzha, and he pestered his mother until she took him to the small rooftop room—a converted washing room, in fact—not at all far from the Herzlichs, big city though Tel

Aviv was. Next morning, after returning from Sabbath prayers (he didn't dare risk the *fetter*'s wrath by skipping them), as soon as the *kiddush*—the blessing over wine—had been said at the table (he didn't dare miss it either), Nachman ran off to Ruzha's again.

As soon as he entered he knew the whole truth, but it was already too late to escape: in a flash Ruzha ran to meet him with a cry of joy, while Volush mumbled something in Polish to their friends, who were seated on the bed, on the two stools, and on the wicker mat on the floor. They choked back their laughter, the smoke from their cigarettes hanging in the room like a cloud. With his own eyes Nachman saw the terrible sin they were committing, which was punishable in the days of the Temple by stoning and now by an early death. He didn't want to have to see or to know, but Ruzha had already kissed him on the forehead, put one arm around him, and pulled him after her to the couch.

He now saw the little table in the middle of the room too. It was covered with one of Ruzha's embroidered tablecloths, on which was a rye bread, some hard sausage of the kind that people brought from Poland, a tin of goose fat, a slice of salty Safed cheese, some yellow Latvian butter, a plate of sour pickles, and a bottle full of water, though Nachman knew very well that it wasn't water at all, nor even the fiery spirits that old man Becker liked to toss down his throat. It was the drink people brought from Poland—*vudka*. It wasn't this that made him stare, though, but the sausage and the butter. *Treifah*—unclean. Ruzha sat down next to him while the company went back to its talk and to taking thin slices of bread and butter, placing a small coin of sausage on top of them, and swallowing them in two bites. Nachman looked down and then up again, aghast. Unclean. Unclean.

Ruzha buttered a slice of bread for him, but he shamefacedly refused it, his ears on fire.

"Ruzha," scolded Volush, "what are you giving the boy to eat? He's just come from synagogue."

"This is good kosher Polish sausage," said Ruzha.

"Kosher sausage with butter is *treif,* you *goyeh,*" said Volush, reaching out for the slice of bread. "I myself, it so happens, am both *treif* and hungry."

Nachman didn't know how to extricate himself, but fortunately he was distracted just then by the sound of a harmonica in the mouth of one of the boys. The harmonica player sat on the mat with his legs crossed in front of him, a curly shock of hair like *mimeh* Herzlich's wig on his head, a veiled look in his eyes as though they had taken in smoke. The joints of his fingers were angled like Pinocchio's limbs. He cradled the harmonica between his lips in the palm of one hand. Its strains made Nachman shiver. At first everyone fell silent, moved by the melody, but soon the silence turned to humming and the humming to a song. Scarcely had one song ended when there was a request for a second and a third. Some of them were new to Nachman but others he had heard before. *Volga, Volga. Mein Shtetele Belz. Bei Mir Bist Du Schoen. Ah, Beautiful Nights of Canaan. Ein Lied Geht durch die Welt. It Happened in the Fields. Gariachi Bublichki. . .*

Nachman forgot that he had left the Herzlichs' only for the short break between *kiddush* and lunch, just as he forgot that the room was full of cigarette smoke. Ruzha buttered some bread for him, and this time he couldn't say no and make everyone feel unclean. Anyway, the bread itself was kosher, even if the knife had been used by them all.

"Leave the boy alone," said Volush.

"We won't breathe a word to your uncle," whispered Ruzha in Nachman's ear. "You'll leave here as kosher as you came."

Nachman took the piece of buttered rye bread and bit gingerly into it, nibbling at the crust. He was sinning horribly. For a second the bread stuck fast in his throat as though its poison were already spreading through his doomed body. But nothing happened. It was just a piece of buttered bread which melted deliciously in his mouth. The harmonica player played marvelously on his little instrument, and everyone sang with feeling and helped finish off the sausage and the cheese and the bread and the butter and the goose fat on the embroidered tablecloth. Between songs they sipped *vudka* and asked Magid (which was the harmonica player's name) to tell them what he had seen on his recent trip to Poland. His deep voice held Nachman spellbound like his music, even when he spoke in low tones. The air in Poland was electric with tension. The Jews lived in fear and didn't know what tomorrow would bring. In Radom there had been a pogrom, and Jews traveling in trains had had their beards cut off. But that wasn't the worst of it. There was a smell of war in the air. If they didn't get out soon, on the very first ship, it would be too late. War. Spain. War. Ethiopia. Manchuria. War.

Nachman sat listening to the strange, incomprehensible words that were pregnant with allusion to distant worlds. When Ruzha and Volush's friends spoke, it was like in the newspaper, like in books. When they laughed, it was full-throated. When they argued, they practically came to blows. But in another minute they were singing again to the accompaniment of Magid's harmonica. Nachman hardly noticed that he had eaten another slice of bread and that the time had flown. It was Ruzha who suddenly had to remind him that they must have already finished lunch at the Herzlichs'. He jumped to his feet in a sudden fright, as though his tardiness were sure to betray his having eaten *treifah* at Ruzha's.

Yet not really, he reassured himself, as he ran down the empty, noontime Sabbath street. Just a slice of bread and butter. Only the knife, which had been used for the goose fat and sausage too, was unclean. It wasn't like eating something really unkosher, he told himself, feeling how he had lost his heart to the young men and women at Ruzha and Volush's, to their singing, to their talk that fired his imagination. It seemed to him that the *fetter* was bound to read his thoughts as soon as he stepped through the door, which frightened him even more than the danger that someone might notice a telltale smudge of butter in a corner of his mouth.

He could tell by the look of the table when he entered that they were already done with the soup. His mother threw him a piercing glance, but the *fetter* and the *mimeh* innocently sought to convince her it was nothing. "There's a boy for you!" said *fetter* Herzlich to his sons and their wives. "He's always off in some corner, lost in another world. Do you remember," he asked Nachman's mother, reminding her of the incident that he was never allowed to forget, "how he ran away that day from the Talmud Torah all the way to the orange groves and sat there without moving through that terrible storm?"

"Do I?" nodded his mother. "I only hope that the pneumonia he came down with doesn't stay with him as a souvenir for the rest of his life."

They sang Sabbath hymns and ate what the *mimeh* had made them. *Cholent* and stuffed chicken necks and baked potatoes and beans and a roast. Candied carrots and stewed plums and slices of dried apples from California. Between one course and the next they sang more hymns, and between hymns the Herzlichs' two sons and their wives told stories about Nachman's grandmother and about the rest of his mother's family in Poland. Nachman wasn't asked a thing about his visit to Ruzha's, neither what he ate there nor whether he saw anyone smoking, so he had simply to say nothing and dissemble his feelings with an innocent look. The brisk, clear Hanukkah Sabbath shone through the window as though nothing had happened at all. He could feel the secret hardening within him, deep down, as though a splinter had lodged there and gotten infected—a secret that nobody else could even imagine. Yet how strange it was too that despite his terrible sin he looked no different from before and seemed the same Nachman as always to everyone. No one could tell. The sky in the window was as pure as it had been that morning. Volush and Ruzha had seen him, but if it weren't for them, the slice of bread could just as well not have existed.

Unless, that is, the clear Sabbath skies were just a camouflage, and up there, high in heaven, his sentence of early death had already been secretly passed. No one would ever know, neither before nor after its execution. Only God. Nachman shuddered imperceptibly. His mother and *fetter* Herzlich didn't know, but he did. Minutes ago he had crossed the fearful border between the permitted and the forbidden, and now he would find out what that invisible, all-seeing Eye had seen, if anything at all. He softly joined *fetter* Herzlich and the rest of the family in singing the final hymn before grace, but an inaudible something continued to echo inside him. So the great explorers must have felt at that precise moment when the wind caught their sails and their ships first set out westward for the open sea. What would they find there at the sea's end? Would it be India or a yawning gulf from which no one ever returned to tell the tale?

25 | *An unfinished story*

The secrets mounted between Nachman and his father. Each rooted deep like a broken thorn that drew a yellow abscess around it. Nachman learned to keep them to himself, to hide behind them, to listen to the dull throbbing of each infected sore.

He did and he didn't. He was not by nature the type to torment himself day and night over what had happened that Saturday in Tel Aviv at Ruzha and Volush's. What could he do if he was naturally quick to get upset and quick to get over it, so that one eye would already be smiling before the other had done with its tears? And this year especially, which was full of changes and transformations even before the autumn holidays, from the end of summer on.

His father had kept his promise and enrolled him in the Moriah Grammar School. He wasn't running away from the Yavneh School the way he had from the Talmud Torah, but he had no regrets about leaving it either. His memories of the three years he had spent there readily yielded to imagined scenes of the Moriah School, whose very name filled him with anticipation for something superior and grand. At long last he would be one of those boys and girls, so different from the pupils at Yavneh, who passed him every day on their bicycles in their light blue uniforms that made them look so much nicer and taller and handsomer and gayer than anyone else. The boys all had hairy legs and the girls long braids. Soon he too would be tall like them, with a uniform of his own. Perhaps—after his bar mitzvah—he would have a bicycle too and would also (but this was a secret even from Arele Holzberg, who was green with envy as it was, even from Ehud Karniel, who was now in the grammar school too) go out with girls.

The school year began in August and was soon in full swing. He rose early on the first day of school, wet his hair beneath the faucet, combed it well, set his beret carefully on it so as not to muss it all up, and started down the new path to his new school with his new uniform and knapsack. The uniform hadn't been acquired without a fight. "Who ever heard of buying clothes for just one month?" asked his mother. "By the time the holidays are over, it will already be winter. How can he go around then with thin khaki pants and no sweater? And Nachman grows like such a bean stalk that by next summer he'll be too big for both the shirt and the pants. Just because we can finally afford to eat three square meals a day and send the boy to grammar school doesn't mean that we have to throw money out the window!"

In the end, however, the new boy who left the cottage that morning wore a light blue shirt on whose pocket the school emblem was embroidered in navy blue and silver: a shield with the word "Moriah" at the top, an open book and a plow below, and the words "Judaism and Humanism" in silver letters on the book. According to Nachman's father, this same motto was inscribed over the front door of Professor Klausner, one of the great scholars of Jerusalem.

"I certainly hope," he added, his face taking on that special expression it had whenever he was about to say something grave, "that it will be your guiding light on the new path you're about to embark on. To combine what is best in our Jewish heritage with what is best in world culture is a very lofty ideal, and one which I myself have always strived to achieve."

Now Nachman started down his new path, his eyes darting about him to see if the change had been noticed and dropping to the emblem on his chest that symbolized the upheaval that would undoubtedly lead to all kinds of wonderfully exciting things such as Professor Klausner had in mind. Wasn't this the very name on the masthead of the crumbling journal in his father's bookcase—*Ha-Shiloah?* Yes, he would show his father that he too, Nachman, could be both a good Jew and a well-rounded human being—just as his father himself had been when serving in the army back in Catholic Poland. He had refused to eat all those revolting nonkosher dishes and had proudly asserted his Jewishness, and because of his dignified stand even the most anti-Semitic officers had come to respect him. No, Nachman didn't care if all the other children in his class sat with their hats off, as was the custom in the new school. His would stay on.

There was the Moriah School itself, gleaming in the distance. It was a new two-story building of reinforced concrete, like the ones that his father and Uncle Rifael and Kravitz plastered in Tel Aviv: straight lined like a giant brick, with long terraces that hung out in front of the classrooms, one above the other. It wasn't at all like his old school, Yavneh, with its thick, yellow, peeling walls. Here everything was modern, with metal-framed windows that stretched along the entire left wall. There wasn't a single pencil or nail mark on the brightly whitewashed walls. In the main entrance stood a middle-aged man, his face scratched from his morning shave. Despite the bell that he held in his hand, he didn't look like an attendant. He didn't talk like one, either, but with a thick German accent. "Goot mornink," he said, bending down over Nachman. "Vich klass, neu stutent?"

Now he was in the classroom, which was already full of strange children with shiny, scrubbed faces and neatly pressed clothes. They were not confined to the stocks of the usual black school desks with their penknife scars of immemorial students but were seated separately in chairs, two by two before light wooden tables. There were both boys and girls, but not side by side. Nachman felt frightened for a moment by the strangeness of the faces, the whiteness of the walls, and his own utter loneliness, but before he knew it, his name was being shouted above the din by someone. There sat Ehud in uniform, the kinky hair freshly trimmed on his bare head. Here would be someone for Nachman to sit with.

After that, everything went smoothly. There was a bell, followed by the hushed murmur of the first day of school, the excitement of the initial mystery to be solved: Who would be the new teacher? One could tell who the old students were because they traded whispers while the new ones sat silent. Adon Rubin, they whispered. In the doorway stood a man who would forever be recorded in Nachman's memory as follows: A head of hair—the color could have been either gray or a yellowish rust—that flowed out from under a sandy straw hat to rest on his ears and curl in tufts on the back of his neck. Bushy brows, yellowish too, which bristled over his eyes in the middle of a broad forehead. A broad nose, on either side of which were not wrinkles but deep-set notches. Another notch in his square chin and more above his eyes, between the brows. And this too: A brown suit that hung limply on his slouched shoulders. Baggy pants encircling a paunchy girth. A broadly knotted tie pulled to one side above an unbuttoned collar. Pudgy fingers grasping a faded black briefcase and a brand-new teacher's notebook. And yet: That first time and every time after that he saw Adon Rubin mount the low platform in front of the class, his briefcase laid on his chair and his straw hat on his briefcase, it seemed as if those eyebrows had been pasted on, those notches penciled in, the color powdered on his cheeks. Like the actors on the picture cards in the Dubek cigarette packs. Like the time Ruzha and Volush had taken him to see *Liliom* in the theater.

Adon Rubin entered the classroom slowly, nonchalantly removed the hat from his head, and signaled the children to be seated with a limp wave of his hand. He placed his briefcase on his chair and his hat on his briefcase and stood silently surveying his students with a look on his face that seemed equally comical and sad. Like his suit. Or his tie. Or the freckles on his face and hands. Or his brown—or were they yellow?—eyes.

"What sweet children," he unexpectedly said, as though talking to himself.

Just as offhandedly he threw out a question, and then a second and a third, until a conversation had quickly sprung up. Were all the children in the class born in town? he asked in a tone of surprise. What, there were some newcomers too? From where? Somebody's name was Birman? Which Birman? Back in his student days in Vilna he had known a Birman too, a handsome, likable fellow with a lovely voice. Could it be the same person? "Someone told me he was here now. And you, my sweetheart with the braids, where are you from? From here? And your father? And your mother too? Thank goodness for that! At least your mother was born in exile, just like me. . . ."

Adon Rubin reached for his notebook and called the roll, matching each name with each student. His warm, hoarse voice cast a bright net of soft words over the class in a Hebrew that was not so foreign-sounding after all, though it did have a lot of bookish words. Now he was informing them, with the same nonchalant air, that he would teach them Bible and Hebrew. They would study some grammar with him too, but just a wee bit. Mostly they would read poems and stories, and after the holidays, as the school year progressed, they would try other things too. The students themselves would write stories. "Yes, from your imaginations.

Or if you like, I might begin a story and you'll all have to finish it, any way that you like. It'll be fun, don't you think?"

More than anything else this promise brought home to Nachman the change he had so eagerly awaited. Never in his life had he seen such a teacher before, with his intriguing, theatrical face, his uncovered head, his high, freckled forehead, and his shock of yellow—or was it sun-bleached?—hair that spilled down over his ears and the back of his neck. He never raised his voice when talking to the class. You couldn't tell if his brown eyes were funny or sad, and his fleshy, lightly fuzzed ears always listened attentively to what the students had to say. Where had Nachman had such a teacher before?

And yet there was an even nicer surprise than this during these first two hours with Adon Rubin. As the roll was read the name Balfour Mendelevitch was called out, but the boy who rose was not the same roly-poly Mattathias the Maccabee whom Nachman remembered from that Hanukkah morning in his striped robe and the beard made out of flax. He was a different, much bigger boy, one of the tallest in the class, with a roundish head and curly blond hair cut short on the sides and the back in the British style, slicked down with a straight part in the middle that descended over the forehead, a little to the left of the nose. A different Balfour seemed to inhabit Nachman's memory, yet something about the large, gray, tranquil eyes, the smooth, unmarked, unruffled face was perhaps the same. Though he didn't know why, Balfour's unexpected reappearance in his class stirred him deeply, as though it too were part of the change he had looked forward to.

"Balfour," said Adon Rubin with a smile, "is not a newcomer, neither in our school nor in our country. He bears a family name that is known far and wide, and we all expect him to live up to it."

The subject had changed now from the Hebrew lessons they would have to the fighting that had broken out all over the country late that spring and had taken a heavy toll of lives all summer long.

"Above all, in times like these we need young Jews who will be as bold and brave as Balfour's grandfather, Adon Mendelevitch. What a mere handful of Jews were here in those days when Balfour's grandfather put the fear of God into those savage marauders! And today there are so many boys and girls like you in schools throughout the country." Adon Rubin's face wrinkled and his bushy brows declaimed:

Whose blood do I feel in my veins?
It is the blood of the conquerors of Canaan,
Which flows and gives me no rest!

His yellow-brown eyes reemerged from underneath their brows. His voice, which had made the children shiver, reverted to a smile, and he said with a twinkle in his eyes, "That's one of the poems we'll be learning this year. Do any of you know who Shaul Tshernichovsky was? 'And you shall forge a homeland forever for those who come after.' He wrote that too, boys and girls."

Ever since they had moved to their cottage—no, even before that—Balfour had lain sunken in the depths of Nachman's memory. Now it was all coming back to him. The yard. The parlor. The gramophone. Young Madam Mendelevitch's perfume that always announced her presence. The night of the Ninth of Av, Adon Mendelevitch and two other men riding through the sand on their horses. The hot cocoa. The songs that Balfour's mother used to sing and the way she played the piano. Except that now Nachman was no longer the same child, but a grown boy who read and knew all kinds of things and could make the proper connections. The same old man whom his father used to argue with under the mulberry tree, to whom he had brazenly replied, "Why don't you invite Abed for a glass of tea and give me a day of work," was none other than the legendary Mendelevitch, one of the first pioneers in the Land of Israel along with Michael Halprin and Joseph Trumpeldor and Aaron Aaronsohn and Abraham Shapira and Alexander Zeid and Sender Haddad. There was something of all of this in Balfour, and something of that wistfulness that rose now too from the depths of his memory, of Mister and Missus Blackman and the legend of the fortune that had flown through their fingers like a bird.

At first Nachman stuck close to Ehud Karniel, but because Ehud and Balfour also knew one another, the three of them began walking home from school together early in the year, as far as the corner where Ehud turned left and Nachman and Balfour turned right. The two of them would continue to Balfour's house, where Nachman would cut across the empty lot that had stretched between them in the past years like the Sahara desert, but that now turned into a shortcut between their houses, and which they now crossed a few times a day.

It may not have happened early in the year, or even not by the second trimester, but before Passover had come around again Nachman and Balfour were fast friends who seemed never to leave each other's side. They went to school together and walked home together, did their homework together and played together—as a rule in the isolation of the huge clerestory of the barn in Balfour's four-dunam yard, where the fodder was stored and which made a perfect hiding place when partly empty. Nachman's old world again took a large turn: he now faced away in his thoughts from the little market and the creek to high school, Ehud's and Balfour's houses, the library, and the many new children who had rapidly become a close-knit gang.

Above all, there was the classroom itself, with Adon Rubin, their homeroom teacher, and other instructors. Adon Rubin taught them Hebrew grammar and Bible, but the best days of all were those when he put aside the textbook, not even opening the tattered briefcase underneath his hat (in winter a gray fedora, the discolored brim rakishly pulled down), and stood in the corner of the room, oblivious to the children and the whole classroom, his wrinkled, powdery-colored face pressed to the window, gazing at the low dark clouds in the sky. In a moment, they knew, he would be telling a story of his own invention, which he would unpredictably break off in the middle, leaving its hero dangling in midair. Would he be caught by his pursuers? Would he manage to cross the raging river safely and mobilize reinforcements? Would his most hidden desire be fulfilled? Would the train be able to stop before it reached the destroyed bridge? What secret message was contained in the hieroglyphics on the parchment scroll? Could the young lad successfully liberate his people from bondage?

Adon Rubin's resonant voice broke with an ingratiating hoarseness, flooding the room from the corner where he stood and causing a hush even in the back row. Every feature of his face joined in the narrative: his yellow brows, which winced with danger, lifted with amazement, beetled over his eyes in dejection; his lower lip, which folded fleshily downward when all was lost, pouted in anger like the spout of a kettle, caught itself in his teeth when the hero overwhelmed his captors; his eyes, which danced merrily with a yellow light when the sun came out of the clouds and turned almost black when it vanished again.

The stories that Adon Rubin let the children finish as they saw fit always had some connection with the turbulent world of current events, such as the Lord Peel Commission, before which the leaders of Palestine Jewry were now testifying, so that their declarations appeared daily in the newspapers, or the Arab raiders who swooped down from the mountains to set fields and forests afire while the English and the local constabulary fought to stop them—Abu Jilda, Abu Dura, Kawkji, and still other marauders. Once Nachman wrote a poem about Joseph Trumpeldor at Tel Hai, which so excited his father that he showed it to Adon Sharoni and

Adon Karniel. The newspapers and the radio and Adon Rubin were full of stories about the brave pioneers in the countryside and their improvised forts with lookout towers in the middle and palisades of wood. Like in the Wild West movie with Wallace Beery he had seen or the story they had heard from Adon Rubin about the mysterious horseman the young pioneers had found by the Jordan with a tiny scroll in Rashi script hanging from a leather pouch around his neck, though he dressed and looked and spoke just like a Bedouin. What a wonderful story that had been! Or the one about the Jewish refugee from Germany who had gone to Spain in search of his ancestors only to find himself suddenly in the middle of the Civil War in Toledo. What happened next? What did he do then? What did he discover in the end?

Everyone was talking about Spain these days. They even had a fierce argument about it at home. Ruzha and Volush said that it was everybody's duty to go and fight the Fascists, while Nachman's father and Uncle Rifael said that it was high time the Jews stopped shedding their blood for the rest of the world. "Let them kill each other off if they like," said Nachman's father. "As far as we're concerned, there isn't any difference between the Bolsheviks and the Fascists. They're all haters of Zion."

About that time an incident took place that stirred Nachman so deeply he wrote a story about it. Mute Baylin, who lived nearby with his mother, suddenly left one morning for Spain. Nachman's mother saw the old widow crying bitterly one day in her yard and ran over to ask what had happened. Her son had risen early that morning, she said, put on his old suit that always hung in the closet, and informed her without any warning—after years of not even so much as saying hello—that he was leaving for Spain that same day. The old woman screamed and pulled at her hair and threw herself down on the threshold but none of it did any good. "I'm sorry, Mother," Mute Baylin had said. "I may not talk but I still have my eyes and ears. I can't go on grafting oranges in silence. I'm going to Spain." From then Nachman's mother dropped in on the old lady every day to bring her a bit of soup and some food and to listen to her stories about all the years she had buried in the town and about her husband who had suddenly died from hard work and typhus and filth. Nachman's mother told her that her son was sure to change his mind and turn up again in a day or two, but the weeks went by, the terrible war in Spain remained in the headlines, and Mute Baylin never returned.

Almost without thinking, Nachman sat down and worked everything he had heard about Mute Baylin (whom he called, however, Peli) into a continuation of Adon Rubin's story about the refugee from Toledo: the books he had voraciously read, his solemn oath not to speak, his farewell from his mother who lay prostrate in front of the door, and his death (the ending seemed inevitable) on the field of war. Adon Rubin asked Nachman to read the story out loud to the class, an honor reserved for the best compositions and one that had hitherto eluded Nachman. After he finished, Adon Rubin asked the children what they thought about Peli. Did they really think he was a hero? Was he really so glorious? In the end he disclosed his own negative opinion:

"Any life lost on foreign soil at a time when every worthy man is needed right here is a life wasted. Soon the Peel Commission will hand down its verdict, and God only knows what trials await us, what battles we shall have to fight in the years ahead. We're all living in a state of siege here, and whoever deserts across the lines commits treachery."

Nachman was confused by Adon Rubin's comments. He had just said to himself that if only he were somewhat older, he too would follow Mute Baylin to Spain, whereas now he felt that the fate of the Jewish community in its struggle for survival was his personal responsibility. "You are our Maccabees," Adon Rubin had quietly said, right after which he remembered to add, "That's a fine story you've written here, Shpiegler. A fine story."

These were the times for stories. On Saturdays, or after school, when they sat in the dim light of Balfour's barn, they swapped tales about the great heroes whose adventures were written about in *Dreamers and Fighters* or some other such book, or spun new yarns about what they themselves would do one day. There in the barn they talked about these and other things. Girls, for example.

It should be mentioned at this point that Nachman and Balfour were frequently joined by two other friends. One was Ehud. The other was Amichai Pinski.

No one wrote as grandly as Amichai, who inscribed his compositions with a gold-tipped Waterman pen that had a transparent inkwell, in small, round letters and marvelously straight lines, without a single stain or smudge of ink. Adon Rubin praised his writing highly, just as Adon Lev-Shoshanim, the music and art teacher, praised the way he played the recorder, the ocarina, and the Arab flute. This was one side of him, but Amichai had another, even greater talent. Though he was short and broad-hipped, with a pale complexion that looked as though it had never been exposed to the burning sun and was easily given to blushing; though his prominent ears stuck up from his delicate face; though he blinked and twitched his shoulders and neck strangely whenever he stood up to read his compositions in front of the class, which made many of the children laugh at him, as did his compositions themselves and his elegant handwriting; though he never made the class dodgeball or stickball or soccer or johnny-on-the-pony teams; and though he caught a ball like a girl and jumped over a gym horse like an old woman—nevertheless, the way to the girls led to Amichai.

Their class was co-ed. The boys and girls sat at adjoining tables, practically touching. But how was it possible to talk to a girl without losing your tongue? How could you be seen with one without being laughed at? The girls were all reaching their twelfth birthdays now, and Nachman was discovering a new custom: the birthday party. The parties were always on

Saturday afternoons and the boys were invited too. What did you do at a party? The boys grabbed all the goodies and shoved each other at the girls. Ruti Segal had a head full of curls like Shirley Temple, which the boys were constantly after, but Tamar Levin had a different kind of hairdo, smooth and silky, that came down her neck in the back while in front it was pulled back and tied with a wide silk bow, just like Deanna Durbin. This ribbon gave the boys no peace until they had untied it and reduced Tamar Levin to tears. Shamefully enough, the first birthday party ended in blows, not all of which were dealt by the boys.

In its aftermath, Adon Rubin urged the class to elect a party committee. Amichai Pinski was the choice of the girls, while the boys picked Ehud Karniel, who was a comedian with his funny whistles, his buzzes, and his five imitation voices. He could talk through stuffed nostrils with a nasal trill like Reb Moshe Hayyim Gutman, the town mayor; he could rasp hoarsely in his throat like Missus Blackman; he could make a hollow sound like the echo of a dry well or of ghosts; he could chirp in a falsetto like Little Red Riding Hood; and he could mimic a Yemenite. In addition, he could crow like a rooster, bray like a donkey, howl like a jackal, and yammer like a cat in heat, to say nothing of roaring like the MGM lion in the movies. No party was complete without Amichai's flutes and Ehud's imitations.

Planning the birthday parties gave that winter a special flavor of its own. One of the new children from Germany, Hanan Frankfurter, had a magic lantern into which you could slip drawings on glass slides. They made up entire cartoons, which were accompanied by Amichai on the flute and Ehud's different voices. Or else they stood behind a sheet and put on silhouette shows. Only where was the script to come from? For that they sat in Balfour's barn and composed skits. On the new port in Tel Aviv. On Trumpeldor. On Purim. Or else they wrote funny rhymes about the teachers and the girls. Or planned a class newspaper. The same boys who rehearsed together also played together in backyards, went together to the movies, walked together to the orange groves on Saturday afternoons, wagered together who could eat more oranges, watched soccer together, strolled together down those streets where the chances were best of meeting the girls from their class.

The girls. That was the main thing. How could you tell who loved whom? Only indirectly, through complicated hints, because real lovers never revealed their love or went off by themselves, but kept a calculated distance. One way was to put the two names next to each other and cross out all the letters they had in common. If both names were crossed out—either mostly or entirely—it was a sure sign that the love between them was eternal. Nachman wasn't sure whether he loved Ruti Segal, who looked like Shirley Temple, or Tamar Levin, who looked like Deanna Durbin. A comparison of first names showed that he and Ruti hadn't a single letter in common, while he and Tamar had only common *a*'s. When it came to last names, however, his chances with Ruti Segal were better: of her name only the *a* remained, and of his, *h, p, i,* and *r*. Indeed, it seemed to Nachman that he really did love her, curls, plump body, good-natured giggles and all. Both Ehud and Amichai, though, were in love with Tamar Levin, who had long legs and breasts that showed clearly beneath her dress, and who already wore a brassiere. Perhaps, Nachman wondered, casting about for other signs, he loved her too.

Nachman's mind was troubled and full of forbidden thoughts. He stubbornly insisted on sitting with his beret on, though this made him the only boy in class to wear a hat. He knew that it was forbidden to pick oranges on the Sabbath or even to eat the fruit that Balfour and Ehud had picked, but what kind of fun was it to go to the orange groves without sucking the juice of a well-squeezed blood orange, or eating tangerines, or mallow seeds, or anything? Nachman would make little exceptions for himself—and then regret them. He swore not to betray his vow to be both a good Jew and a well-rounded human being like his father, but he could see his father changing too. First he had lost his beard, then he had exchanged the smelly depilatory with which he shaved for a razor, then he had stopped going to synagogue on the Sabbath, and now he even went to visit Uncle Rifael on Saturdays, far past the limits you were supposed to walk. How much worse could it be to pick an orange?

The Moriah School was completely different from Yavneh, which it now seemed to Nachman he had never gone to. The little market and the creek were like a distant dream. Before he knew where the time had gone, the winter was past, the Passover holidays were over, and the last trimester had begun. The oldest boys were nearing bar mitzvah age and the oldest girls were beginning to show womanly signs. In the dim light of the barn he and his friends conversed in whispers, asked forbidden questions, and examined themselves over and over to see if the symptoms of manhood had already appeared on their bodies. Not only boys and girls—the whole world was now divided into male and female: the cows and the mare in the barn, the hens and roosters in the yard, the pigeons in the dovecote, everything, even the flies, were assigned by their acts to one group or the other.

Nachman's days were crowded and full of forbidden thoughts. With the first heat wave, ugly boils began to break out on his skin, hard red swellings with pussy heads that hurt terribly. His mother forced him to swallow yeast pills and cod-liver oil, but despite all the pain and the pus and the Ichthyol and the gauze on his arms and legs, Nachman relished hearing it said. "They all get sores at this age. The boy is simply growing up a little faster than usual."

26 | *Doctor Herzl's diary*

He was sure that each new boil would be the last, that finally, as his mother explained it, his body would have cleansed itself of the last of its dirty blood. Yet in the middle of that summer an entire cluster of them suddenly sprouted on the inside of his thigh, sore within sore and pain within pain—a carbuncle, said the doctor. And it wasn't just there that he felt as though a sewing machine were jabbing its needle into his flesh; his whole leg ached and a swollen gland in his crotch turned his flesh red and hard as a rock. He lay on the couch by the window feeling as though he were on fire, smeared with black Ichthyol that sucked out the pus from his sore, which ticked like a soundless clock. The doctor came, prescribed some pills, and gave him a shot in his backside. The fierce summer heat invaded the cottage, and he languished feverishly hurting on a sweat-drenched sheet. "It's only a boil," said his mother. "It won't cripple you for life." The doctor came every day to give him an injection and tell him that he was getting better. "It's practically ripe now," he said. "Tomorrow or the day after it will open completely."

One night, indeed, the carbuncle opened. The pus began

to flow out and the pain diminished. "Your body will get rid of all its dirty blood now," said his mother. But now that his fever and the swelling had gone down, it was deathly boring to have to lie there in the heat. Toward evening Balfour, Amichai, and Ehud would drop by to look in on him through the shutter and ask how he was. The day the carbuncle burst he asked them for something good to read, something different from the books in his father's bookcase, half of which he had already read and the rest he never would.

"Just you wait," said Ehud. "I'll be back in half an hour."

Before the half hour was up, Ehud returned to slip a well-tied cardboard portfolio through the open shutter between the wall and the couch. In it, he whispered, were more than sixty novelettes, in the series of *The Shanghaied Beauty of Tel Aviv*, *The Twentieth-Century Crime Library*, and other love and murder mysteries. There would be plenty for Nachman to read.

Such books had never crossed their doorstep before, for Nachman's father had a single word for them all: smut. Amichai and Ehud and Balfour all had rooms of their own in their homes where they could lock themselves up and do whatever they pleased; but here, where they all lived on top of each other, his father was everywhere and had an opinion on everything. Once his father had seen Ehud with a detective story in their house and when Ehud left he delivered a speech. "Do you think your mother and I are scrimping on every meal to send you to grammar school so that you can grow up to read such trash? Do you suppose that Eliezer Ben-Yehudah revived the Hebrew language for the sake of such disgusting smut? Is that why generations of Jews martyred themselves at sword's point—so that *Sabina* and *Regina* could be printed in the Land of Israel in the twenty-two holy letters of the Hebrew alphabet?"

The secrets grew between Nachman and his father. Little lies cut between them like the grooves of a phonograph record. Not that he dwelt on his sins all the time or tormented himself with the fear that lightning might strike him dead any minute and turn him into a heap of cinders. Yet it was still not easy to cheat behind his father's back—not easy at all. The Berkovitzes, who owned the egg stall and the wagon, had moved out of the old packinghouse that spring and gone to live at old Widow Baylin's place. They did not live on their eggs and their wagon alone any more, because all their sons—including Nachman's old classmate Pesach—were now working and the family was growing richer and richer just as Nachman's mother had predicted. They had even bought a gramophone, and on summer evenings, particularly Saturday nights, the Berkovitz boys sat outdoors with their friends, cracking sunflower seeds and eating watermelon and listening to the sweet strains of the record player, especially to the two songs that were currently everyone's favorites: *Bei Mir Bist Du Schoen* and *Mein Shtetele Belz*. They had played them so often that the records were now badly worn, so that the needle would suddenly jump and hiccup metallically as the sweet, familiar melodies flowed out into the warm evening air. Hic! Nachman felt the same way when he was about to do something wrong. Hic! A Lie. Hic! A secret. Hic! A sin.

There were bad secrets now between him and his father, and the fear that they might be discovered crawled over him like an ant. And yet at the same time he derived a curious pleasure from them. Not only that: just as he liked to see if he could pass his finger quickly through a candle flame without being burned, so he felt an uncontrollable impulse to do whatever seemed dangerous or forbidden.

"I don't care what you do," his father had once said, his finger aimed between Nachman's eyes like an arrow, "just as long as you don't lie. Tell me that you don't feel like doing your homework, tell me that you'd rather go out and play, tell me that you're lazy or that you forgot, tell anything at all as long as it isn't a lie. Sooner or later every liar gets caught and then I don't envy him. Even when he tells the truth no one will believe him anymore, just like the man who cried wolf.

"I want you to know," he went on, his finger still aimed at Nachman's eyes, "that I always know when you're lying. Even when you think that I don't it's written all over your face. There's nothing I hate more than a lie. This isn't something that's made life easy for me, believe me, yet I've never regretted it for a moment. Once you get used to lying, you're caught in an endless net. You can do what you like, Nachman, but never, never tell a lie!"

Nachman couldn't help agreeing, yet things were not that simple. The family row that would have broken out had he told his father what had happened at Ruzha and Volush's that Saturday in Tel Aviv! And he hadn't even lied then but just not told the truth. Had his father asked whether anyone ate sausage with butter and had he said no—that would have been a lie.

Some secrets were so deep that Nachman didn't even dare tell them to himself, such as that day at the Herzlichs' in Tel Aviv when the children all played in the storeroom behind the new house that *fetter* Herzlich was building for himself and his family from Poland. They had gone there as usual to act out the Arlosoroff murder trial. There was an English judge and the defendant Stavsky and a police inspector and an Arab tracker. That day, however, they lost interest in the game, which they already knew by heart. Most of the children went off somewhere else, leaving only two boys and a girl in the dimly lit shed. Even now Nachman's ears burned when he remembered how one of the boys persuaded the girl to play doctor. This boy was *fetter* Herzlich's grandson Milik, who was covered with rusty freckles and spoke only Polish and a few words of Hebrew. The girl was Milik's cousin Lola. Milik closed the storeroom door, but Lola said she didn't want to in the dark. If they stood for a moment with their eyes shut, Milik suggested, there would be enough light to see by when they opened them. And indeed, when they looked again there was a trickle of light through the cracks in the walls of the shed. Lola said they couldn't examine her unless Milik and Nachman played sick and let her examine them too. No, Nachman said, he didn't want to play. Yet he stayed where he was and watched Lola lie down on the sack that Milik spread on the floor and let him raise her dress and examine her with his fingers. Even in bed at night, under the blanket, Nachman was ashamed to admit how much he remembered, such as Lola's little hand that promenaded over his body, or his own hand as it touched the forbidden parts of hers. How could he ever tell his father and not let the secrets mount higher and the lies cut deeper? *Hic!* A lie. There were stories in the Bible that they skipped in school, but Nachman had read the one about Lot and his daughters more than once. They had uncovered their father's nakedness. And hadn't the same thing happened to Noah when he was drunk? Lola, thought Nachman, had done to him what Tamar, Er's wife, did to Judah. And yet, he thought again, it was nothing, just a before-dinner game that he had long ago forgotten. There was no need to stare down at the floor when his father looked at him with all-knowing eyes. He need simply whisper to himself that nothing had happened, make sure his facial muscles were under control, and look straight at his father, who could not possibly hear the needle as it jumped in its groove. Hic! A lie. Hic! A lie.

Ehud and Amichai and Balfour now sat by his side and worked out a scheme with him for sampling the treasure trove that lay between the couch and the wall. Ehud looked around and noticed the bookcase. Which volume would serve best? *Ha-Tekufah* was too bulky. *The Science of Life* might seem suspicious.

Nachman had a sudden brainstorm. "Give me Herzl's diaries," he said.

That evening he heard his father boast about his only son to Sharoni the teacher, who was sitting with him in the yard, underneath the window.

"He's truly an extraordinary boy. No sooner did his carbuncle break and the pain go away than he started to read again like mad, And what is he reading? Doctor Herzl's diaries!"

At that exact moment Nachman's hand was groping in the narrow space between the couch and the cottage wall, returning *The Vampire* to its cardboard portfolio, and expertly extracting a new penny novel, which he slipped between the pages of the blue-jacketed memoirs of the visionary of the Jewish State. What had he come up with now? The title was promising: *The Case of the Black Hand Murder.* Nachman's pains were immediately forgotten as soon as he set forth in one of these forbidden books—whose graying pages had been cut not with a knife but with a finger that shook with excitement—and followed the adventures of keen-witted detectives as they chased after pathological killers, hashish smugglers, pyramid robbers, inscrutable Chinamen in opium dens, deserters from the Foreign Legion, women in transparent silk slips who tried their tricky wiles on Scotland Yard inspectors. Revolvers with special silencers, poisoned arrows, secret X-rays, artifacts from lost Africa that sowed death and destruction—what was one carbuncle compared to the hair-raising perils that lay in wait hour after hour for the heroes of the sixty novels in the cardboard portfolio between the wall and the couch? And all this (ah, the added attraction!) while lying cozily in bed right under his father's eyes.

At the first sound of his father's footsteps he would flip fifty pages and plunge deep into Theodor Herzl's diaries. The flag of the Jewish State would have seven gold stars to symbolize the seven hours of the working day. In the Jewish State his father would no longer have to get up at five o'clock in the morning the way he did now and come home from work at six in the evening. And how carefully Herzl had planned all his meetings with leaders of state: what he would wear, how he would enter, the things he would say to them. It was a pity he had died so young, Nachman's father said, burned out by his own inner flame and by the politicians who gave him no peace and hastened his end. If only a man like Herzl were alive nowadays, said his father, there would be none of the fratricidal feuds among Jews that had been going on ever since Arlosoroff had been murdered. Yes, if Herzl were alive, there would be no killing of Jews today in the Jewish homeland. Maybe there would even be a state, with an army and a flag of its own. Nachman thumbed through the glossy pages, traveling with Herzl from Vienna to Paris, from London to Constantinople, from Rome to Jerusalem, from St. Petersburg to Basel. When he grew up he would like to be tall and handsome like Herzl too, and to travel a lot, and have fine ideas, and be the savior of the Jewish people. . .

His father would come sit by the couch to chat with him, to have a look at the open carbuncle and feel how the swelling had gone down. His eyes shone with satisfaction at the sight of the open book in his son's hands. Just let him not pick it up now and find *The Microbes of Doctor Koch* among its pages! But Nachman looked his father calmly in the eyes, his face as inscrutable as a Chinaman's. His father was telling him how he had heard of Herzl's death, improbable though it seemed that he could remember such a day because he was only three or four years old at the time and his own father thought Zionists were no better than apostates. "And yet I really do remember," he said, "because even an infant like myself must have somehow sensed that the entire nation was mourning its lost prince." Nachman liked the way his father sat chatting with him by the couch as though he were grown up. Only now did he realize how long ago it was that Doctor Herzl had died, when his father—but how difficult it was to imagine—was only three or four years old. How funny it seemed.

The next day too Nachman devoured one novel after another, transferring them from the cardboard portfolio to the pages of Herzl's diary. He wasn't sure exactly when it was that he dozed off, but it must have been sometime in later afternoon when the sun glanced directly off the cottage wall, heating the air of the room and drugging his senses. Perhaps it was only for a second that he had let his lids drop and given his imagination free rein to show him the Shanghaied Beauty of Tel Aviv in the flesh in her hiding place in Beirut. Through her filmy slip she looked like Ruzha the time he had accidentally seen her in the shower. Perhaps it hadn't been long, but when he opened his eyes it was already dark in the mosquito-netted window and the electric light was burning above the table, where his father sat doing accounts in his black ledger. As soon as Nachman looked at him, he glanced up too.

"Feel better?" he asked. There was a hard tone in his voice and the look on his face announced that he already knew all. Nachman fumbled in a fright over the sweaty sheet. His fingers collided with the hard binding of Herzl's diaries.

"Much better," he said, his face as inscrutable as a Chinaman's.

"I see you're still reading Herzl. Tell me what you read today before you fell asleep."

His father's voice was still low, but the hard tone threatened to lash out at any moment like the blade of a knife. Nachman was certain now that the novel was not in the book and that his father must have it in his ledger. Every additional word meant an additional lie. And yet perhaps it was only his imagination. He kept silent.

"What did you read? I want you to tell me."

"I read that Herzl went to Constantinople, and there he met . . . he met . . ."

"The Shanghaied Beauty of Tel Aviv!"

He pulled out the tattered novel, whose paper binding had already come loose, and held it between two fingers like a dirty rag. His face, which was lined with long creases, wore an expression of pain. The books, whispered a panicky voice in Nachman's ear. Ehud's books. Above all, he must save the books.

"It's too wonderful for words. At long last we have a son we can be proud of. Our little prodigy, who was too good to study in the Yavneh School like all the other boys, who had to go to grammar school, has finally proven his worth. Your mother and I count every penny so as to be able to afford your tuition. She worries all the time that you'll spoil your eyes by reading too much, and I—I was just boasting yesterday to Sharoni about my son who reads Herzl."

His voice was still low, but the hard tone had crumpled and his dark eyes were glistening moistly. Nachman couldn't bear the anguish in the corners of his father's tight lips and the long lines that ran from his chin to just beneath his eyes. His own eyes filled with tears too.

"Papa. . . I"

"You what?" His father's voice broke in a single hoarse cry and the network of veins on his receding forehead stood out like fat worms.

The carbuncle pulsed in his thigh and fear in his heart. He should have known he'd be found out. *Hic!* A lie. *Hic!* A lie.

"You what?" The voice was lower again. "If this is what you want to cram your head with—this garbage, this junk, this *shund*—that's your business. I can't do any more for you He held the book between his fingers a little longer, as if it were the tail of a dead mouse, and then tossed it toward Nachman on the couch. For a moment Nachman let himself hope that this was the end of it. He wouldn't lie any more. He would promise never to again. Just let him be allowed to give Ehud his sixty books back. Yet only for a moment, for then a new thunderclap descended:

"But to contaminate Doctor Herzl with this filth! *The Shanghaied Beauty of Tel Aviv!* Do whatever you like, please, but don't lie! Who, tell me, who taught you to lie? Your mother? Myself? Who?"

It grew so depressingly silent now that the world seemed empty. It was so empty that the ticking of the pumps in the orange groves could be heard from far away.

"I'm still waiting for an answer, Nachman. Who taught you to lie? How long is it that you have been lying to me?"

White foam gathered in the corners of his chapped lips, and to Nachman it seemed that he could see the pulsing of his swollen veins.

"If you'd rather not have an education, if you don't want to become a man, fine, go roll in the mud with that drunkard Kashani. Go work in the garage. But to use Doctor Herzl as a cover-up for the Beauty of Tel Aviv! I never thought I'd live to see the day."

The thunder and lightning were gone now, their place taken by mourning and lamentation. As on the Ninth of Av, the day the Temple had been destroyed, the day Uncle Rifael had brought the letter about grandfather's death, Nachman's father was now rocking back and forth in his chair and shadows were dancing on the wall. It was as if his father was sitting now in mourning after him, and Nachman could not hold back his tears. He was crying for his father who was mourning after him.

But his father had risen from his chair and was standing before the couch. In a cold voice he said, "It's too late for tears. Where did you get this book?" He had been expecting the question, but though he might be a liar in his father's eyes, he would not be a tattletale. He could do what he liked—take a strap to him, skin him alive—he wouldn't squeal and he wouldn't tell.

"You have more of them?"

It wasn't clear to Nachman from the tone if he was asking or stating a fact. Neither Ehud nor Balfour had been by yet that day, and if either of them should turn up he could slip the portfolio to him through the shutter. But what was he to do now? If he revealed the books, his father would destroy them all. Though he had just sworn never to lie to him again, he whispered, "No. Just this one."

"Just one? You didn't hide any others in the pages of the Talmud? Or the Bible? Or *Ha-Tekufah?*"

Perhaps he should confess at once, right now, before the portfolio was discovered. But what would he say to Ehud if his father should burn all the books? Before he could reach down between the wall and the couch, his father had pounced on the latter, pushed it aside, and discovered the hidden cache.

"Good God!" he murmured at the sight of the overflowing portfolio. "Who would have imagined it?"

"I swear, papa," pleaded Nachman. "I swear I'll never read another again."

"Don't swear in vain."

"Then punish me. Any way you want. Just let me give them back."

"To whom? Who gave you this smut?"

Let him hit him. Let him transfer him out of the grammar school. Let him do with him what he wanted. He could not make him tell.

"You're not going to tell?"

Silence.

"Very well. If this trash doesn't belong to anyone, I can burn it right now." He turned and headed for the door, heedless of Nachman's entreaties. He was already on the porch when Nachman's mother appeared there too, but he brushed off her frantic questions and stormed outside, determined to put everything to the match.

Nachman hadn't budged from bed for two weeks and his carbuncle had only opened yesterday, but forgetting now that his leg was sore and lame, he rolled off the bed, stood on his good leg, and began to hobble outdoors. His mother tried to stop him, but he pushed her away and continued to appeal to his father. "I swear to you, papa. I'll never look at a mystery again. Punish me. Do what you want. Just let me give them back."

He stood in his underwear on the front steps, leaning against the doorway, while now it was his mother's turn to shout. "I want to know what's going on in this madhouse,

Shalom. I haven't been gone for half an hour and already you've both gone stark crazy. What's happened to the boy, Shalom?"

Nachman's father turned around at last. The portfolio was already on the ground. In another moment it would go up in flames. "I'll tell you what's happened to the boy. He lay there all the time on the couch holding Doctor Herzl and reading this garbage. A whole collection of it." Before she could grasp what he was talking about, he added, "Get back into bed this minute, Nachman!"

Despite his painful leg, Nachman did just the opposite. He vaulted down the stairs, coming perilously close to losing his balance, and hopped straight toward the portfolio. His father ran toward him, grabbed him in his strong arms, and swept him into the air just as he had on that day when he had burned himself lighting the play cigarette. There was a smell of dried plaster and sour sweat and the prickle of a stubbly beard. Nachman whimpered into his father's shirt, crying from shame that a big boy like him should be caught in a lie, crying because his father had made him cry.

"You're awfully heavy," said his father, surprised. Nachman was glad that he was barely able to carry him to the couch. Only now that he was on his back again was he conscious of the throbbing in his open sore. His mother carried the portfolio into the room. His father took the corner of the sheet and wiped Nachman's wet brow.

"Promise me you won't touch it again until you return it to whoever it belongs to."

"I promise. I swear."

"Don't swear. I believe you. And you won't ever lie to me again?"

"Never, Never."

Nachman shut his eyes and let himself feel his father's rough fingers in his damp hair. They brushed against his cheeks and the dry callouses tickled his skin.

"Do anything, anything at all that your conscience is clear about, but never, never be a liar or a cheat. Our whole life here is nothing if we can't live it in honesty and truth. Nothing you ever do or say can hurt me as much as a single lie. Will you remember that, Nachman?"

"Yes, papa."

"And you'll never try to deceive me again?"

"Never, papa."

"Or to lie?"

"Never. Never."

27 | *The* Meshulach *from* The Dybbuk

The attack of boils vanished as suddenly as it had come, so that Nachman was soon up and about, in school, in the Mendelevitches' barn, among the permitted and the prohibited books in the Karniels' house, in the labyrinth of rooms at the Pinskis'.

Everyone knew that nothing really cured boils, neither cod-liver oil, nor yeast pills, nor ultraviolet rays, nor lancing—just as everyone knew that boils were the most painful part of growing up. The summer heat, the sand, and the flies—these were all perhaps contributing factors—but the main thing was that in puberty the whole body changed: the voice got deeper, the arms and legs got longer, hair sprouted all over one's body, and the blood, said Nachman's mother, the blood got thick and dirty.

But not all boys got boils. Balfour, for instance, who was about to celebrate his bar mitzvah early that spring, hadn't a single boil yet. At most an occasional pimple the size of a pinhead appeared on his forehead and chin, but Balfour's mother had taught him to wash them with rubbing alcohol and not to touch them except with the absorbent cotton she kept in a closed jar just like they did in a doctor's office, and never, never with his fingers, even if they were clean. All infections were caused by dirt, which was swarming with germs.

Cleanliness, Balfour's mother reminded Nachman whenever he came to visit, was more important than anything else. His own mother said so too, but coming from Madam Mendelevitch it sounded like a rebuke, as if therein lay the difference between their own one-room cottage and the Mendelevitches' house, which stood on a high foundation surrounded by tall trees and had a parlor and separate bedrooms for Balfour and his parents and his little sister and a kitchen and a dining room and a bathroom in the yard that looked like a small cottage in its own right. Even on ordinary weekdays Madam Mendelevitch wore flowery dresses and was unruffled and patient, in spite of which—Nachman had no idea how—her house was always spick-and-span. The furniture was just where it should be, and there were carnations or snapdragons or chrysanthemums in the parlor and dining room and a fresh tablecloth on the table and a clean, cool, immaculate smell throughout the house. The same smell was in their cottage on Friday afternoons when his mother ran wearily about in his father's old leather slippers to finish the Sabbath cleaning, her fingers red and chafed from the soap, her blue cotton dress wet around the waist from washing the floor and the dishes and the dirty clothes, and wet above her breasts and under her arms and down her back from the perspiration she exuded as she raced against the clock to leave an hour before sunset in which to shower, put on the print dress that Ruzha had sewn her out of the imitation silk sent by Nachman's aunt in Lodz, spread the white Sabbath tablecloth on which she stood the silver candlesticks that Nachman had cleaned with silver polish and newspapers, and lit them with an exhausted smile like a marathon runner entering the stadium with his burning torch in his hand. But in Madam Mendelevitch's house there was never a fuss and yet it was clean all the time.

Nachman was keenly aware of the difference, just as he was of the rebuke in her remark that cleanliness was more important than anything else. And though he might bristle and even suspect that Balfour's mother wasn't happy about his friendship with her son, such moments were rare. His second year in the Moriah School, which was now beginning, was to be one long, happy, active, and very mischievous year that was constantly full of surprises. It went without saying he and Balfour were best friends. He knew from both his own and the family's memory that once they had lived nearby, somewhere between Balfour's house and Mister and Missus Blackman's, but memory was one thing and reality another. Mister and Missus Blackman's house was long gone, as were the store and the barred fruit garden that Mister Blackman had wanted to leave him. A bright two-story building had risen in the yard, which was surrounded by a new mesh fence—one of those Tel Aviv buildings that were now invading the town with their flat roofs and shuttered terraces that hung out over the street like open drawers. Yes, the fruit garden, whose gate had always been locked, was gone, and in its place was a patch of lawn, a concrete walk that passed between two low hedges of myrtle, some rose bushes, chrysanthemums, and two cypress trees. Where was the fig tree he remembered, or the mulberry? Under the foundation of the building, joked Balfour. Doctor Stockhammer, the veterinarian, and his tall English-type wife with her raised hip that looked as though it had been broken in two had tried to convince Balfour's parents to cut down their fig and mulberry trees too because the fruit attracted flies. Dopey Germans, said Balfour. They and their three daughters, who were all big and fat and had breasts that shook back and forth like the udders of Guernsey cows.

Memory was one thing and this year another. In his

memory old Adon Mendelevitch had always sat outdoors, under the fig tree. Now, however, Nachman learned that the old man and Balfour didn't even live in one house. Years ago, Balfour explained, his grandfather owned nearly the entire street, which he divided among his children when they married so that each could have a house of his own. Now the land was worth more in itself than the vineyards, or the orange groves, or anything else you could grow on it. Old Adon Mendelevitch lived at one end of the street, and two fenced, built-up lots separated Balfour's house from his. Even now, mused Nachman, the Mendelevitches had much more than his father's single dunam—except that they kept selling and living off the proceeds.

Nachman now noticed other things as well. Young Adon Mendelevitch's youngest brother, one of Balfour's uncles, had lived for years in London, where he studied to be a lawyer. Sometimes he would come to visit, dressed in his plaid jacket and pants, smelling of his briar pipe and after-shave lotion, just like a British police officer in mufti. Young Adon Mendelevitch himself, whom Nachman remembered from that moonlit, summery night mounted on his horse with a broad-brimmed hat and a rifle jammed butt-up into his saddle, no longer rode about on horseback, though he still kept a horse in the barn. He was no longer the head of the defense force either. Ever since the Arab uprising the town was full of *gaffirs*—special constables, without the shiny police number on their chests, and the *kolpaks* on their heads were brown, not the police blue. They were never seen unarmed, and unlike the regular police force, everyone was friendly to them, for they were drawn from the ranks of the townsmen themselves. At night they drove off the Arabs who attacked young orange groves and uprooted the tender plants, or set fields and forests aflame. Balfour's father wasn't one of them now; he was an important official on the town council.

"He's a good-for-nothing," said Nachman's mother, "even though he does make eighteen pounds a month."

"But he bust do sobething to earn that buch boney, wouldn't you say?" Kravitz asked, his nose stuffed as usual.

"He is supervising the town wells," Nachman's father replied.

"Sure," said his mother. "He calls on them every morning to check that they haven't been stolen." She still nursed that mysterious grudge against both him and Balfour's mother, whom she referred to only as "madam."

"It doesn't stand to reason," said Kravitz, "that they should pay a ban eighteen pounds a bonth just to look at sobe wells."

"Do you think it's easy to walk around all day long with the name Mendelevitch on your back?" asked Nachman's mother.

"The truth is that he always hated honest work. Riding horses is what he liked," put in Nachman's father.

"Noblemen aren't supposed to work, they are supposed to live like noblemen. He and madam—noblemen!" said his mother cuttingly.

His parents could mock the Mendelevitches all they wanted, but for Nachman the word "nobleman" actually expressed everything he felt about Balfour's spacious house, about the cool scent that seemed to be stored within the thick walls, about the cleanliness, the quiet, the meticulous schedule of the day, about Madam Mendelevitch's elegant Hebrew, about the black piano that was always closed, and the radio in the parlor, and the newspaper that always lay on the dining room table, and the glass dome of the clock that stood on the buffet, and about the leafy trees in the yard, and the metal gazebo with its trellised grapevines, and the barn with its horse at one end and its cows at the other. Noblemen.

But this was only at first. By his second year at the Moriah School Nachman's self-assured world was a series of concentric circles: the school, the class, and his own little circle of Balfour, Amichai, and Ehud. Above all, Balfour, with whom he had sworn to be eternal friends.

The big empty lot between Nachman's cottage and Balfour's house was still a jungle of trampled dirt and broken thorns in the summer and of high grass and standing water in the winter. One side bordered on Guberman's dairy and the other on the Hasidic synagogue, but mainly it served now as a land bridge between Nachman and Balfour, who crossed back and forth several times a day. Nachman's mother insisted that the two boys' relationship be on an equal footing and that Balfour visit them as well. "We too have a house, God be praised," she said, "and you can shut yourselves up here too and do your homework without being bothered." Deep down Nachman preferred Balfour's house, but Balfour was fond of the cottage, where he suddenly threw off his good manners, horsed around, told naughty jokes, and dressed up in costumes with Nachman.

He was not the voracious reader Nachman was, but he liked to listen to Nachman's tales about the books he had read and better yet, to his own imaginary stories, which borrowed liberally from fictional heroes and plots but which included what Nachman himself would do when he grew up: He would go to sea like Young William; or he would venture across deserts of sand and ice like Marco Polo, Sven Hedin, Captain Scott, and Nachum Sluszcz; or he would visit his Uncle Elyakum in Chicago and meet all the gangsters; or he would dress up as a Bedouin and live for several years in the desert, stealing into the forbidden cities of Mecca and Medina and discovering the lost Jewish kingdom of Yusef Abu Nuas, which he would lead back to Palestine, Jews, horses, camels, and all. Balfour's mother knew all the great Jewish heroes of the day personally, for though she had grown up in Jerusalem, she had family all over the country who stayed at her house whenever they came to visit from the Galilee, or Zichron Ya'akov, or Petach Tikvah, or Rechovot, or Rishon Le-Ziyon, while she herself had once gone touring the country with a party of friends and had stayed with them too. This was already in the time of the English, after the death of Aaron

Aaronsohn, whose plane they sabotaged because he knew too many secrets. Balfour would tell all the stories he had heard from his mother and his father and old Adon Mendelevitch his grandfather, the famous hero, and Nachman would tell tales he had found in books or spun from his own imagination. In the bottom drawer of the couch were his parents' old clothes from Poland: his mother's fox wrap; her black silk dress and another silk garment in purple, like the robes the Arab women wore; a large woolen shawl, all different colored flowers; his father's black suit; striped shirts and starched collars; felt hats that belonged to his mother and a cracked panama hat of his father's; white lace gloves and a heavy cotton nightgown, with a lace collar and bows at the cuffs of its short sleeves. The smell of mothballs, the locked door, and the closed shutters only deepened the air of mystery.

This year, unlike the last, they would put on real performances with costumes and a curtain and perhaps even colored spotlights. Balfour thought that Nachman should write a play. It could be from one of his stories or from the imaginary conversations they held while dressed in the clothes they had taken from under the sofa to look like Cossacks, Bedouin sheikhs, Mata Hari, Al Capone, Buck Jones, Joseph Trumpeldor, Samson and Delilah, Lawrence of Arabia, the mysterious messenger-*meshulach* from *The Dybbuk* . . .

Ah, the *meshulach*. Once every week now Balfour and Nachman went together to the movies. Nachman's parents looked askance at this extravagance—thirteen mils for the afternoon show, two piasters for the cheapest ticket in the evening. They themselves never went to the movies at all, partly because they were always too tired, partly because it was foolishness anyway, and partly because you had to think twice before spending four piasters. It was different, however, if a Polish film like *Zanachor* was showing, or something in Yiddish. It was different too if a play was in town. Before the new movie house opened, there were hardly ever live performances in town—not since *Jacob and Rachel* had been put on in the old corrugated tin hall (was this distant memory his or the family's?), in which the biblical patriarchs looked and dressed like Bedouin and sang beautiful songs to the accompaniment of a shepherd's flute ("O fair maiden by the water, art thou Rachel, Laban's daughter?"), or since the revue from Tel Aviv that satirized the Jewish farmers, who came armed to the performance with their pockets full of rotten eggs and tomatoes and spattered the stage with yellow yolks and red juice as soon as the offending lines were uttered. Now, however, all was forgiven, and every Thursday was a movieless day on which some troupe from Tel Aviv came to town. Nachman's father was terribly fond of the theater, and it was from him, Nachman's mother claimed, that Nachman himself had inheritied the childish urge to dress up in all kinds of clothes and make a clown of himself. But tickets to the theater started at forty-nine mils, which meant nearly nearly two shillings for a couple. His father still earned a good living when there was work, but who knew what the morrow might bring? Two shillings were no laughing matter. They went to see *The Threepenny Opera. Yoshe Kalb*. An occasional revue. But to go every week?

Nachman and Balfour went to the movies every week. Almost. Nachman would do his mother's shopping at the store, come home dragging a full basket, and keep two mils for himself. He would scrounge another mil here and another mil there and half a piaster for a *pita* (so as not to have to eat at Madam Mendelevitch's, he would cajole his mother) until he had the thirteen mils he needed. How could he skip a Buck Jones Western? Or miss seeing Flash Gordon? Or Shirley Temple? Or Freddie Bartholomew in *David Copperfield* and *Captains Courageous*? Or *Boys Town* with Spencer Tracy? Or Clark Gable? Or Paul Muni? Or Mickey Rooney? Or Deanna Durbin and Bobby Breen? Or *The Ziegfield Follies*? Or *Modern Times*? Or *The Dybbuk*?

They came early as usual that wintry day in the second trimester to stand at the head of the line and be first inside, so as not to miss the newsreel or the cartoons. It had rained that morning and seemed sure to rain again—the sky was still threatening and gray—before the day was done. Nachman had run straight home from school, eaten standing up, and run off to Balfour's in his green sweater (the one with the zipper and the crew-neck collar) with the help of the standard alibi that he needed coaching on his English from Madam Mendelevitch, who had studied the language in Jerusalem with the well-known Miss Landau. They speedily conjugated a verb, copied out a few sentences, translated from the *New Method Reader*, did twenty arithmetic problems, wrote a composition, learned a poem by heart, dashed out the door, and were breathlessly standing at the head of the line at three o'clock sharp, Nachman in his green sweater, Balfour in his navy blue slicker, which looked like an English policeman's.

The children's screams were deafening, as if they meant to blow the new movie house roof right off its moorings—the same roof that slid open on summer nights to let in the fresh air and the starry sky. They screamed their way through Popeye the Sailorman, through the Tour de France that slithered through rain and mud, through the German bombardment of Spain, even through the shots of the Maginot Line, the French fortifications that made a laughingstock out of Hitler and his empty boasts.

Then the main feature, *The Dybbuk*, began and a hush slowly descended. Nachman wasn't sure afterwards what had frightened him and Balfour so much, because they generally loved thrillers. Perhaps it was the *meshulach* who stayed far behind and yet magically overtook the galloping carriage to emerge suddenly from the dark, a mute witness to the cemetery scene. Perhaps it was he—and perhaps it was the thunder and lightning in the movie, which now mixed with rumbles of thunder outside and the hailstones that drummed on the convertible tin roof. The *meshulach* supernaturally came and went. Hanan's soul was alive in Leah's body. (Though he knew it had no connection, Nachman couldn't stop thinking of the fact that this was his mother's name too.) Or perhaps it was the cemetery, that mysterious place outside of town that the children were forbidden to explore. Children whose parents were alive, his father told him, were not allowed in a cemetery. Neither were the *kohanim*, because the dead were unclean. So many prohibitions, which he strove to outsmart yet always ran into anew. So much fear, of what he himself didn't know.

Surprisingly, Balfour was frightened too, and Nachman didn't know whether to be disappointed or glad. True, all through the movie he had sat staring calmly at the screen, and Nachman saw out of the corner of his eye how he didn't even flinch when Leah's scream made all the children shiver. But not when they stepped outside.

It had been light out when the movie started but now it was dark. The thunder was gone, the hail had stopped, and it wasn't even raining. Yet silent lightning flashed through the sky and eerily lit up the low-lying clouds. The lights from the stores that were still open shone into the street, but once they had left the center of town and passed by the little market, whose stalls glowed yellow and blue with kerosene and alcohol lamps, the darkness thickened around them. Toward the end of summer, work had begun on paving their street, but it had proceeded so slowly that even the undersurface still reached only as far as the Hasidic synagogue. From there on the empty lot stretched away into total blackness. What now? It was Balfour who had to cross it to get home.

"Do you want me to walk you?" asked Nachman, hoping that Balfour would be gallant enough to decline.

"You don't have to," said Balfour, but Nachman could hear the tightness in his throat. He thought of the time he had broken his cork helmet and strove to overcome his fear, but still it was there.

"I'll walk you to the middle of the lot," Nachman said, "and we'll say good-night there."

Balfour didn't refuse but simply asked, "And then I'll walk you back again?"

They laughed into the darkness and started down the

muddy trail that was lit by mute lightning. They had barely alluded to the movie and hadn't mentioned the *meshulach* at all, yet suddenly Nachman was sure that he saw him, silently waiting at the far end of the lot. They were about to part when Balfour remembered that Nachman had left his books at his house. The sensible thing would have been for him to bring them to school the next day, except that now they had an excuse to remain together a while longer. They reached the cypresses by the Mendelevitches' yard. There was a man standing close behind the trees and Nachman froze in his tracks.

"Did you see something?" whispered Balfour.

"What makes you ask?" Nachman whispered back. "Did you?"

"I'm not sure."

"Me neither."

"Behind the tree . . ."

"Something's there . . ."

"Let's wait here quietly for a minute," whispered Balfour. The two of them stood there suppressing their fear, each trying to act the seasoned warrior, like old Adon Mendelevitch, like the Nili heroes, like the brave pioneers in their forts. Lightning flashed over the lot, the tall cypresses, Doctor Stockhammer's white house, the diagonal line of the Mendelevitches' house among the trees.

"It's nothing," said Balfour, walking faster now.

"It must have been the *meshulach*," said Nachman, attempting a joke.

Still, they felt better when they were inside the house with the door shut behind them. Except that Nachman had eventually to go home too.

"I'll walk you halfway," Balfour said.

Nachman didn't say no but answered as though in jest, "And then I'll walk you back again."

They both laughed out loud like grown men, yet Nachman couldn't help glancing quickly into the hedge line as they passed between the cypresses. He was sure someone was there. Maybe Balfour had seen him too, but they hurried to get to the middle of the lot without exchanging a word. There it felt safer, and it was possible to make out a patch of yellow light from the dairy, where a bulb on a wire made the shadows dance in a sudden gust of wind. The silent lightning lit up the black rain clouds overhead. As always on such nights the mournful howl of an Arab dog suddenly cut through the air and made Nachman's flesh creep. Yet they continued to walk like two grown men, with measured if slightly longer and quicker steps than usual, as far as the middle of the lot, facing the dairy.

"Now," said Balfour, "we'll race to see who gets home first."

"We'll outfox the *meshulach*," said Nachman. "He won't know which of us to chase." And he added, "Do you want me to walk you back?"

"Don't be a jackass. On your mark, get set . . ."

"Go!"

28 | *Troubled times*

Fear had caught them by surprise between thunderbolts, amid the shadows underneath the trees, but they weren't little boys anymore, and the morning after they swore to each other by broad daylight that it hadn't been so.

At a time so dense with heroic thought, how could they possibly admit that they had been frightened by a bogeyman from a story that took place in a distant land, a story in a movie? Between them they reached an agreed interpretation: they hadn't been frightened at all, they had run only because it had started to rain again, and that anyway you had to be pretty dumb to believe in ghosts.

"I'll bet you," said Nachman, carried away by his bravado, "that I can walk by myself through the orange groves at night all the way to my uncle's and back."

"When my father became bar mitzvah," said Balfour, "my grandfather put him in a wagon and sent him off by himself through all the Arab villages, with nothing but a dagger and a lemon club, to test if he was already a man."

"My uncle makes the rounds of orange groves every night on his bicycle. All by himself, with only an English rifle."

It was true too. Uncle Rifael was no longer a partner in the plastering team. Now that a day didn't pass without shots being fired into some house, or young orange groves being torn up, or ambushes sprung on Jewish laborers coming home from the fields, Uncle Rifael had decided to become a *gaffir* in the night patrol. It was to Adon Sharoni that Nachman's father confided in a lowered voice that Uncle Rifael wasn't just another watchman but had a highly important job, which was to organize the town's defenses against an attack from the east, from the Arab villages at the foot of the mountains. He now passed by almost nightly on his bicycle, a rifle slung diagonally over his shoulder and a bandolier across his chest. There was no longer dry mud underneath his fingernails or a fine layer of cement on his clothes, which now included a pair of well-polished black army boots and rough khaki puttees that were wound around his legs. Sometimes he left his bicycle at their cottage and walked into town for a while, and sometimes he sat to chat with Nachman's father about the Arab riots. Nachman's father was very proud of Uncle Rifael, whom he called a pioneer in the truest sense of the word, a man who dedicated himself to defend the town against Arab marauders in the same spirit of self-sacrifice with which he had originally gone to farm among the dunes.

Nachman's mother, on the other hand, sighed each time she saw him. "The man's no longer a youngster," she said, "and he does have certain responsibilities, if not to Tsipoyrele, then at least to his two children. What is he trying to prove out there in the orange groves every night? What good is a rifle or a bicycle if you suddenly run into an ambush?"

Nachman would look at Uncle Rifael—whose whole appearance had been changed by his uniform and his *kolpak*, which together with the two deep furrows that fanned out on either side of his nose and lips made him look like a fearless warrior—and grieve that the Arab uprising would be over before he would be old enough to wear a *kolpak* and carry a rifle too. Sometimes Uncle Rifael would let him pick up the rifle, the *kolpak* coming down to his eyes and ears, and would break into that special laugh of his, which sounded like gravel being poured down a chute. The rifle was heavy for Nachman and its butt came down to the floor when he tried to sling it over his shoulder. Yet to judge by the first signs of puberty that were now sprouting on his body, and by the new pair of shoes he had gotten in the fall and had already outgrown by early spring, Nachman was convinced that it wouldn't be long, just another year or two, before he would be big enough to shoot a gun. Balfour's father had just turned thirteen when old Adon Mendelevitch sent him off in a wagon to Jaffa. The uprising was already two years old, and if recent events in the weeks since the arrival of the new high commissioner, MacMichael, were any indication, it wouldn't be over too soon.

They all read the newspapers nowadays. On weekdays they bought the late editions and listened to the radio at the kiosk or at Adon Sharoni's, and on Fridays Nachman's father bought the Sabbath edition of *Davar,* which he traded after reading for *Ha-Aretz,* which Sharoni received every day. Balfour's parents subscribed to a daily paper too, *Ha-Boker,* and Nachman read all the news in it whenever he came to visit and found it on the dining room table. 40 TERRORISTS KILLED, 14 CAPTURED, IN FIERCE BATTLE BETWEEN ARMY AND GUERRILLAS NEAR JENIN. "Josiah Wedgwood said in Parliament yesterday that the Jews' sole desire was for the Balfour Declaration to be honored." HITLER TAKES AUSTRIA BY FORCE. BOLSHEVIK LEADERS EXECUTED IN MOSCOW. "Hanita, the new Jewish outpost on the Lebanese border, was attacked from three directions last night in bright moonlight. The light tents of the settlers were an easy target for the marauders' bullets."

They read all the papers and discussed what was in them. His mother was afraid of a war, as were the Beckers, who stopped by their cottage in an agitated state on the night that the *Anschluss* was announced. All evening they sat and talked about a world war. As bad as the Germans might be, said

Nachman's mother, the Russians were even worse. She was especially worried because if war broke out she would have to put off visiting Nachman's grandmother in Poland for God only knew how long, and his grandmother was no longer so young.

His father didn't believe there would be war. It was all pure bluff. The Germans were a practical people who always looked before they leaped. They were sure not to run any risks that might end in disaster because anyone who knew them knew that this wasn't in character. It wouldn't come to war.

Nachman read the papers and listened to the grown-ups' conversations, but he didn't feel frightened in the least. The fact of the matter was that he envied whoever had been in a war, even old man Becker, even his father, who had been a soldier in the Polish army. There was no one more splendid in his eyes than the English soldiers who were frequently seen in town nowadays on their way to fight the guerrillas in the mountains around Jenin and in the Galilee. He hoped that he would get to be a *gaffir* in time, like Uncle Rifael. Once he heard his father read a lengthy article from the newspapers to Kravitz and Volush and Ruzha in the middle of an argument over how long Jews in Palestine would have to go on being killed: "Despite all the aid received from both overt and covert friends near and far, the enemy has been thwarted. The Jewish community has not gone hungry; transportation has not been disrupted; not a single Jewish settlement has been abandoned; not an outpost has been lost. Not one of the goals set by the leaders of the Arab resistance has been achieved by the bloody tactics they have called for." Nachman's father agreed with the article and Nachman agreed with his father. It made him feel heroic.

Fear had overtaken him and Balfour between the thunderbolts, amid the shadows underneath the trees, but the times called for feeling heroic. They agreed that they hadn't been frightened at all, that they had run because it had started to rain, that you had to be pretty dumb to believe in some *meshulach* from a movie. They thought about Hanita, where the brave Yehudah Brenner had died, about Juara, about the ship *Polonia* that had disembarked the first passengers in the new Jewish port in Tel Aviv, about the money they had collected for the Jewish National Fund to replant the forest that had been burned and torn up. They thought of how they would soon be heroes themselves.

29 | *Big plans*

If the wheel of fortune had begun to spin around again, Nachman failed to take notice. On the contrary, everything flowed on as before toward the unwinding future with its thousand possibilities, each one equally tantalizing, equally attractive, equally within reach. Nachman let his imagination carry him onward like Huckleberry Finn on his raft. He imagined he was like Clark Gable in *San Francisco*, like Tyrone Power in *The Rains Came.* He imagined he was like Sholem Aleichem. He imagined he was a sailor in the South Sea Islands. He imagined he was head of the defense force, more of a hero than Uncle Rifael, more even than old Adon Mendelevitch—a hero like Trumpeldor perhaps. He too would die in battle after having fired his last bullet. The whole country would turn out at his funeral, so that the streets would be dark with people and the entire front page of the newpapers would be rimmed with black. As was done for Beilinson, for the Baron de Rothschild, for the executed patriot Ben-Yosef. He imagined he was an actor in the theater, a different person in each performance, unrecognizable beneath his costume and his makeup. An actor—yes!

His friendship with Balfour had by no means weakened, yet Nachman felt increasingly drawn to Amichai Pinski, even if he did have a pale, white complexion that made him look like a convalescent from some illness, big, practically transparent ears, and prominent, red-veined eyes—yes, even if he preferred the company of girls to boys and his flute and black notebook of poems to playing ball and long walks through the orange groves and gymnastics and face-to-face combat and casting lead knuckles in homemade molds. Nachman didn't really care for Amichai that much, but something about him spurred his imagination, soothing and inflaming it at once.

The Pinskis' huge mansion in the center of town was different from any other house, just as the Pinskis were different too. The house had two stories. The bottom one was occupied by shops and storerooms, while the top one, which could be reached either by a broad wooden staircase in the back or a stone staircase that fronted on the street, was inhabited by the family, whose exact size was as much a mystery as the number of rooms in the house. Indeed, according to some people, even the Pinskis themselves weren't sure. It was common knowledge that Amichai's father had inherited a large fortune in Russia and had come many years ago to Palestine with his money and his first wife, along with the children she had borne him. Not many years went by before she died in some epidemic, and because he had a house full of children, he married again to keep his brood from running wild in the streets while he looked after his orange groves, his lumber and scrap iron sheds in Jaffa, his fertilizer, building materials, and work-tools business on the ground floor of his mansion, and his affairs on the town council. In the course of their ten years of marriage his second wife contributed a few children of her own, but during the difficult days of the World War she died while bringing her last one into the world. A young man no longer, and having already buried two wives, Pinski swore never to bring another into his ill-fated house. But who would care for his children and raise the infant that his second wife had left behind? He would have been happy to make do with the Arab wet nurse whom he installed in the back yard together with her children, but the town elders and their wives gave him no peace until he had agreed to take a third wife, a young woman from Jerusalem whose husband had run off to America, where he had been found and made to grant her a divorce only with the greatest of difficulty. This woman was Amichai's mother and the mother of several bigger and smaller brothers and sisters—the exact number was anyone's guess.

It was especially difficult to reckon the members of the Pinski family both because of the endless number of rooms that branched off from the great main hall in the middle of the second floor and because there was never any telling who actually lived in the house, who had merely come to visit, and who were Pinski's own children as opposed to his grandchildren, several of whom were older than Amichai. Though they all comprised one family and lived under a single roof, each of the Pinskis had his own separate room, led his own private life, and was involved with his own affairs, coming, going, eating, waking, and sleeping whenever he pleased, as though the house were some sort of hotel.

It was a strange and captivating mode of existence for Nachman—most of all Amichai's own little world, which was confined to his room behind blinds that were always half-lowered and a door that was always locked. While Nachman's mother always worried about their overcrowded cottage attracting dirt, bugs, and other filth-loving creatures and constantly kept moving the furniture about, pouring kerosene on the floors, spraying the house with insecticide, and airing things out in the sun, everything at Amichai's stood in semi-darkness and smelled of stale air, heavy walls, bedclothes, and books. Writing pads, recorders, volumes of poetry, and articles of clothing were scattered over his desk and floor. At night, Amichai told Nachman—and the scribblings in the margins of his black notebook bore him out—he would sit and write poems. He was in love with Tamar Levin to the tips of his funny ears, and all his round-lettered, straight-lined pages of verse were dedicated to her beauty that was even greater than Deanna Durbin's. Amichai read his poems out loud to Nachman, Balfour, and Ehud, so that the whole class knew about them and his great love. Tamar Levin knew too, yet her only response was the same frozen smile on her full lips, the same veiled look in her blue eyes that were as smooth as the sea on a summer's day.

Nachman was entranced by the black notebook in which Amichai scribbled late at night, by the marvelous way his fingers moved over the recorder, by his dimly lit room in which no member of his family, not even his mother or his aging father, was admitted without permission. Yes—and by Amichai's knowledge of girls. Not that he couldn't talk with Balfour about girls too, but only Amichai thought about them constantly, not just about Tamar Levin but about *all* of them, down to the most intimate things such as those that were mentioned in the book that lay open on his desk, *The Sexual Life of Woman*. Only Amichai was able to help Nachman to cross—under a cover of studied indifference—the threshold of that deepest of all secrets, that darkest of all prohibitions, which soothed and inflamed him in turn. That year he and Amichai became good friends.

Nachman often went to the afternoon show at the movies with Balfour and the other boys and girls in their emerging gang, but only Amichai joined him in another adventure, which was sneaking backstage on Thursday nights when a traveling theater troupe came to town. "Why should I be afraid to go with you at night?" scoffed Balfour. "I just don't want to sneak backstage. It won't by any fun if they catch us without tickets, and anyway—what's the good of seeing a show from behind?"

Nachman then confided to Amichai how he slipped away

from home on Thursday nights or managed to make believe that he was staying with friends to do homework. A little after seven he would arrive at the movie house, which converted into a theater by having its white screen taken down. At one end of the stage, in front of an iron door that was opened only on such nights, the actors' prop truck was parked. The actors gathered around little tables backstage, in the large room that was used as the Workers Club during the rest of the week. They opened their handbags and began to make themselves up, rubbing their faces with red pancake, drawing age lines with brushes and pencils, sticking hair on their heads, false lashes over their eyes, and beards on their chins. The curtains on the windows were drawn against inquisitive passersby, but Nachman always managed to find one that wasn't lowered all the way, or a crack in the door, through which he would peek while perched on two cinder blocks. In front of his eyes the young actors might be turning into Hasidim. Hocus-pocus. Beneath their silk caftans they wore no clothes but only false collars and cuffs. Nachman stood there as though in a trance, his astonishment in no way diminishing once he had figured out where the sleight-of-hand lay. Again and again he came back to watch with no less enjoyment than he would have gotten from sitting in the theater itself had he been able to pluck up the courage to ask his mother for forty-nine mils for a ticket, and had she—unimaginable prospect!—actually agreed.

Nachman told Amichai, and from now on they stole backstage together whenever one of the traveling troupes was in town. When the Habimah returned from its tour of Poland, they would go to see its production of *The Dybbuk*. Meanwhile, with the help of the iron door, they climbed some old crates in a darkened corner, pressed themselves flat against the bare wall, and peered backstage. How wonderful the actors were—and how disappointing. They would stand around smoking or laughing or playing chess backstage when suddenly one of them would jump to his feet, hand somebody his cigarette, and head for the wings erect and with firm steps to be a rabbi, a prince, a British policeman, a Spanish senora, a dreamy young maiden. Or else someone might suddenly shake or strike the large sheet of tin that he held in his hand to send a peal of thunder resounding through the auditorium. It was both exciting and disappointing—yet more the first than the second, really. Amichai and Nachman returned over and over to watch the plays from backstage. When he grew up, Nachman finally decided, confiding his thoughts to Amichai, he would be an actor too. Or perhaps he'd write plays. "Maybe," said Amichai, "I'll write a play too, in blank verse. Or an opera like *La Bohème* with Marta Eggerth and Jan Kiepura."

"Maybe we can write one together," said Nachman. "It'll have music in it, and we'll put it on for the class."

"Maybe we could," said Amichai.

It was Adon Rubin who first suggested that they put out a class newspaper. He'd had something quite modest in mind: just the usual carefully penned notebook pages illustrated perhaps with crayoned flowers and tacked up on the bulletin board—a short review of the week's current events, a few poems, two or three compositions, an interesting book review, perhaps a special page for controversial class issues like cleanliness and discipline, relations between the boys and girls, or the repeated vandalism of the teacher's desk. Almost without opposition the trio of Amichai, Ehud, and Nachman was elected to the editorial board. The class also agreed, though with a murmur of discontent, to the addition of Ruti Segal, whose job it would be to draw the colored flowers in the margins of the pages.

Next Amichai came up with the idea that the newspaper should be typed. Amichai had always been the best in class at collecting money for the Jewish National Fund, and the fact that he was suspected by some of unfairly enlisting the financial resources of his enormous family for the purpose did nothing to detract from his official prestige. On Jewish National Fund Day all the other children would pick up their blue and white ribbons and locked collection boxes, return with whatever they had managed to solicit, wait until the boxes were opened and the coins counted out, and forget all about it until the next collection day came around. Not Amichai, however, who never returned his box before it was full and hadn't room for another cent. The Jewish National Fund representative was especially nice to him and even let him practice typing on the black machine in his office. Just as Amichai's fingers were perfectly skilled on the recorder, so they quickly mastered the knack of the typewriter keys. Thereafter he typed out all his poems as though intending to make them into a book. What he would do with it no one knew, but Nachman suspected that he was planning to present it to Tamar Levin. (That his suspicions were not groundless was borne out by the following quatrain he had found on a clean sheet of paper, each line of which started with a large red letter: "Go forth O ship of youth, and sail/ To the far land of my heart's heaven/ And bring these songs to love's sweet shores/ Where dwells the maiden Tamar Levin.") In any event, once the editorial board had convened, Amichai suggested that they type the newspaper in long, narrow columns with a table of contents and eye-catching headlines. Ehud wrote an editorial on the bloody Arab uprising and the brave stand of the Jewish community that was called "We Shall Not Be Moved." Balfour transcribed one of his grandfather's tales about the settlement's early, heroic days. Amichai composed two new poems, while Nachman sat down and wrote a short story, which he realized upon rereading was taken entirely from his Uncle Rifael's life. Only its sad ending, the death of the hero at the marauders' hands as he tried to save a water pump in the orange groves, was really made up. Nevertheless, he left it as it was, ending and all.

They already had the makings of the paper. Material in

hand, the four editors now went to Hanan, the Jewish National Fund representative, a young man with a tanned, lightly lined face and dark, excitable eyes. He glanced up from the typewriter at the pages they gave him and accompanied his perusal with encouraging exclamations. "Terrific! First rate! Who are all these young talents, Amichai?" Without further ado he suggested an idea they hadn't even thought of. "Listen, all of you. If you've already decided to type up the newspaper, why don't you do it straight on a stencil, so that you can run it off on a mimeograph machine and give a personal copy to each boy and girl in your class? That will be the Jewish National Fund's way of repaying you for all the money you've collected."

Hanan not only suggested the idea, he supplied them with the stencils and a package of paper. When the stencils had been typed and proofread by the editors, all four of them felt a burst of pride. It was then that Amichai had the brilliant idea of turning the paper into a newspaper for grammar-school children all over the country. Ehud's editorial, he said, deserved to be read not just by their own class. No doubt there would be students everywhere who would wish to argue about it. In the coming issues these arguments would be printed, and readers from different schools would send in their answers to puzzles. There could even be a raffle, which would give their paper wide publicity. It might be best to send the first issue to all the upper forms with an attached letter that would explain their idea of putting out a paper by the students, of the students, and for the students.

The idea was inspiring in its simplicity and it occupied Nachman all through the latter half of that winter. Indeed, the first issue was run off right on schedule. Because Amichai lacked experience with the stencils, however, and because the lines were too close together, some of the ink ran from the front of each page to the back of the one above it, to say nothing of the erasures, which created large blots. Because of this, the editorial board decided against circulating the first issue and resolved to do a more professional job on the second and perhaps even to set it in real print. Hanan, the Jewish National Fund representative, thought this a feasible idea and suggested to the editors that they present it before the directors of the Jewish National Fund's educational division in Tel Aviv. They had plans to act on his advice as soon as the Passover vacation was over, except that meanwhile the wheel of fortune was spinning round again in Nachman's house.

30 | *A broken scaffold*

Nachman hadn't the faintest inkling, but the good years were coming to an end.

The wheel of fortune had begun to spin round again long before the accident, but then his father wasn't yet in the habit of repeating the words that later became his motto: "Once a man falls, he falls all the way." True, there was a great deal of talk about the slump, but when hadn't there been some kind of slump in the building trade, or in the orange groves, or in both together? Because of the Arab attacks and the night curfews on the roads, Nachman's father and Kravitz no longer worked beyond the town and its immediate outskirts. To make matters worse, the large immigration of Jews from Germany had now dwindled to almost nothing, for reasons which Nachman was at a loss to understand. Adon Rubin and the newspapers kept talking about the quotas imposed by the Peel Commission, whereas his mother said that she had heard from the Saubers, who had heard from their cousins in Germany, that the Jews there had decided to wait things out for a while. In any case, work was getting scarcer all the time, and the contractors no longer stood in line at his father and

Kravitz's door. They subsisted on odd jobs, a repair here, a renovation there, taking what they could get and doing business even with the least savory of contractors. Somehow they managed to get along. They no longer made a pound a day, or even eighty piasters, as they had when the boom was at its height, but their reputation being what it was, they rarely lacked a day's work. Even when Nachman's father stayed home, he put his time to good use. There was always something to do in the vegetable garden, and he had decided to expand the citrus nursery too: just this year the prices in London had been encouragingly high, and there was talk of planting new orange groves and rejuvenating the old ones. No, the wheel hadn't spun round yet. As for the slump, it couldn't go on forever, and if only times got no worse, they would manage to get by.

This was his father's opinion but not his mother's.

His mother was again full of fears, and the tears came freely to her eyes once more. The times had been bad, she unassertively but stubbornly declared, for nearly two years now. Everyone knew that whatever change there had been, had been for the worse. The end of the Arab uprising was nowhere in sight. On the contrary, in the last few months hardly a day had passed without a new fatality. The world cared only for fighting and blood. There was no hope for little people like the Jews.

Passover was already in the air. They could sit in front of the cottage in the evenings and smell the orange and lilac blossoms or look pensively at the stars. Since he no longer worked out of town, Nachman's father was always home early now. By the time it was dark, he would be washed and freshly dressed. Then he would sit outdoors with Kravitz and Nachman's mother. Uncle Rifael would drop by on his bicycle practically every night, and Adon Sharoni and Ruzha and Volush would sometimes come too.

"Why isn't there," his father asked heatedly, "why isn't there any hope? We have our own house, praise God, which is almost all paid off. We have electricity. We have a paved road. There are three or four times as many Jews in the country now as when we first came. Why isn't there any hope?"

"Aunt Leah," said Ruzha, "is upset over that murder on the Safed road. A mother and daughter. And a seven-year-old boy. They still haven't found the girl."

"It's really sobe tragedy," said Kravitz. As long as Nachman had known him, he had never grown accustomed to his strange appearance, especially in the dim evening light. Not only was he unusually tall, but his limbs were extra large even for a man of his size. He had a head like the Frankenstein monster, hands that seemed carved from wood, and shoes that resembled two rowboats. His bulbous nose was always stuffed, so that all his "*m*'s" sounded like "*b*'s." "We're living here abong savages."

"We all know that," said his father. "But does that mean there isn't any hope? According to the newspapers, it's just the opposite. The English are determined to restore order once and for all. Now that the English and French are working together, the Arab gangs aren't long for this world."

"They'll be sorry they ever started," said Uncle Rifael.

"They already are," said his father.

His mother sighed.

"Who are you sighing for, Leah—us or them?" Everyone laughed, but there wasn't a hint of a smile to be seen on her face in the darkness.

"I'm sighing," she said, "for one reason only. I'm not ambitious and I thank God for what we have. But my one dream is to see my mother and our old house again. Nachman will be bar mitzvah next summer and she hasn't ever seen him. If only she could."

"The sabe here. We cabe here albost sixteen years ago. I'd give anything for one last glibse of hobe. Let it be for two weeks, even for one—just to see and cobe back!"

"Me too," said Nachman's father. "I'd also like to go back just once."

Nachman was always to preserve this moment in his memory: a springlike night, the heavens ablaze with polished stars, the moon just risen or set. The night he heard his father say with open nostalgia that he too would like to go back just once—his father, who always used to insist, "There isn't a single thing about that unclean country that I miss. It's true that I was physically born and bred there, but in spirit I was always here. If they want to see us, there's nothing easier than for them to come here."

"It really doesn't cost that much," said Volush. "Plenty of people go every summer on a round-trip tourist fare."

"And now," laughed Kravitz, "you can sail direct frob Tel Aviv on the *Polonia.*"

"I'll tell you what," Nachman's father suddenly announced. "Go this summer with Nachman."

"Really, Aunt Leah!" Ruzha excitedly urged her.

"I'm ready to go tomorrow," said his mother. "It's only a matter of money."

"We'll get the money somehow. We've paid off almost all our debts and we can always get a loan against our property. Seriously, Leah. Take Nachman and go for the whole summer. I'll live it up here by myself."

"Don't start making plans. I'm not going yet."

"Why don't you go, Aunt Leah?"

"It's not just a matter of money," his mother said.

"What else?" His father's voice was suspicious, ready to pounce.

"Suppose, God forbid, a war breaks out. We'll be there and you'll be here."

"Now you see!" his father exclaimed triumphantly. "All these years Leah has been dying to go to Poland, but as soon as you say to her, 'Go right ahead, we'll find the money somewhere'—right away she has a new excuse. 'Suppose a war breaks out!' There won't be any war."

"All right," said his mother. "All right. But the ship isn't sailing tonight. There's still time to decide."

Uncle Rifael put on his *kolpak*, got to his feet, and shouldered his rifle.

"What about you, Rifael?" his mother asked. "Don't you ever think of going back for a visit too?"

"Going back for a visit? Of course, sometimes, but *a mentsh tracht un Got lacht*—man plans and God laughs. I'll think it over while I make the rounds of the orange groves." He laughed his broken laugh and turned to go. Kravitz rose too and stretched his giant frame. Suddenly Uncle Rifael came back and said to Nachman's father and to Kravitz, "By the way, if I were you I'd sign up with the Histadrut, the sooner the better."

"What made you think of the Histadrut all of a sudden?"

"I ran into Werfel before. You still have work now and so you think you can shrug your shoulders, but if things don't get any better, you're going to be in trouble. Werfel begged me, for your own good."

"I have my own ideas about the Hebrew workingman. I'm not going to be pressured into joining the Histadrut or any other political party."

"Ask him what he'll do, Rifael, if he finds himself out of work one day."

"Take my word for it, Shalom. Werfel is a fine fellow. He's only thinking of your own good."

And so the evening ended inconclusively, like so many others before it. His father thought that things were looking up and couldn't understand his mother's growing anxiety. "We've been through worse," he would say, "and thank God, everything's always worked out. No one who isn't afraid of a hard day's work has ever had to worry about starvation here or ever will. And as far as the Histadrut is concerned, the way I look at it the Jewish workingman in his homeland doesn't have to wave a red flag just because it's the custom elsewhere. We have our own socialism and the Prophets of Israel are thousands of years older than Karl Marx. It's a theme that repeats itself throughout history: along comes some apostate who plagiarizes the most lofty ideas in Judaism and peddles them as his own invention. But the *goyim* are by their very nature unable to assimilate the profoundest aspects of the Jewish religion, such as love of your fellow man, or true equality, which isn't based just on how much you earn but on your being created in God's image, even in these distorted apostate forms. What was the original Christianity of Jesus if not Judaism? When I was in the Polish army, there was an officer, a certain Pan Jerzinsky, a very intelligent fellow who came from an old aristocratic family. He did his best to fight against the anti-Semitism in his blood which every Gentile drinks with his mother's milk. 'Pan Jerzinsky,' I used to say to him when he would ask me about the Jewish religion, 'let me give you an example. The two of us are now standing in front of a window and our eyes are practically blinded by the bright summer light, even though the sun is hidden from us by the walls of this room. Suppose now it's that way with God: the divine reality is always revealing itself to us, but we're shut up in the narrow room of our human understanding, which has only a little window through which we can look. And it's here that you'll find the difference between yourselves and us. It's not that we see more than you, but simply that we're aware that such brilliance must come from an immeasurable source of light. Whereas you—you take a piece of wood with some sulfur on its tip, scratch it till it burns, and say, *There's the light!* Begging your pardon, Pan Jerzinsky, this is the difference in a nutshell between the God of Israel and all the imitation idols.' He liked my analogy so much that he patted me on the back and said, 'Shpiegler, you're all right!'—And really, it's as simple as that. That's exactly what happened with Karl Marx, and it's what happened with that contemporary apostate of ours too, Lev Bronstein, alias Trotsky, who was the first high priest of the Bolsheviks far more than Lenin or Stalin. There are people in this country whose world was

working overtime from dawn to dusk. In normal times Nachman's father would never even have considered working for this particular contractor, who would gladly have committed mayhem for a penny and was known to be an impossible man, but nowadays one couldn't afford to be choosy. You thanked the good Lord if there was work at all.

"This Sabbath," he answered with a smile, "this Sabbath I'll get hold of Werfel by the synagogue."

Nachman knew why he smiled. Werfel was one of the labor leaders in town, but his father said that he was different from the others in every sense of the word. "I respect him the way I do," said his father, "both because even though he has a lawyer's degree he's completely devoted to the interests of the workers as he sees them, and because he's a cultivated man with a sense of humor with whom you can talk as an equal on any topic at all. But what really lends him stature in my eyes is something else, something which may not seem to be the most important thing in the world, but which is not without reason one of the Ten Commandments—I mean honoring thy father and thy mother. It's no accident that this commandment is the only one of the ten to be followed by the promise, 'That your life may be long upon the earth that the Lord thy God hath given you.' There's a very deep moral here. Whoever cuts himself off from his father and mother and thinks only of himself loses his connection with both the past and the future and so his life seems very short. But whoever honors his father and his mother and takes care of them in old age prolongs both their life and his own. His life stretches back into the past, down the chain of the generations that links his father and his forefathers, and forward into the future, toward his sons and grandsons. Whoever lacks a feeling of obligation toward his parents or his children is like a weed that gets hoed up and uprooted in the end. Werfel is really a man of culture."

All this Nachman or anyone else could see for himself on holidays and Sabbath eves. During the week Werfel walked about town in a simple Russian tunic, khaki shorts, and khaki socks that came nearly up to his knees, which were burned black by the sun like his arms and his shiny bald pate. On Sabbath eves, however, he wore his gray pants and over them a Russian blouse of black silk, which he belted with a silk rope that looked like the cord old man Becker tied around his black caftan. A workingman's cap on his head, he would guide his old mother to the Hasidic synagogue. She toddled along, step by step, her black dress hanging on her withered, shrunken frame as though on a scarecrow. Werfel held her arm, walking beside her as far as the top of the stairs that led to the women's gallery with small, measured steps that were completely unlike the way he gadded pell-mell about town the rest of the week. He himself remained outside the synagogue, but as soon as the service was over he was waiting at the top of the stairs to take his old mother by the arm again and toddle back with her, step by step, to their house in the new workers' quarters that had been built down the street. It was this time of day that Nachman's father had in mind when he said he would speak to Werfel on the Sabbath, by the synagogue.

It never came to that, however. The wheel of fortune spun round all at once and what was up was suddenly down. Quite literally so. One day Nachman came home from school in a hurry to eat and run over to Balfour's so that they could finish their homework in time to make the afternoon show. When he tried the front door of the cottage, though, he found that it was locked. He searched for the key on the kitchen windowsill, behind the half-closed shutter where his mother would have left it, but it wasn't there. She was almost always home at this time, and she never forgot to leave the key behind if she went out. Nachman circled around the cottage and peered inside through a crack in the back shutter. The window was open. He unhooked the shutter with a stick, threw his knapsack inside, and started to boost himself after it.

"Nachman!"

He turned around to look and noticed for the first time that Mute Baylin's mother and Berkovitz's wife were standing and staring at him. Only now did the frightening thought occur to him that something must have happened.

"Where's my mother?"

"It isn't her," said Mute Baylin's mother.

"It's nothing," said Berkovitz's wife. He could feel the fear crawl through his body. "Don't be afraid, it's nothing. The scaffold broke and he fell."

"My father?" Scenes flashed before his mind. Black-bordered placards on the streets. Photographs in the newspapers. The stores in town shut down. Hundreds of people crowding in front of the Great Synagogue, straining to make out the words of the mayor's nasal eulogy. His father.

"You needn't scare the boy so," said Mute Baylin's mother. "Your father did fall off the scaffold, but it's nothing serious. Kravitz came and took your mother to the hospital. She said you should make your own lunch."

"Which hospital?" He didn't know how, but he knew right then that it wasn't nothing and that their whole world had come crashing down with the scaffold. Despite himself he kept picturing his father lying in the hospital, his face covered with blood, weak, windy groans escaping through his lips. "Which hospital?"

"The new one," said Berkovitz's wife. "The Histadrut hospital, the one . . ."

"Where are you running to, Nachman? Eat something first. You don't even have money for your bus fare. Nachman, come back."

31 | *Brother to brother*

The two of them stood before the screen door that said "Emergency Room," still out of breath from racing downhill on Balfour's new bicycle and running with it uphill. Each time a stern-looking doctor or a chattery nurse in starched white came through the door, Nachman retreated a step toward Balfour, then returned to his post. His mother stood inside, in front of a pair of doors that swung open and shut on their hinges to admit and discharge an endless flow of people and stretchers. She stared at them red-eyed as they brushed back and forth, her body a frozen mass, her fingers pressed to her cheeks as though she had a toothache. Behind her stood Kravitz in his white workclothes, which were so torn and patched that even the patches had tears. His father had been brought through these doors for X-rays long before he and Balfour had arrived. Nachman tried to imagine him hurtling helplessly from the broken scaffold to smash against the ground. He must have cracked up on the iron construction rods, like the wagon driver Nachman had heard about who felt so sorry for his mule that he hitched himself to a wagon full of building rods to help it carry them downhill;

the rods slipped off the top, doubling him over and running him through before the wheels crushed him completely. But perhaps his father had been lucky and fallen on a pile of gravel or clean sand. When he'd asked his mother how he was, she had simply hugged him close to her and murmured without tears, "I knew it would happen. Our luck was bound to run out."

"Please, Leah, listen to be for a bobent. It's nothing serious. I probise you, he'll be all right. I saw exactly how he fell." The giant Kravitz was as white as his plasterer's clothes, as white as the dry clots of whitewash on his ears and his bushy brows. His wooden fingers kneaded his caked cap and he stubbornly said again, though the words sounded less than convincing through his stuffed nostrils, "I probise you, there's no internal dabage. It's nothing at all."

"Even a stronger man than he couldn't get away with a fall like that. He didn't even recognize me. I tried talking to him but he just lay there as white as a sheet. And those eyes . . . How many times did I tell him that it wasn't any work for him, climbing like that over scaffolds with buckets of plaster in his hand! What's to become of us now? What has he done to himself?"

"Please, boys, this is no place for children. Why don't you go sit sobewhere outside, in the shade."

"What's to become of us, Nemmale, what?" His mother was a grown woman who was never at a loss for something to do. Now that she threw her arms around him and hugged him close to her soft body, he shivered strangely. A distant scene passed before him, as though he were remembering it from a movie or a book. A warm bed early in the morning, underneath the feather quilt. He lay snuggled against the body of his mother, who was sleeping on her side. It must have been after he had been burned and the bandages had been removed from his eyes—yes, after. His eyes were open. Rays of sunlight fell on the warm bed through the slats in the shutters. His mother was hot and kicked off the quilt in her sleep. Through the opening of her nightgown he could see two round globes with two dark, wrinkly coins at their tips. He buried his head in their softness. "What, Nemmale, what," she whispered in her sleep, throwing her arms around him.

Nachman wrenched himself free from his mother's arms. When he stood right next to her, his head came up to her shoulders. Kravitz stood behind her.

"I'll wait outside."

"Have you eaten lunch? I asked Widow Baylin . . ."

"I've eaten, I've eaten," he called back, passing through the screen door.

Now they stood outside, silently waiting. His mother remained at the far end of the room, her eyes on the swinging doors, through which men in white and green smocks kept coming and going. Nachman couldn't see her eyes but he knew they looked like big, frozen tears. He thought of the time long ago when she had had to stand by herself from morning to evening, without his father, in the store Mister Blackman had built them. The perspiration that had drenched his body as he ran in a panic to the hospital before Balfour caught up with him on the bicycle had dried now and no longer crawled through his hair like yellow ants beneath his hat. Fear crawled through his body instead. His mother's stonelike stance, as though she were hypnotized by the swinging doors that brushed each other back and forth, made those half-forgotten times when something bad had come between his parents float again to the surface of his memory: his father's trips to Jerusalem, the long silences at home, his mother's bitter whispers in the night and her eyes that were as red as a chinchilla's all day long. Fear climbed silently over him with catlike stealth and Nachman fought to drive it away. He was sure his father wouldn't die. Kravitz knew what he was talking about. But suppose he had broken his legs and couldn't walk again? Or his arms, and couldn't work? The newspapers were full of stories of horrible accidents. He couldn't stop imagining his father lying crippled in bed, a living corpse for the rest of his life. Why hadn't he recognized his mother when they brought him in on the stretcher?

He kept imagining his own future too, as though he too had toppled off the scaffold. The wonderful year he had been having in school, which was still far from over, was now smashed to smithereens. He would not be going with Amichai to Tel Aviv anymore to arrange for a students' newspaper. *Our Future.* A fine future awaited him indeed—wrapping oranges like Pesach Berkovitz, or working as an apprentice in the garage like Peterzail, or selling nuts in front of the movies like Kashani the drunk's eldest son! The empty lot between his cottage and Balfour's house seemed to stretch to infinity, like the great deserts of Africa and Asia.

"You really don't have to wait anymore," said Nachman to Balfour.

"I don't mind."

"I'll be staying here with my mother anyhow. There's no way of knowing when we'll find out how he is. You really don't have to wait."

He wasn't trying to be considerate of Balfour. He just wanted to be by himself. He hadn't even asked for this show of friendship, which was beginning to unnerve him. It had been pure chance that young Adon Mendelevitch passed by the building, noticed a crowd there, and learned the news. Balfour had sat down to eat the minute he got home from school, so that he would have enough time to do all his homework before the afternoon show. His father, he said, had casually mentioned Adon Shpiegler's fall from the scaffold only in the middle of the meal. By the time he reached the Shpieglers' on his new bicycle, Nachman was on his way to the hospital. Balfour sped after him, caught up, and sat him in front of the handlebars. They took the downhills and level stretches as fast as they could and ran uphill by the bicycle's side. Nachman knew that Balfour was a true friend, yet something rankled inside him nonetheless. Why didn't he go back to his big house already, where he could bask all he liked in the quiet coolness of the large rooms, in Madam Mendelevitch's lemony scent, in old Adon Mendelevitch's glory?

"We're bound to be here for a long while still. I'm going inside." He had already opened the screen door, leaving no room for argument.

"Come over tonight then to let me know. It doesn't matter how late."

Once Balfour had mounted his bicycle and left, a hard lump stuck in Nachman's throat. Whatever happened, it wouldn't be good.

He was still standing in the doorway of the emergency room when the white swinging doors opened wide and through them a man in green clothes pushed a bed that was covered with a blue hospital blanket. Nachman's mother and Kravitz ran to its side. Nachman too hurried over, the yellow ants crawling over him once more.

He could only see his father from the chin up. His balding head lay on a white pillow, a thick stubble on its cheeks. There had always been a hat on his father's head and a definite line ran between his sunburned face and his scalp, which was colored a grayish-whitish blue as though it had the same glassy surface as their heavy milk dishes. Streaks of congealed blood ran down toward his ears like phylactery straps. His wide-open eyes had their usual brown glow and even smiled at Nachman's mother as she bent over them.

"Have you been here long?" he whispered. To Nachman it seemed that it hurt him to talk.

"Where else did you think we'd be? Nachman's here too. Let your father see you, Nachman. And Kravitz."

"You busn't try to talk," said Kravitz before his father could utter a word. He thrust his gigantic head before his father's eyes, so that he shouldn't have to move them. "Try not to talk. This Sabbath I'b going to say a blessing in the synagogue that you cabe through all right."

"Nachman," his father whispered anyhow.

Nachman squeezed between his mother and the bed, craning his neck to see. His father rolled up his eyes at him. Perhaps he even tried to move his head, because suddenly his face contorted and his eyes shut tight.

"He's in terrible pain!" his mother practically screamed in her fright. "Where are the doctors?" But his father's eyes were open again and looking straight at him. Nachman had always associated them with the "burning coals in their sockets" that he read about in books, but now he discovered that they were not only brown but had little bits and drops of honey scattered all over. They weren't burning at all, or even glittering, but dusky, like a sooty lamp. He had never known before that his father's twinkling eyes were so sad.

"You have a broken papa," his father whispered. "I was always careful not to work for that son of a bitch. The wood on his scaffolds is rotten. It broke right under me and I fell and smashed myself like a bottle."

"You're talking nonsense, Shalob!"

"I'm not a child, Kravitz."

"You're a lucky ban that you fell in the sand."

"The luck of a Jew. Nachman! You'll have to be the man in the house now."

"Did you ever see such a person? He's worried about us! You'd do better not to talk so much and to worry about getting well soon yourself!" Though he was standing with his back turned to her, Nachman could hear the tears in his mother's voice.

"I'm a natural wonder. Animal, vegetable, and mineral all in one."

"If he's already making wisecracks, it's a sure sign he's all right."

This remark came from Uncle Rifael, who had entered unnoticed in his *gaffir*'s uniform, his gun on his shoulder.

"So you've come to see the *shlimazel* too!"

"*Shlibazel!* He falls frob the second story into a yard full of betal rods, sits up and begins to joke two hours later, and calls hibself a *shlibazel!*"

"What did the doctors say?" asked Uncle Rifael.

"We haven't even seen a doctor," said his mother. "Someone brought him back in here and went away."

"We'll find out in a minute," said Uncle Rifael, but he continued to stand there looking quietly at Nachman's father. For a moment it seemed to Nachman that a smile flitted across his sunbeaten face, whose wrinkles had plaster and dried clay in them no longer.

"You're laughing at me," his father unexpectedly whispered too.

"Why on earth should I laugh?" He was disconcerted. "You might say just the opposite. I was thinking . . ."

"That you expected this to happen from the first day, eh? That you were always sure I'd never make a workingman, eh?"

"Please, both of you! He isn't allowed to talk."

"But I am, Leah. I was thinking the exact opposite. What makes you say that I laughed? It's just the other way around. Who else do I have here besides you? The ways things are nowadays, who's to say that tomorrow I won't need you, God forbid? Having a brother like you here makes all the difference for me. And not just a brother, but a man I really respect, *a mentsh!*"

"A *tsebrochener mentsh!*" whispered his father. A broken man.

"Please, Shalom, you mustn't talk like that. I beg you. Everyone says it's nothing. You'll be all right."

"You hope," whispered his father. "Once a man falls, he falls all the way."

32 | *Once a man falls, he falls all the way*

"Once a man falls, he falls all the way! It's as simple as that. The wheel spins around, and you can save all your questions and your answers and your complaints. The fact that my whole world is in shambles, that I have no idea for what I'm being punished or how I'm supposed to atone for it, is completely irrelevant. Why did it happen? *Azoy vil er*—that's God's will. That is, if He really exists and cares at all, then things don't happen just like that: a rotten board breaks, a man falls off a scaffold, and finished, *oys!* Just like that. Do you hear me, Sharoni? I've been rotting away in this cast for weeks. The heat and perspiration are eating me alive and I can't even move, to say nothing of going outside to water the vegetables or even making myself a glass of tea. I can't even take a leak without help. I lie here and I look at a book now and then and I think: Why, why did it have to happen to me? What was I asking for, after all? To be a big orange grower? A delegate to Zionist Congresses? The Chief Rabbi of Palestine? All I wanted was to be a plasterer, a simple workingman, to be allowed to earn my bread by the sweat of my brow. So why me? *Oy vay vay,* the fall that I've taken! To tell you the truth, even before the accident I was beginning to have my doubts. Just to have seen what that Kutter did to Missus Blackman was enough to make a man conclude that it's all one big hoax! Or perhaps it's like Spinoza says, that God isn't all-merciful, all-compassionate, all-etcetera, but that He simply reveals Himself in nature, or maybe He even is nature. In other words, if you don't pray every day or wait six hours between eating meat and milk, it's no shock to Anyone up there. God is a sort of philosophy, *efshir iz er, efshir iz er nit*—maybe He exists, maybe He doesn't. But now that I've been ruined and can see for myself how we're stranded high and dry—and now of all times when there's no work to be had and fighting everywhere and a danger of world war!—I'm beginning to think that there must be a God after all, some kind of power up there that looks down just on me and knocks me over the head each time I'm about to straighten up. Everyone comes to congratulate me for my miraculous escape. Some miracle! So what if I may never be able to bend my arm again because the elbow is fractured or lift it more than forty-five degrees because my shoulder is smashed—that's a tragedy? That's a miracle, the hand of God! *Yoh, ikh zay shayn oys*—I'm some beauty. If I owned a few orange groves or bought and sold real estate that wasn't mine and made a commission, I could get along fine with my two broken legs and my arm—even with two broken arms. But I'm a plasterer. I never had such good years as the ones I spent on the scaffold and I never will again. The late Shalom Shpiegler was thirty-two years of age when he first held the plasterer's spade and lived barely four years more. May God's will be done."

Nachman sat somewhere off on the porch or outside the window, but he kept an ear on his father's conversations with Sharoni, just as he did on all his endless talk. His father had come home from the hospital long ago and now sat up in bed with his arm in a cast that was cradled in some strange apparatus that rested against his chest, while his two legs were in casts up to the knees, which made it seem as though he were wearing white boots. He hadn't had a concussion, his ribs were all right, and the worst that could happen, the doctors said, was that he might lose partial use of one arm. So they said, but he still found it hard to move about and never left the house. Even with a crutch under his right armpit, he had to be held onto when he walked. Several times a day he withdrew under an old blanket while someone brought him a chamber pot. He let his beard, which was now shot through with gray hairs, grow all week long and shaved only on Fridays with the help of Nachman's mother. The summer seemed to last forever that year and splotchy red hives covered his body, which was irritated by the cast and the heat and the sheer aggravation. On the other hand, it was just as well that he needed to wear only a pajama top and a pair of khaki shorts, which were easy to put on and take off. The shorts were baggy and came down to his knees, where the white skin of his flabby thighs—which seemed too frail to carry his thin body—showed through above the cast. His chest muscles too seemed flabby beneath the pajama top, whose limp left sleeve was buttoned beneath the plaster cast. He couldn't really walk, but he couldn't lie in bed all day long in the heat either, and so he went from chair to chair, from the window that looked out on Widow Baylin's house to the porch, which got a westerly breeze after sunset. He spent most of his time reading books and newspapers and began to perk up only when visitors came.

Sharoni was now a regular visitor. So was Uncle Rifael, but it sometimes seemed to Nachman that his father enjoyed talking to Sharoni best of all. There was no one else with whom he felt free to converse about any topic at all and not just about the terrible accident that had turned him into a zombie. When he sat with Sharoni, who wore only a tiny skullcap on his sleek, wavy chestnut hair and carefully, unhurriedly enunciated each word, his own voice too became deeper and more formal, as though he were reading the news on the radio. Nachman might be off somewhere else, but he would manage to catch every word. Sharoni had come to Jerusalem with his parents as a small boy, before the last war, and he had countless stories to tell about the city and the special character of its inhabitants, of whom the Sefardim, who weren't really like Sefardim, were even snobbier than the Ashkenazim, who weren't really like Ashkenazim. He also liked to tell about his wife's large family, which claimed descent all the way back to one of the eminences of the Spanish exile (Nachman's mother said behind his back that he had married her only for her pedigree and because he mistakenly thought that she could provide him with a good job and an easy life in Jerusalem), about his teaching years in the remote Upper Galilee, and about the article he had published several years before in *Education*, which made such an enormous impression that he was besieged with requests to lengthen it into a book.

His father's conversations with Sharoni lasted so long that Nachman sometimes suspected that he enjoyed being an invalid. But there were other visitors too, such as the old Beckers, or Holzberg the plumber, Arele's father, or even Chupchik, who had been willing to forgive and forget ever since the accident and now came to see Nachman's father through a hole he himself had opened in the disputed fence. Yes, even Blind Koppel, who was still awaiting the Messiah as eagerly as ever. A milky fire burned in his sightless eye each time he set out to prove that the days of Armageddon were truly at hand. Look at Austria. Look at Chamberlain's trips to Hitler. His blind eye turned in its socket while he spat out verses from the Bible that strewed his short beard with froth. "For I have a contention with the dwellers of this earth, for there is neither truth nor human kindness nor knowledge of God among them. For they swear and deny, murder and rob and whore, until blood laps against blood."

The Herzlichs too came to visit. They would heave a

sigh of sympathy and ask Nachman's father if he had decided about looking for work. "You'll never return to the scaffold," they told him. "It's not even worth thinking of. The best thing would be for you to open a small shop of some sort, but these aren't the times for shops. Whenever there's a new rumor of war, everyone runs to hoard food and the prices soar sky high, while when the rumors die down, everyone's still out of work and you have to give credit if they're going to buy at all, which takes a lot of money. Perhaps," said *fetter* Herzlich, stroking his red beard, "perhaps you could find a job as a teacher again."

Nachman's father didn't answer. He was feeling too broken and blue to run the risk of a fight. "I don't know what to say anymore," he said. "I don't know where to turn or whom to ask for help. All I want is some source of income, so that Leah doesn't have to wash strangers' underpants and Nachman can continue at school."

When the Herzlichs were gone, though, he let his true feelings out. He could see well enough the malicious, vengeful pleasure in their yellow eyes! To this day they hadn't forgiven him for selling the store and not indenturing himself and Nachman to them for life.

His mother took offense. *Fetter* Herzlich, she said, was their only close relative in the country. He had already helped them once when they had been in trouble, and she couldn't understand what Nachman's father wanted from him. "He's only thinking of our own good. We can use a helping hand right now. I beg of you, Shalom, don't start up with him."

Nachman's greatest fear was that the something bad between his parents might return again. It was already in the air. Why wasn't his father more careful of what he said, like Uncle Rifael? How had he fallen off the scaffold anyway? What made him so brittle and so full of self-pity? Uncle Rifael went out to patrol the orange groves every night, but you never heard him complain how dangerous it was. And there was Volush and Ruzha, who had grown so tired of living in town and going to the work lineup every evening that they decided to join one of the new kibbutzim on the embattled banks of the Jordan. When they had come to say good-bye, they seemed as jolly as if they were going off on a picnic. Why did his father have to make such a big thing of his accident? Why was he being so hard on his mother? Shouldn't he really be thinking of some kind of work?

Nachman was beginning to think unkind thoughts. It scared him and he tried not to, but he couldn't help seeing his father in a different light these days. The long weeks he had spent shut up in the cottage had robbed his face of its tan and slackened the fine wrinkles—like Uncle Rifael's—that had formed in the corners of his eyes. Where his body showed through it was flabby and white, and he seemed to have shrunk to half the size he had been before his fall. The contrast was especially striking when he was visited by Kravitz with his huge, square skull that was crowned by a great mass of hair, and with his ears, nose, and jaw that seemed too big even for his head, which in turn seemed too big for his body. Kravitz would sit there with his hands on his knees, every finger of which looked like a tent peg. How pitiful his own father's fingers seemed in comparison, how delicate and weak and almost transparent! With hands like his, Kravitz could have slain Goliath without the help of a slingshot. He was a simple soul, but though the few words he managed to get out always sounded funny, what he said to Nachman's father made good sense. The truth of the matter, he said, was that even if he hadn't fallen off the scaffold, he wouldn't have stood on it much longer. There was less and less work to be had these days, and what there was, was a crime to accept. The good years in the building trade were over and done with. He himself had been working with his hands for sixteen years, the last ten in the orange groves and construction, lifting crates of fruit, digging wells, quarrying, mixing cement—and now he was right back where he had started. The one solid offer he had was to drive a kerosene cart from door to door. "The trouble is, though, that then I'll have anibals to take care of. All I want is sobething with regular pay that I know is steady and not too hard. If it's not one thing, it's another. When tibes are good everyone fights over you, and when they're bad you can't find a thing. Who knows, if nothing better turns up, baybe I'll drive the cart."

His father seemed to listen yet he didn't really hear. In reply he told Kravitz about Uncle Herzlich's suggestion, which had shocked him to the quick.

"They think it would be idyllic, that the Messiah would already come, if only every Jew owned a shop of his own. Why do you think I left my father's house and all my family in the first place? It was only because that was exactly the future that awaited me there: either to go into business, or to become a teacher, or to live off the Jewish religion. Tell me your opinion, Kravitz. What can I possibly work at when they take this contraption off my feet, eh? What?"

Kravitz told him. So did Uncle Rifael. So did Sharoni. So did Karniel. So did all his friends and acquaintances. Whatever advice they gave, however, he always found something wrong with it. Everyone agreed that hard physical work was out of the question. Perhaps he should go to Jerusalem and study in the teachers college. What, now that he had to prepare his own son for his bar mitzvah? Maybe he should consider becoming a bookkeeper. Who needed a bookkeeper and who was there to teach him anyway? Well then, let him be a broker of some sort. That was easily said, but what kind of broker? Why not an insurance broker, for example! Many people did quite well, even became wealthy, selling insurance. Jews liked to be insured; they might not have a penny to their name or know if they were coming or going, but they were always ready to take out a policy. "That's it!" said Karniel. "It's just the thing for you. You're a man who likes to talk with people, and I'm sure you're a man whom they'll trust."

"I can just see them looking at me and thinking: 'Get a load of who's coming to insure us—it's Shpiegler, who broke his arms and legs in that accident and got nothing for it except the right to curse out the contractor.'"

"On the contrary," said Karniel. "Tell them about how you came to sell insurance, about your own bitter lesson. It'll go over big."

Nachman's father liked this idea, especially since Karniel promised that he could get him a job with a large English company whose chief agent in Palestine was a cousin of his. He could already see himself insuring the whole town, the area around it. Everything would work out fine. Nachman's mother heaved a sigh.

"What are you sighing for now?" asked his father.

"I'm not so sure," she said. It was plain to see that she was already against the new plan.

"You're not so sure about what?"

"You'll have to go from house to house. You'll have to knock on every door. And with your legs."

"My legs will get all better," said his father with surprising self-confidence and just a trace of resentment.

"It's not just your legs. It's the times. Everywhere there's shooting, burning, destroying. War might break out any minute. What insurance company would want anything to do with our problems?"

"So what are you suggesting?" He sounded angry but he clearly took her words to heart.

"I don't know." And after a moment's silence: "I asked you so many times to join the Histadrut, to talk to Werfel."

"What does Werfel have to do with it? Why must you keep badgering me that I didn't join the Histadrut? What would Werfel have done for me? What?"

"It makes no difference any more."

"If it makes no difference, why must you keep harping on it?"

Nachman sat off somewhere listening. The something bad between his parents was happening again. He didn't want to hear any more. He would go to Balfour's or to Amichai's and not come home until late. Except that then too his shrunken, half of a father would be sitting up with some visitor, to whom he would be telling the tragic story of his life. Nachman knew exactly with what words he would begin and end, the lilt that they would have, the sighs that would encase them like absorbent cotton: "Once a man falls, he falls all the way!"

33 | *Eighth grade anyway!*

Yes, eighth grade! The year of the bar mitzvahs and the bicycles; a crisp, mischievous year, and as far as Nachman was concerned, a Janus-faced one; a stolen year, a gift year he hadn't expected; and therefore, perhaps, a year of fierce tensions, whose every milestone seemed the last, whose every hour—a farewell.

He was one of the eighth grade's biggest pranksters. Every day they thought up some new escapade. The table for example. The grammar school, they all knew, charged their parents a small fortune—and yet look at the table they had been given this year in their new classroom! Touch it—and it wobbled. Move it—and it groaned and creaked. Move it a little farther—and it broke down into its component parts like an arithmetic problem. Then why not really take it apart, right away, into such tiny components that it could no longer be put back together again? And why not carry its corpse downstairs, part by part, and present it to the janitor with full honors? After such a splendid funeral, there would be no choice but to bury it for good.

The inspiration for the funeral was Nachman's. The

master of ceremonies was Ehud. The grand eulogy was given by Amichai during the long intermission, while every eighth grader held a piece of the dead table in his hand. When the speech was over, the funeral procession descended the stairs from the second floor. Nachman went at the head of it, brandishing a table leg in one hand and chanting sweetly, "Pray for poor sinners in the hour of their death!"

Each student deposited his piece of table before the janitor's door. Amichai recited the *kaddish* and refused to be interrupted even by the irate janitor. The whole class was laughing uproariously, and word of this latest prank spread quickly through the school. The upshot of it was that Adon Ben-Shalom himself came to their classroom and demanded to know who had broken the table.

Adon Ben-Shalom was a class above all the other teachers, even Adon Rubin. He was a giant of a man, two meters tall or more, with kinky hair like an African's and brown eyes that took in the entire classroom at a glance, stopping every bit of horseplay. He taught history as though it were a detective story, told jokes, presided over arguments, even invited students to his home for long talks. And that wasn't all. He rode to school on a bicycle. He played soccer. It was even whispered that he was a secret commander in the Haganah. And *that* wasn't the whole of it, either. It was impossible, for example, to cheat on one of his tests. How could you when he announced in advance that he had full confidence in you—and walked out of the classroom? In a word: Handsome. Young. A prince of a man.

Now he sat in his chair, holding his notebook on his knees since there wasn't any table, and quietly asked, "Who broke the table?"

The eighth grade was a Janus-faced year for Nachman, for he knew that inside himself, hidden from sight, was another Nachman who turned an appraising eye on everything and held a silent but steady dialogue with the Nachman everyone knew. Seen by Adon Ben-Shalom, he was a bashful young boy who could hardly do wrong. Seen by his parents, he was still a mere child who was quick to catch cold, prone to get boils, and overly given to reading, which threatened to ruin his lovely eyes. The inner Nachman, however, looked coolly out and saw things he hadn't even known existed a year before, things that gave him a catch in his throat and butterflies in his stomach, things he alone, as though under a private curse, seemed to see.

Take his father, for example, whose legs and arms were now released from their casts and enforced rest. Gone were his white workclothes, while the tools of his craft—his spade, his pallet, and his level—lay forgotten in the shower stall outside. No longer did Nachman's mother prepare a lunch basket for him every evening with hamburgers, peeled cucumbers, hard-boiled eggs, slices of bread, a pinch of salt, and a bottle of tea. No longer did he rise in the darkness to go off early to work, or return in the evening with the pungent smell of dry plaster on his body, or the scent of the turpentine with which he cleaned the lime and cement from his hands.

When his father rose in the morning now, it was to don an old green bathrobe that had been tucked away in mothballs all these years in the bottom drawer of the sofa along with his parents' other clothes from Poland and his mother's fox wrap with its two long tassels. The faded wool robe hung on his father's gaunt body over the long woolen underwear in which he slept. Nachman would have preferred not to watch, but his cool eye that was always open saw his father's feet as they dragged themselves in his mother's floppy slippers from the kitchen to the porch and back again, saw his hands slicing bread and making sandwiches, which he wrapped in paper from the packinghouse, saw them carefully peel an orange and put everything into the lunch bag that he took with him to school, after which they handed him a piping hot cup of thick cocoa. Nowadays it was his mother who left the house early, in order to be at Doctor Stockhammer's promptly at seven. None of his father's protests had dissuaded her from taking on work, any work at all, at least until things looked up a bit. He argued with her loudly, swore by his life and Nachman's, but to no avail: they couldn't afford, she insisted, to pass up three and a half pounds a month, lunches included—and off she went. Nachman didn't mind that his father stayed home in the mornings and served him breakfast, but the half-shrunken sight of him in his old robe and the yellow woolen underwear on his thin legs made him want to look the other way.

Not that his father stayed home all day long. On the contrary, as soon as Nachman left for school, he put on the suit that the tailor had turned to make it look nearly new, knotted a tie, placed a hat on his head, and went into town to look for something to do. So far he had managed to find an odd job here and there, but he was still looking for steady work, which was bound to turn up in a few weeks or a month. It was on this basis that they were keeping Nachman in the Moriah School, though God only knew, said his mother, how they would ever pay the bills. "Believe me," his father said, "I'd sooner steal than see him drop out of school, because I'm only now beginning to realize how a man without an education, or more exactly, without a diploma—because it's the diploma, after all, that counts—is a complete nobody. If only I had some kind of degree, I'd be in a completely different position today. I could get a teaching job. I could be a corresponding secretary for some institution. I could work in a bank as well as Karniel. But that's life. In this country too, I'm sorry to say, you have to be rich or have pull to get by without a degree. Mendelevitch, for example, doesn't have one, but he still draws a fat salary from the town council to look at the wells now and then and make sure that they still have their water. But I myself, Nachman, am not Mendelevitch, and you're not Balfour. I may have to steal or mortgage this cottage, but I'll see to it that you finish school and make something of yourself."

Nachman stayed on in school—yes, in eighth grade. He

applied himself to his studies, yet he felt as though he were laboring under a curse. His father, he plainly saw, was a feeble man who ran about town begging people, literally begging them, to help him find some kind of a job, a clerical post, a brokerage, perhaps something collecting taxes, or a position with the town council, or the farmers' association, or the chamber of commerce, or the Histadrut, or anything, anything at all. He did in fact get an offer of selling insurance and newspaper and magazine subscriptions, but who wanted to take on more payments in times like these when everyone was looking for work and work was not to be had?

Nachman stayed on in eighth grade, wondering how long it would be before his father came to tell him that their money had run out.

It was a perfect shame too, because this year, with Adon Ben-Shalom, with all its bar mitzvahs and pranks, had begun so promisingly. What would happen to him if he should have to drop out of school even before his bar mitzvah, before everything? Every two or three weeks now, there was a bar mitzvah party in some boy's house. They would all go to synagogue and the bar mitzvah boy would get lots of presents, and best of all, a bicycle. Nachman himself had no illusions: even if he stayed in school, he would not have his bar mitzvah in the Great Synagogue like Balfour, and he would certainly not get an English racer. If he had to drop out, though, he would have even less. Not a boy would come to his party. He wouldn't get a single gift.

Still, he let himself dream: even in the middle of class, or horsing about with the boys in the schoolyard, the second, hidden Nachman inside him kept spinning out dreams. In his dream his Uncle Elyakum in Chicago might have died and left a huge inheritance (in actual fact, he had sent them a hundred dollars after Nachman's father's accident, which had helped tide them over the winter), all to Nachman. The word spread quickly through town. The sexton of the Great Synagogue came to their cottage and suggested that Nachman read the *haftarah,* the portion from the Prophets, not before the small prayer group to which his father belonged, but in the Great Synagogue, like Balfour. He saw himself sitting in the front pew, exactly where he had sat with Balfour and old Adon Mendelevitch last Purim. He saw the huge interior of the building, whose likes he had seen nowhere else—the two rows of thick, marmoreal columns, like those that had stood in the Temple, supporting the high ceiling, with a round dome rising from the middle. The twelve signs of the zodiac were depicted on the narrow stained-glass windows, while above them were the symbols of the twelve tribes, six along one wall and six along the other. The whole synagogue—so old Adon Mendelevitch told Balfour—was built so that the Holy Ark faced straight toward Jerusalem, indeed, straight toward where the Temple once stood. He saw himself in a gray, custom-made suit, in long pants, in a new beret or perhaps an embroidered skullcap, a silk prayer shawl over his shoulders. Candies in paper wrappers would rain down on him from the women's gallery as soon as he finished the *haftarah.* Then everyone would come to a reception at his house. The cottage would fill up with books, games, tennis rackets, a bicycle, just like Balfour's room. . . . *So it's presents you're after, you dumbbell!* laughed the same chill-eyed Nachman inside him who had just been dreaming. *But if Uncle Elyakum left you all his money, what do you need with their presents?* He had to admit he was right, yet there was one concession that he dreamily refused to make: the gift of a pistol like the one that Balfour had received from his grandfather, the little Parabellum that young Madam Mendelevitch now kept locked away. But Nachman didn't even have a grandfather, to say nothing of one like old Adon Mendelevitch. This dream too was a flop.

It was a Janus-faced year, the eighth grade, and Nachman's world was Janus-faced too. Some days he would shut himself up in the empty cottage—his mother didn't come home from Doctor Stockhammer's until late, and his father was constantly coming and going all day long—and devour one book after another, whatever his friends had gotten for their bar mitzvahs, whatever new he had found in the library. He read *The Story of San Michele* and envied the Swedish doctor who had been to so many places and seen so many strange people. Even his blindness seemed enviable. He was going through a stage of historical novels now: he read *Napoleon,* and *Lincoln,* and *Mary Stuart,* and *The Ninth of Thermidor,* and *Peter the Great,* and *Shlomo Molcho.* Among the old books he came across in the library were several thrilling volumes about the false messiah Sabbatai Zevi, novels that were every bit as exciting as the serialized stories about the great scholars Rashi and Rabbenu Tam in *Der Amerikaner,* the Yiddish magazine his mother borrowed from Rosenwald. *Spartacus* enthralled him, *Samson* filled him with heroic thoughts. Not everything was so cramped and afflicted and confined. Everywhere there were heroes and adventures such as the ones he had read about in *On Heroes, Hero Worship,* and *The Heroic in History.* Nachman read on and on, and the more he read about other people the more he was thrown back on himself, for the world of these heroes was the same as that of the second Nachman inside him, the one who was so hidden that no one even suspected his existence. Secretly that other Nachman too dreamed of glory. In his dreams he wandered like Spartacus from place to place, and in each place he came to, the Jews cast off their bonds of exile and followed, the way they had followed Herzl, doing so under the influence of his oratory, which was as spellbinding as Jabotinsky's, doing so because he would fearlessly die for his homeland, the way Trumpeldor and Ben-Yosef had.

On Jewish National Fund Day, Nachman and Amichai had a contest to see who could collect the most. Amichai won as usual, but it was only because Nachman's box filled up too quickly with one and two penny coins, while Amichai went to his relatives, whose contributions started with a piaster, and some gave as much as a whole shilling. That same day, he conceived his great plan for redeeming the whole Jewish people. He couldn't stop thinking about it all day long. It was so utterly simple that he was astonished no one had thought of it before. After they had returned the collection boxes and he said good-bye to Amichai, he went to the Jewish National Fund office and asked permission from Hanan to use the typewriter. Two fingers at a time, letter after letter, he excitedly began to type his plan. Whoever joined the Society would have to pledge just one thing: to bring ten more young men like himself to the Land of Israel. He, Nachman, would find the first ten volunteers, who would quickly swell to a hundred, a thousand, ten thousand. It would all start with ten, and the ten with just one. Nachman was completely absorbed in his plan, which worked out so beautifully simply, when Hanan suddenly entered the room and came up behind him. Automatically, he pulled the sheet of paper from the typewriter, crumpled it up, and tore it into shreds. No one must see it. Like the second, hidden Nachman who lay curled up inside him, it too was purely his own, a private dream.

It was a Janus-faced year, the eighth grade. While one Nachman dreamed in his secret hiding place, another was swept up in the busy round of class life, with its bustling, self-confident, impudent activity that was different every day. His involvement in all this was an end in itself, and if it accomplished nothing else, it at least kept him out of the house.

There was really no one to keep an eye on him this year, because his mother was working and his father's mind was on other things. There were five, sometimes even six or seven hours of school a day, plus the discussion periods with Adon Ben-Shalom, which nobody in his right mind would want to miss even though they were optional. When it rained they held them indoors, but if it was one of those clear winter days when the moist, quenched earth put out a carpet of green and the trees in the orange groves bent double beneath their burden of gold, the class went out to the hill behind the school, right below the big irrigation pool.

In a casual, roundabout way, between exciting stories and jokes with sudden twists, he would lead the whole class into a serious discussion, which he rode like a master horseman. It happened like that the first time they met, and it happened every time after. Striding into the classroom, two meters tall, he would put his briefcase on the table and not open it until five minutes before the end of the period, when he would take out his black notebook with their homework for next week—an assignment, the class quickly discovered, that he had carefully planned in advance and on the basis of which he had guided the lesson, which was really one long discussion that took off not from some point in ancient history, from the kingdoms of Babylon and Sumer, Israel and Judea, but from the events in that morning's newspapers.

These were the discussion periods, which sometimes bore no connection at all to current events, or even to the two subjects that Adon Ben-Shalom taught, history and geography, but to theater, or psychology, or something else. "The truth is," he would tell them, his thick lip curling upward in a mischievous smile to reveal two columns of big teeth that were yellowed from the cigarettes he constantly smoked, "the truth is that I'm a psychologist by training. History is only my hobby, and so you'd better watch out that I don't read whatever's on your minds." At first they were taken aback, but once he had told them some of the things that the psychologists said about human nature, about the different types of character, about the nervous system, about love and hate, about conscious and unconscious motivations, the children felt—at least Nachman did—that a previously unimaginable world had opened before them, a world that was like an open book to their jolly young teacher, all two meters of him, with his yellow teeth that looked as strong as a beast's. When he grew up, Nachman wanted to be like Adon Ben-Shalom. He was the one hero he had found outside of books, and he measured all the others against him.

Yes, eighth grade! A stolen year. The year of Adon Ben-Shalom. The year of the bar mitzvahs. The year of distant dreamlands. A crisp, mischievous year—the year of the bicycles.

Now that Purim was approaching, practically all the boys in the class had bicycles. Nachman alone had to wait for his bar mitzvah until the end of the spring vacation, which turned out to be no worse a time than the rest of that year, the grimmest they had known in the cottage. He tried to stay out of the house as much as possible, visiting friends, or sneaking backstage of the theater on Thursday nights, or going to look at the Scottish soldiers who were now billeted in the old movie house and in the warehouse at the railway station. Sooner or later, however, he had to come home.

The moment he crossed the threshold, he would be in a different world. His mother would have come home exhausted after a day's work at Doctor Stockhammer's and begun immediately to tidy up the cottage, to clean, to cook, to launder, to iron; if she wasn't working, she would be dozing at the table, a cold glass of tea before her. His father had despaired of the high hopes he had pinned on his friends. Selling insurance had brought him nothing but a pair of worn soles, and he wasn't qualified, it seemed, for an office job. "That's how it goes." he would say, sometimes to Adon Sharoni and sometimes to Uncle Rifael, "when a man refuses to join a party and tries just to be a good Jew. Being a good Jew gets you nowhere here, either. It's like on Passover, when you have to eat the *seder* meal leaning either to the left or to the right. Try sitting up straight with the three matzohs in front of you, which I take to symbolize the three pillars of our existence—the People of Israel, the Land of Israel, and the

Torah of Israel—and you might as well knock your head against the wall. Werfel is a decent fellow, and I know he thinks well of me, but he doesn't owe me a thing. If I manage to keep alive, he'll be glad to come and chat with me—but if I don't, what can he do? And as for our local businessmen and growers, the less said about them the better. They see the whole world through the hole in a piaster coin. Here we are, on this Purim eve, facing a situation as bad as in Queen Esther and Haman's time. Everywhere you look, the Jews are in sackcloth and ashes. It's enough to read that item in today's paper about putting away food for an emergency. Just for three months a family like our own needs twenty kilograms of sugar, ten of honey, ten of oil, sixteen of rice, fifteen of beans, fifteen of lentils, and still more. The one thing they forgot to write was where to get the money if you don't have a job. The growers still think that as soon as things are settled around some table in London, they can bring all their Arab workers back to the groves. As for myself, if I perish, I perish, as it says in the Book of Esther."

Nachman was tired of his father's laments. Seeing that Uncle Rifael intended to stay for a glass of tea, he slipped outside to steal a ride on Rifael's bicycle. The paving of the street was almost finished and lacked only a final layer of asphalt on the pressed gravel. He was still not big enough to sit comfortably in the saddle with his feet on the pedals, and so he rode standing up, the bike tilting one way and he the other. He quickly reached the synagogue, made a U-turn in the middle of the street, pedaled home again, and quietly leaned the bicycle back against the cottage wall. Between stolen rides on Uncle Rifael's bicycle and authorized ones on Ehud's and Balfour's, he had become an expert cyclist. What good did it do him, though, if his mother didn't even know how she was going to pay his tuition?

His last ray of hope was that his father stood a chance of landing a newspaper franchise—which paper he wouldn't say, because he was afraid that this too might slip through his fingers—and if this came through, he would need a bicycle for deliveries. After he had gone and fallen off the scaffold, it wasn't clear that he would fare any better on a bicycle, but there was no reason why Nachman couldn't handle the far part of the route, while his father would take what was near and keep track of the accounts. The possibility was exciting not only because it would enable him to pay his own way through school and perhaps ever more, but also—to himself he admitted: above all—because this way he too would have a bicycle of his own like all his friends.

And in the end he was to get one, though not for a newspaper route or in any other way he could have thought of.

34 | Exit Uncle Rifael

Late one night a heavy knock on the door catapulted them from their beds in a fright. Nachman's father turned on a light and slipped his green robe over his long woolen underwear, while his mother hurried to put on a dress over her nightgown. Nachman thought he could actually see his father's legs tremble as he went to the locked door and asked in a strained voice who was there.

"We're Jews," came the answer, ruling out the possibility that they might be English or Arab policemen. "Shpiegler, we've got something to tell you."

His father's voice changed completely and he growled, "At this hour of the night it better be important."

"It is." Before it could identify itself, his father recognized the voice. "Werfel!"

He turned the large key in the lock and opened the door. Werfel stepped onto the porch, his cap pulled over his eyes. A leather jacket came down to his knees and a big Mauser revolver was strapped to his hip. It was a different Werfel than usual, a Werfel who boded ill. He was accompanied by a sergeant in the *gaffirs*, not one who wore a brown *kolpak* like Uncle Rifael, but one of the new ones, with a broad-brimmed Australian hat. On it and on the sleeve of his shirt was an orange triangular patch.

"What are you doing here in the middle of the night, Werfel?" The dim light of the fifteen-watt porch bulb fell on his father from above. It made shadow tremble within shadow—or was that just his father again? His father's voice confirmed his own suspicion that the two men were bringing bad news. He too stepped out on the porch.

"Get back into bed, Nachman!" ordered his mother, reverting to role right there in front of Werfel and the sergeant. A sack full of oranges, which Uncle Rifael had brought them, lay in a corner of the porch. He rested his bare feet on it before she could tell him to get off the cold concrete floor.

"You'd better get dressed now, Shalom, and come with us."

"What's going on here?" his mother interrupted. "At this hour of the night? Have you gone out of your minds?"

"I think you'd better come with us too, Leah. We've got a car outside. We're going to Tsipoyrele."

"Rifael!" his father shouted fearfully, as though he saw his brother before him and sought to warn him of some impending danger. "Rifael . . ." he began again in a near whisper. "Rifael . . ."

Only now that the sergeant was recounting how they had found Uncle Rifael, the *gaffir* who was with him, and the two men in the trunk, did Nachman begin to imagine how the town would look the next day during the great funeral that would be held for the four latest victims of the times. It suddenly dawned on him that Uncle Rifael would never again drop by their cottage in the evening on his bicycle, his rifle slung over one shoulder and the *kolpak* pulled low on his head. Nor would he ever see him again as he first remembered him, mounted on his little donkey with his legs dangling down on each side, the caked cement on his shoes mixed with the dust from the road. There would be no more Uncle Rifael.

Only now did he get goose pimples all over as he remembered the story he had written for the class newspaper the year before. He had thought he had made it all up, only to realize later that except for the tragic ending, it was simply the story of Uncle Rifael's life. A thought he had suppressed at the time now returned to him: suppose the way he had ended the story could make Uncle Rifael's life end the same way?

"Let's go to Tsipoyrele," Werfel said quietly.

"I knew it," whispered his mother. Two small blood-tears were all that were left of her eyes. "I knew it all along."

His father stood there in his robe, shrunk to half his size, looking as he had that time long ago—when? when? in what distant dream had it been?—when Uncle Rifael had come on his donkey to bring the letter that said that grandfather was dead. Except that now he was whispering "Rifael" instead of "*der tateh*."

"And I was always criticizing him, from the day we got off the boat. Now he's gone and left me all by myself. *Oy vay vay*, Rifael . . ."

35 | *Nachman studies the Prophets*

Every evening he now sat with his father to study the portion from the Prophets he would have to read at his bar mitzvah. He was looking forward to this day, though not with unmixed feelings. From the beginning of the year he had been constantly reminded that he was already a "bar mitzvah boy." Everything he did or was expected to do was judged by the sole light of whether it was fitting for a bar mitzvah boy like himself, who in a sense was already more than a bar mitzvah boy because he was finishing eighth grade, which marked the end of elementary school, and for most children—yes, Nachman, even in more comfortably off families than our own!—their introduction to real life, that is, to work. He had already grown weary of such talk months ago, but now, during the spring vacation, it reached positively floodlike proportions. He was tongue-lashed with his bar mitzvah as though it were a whip, told over and over that the time had come to open his eyes and take a good look around him, so that he might appreciate all that his parents were doing for him. "You're old enough to stop and consider the kind of world we're living in!" The storm clouds were gathering from day to day; who was to say that they wouldn't have war even before his bar mitzvah? How much longer would he go on being such an irresponsible child whose only desire was to play with his friends, to splash in the water hole, to go for donkey rides, to run around wild all day long? "A bar mitzvah," his father would say, waving the whip while they studied his portion from the Prophets, or the blessings he would have to recite before and after reading it, or some point of Jewish law, or on any other suitable occasion, "a bar mitzvah is not just a party and presents. It's the day on which a person says goodbye to his childhood forever. From now on you'll be eligible to be one of the ten Jews needed for a *minyan*, which is no trifling matter, because it also means that you'll be fully responsible for your actions: your good deeds will be all your own, but so will your sins. I want you to understand, Nachman, because you're not a child anymore, that when the father says at the bar mitzvah ceremony, 'Blessed art thou, O Lord, for relieving me of the burden of this boy,' it isn't that he wishes to be absolved of the responsibility for his son's future welfare, but that he's happy that his son is now a responsible person in his own right, a full Jew with all the privileges and obligations that go with it. And the main thing, Nachman, the main thing in every Jew's life is—the obligations. 'Know from whence thou comest, and whither thou goest, and before Whom thou wilt be called to account.' "

"From whence comest thou? From a putrid drop." Nachman suppressed a smile, not just at this saying of the rabbis, but at all his father's endless, wearisome preaching. Ever since his fall from the scaffold he had been a different man, as though not just his legs but something inside him had broken in two. Especially in the months since Uncle Rifael's death, he had been practically unrecognizable. Not only had he begun to go regularly to synagogue on the Sabbath again, to the afternoon service as well; not only had he taken to praying with phylacteries on his arm and head; he actually went now every day of the week to the morning service at the Hasidic synagogue (ostensibly, so he claimed, to recite the *kaddish* for Uncle Rifael), and to the evening service too if he didn't happen to be chasing some new job in town. This wasn't the half of it, either. He was continually humming prayers and singing hymns these days, studying the Talmud and the sayings of the rabbis, talking religion and carrying on generally in such a way that he no longer seemed the man he used to be.

Nachman himself was the principal victim of this transformation. Several long months before his bar mitzvah, as soon as Passover was over, his father informed him that learning to read his portion from the Prophets was simply the icing on the cake. "Soon you'll be entering the palace of Judaism; now that you're standing on the threshold, you should at least be getting a taste of what awaits you inside. I can't predict what path you'll choose to follow when you're grown up and on your own, but it's my duty to equip you for the pitfalls ahead. And the first rule is: know your own faith. Afterwards you can become a freethinker if you want to, but at least it won't be out of ignorance."

Indeed, ever since Passover, Nachman was being equipped without mercy. On Friday nights he went to synagogue with his father, after which he accompanied him at the Sabbath table in the singing of lengthy hymns. His father lingered on each syllable, adding flourishes that stretched out like chewing gum, and Nachman knew better than to try to excuse himself before they had recited the entire grace after meals, though beneath the window he might have already heard the impatient whistles of his friends, who were in a hurry to get to the Maccabee clubhouse or to a rendezvous with the girls in front of Tamar Levin's house. Saturday morning was the same. He was expected by his father, and all his efforts to escape were in vain, to sit through the entire Sabbath service, at the end of which he still wasn't free, because from the synagogue he had to go directly to the red monkey, Adon Pollak, for his weekly Talmud lesson. This last annoyance, which his father had decided on after Passover, led to a great fight between them: after all that his father had said about the Talmud Torah, after all that he knew Nachman went through the day he had run away in the rain to the orange groves from Ozer Lichtig and his slaves, how could he possibly insist that he study Talmud with Adon Pollak of all people? But his father, who was surly and irritable nowadays and listened only to himself, simply answered, "Believe me, nobody ever died from a few pages of Talmud. It won't do you any harm to study with a simple, honest scholar of the old school, a man who has spent his life laboring in the vineyards of the Law. Either you study with him or you stay inside the house all Saturday. Take your pick."

As luck would have it, however, this new arrangement lasted barely a few weeks. Indeed, perhaps it was really too bad that it didn't last longer. Adon Pollak lived with his numerous progeny and his wife, who was again big with child, in one of those old, low, ramshackle, straw-and-clay houses behind the Great Synagogue. The family had only one room, which was piled high with beds and mattresses and decorated with hats and coats hanging from nails in the walls. In the one cleared corner stood a table and some chairs, all of which wriggled because of the sinking floor. Nachman would sit there longing for his friends, who at this very moment were sure to be off somewhere new, up to some escapade that could only be hatched at such times and that was the exclusive property of its creators. His resentment of his father weighed like a heavy stone on his heart, yet strangely enough, he had come to see Adon Pollak in a different light. The overcrowded room was full of smells. There was the smell of the musty mattresses, of the fingerworn Talmud, of Sabbath clothes, of Adon Pollak's yellow beard as he nearsightedly squinted at his book, and above all—of the *cholent*, the Sabbath stew that had simmered overnight on the low kerosene flame. Adon Pollak's soft, tired voice shook waveringly like the kerosene wick. It too would sputter out for good some day. Nachman knew that his father was paying for this weekly lesson, and though he knew that his own family was badly off too, he felt a surge of compassion for Adon Pollak. Why should he begrudge him the few extra piasters a month that he made by shuttling back and forth over his Talmud? He suddenly remembered the stories that were told about Adon Pollak in the Talmud Torah, how at night he sneaked over to Crazy Sima's mud shack and did things to her that were too awful even to mention. A thin smile flitted over his lips as he looked at this haggard man, who spoke in a shaky waver while his yellow finger traveled feebly from line to line. He saw Adon Pollak through eyes that had matured in a sudden burst and an almost audible sigh of relief escaped from his lips at the thought of this grotesque memory. How funny, how really funny it was.

It was all over in a matter of weeks. One Saturday in late spring Nachman arrived at Adon Pollak's lowly house beneath the sidewalk and street to discover that a new baby girl had augmented the swarm of children who already more than filled the Pollaks' one room, their tiny kitchen, and back yard. For the time being—which of course meant forever—his weekly Talmud lesson with Adon Pollak was discontinued. For the time being—until he found another teacher—his father was forced to relent, though he tried to make up for it by teaching Nachman a bit of Jewish codes, reviewing the weekly Torah reading with him, studying the Book of Ruth, and indulging in still other experiments, all of which sooner or later ran aground. The most successful tactic of all, Nachman quickly came to realize, was not to fight back but simply to roll with the times, which were out of joint themselves and played havoc with even the best-laid plans.

It had been a bad year in general, but to Nachman it seemed that the floodgates opened for real on that night before Purim when Uncle Rifael was killed. Ever since then, all news sounded different to his ears and there seemed to be no end to the black-rimmed mourning placards, the protests strikes, the funerals, the demonstrations, the curfews. Scenes from these packed days were forever to remain confused in his memory, and all would remind him of that afternoon in front of the Workers Club, from where they had started out behind the coffins that were borne on two pickup trucks.

Tsipoyrele wasn't crying, yet not until now did Nachman realize how much she had changed since that winter Sabbath when he and his mother had crossed the sea of dunes together for the first time. How small and thin she was! Her face was expressionless beneath the black kerchief with which Nachman's mother had covered her bunched braids. His mother held onto her on one side, and Ruzha, who had come straight from the kibbutz, on the other. Volush and Kravitz supported his father, who wept bitterly and without shame in front of the large crowd. The whole town had turned out. The siren on the town well wailed across the blue winter sky, the same whistle that used to signal the beginning of the work day, the afternoon lunch break, and the start of the Sabbath, but that now blew only to summon the townsmen to lock up their shops and houses and pay their respects to the latest victims of the times, or to gather for a rally at the town hall or Great Synagogue. Today it wasn't really needed, for the shops were already all closed. The street turned black with people as the procession moved slowly along. This was Nachman's first funeral, his first mass demonstration too, and when he was to look back on this day in the future, his first recollection of it—though he knew it had been wrong of him to feel it—was always of a sense of great importance, of great power. The coffins went first with their honor guard of *gaffirs*, followed by his father and Tsipoyrele and the families of the other murdered men. Nachman walked right behind his father, feeling how the whole great crowd that filled the street behind him had come to pay its last respects to his Uncle Rifael. His inner eye surveyed the scene almost grudgingly, encountering the name Rifael Shpiegler again and again in its black frame, on billboards, on walls of houses, on electric poles, on fences, astonished each time to see it written so clearly. More than confirming that Uncle Rifael was gone forever, it seemed to proclaim the birth of a new hero and martyr, Rifael Shpiegler, his very own uncle. There were mourning placards on behalf of the Workers Association, on behalf of the town, on behalf of the bereaved families, on behalf of all kinds of organizations. Still wet and shiny with paste, the placards had been slapped over older proclamations of mourning and took their place among giant notices which said things like IN THE NAME OF THE JEWISH PEOPLE! WE SHALL NOT YIELD, TO THE COMMUNITY! ALL-DAY PRAYER VIGIL, and GENERAL STRIKE. When they reached the town hall, the mayor and Werfel and old Adon Mendelevitch gave speeches from the balcony, on which the high commissioner had once stood and down whose railing Nachman and his friends used to slide whenever they came to borrow books from the library. Then they all proceeded to the broad steps of the Great Synagogue to listen to the rabbi deliver an oration in a strange mixture of Hebrew and Yiddish, which was followed by the cantor singing prayers and psalms in an operatic voice that recalled the High Holy Days. Now the great crowd moved on again, first down the new asphalt road, then down the old cobblestone one, and finally on the soft sands, among the orange groves, breathing in the clean air of this day that only seemed bluer because of the scattered clouds, breathing the rotting scent of the last fallen fruit and the pungent fragrance of the first new blossoms, continuing as far as the cemetery, the first time Nachman had ever been there, his father having not only granted permission but expressly bade him to come.

Ever since then, so it seemed to Nachman, there had been no end to the bad news, which he now heard with a different ear. When part of Czechoslovakia had been handed to Hitler, the radio and newspapers explained that peace was assured. Now, on the morrow of the funeral, it was announced that perfidious Albion had once again betrayed its promise to the Jews. IMMIGRATION TO BE CHOKED OFF, SEVERE RESTRICTIONS ON LAND PURCHASES, JEWISH POPULATION TO BE FROZEN AT 30%, announced the newspapers. That same day the listeners gathered around Rosenwald's kiosk heard the radio announce, "The German army has entered Czechoslovakia, Moravia, Bohemia, and Slovakia." There hadn't been a day since without its share of bad news. Where did Hitler intend to strike next, everyone, all the newspapers, were asking: in the east or in the west? And meanwhile the Arab gangs were still on the rampage. The funerals, the prayer days, the general strikes, the demonstrations, continued one after the other.

The spring vacation came round and Nachman now sat every day with his father, studying the portion from the Prophets he would have to read on his bar mitzvah, which was less than six weeks away. His mother had tried suggesting that given the times, a big celebration would be out of place. Not only because they simply didn't have the money, but equally because there was no one to make it for: their whole family was in Poland, where it was sitting on a powder keg that could go off, God forbid, any day, while here there was Uncle Rifael, to say nothing of new troubles, which came when you least expected them. Nachman's father, though, wouldn't hear of it. "We have only one son," he said, "and we'll make him a proper bar mitzvah if we have to pawn everything we own. As long as we have even a bit of family here, we have to stick together. Don't you worry, the Jewish people have been through worse times than these without changing their customs or losing faith in the future! So the English have clamped a curfew on us, so what? So we'll spend three days at home. When Rosh Hashanah falls on a Thursday and Friday, as it will this coming year, everything stops dead for three days too."

The curfew had come all at once, giving Nachman a sudden glimpse of a violent reality whose thunderpeals had previously been heard approaching from afar. The summer vacation was above all a time of long, carefree days, if only he could manage to get out of the house, with or without a good excuse. Early that Thursday afternoon he had slipped away to go with Ehud to his uncle's orange grove, which had a magnificent irrigation pool that was neither too deep nor too big. At this time of day, when it was filling up from the well, it was a perfect place to steal down to and learn to swim. Nachman was just a beginner, but he could already float and dog-paddle and do a bit of a crawl. They took their time swimming and drying out in the sun, which was already low in the sky as they started out for Amichai's with a new idea in their heads: to sneak backstage of the new revue that would be at the theater tonight. They walked back through town without noticing any change, arguing about the bombs that had recently gone off in the marketplace in Haifa and in a coffeehouse in Jerusalem, wounding and killing dozens of Arabs. Ehud said that he had just read an idiotic, cowardly editorial against the bombings in the morning paper, under the caption MURDERERS. "That's just great!" he said. "They can kill us all they want, and we're supposed to sit back and take it like in a pogrom!" Nachman was glad that the Arabs had been given a taste of their own medicine, but at the same time he thought it was a terrible thing that a lot of poor people who had come to the market, even women and children, should have to be killed whether they were guilty or not. "It's beyond me how you of all people can talk that way!" Ehud angrily interrupted. "Did anyone ask your uncle what he was guilty of before they murdered him out in the groves?"

The entire conversation, however, was now interrupted by something else, whose nature they at first failed to fathom. People were rushing frantically by them, signaling them to get off the street. Only now did they notice that the shops were all closing, their heavy iron shutters clanging noisily shut—yes, only now did they see the line of mounted British policemen advancing toward them at a gallop from the direction of the Great Synagogue, charging into the pedestrians

Baylin's, opened as though by itself and a bloody figure leaped in out of the night. It picked itself up off the floor with wonderful agility, sprang to its feet, and closed the shutter behind it. The three of them made it out together beneath its bloody mask. It was Ozer Lichtig.

"They're after me," he whispered, scanning the room with his beady eyes. In a flash he was flat on the floor again, vanishing under the double bed. Nachman's heart leaped to his throat with excitement.

"It's that hooligan!" he read on his father's lips, which had turned ash gray like a corpse's. "What are we supposed to do now?"

Never before had he seen his mother so quick and decisive. She dashed into the kitchen, and a moment later they heard a dull thud, as though something heavy had fallen to the floor. Nachman ran after her. From the doorway he could see what she had done: she had spilled the large pot of chickpeas, boiling water and all, onto the porch floor, from which steamy vapors now arose like in the hot springs he had read about in books.

"They're coming," she whispered.

There was a knock on the door.

"Oy, all I need is visitors!" she said in a loud voice. "Who is it?"

"Police," said a voice in English and added several more incomprehensible words. His mother tiptoed to the door, taking care not to scald herself in the hot water or to step on the chickpeas that lay scattered all over the floor, and opened it. A soldier planted a foot in the doorway. His helmet fell over his perspiring face and the barrel of his rifle pointed straight into the house. He took one look at the floor and at Nachman and his father bent over the mess, growled something that sounded like a curse, and disappeared.

This was the biggest adventure of that summer, in which his mother came through as a braver, cooler, more resourceful woman than anyone would have imagined. For days, no, years afterwards, she had only to put up some chickpeas to soak for them to recall the story of how she had outfoxed the English and rescued that hooligan, Ozer Lichtig, from their clutches, though he didn't really deserve to get out of the fix he was in. Nachman rejoiced in his mother's courage, and when he later found out that Ozer Lichtig was wanted by the British for having jumped one of them in the darkness and cracked open his head with a brick, he forgave him all his old sins. Ozer himself said nothing. Shortly after his pursuers went away, he leaped out from under the bed and vanished as he had come by jumping nimbly through the window, without even letting them bandage his bloody head.

Nachman sided with his father on the question of the bar mitzvah and of the grand production he wished to make of it, but he agreed with his mother that there was going to be a war. Unlike both parents, however, he looked forward to the latter as to a particularly thrilling adventure.

His father eagerly kept track of every piece of reassuring news. It was a fact, he pointed out, that no one had returned his travel tickets despite the panic over Danzig, and according to the newspapers, four or five hundred delegates from Palestine alone were preparing to set out for the Zionist Congress in Geneva. If the danger were so great, did anyone think all these leaders would really be going off now to take part in Zionist elections? Or take the reports coming out of Poland in the newspapers, which he personally accepted at face value. "And I'm not even referring," he said with a smile, "to that famous fortune-teller Ossowietzky, who's never been wrong, and who just came out with a statement that there won't be war this year. I'm talking about what informed sources are writing from Warsaw. 'Should war break out, a German defeat is inevitable. It will take the Germans a generation or more to recover from such a rout.' What more needs to be said? We've wasted enough time already, Nachman. Open your book and let me hear you read the *haftarah.*"

A week after the curfew there was a great rally and demonstration in town, whose slogan was FREE IMMIGRATION! Nachman went on studying the Prophets. A few days later there was another three-day curfew. Nachman went on studying the Prophets. Suddenly the whole town was talking about the report in the British press that Hitler was planning to attack Poland in two more weeks, that is, exactly on the day of Nachman's bar mitzvah. Late that evening, in the summer heat that didn't let up day or night, he heard Adon Sharoni tell his father as they sat outside that it said in the papers that Hitler had ordered all roads leading to the Polish border repaved by the first of September. "If that doesn't mean war, tell me what does?"

But Nachman's father angrily retorted that one had to read between the lines. "I saw the same item too," he said, "but right next to it there was another report that came from a reliable source in Germany itself, and to my mind it's more plausible than all the scare stories that the newspapers make their money on. It said that Hitler, may he rot in hell, is suffering from attacks of dizziness and melancholy. True, it's been denied that his illness is serious, but something tells me that one of these days we're going to wake up and hear that another anti-Semite has bit the dust."

Come what may, Nachman went on rehearsing his portion from the Prophets, and his bar mitzvah was now around the corner. His father composed and sent invitations to the entire family in Poland, Germany, and America. "If only they could come," sighed his mother, who was clearly not excited by the prospect of the approaching day.

"Even if they can't," said his father, "the invitations have to be sent. It's a waste of breath to talk about it now that immigration has been cut off, but how many times did I beg them to come when they could have? If they were here with us now, we'd all be feeling happier, both them and us."

36 | *There'll never be a war*

The silence that had descended over Nachman's mother continued, despite his father's best efforts to break through it. But her depression was one thing, and preparations for the bar mitzvah were another. She marinated herring in vinegar and baked sugar cookies in Tuvim's oven, putting them in airtight biscuit tins to keep them from getting soggy and losing their fresh, crisp flavor. Then she wracked her brain over what else to make and how. It would have been nice to invite the whole congregation to their house after the service, as Nachman's father wanted her to do, but it was clear from the start that the practical thing was to bring two cakes and some wine to the synagogue and hold the *kiddush* there. The main problem was all the relatives who would be coming from Tel Aviv and from Haifa, from the kibbutzim and from town itself—how would she feed them all? What would she make for the Sabbath eve meal and what for the Sabbath noon meal? And what would she serve Nachman's friends, for whom he wanted to make a special party of his own on Saturday afternoon? Where were they to get the money for it all, and who would do all the work?

On the Sunday before the bar mitzvah, *mimeh* Herzlich arrived from Tel Aviv, her wig on her head and two bulging handbags under her arms. Though she had walked all the way from the station at high noon in the worst heat there had been in weeks, she took charge of things as soon as she entered the house. The first thing she did was to head straight for the shower, from which she emerged in a summery housedress with her head wrapped in a kerchief, carrying her clothes, her wig sitting on top of them, before her. For five full days she helped Nachman's mother shop and peel and squeeze and grind and chop and pickle and knead and stuff and bake and cook. The two of them, Nachman observed (though it was actually the *fetter* and not the *mimeh* who was related to his mother), were cut from the same cloth: neither went in for idle chatter, and it was only as they worked, or over a glass of tea, that they reminisced about their family in Poland and the wealth that it enjoyed there. By the time Thursday had arrived, all manner of baked and cooked delicacies stood ready, covered with newspapers and piled in the corners of the cottage, stuck into ice buckets and insulated with sacking, or farmed out to the neighbors' iceboxes: dark honey cakes and tawny pound cakes made with folded egg whites for the *kiddush*; huge sweet hallahs for the family banquet; heaping portions of gefilte fish, well peppered, nicely onioned, and sweetened to perfection; two enamel casserole dishes of jellied calf's foot; noodles for the soup and a *kugel*—a baked noodle pudding with raisins and cinnamon; stuffed chicken necks and chopped liver; meatballs for the many guests and generous helpings of chicken for the older guests of honor; and a special fruit compote for dessert, whose main ingredients were dried apples and prunes from California plus lots of apricots and grapes. This was the formal menu, in addition to which there were plates of crunchy cookies, nuts, seeds, fresh fruit (luckily it was the end of summer, so that grapes, figs, apricots, and watermelon were available in abundance), and sucking candies for the children and whoever might drop by later in the day. When Nachman's mother and *mimeh* Herzlich stood to light the Sabbath candles that rested on the long table—a makeshift structure of scaffolding boards spread with white sheets that stretched from nearly one end of the cottage to the other—they were so exhausted that they could barely stay on their feet. Still, the feast on the table that night and the day after would put neither the bar mitzvah boy nor the Herzlich family to shame.

They were joined for the Sabbath eve meal by *fetter* Herzlich, the Herzlichs' daughter Toybe, and their two sons with their wives and children, including Milik and Lola, who already had a woman's body though she was younger than both Nachman and her cousin. Tsipoyrele too came with her children, though not before Volush—who had arrived from the kibbutz with Ruzha that afternoon—had told her that she would ruin everyone's good time if she didn't. Ever since word reached Nachman's parents following Uncle Rifael's murder that she had spoken to Werfel about selling Uncle Rifael's farm and going back to her family in Poland for a year or even more, there had been bad feeling again between them. Nachman wasn't sure why she still lived beyond the dunes and had put off her trip to Poland, at least for the time being, but in any event his father now embraced her when she came with her children and kissed her on both cheeks before running out to wipe away his tears. Nachman's mother kissed her next and ran back to the kitchen to wipe her eyes too. Only Tsipoyrele's dark eyes seemed to glitter dryly, perhaps because of the electric light and the many candles. (Besides the Sabbath candles lit by his mother and *mimeh* Herzlich, there were candles for Toybe and the Herzlichs' daughters-in-law, as well as for the three other women at the Sabbath eve meal, Ruzha, Tsipoyrele, and old lady Becker.) In a high, sharp voice she said, "Well, Volush, why don't you go show Nachman his bar mitzvah present already."

Volush, who had grown terribly thin since he joined the kibbutz, and was as deeply sunburned as Uncle Rifael, or like

Nachman's father before his accident, smiled to himself, the wrinkles fanning out from the corners of his eyes. "You brought it, Tsipoyrele, and you'll give it to him."

"Run outside, Nachman," said Tsipoyrele, "and see what's leaning against the cottage wall, out back. Well, what are you waiting for? It's for you."

Nachman guessed at once though he pretended not to. Ever since he went with his parents after the funeral to visit Tsipoyrele and saw the riderless bicycle standing on the porch . . . His ears burned with shame at the thought of his duplicity, at the lie he was living by feigning to be in the dark.

Tsipoyrele came over and hugged him hard. At last she too had tears in her eyes.

"I brought you the bicycle," she said. "It's not from me. It's from your uncle. I hope it brings you luck and long life."

She crossed back to her two children, who were sitting with Ruzha on the couch, and buried her head among them. Just then both his parents reentered the room. When they heard of Tsipoyrele's present, they hugged her again. This time they didn't dry their tears so quickly. The whole family stood around while eight pairs of Sabbath candles flamed and danced before their moist eyes.

That Sabbath eve was unlike any other he remembered. The whole family feasted together, and after they had eaten the last of the king-sized courses and sung Sabbath hymns and talked themselves hoarse, they scattered to the houses of relatives and friends. The old Herzlichs and Tsipoyrele and her children stayed in the cottage to sleep. Nachman's parents slept at Adon Sharoni's. Nachman himself slept on the folding bed on the porch. The young Herzlichs slept at the Holzbergs' and the Kravitzes'. Ruzha and Volush went to the Beckers'. Not just that evening, that whole night too, was different from any before.

The next day was even grander. It began in the synagogue, with the family and all their friends and Balfour and

Ehud and Amichai, who came to hear Nachman read his portion from the Prophets in his brand-new shoes and new custom-made pants, Milik Herzlich's silk prayer shawl draped over his shoulders. The service was followed by a *kiddush* in the synagogue. Then the whole family trooped back to fill the cottage and the yard, while friends and acquaintances came and went to have a piece of cake, munch a few cookies, crack pumpkin or sunflower seeds, sip a bit of wine, press a present into Nachman's hands, and take their leave. Then came the great banquet itself, the likes of which their cottage had never seen before. *Fetter* Herzlich blessed the wine in his black silk caftan. Old Becker downed glass after glass of whiskey, stamped his boots and sang, "tum-ta-ra-rum, tum-ta-ra-rum, ta-ra-ra-ra, tum-ta-ra-rum." Nachman stood at the head of the table and gave the bar-mitzvah speech that his father had composed for him. "Dear parents and honored guests," it began, "today I am thirteen years old and I bid a fond farewell to my happy years of childhood innocence. . . ." Ruzha and Volush guffawed out loud. His father called for quiet. The women came and went with heaping platters. *Fetter* Herzlich looked up at the picture of Grandfather Herzlich on the wall, shook his head, and said, "Oy, what a handsome young lad he was, as straight as a tree! And all of a sudden . . . just like that . . . to this day, to this day I can't understand it. . . ." Finally, Nachman's father could control himself no longer, and between the soup course and the meat course he rose to give a speech of his own.

"I've been thinking," he said, "about the chapter from Isaiah that Nachman read today. I have in mind the verses where he says: 'My people went down aforetime into Egypt to sojourn there, and the Assyrian oppressed them without cause. Now therefore, what do I here, saith the Lord, seeing that My people is taken away for nought?' What does 'What do I here' mean? What it means is, Why do I stand aside and not come to the defense of My people Israel, why don't I do something? And so the prophet continues—stressing that it will be 'on that day,' that is, on the day when things are so bad that they can't possibly get any worse—'Therefore My people shall know my name; therefore they shall know on that day that I, even He that spoke, behold, here I am.' Yes, on a day like the one we're assembled here on, when it seems as though everything has joined hands against us, the Arabs, and the White Paper, and Hitler, and my fall from the scaffold—on such a day, God speaks. There's a wonderful symbolism in the fact that here we all sat today, the representatives of our great family in Poland, and listened to this chapter from Isaiah, which seems addressed directly to us. 'What do I here?' asks the prophet, speaking in God's name—in other words, You who are everywhere, You who are every place, why don't You reveal Your true powers to Your people Israel? This is what the prophet asks, but right away he answers: 'How beautiful upon the mountains are the feet of the messenger of good tidings that announceth peace, the harbinger of good tidings that announceth salvation.' Yes, this is what the prophet has to tell us. The tidings are good. There will be peace."

His father's unexpected sermon took them all by surprise. Even his mother and the other women, who were standing in the doorway with their platters of meat, didn't dare disturb him by serving the food while he spoke. There was a profound silence when he sat down again, as though a single word might be enough to thwart his promise of peace.

A minute later, though, they were already deep into the meatballs and stuffed neck, dipping them in the horseradish, blowing on the steamy hot carrots, arguing, getting up from the table to bring the Friday newspaper, which proved that it was senseless to hope: there was bound to be a war. Danzig was at the boiling point. There were eight-and-a-half-million men under arms all over Europe. How could there not be a war?

But Nachman's father, who didn't need to bring proofs because he felt in his bones that there wouldn't be a war, declared that he had read the newspapers too. Was he by any chance referring, *fetter* Herzlich interrupted, to that ad in Wednesday's paper with the headline THERE'LL NEVER BE A WAR, in which some speculator had offered to buy back from the public all the food and preserves that they were hoarding before it spoiled? He could be reached, the ad said, from seven in the morning until nine at night, and not only that, he actually wrote at the bottom, "The highest prices will be paid." If there wasn't going to be any war, why on earth did he want to pay the highest prices?

Not at all, answered Nachman's father. He was thinking of the report from Warsaw he had read, which said that the Jews no longer knew which to fear more, war or peace. A joke currently making the rounds there was that the Jews would be the first to know if there would be peace, because as soon as the danger of war had passed the Poles would start beating them again.

It was with this joke, which his father had read in the newspaper, that Nachman's memory brought the great family banquet on the day of his bar mitzvah to an end. And yet, could it be that this too, like so many of the other things he was to carry forward into manhood (had not his childhood been sealed on this day?), was really the product of another hour, of another time (only when? was it now already another time?) when everything was turned upside down?

The day seemed to last forever. The guests kept coming with their presents all afternoon, which Nachman spent out back at the party he gave for his friends. He showed all of them Uncle Rifael's bicycle which he had gotten from Tsipoyrele, but he had to wait patiently for the Sabbath to be over before he could ride it. It was the richest, jolliest day of his life, but the times were no longer the same. Everything was now upside down.